Nathaniel Southgate Shaler

Outlines of the Earth's History

Nathaniel Southgate Shaler

Outlines of the Earth's History

ISBN/EAN: 9783742810687

Manufactured in Europe, USA, Canada, Australia, Japa

Cover: Foto ©Andreas Hilbeck / pixelio.de

Manufactured and distributed by brebook publishing software
(www.brebook.com)

Nathaniel Southgate Shaler

Outlines of the Earth's History

OUTLINES OF THE EARTH'S HISTORY

A POPULAR STUDY IN PHYSIOGRAPHY

BY

NATHANIEL SOUTHGATE SHALER

PROFESSOR OF GEOLOGY IN HARVARD UNIVERSITY
DEAN OF LAWRENCE SCIENTIFIC SCHOOL

ILLUSTRATED
WITH INDEX

NEW YORK
D. APPLETON AND COMPANY
1898

PREFACE.

THE object of this book is to provide the beginner in the study of the earth's history with a general account of those actions which can be readily understood and which will afford him clear understandings as to the nature of the processes which have made this and other celestial spheres. It has been the writer's purpose to select those series of facts which serve to show the continuous operations of energy, so that the reader might be helped to a truer conception of the nature of this sphere than he can obtain from ordinary text-books.

In the usual method of presenting the elements of the earth's history the facts are set forth in a manner which leads the student to conceive that history as in a way completed. The natural prepossession to the effect that the visible universe represents something done, rather than something endlessly doing, is thus re-enforced, with the result that one may fail to gain the largest and most educative impression which physical science can afford him in the sense of the swift and unending procession of events.

It is well known to all who are acquainted with the history of geology that the static conception of the earth— the idea that its existing condition is the finished product of forces no longer in action—led to prejudices which have long retarded, and indeed still retard, the progress of that science. This fact indicates that at the outset of a student's work in this field he should be guarded against such misconceptions. The only way to attain the end is by bringing to the understanding of the beginner a clear idea of successions of events which are caused by the forces operating in and on this sphere. Of all the chapters of this great story, that which relates to the history of the work done by the heat of the sun is the most interesting and awakening. Therefore an effort has been made to present the great successive steps by which the solar energy acts in the processes of the air and the waters.

The interest of the beginner in geology is sure to be aroused when he comes to see how very far the history of the earth has influenced the fate of men. Therefore the aim has been, where possible, to show the ways in which geological processes and results are related to ourselves; how, in a word, this earth has been the well-appointed nursery of our kind.

All those who are engaged in teaching elementary science learn the need of limiting the story they have to tell to those truths which can be easily understood by beginners. It is sometimes best, as in stating such difficult matters as those concerning the tides, to give explanations which are far from complete, and which, as to their mode of presentation, would be open to criticism were it not for the fact that any more elaborate statements would most likely be incomprehensible to the novice, thus defeating the teacher's aim.

It will be observed that no account is here given of the geological ages or of the successions of organic life. Chapters on these subjects were prepared, but were omitted for the reason that they made the story too long, and also because they carried the reader into a field of much greater difficulty than that which is found in the physical history of the earth.

N. S. S.

March, 1898.

CONTENTS.

v

LIST OF FULL-PAGE ILLUSTRATIONS.

OUTLINES OF THE EARTH'S HISTORY.

CHAPTER I.

AN INTRODUCTION TO THE STUDY OF NATURE.

THE object of this book is to give the student who is about to enter on the study of natural science some general idea as to the conditions of the natural realm. As this field of inquiry is vast, it will be possible only to give the merest outline of its subject-matter, noting those features alone which are of surpassing interest, which are demanded 'for a large understanding of man's place in this world, or which pertain to his duties in life.

In entering on any field of inquiry, it is most desirable that the student should obtain some idea as to the ways in which men have been led to the knowledge which they possess concerning the world about them. Therefore it will be well briefly to sketch the steps by which natural science has come to be what it is. By so doing we shall perceive how much we owe to the students of other generations; and by noting the difficulties which they encountered, and how they avoided them, we shall more easily find our own way to knowledge.

The primitive savages, who were the ancestors of all men, however civilized they may be, were students of Nature. The remnants of these lowly people who were left in different parts of the world show us that man was not long in existence before he began to devise some explanation concerning the course of events in the outer world.

Seeing the sun rise and set, the changes of the moon, the alternation of the seasons, the incessant movement of the streams and sea, and the other more or less orderly successions of events, our primitive forefathers were driven to invent some explanation of them. This, independently, and in many different times and places, they did in a simple and natural way by supposing that the world was controlled by a host of intelligent beings, each of which had some part in ordering material things. Sometimes these invisible powers were believed to be the spirits of great chieftains, who were active when on earth, and who after death continued to exercise their power in the larger realms of Nature. Again, and perhaps more commonly, these movements of Nature were supposed to be due to the action of great though invisible beasts, much like those which the savage found about him. Thus among our North American Indians the winds are explained by the supposition that the air is fanned by the wings of a great unseen bird, whose duty it is to set the atmosphere into motion. That no one has ever seen the bird doing the work, or that the task is too great for any conceivable bird, is to the simple, uncultivated man no objection to this view. It is long, indeed, before education brings men to the point where they can criticise their first explanations of Nature.

As men in their advance come to see how much nobler are their own natures than those of the lower animals, they gradually put aside the explanation of events by the actions of beasts, and account for the order of the world by the supposition that each and every important detail is controlled by some immortal creature essentially like a man, though much more powerful than those of their own kind. This stage of understanding is perhaps best shown by the mythology of the Greeks, where there was a great god over all, very powerful but not omnipotent; and beneath him, in endless successions of command, subordinate powers, each with a less range of duties and capacities than those of higher estate, until at the bottom of the system there were minor deities and demigods charged with the management of the trees, the flowers, and the springs—creatures differing little from man, except that they were immortal, and generally invisible, though they, like all the other deities, might at their will display themselves to the human beings over whom they watched, and whose path in life they guided.

Among only one people do we find that the process of advance led beyond this early and simple method of accounting for the processes of Nature, bringing men to an understanding such as we now possess. This great task was accomplished by the Greeks alone. About twenty-five hundred years ago the philosophers of Greece began to perceive that the early notion as to the guidance of the world by creatures essentially like men could not be accepted, and must be replaced by some other view which would more effectively account for the facts. This end they attained by steps which can not well be related here, but which led them to suppose separate powers behind each of the natural series—powers having no relation to the qualities of mankind, but ever acting to a definite end. Thus Plato, who represents most clearly this advance in the interpretation of facts, imagined that each particular kind of plant or animal had its shape inevitably determined by something which he termed an idea, a shape-giving power which existed before the object was created, and which would remain after it had been destroyed, ever ready again to bring matter to the particular form. From this stage of understanding it was but a short step to the modern view of natural law. This last important advance was made by the great philosopher Aristotle, who, though he died about twenty-two hundred years ago, deserves to be accounted the first and in many ways the greatest of the ancient men of science who were informed with the modern spirit.

With Aristotle, as with all his intellectual successors, the operations of Nature were conceived as to be accounted for by the action of forces which we commonly designate as natural laws, of which perhaps the most familiar and universal is that of gravitation, which impels all bodies to move toward each other with a degree of intensity which is measured by their weight and the distance by which they are separated.

For many centuries students used the term law in somewhat the same way as the more philosophical believers in polytheism spoke of their gods, or as Plato of the ideas which he conceived to control Nature. We see by this instance how hard it is to get rid of old ways of thinking. Even when the new have been adopted we very often find that something of the ancient and discarded notions cling in our phrases. The more advanced of our modern philosophers are clear in their mind that all we know as to the order of Nature is that, given certain conditions, certain consequences inevitably follow.

Although the limitations which modern men of science perceive to be put upon their labours may seem at first sight calculated to confine our understanding within a narrow field of things which can be seen, or in some way distinctly proved to exist, the effect of this limitation has been to make science what it is,—a realm of things known as distinct from things which may be imagined. All the difference between ancient science and modern consists in the fact that in modern science inquirers demand a businesslike method in the interpretation of Nature. Among the Greeks the philosopher who taught explanations of any feature in the material world which interested him was content 'if he could imagine some way which would account for the facts. It is the modern custom now to term the supposition of an explanation a *working hypothesis*, and only to give it the name of theory after a very careful search has shown that all the facts which can be gathered are in accordance with the view. Thus when Newton made his great suggestion concerning the law of gravitation, which was to the effect that all bodies attracted each other in proportion to their masses, and inversely as the square of their distance from each other, he did not rest content, as the old Greeks would have done, with the probable truth of the explanation, but carefully explored the movements of the planets and satellites of the solar system to see if the facts accorded with the hypothesis. Even the perfect correspondence which he found did not entirely content inquirers, and in this century very important experiments have been made which have served to show that a ball suspended in front of a precipice will be attracted toward the steep, and that even a mass of lead some tons in weight will attract toward itself a small body suspended in the manner of a pendulum.

It is this incessant revision of the facts, in order to see if they accord with the assumed rule or law, which has given modern science the sound footing that it lacked in earlier days, and which has permitted our learning to go on step by step in a safe way up the heights to which it has climbed. All explanations of Nature begin with the work of the imagination. In common phrase, they all are guesses which have at first but little value, and only attain importance in proportion as they are verified by long-continued criticism, which has for its object to see whether the facts accord with the theory. It is in this effort to secure proof that modern science has gathered the enormous store of well-ascertained facts which constitutes its true wealth, and which distinguishes it from the earlier imaginative and to a great extent unproved views.

In the original state of learning, natural science was confounded with political and social tradition, with the precepts of duty which constitute the law of the people, as well as with their religion, the whole being in the possession of the priests or wise men. So long as natural action was supposed to be in the immediate control of numerous gods and demigods, so long, in a word, as the explanation of Nature was what we term polytheistic, this association of science with other forms of learning was not only natural but inevitable. Gradually, however, as the conception of natural law replaced the earlier idea as to the intervention of a spirit, science departed from other forms of lore and came to possess a field to itself. At first it was one body of learning. The naturalists of Aristotle's time, and from his day down to near our own, generally concerned themselves with the whole field of Nature. For a time it was possible for any one able and laborious man to know all which had been ascertained concerning astronomy, chemistry, geology, as well as the facts relating to living beings. The more, however, as observation accumulated, and the store of facts increased, it became difficult for any one man to know the whole. Hence it has come about that in our own time natural learning is divided into many distinct provinces, each of which demands a lifetime of labour from those who would know what has already been done in the field, and what it is now important to do in the way of new inquiries.

The large divisions which naturalists have usually made of their tasks rest in the main on the natural partitions which we may readily observe in the phenomenal world. First of all comes astronomy, including the phenomena exhibited in the heavens, beyond the limits of the earth's atmosphere. Second, geology, which takes account of all those actions which in process of time have been developed in our own sphere. Third, physics, which is concerned with the laws of energy, or those conditions which affect the motion of bodies, and the changes which are impressed upon them by the different natural forces. Fourth, chemistry, which seeks to interpret the principles which determine the combination of atoms and the molecules which are built of them under the influence of the chemical affinities. Fifth, biology, or the laws of life, a study which pertains to the forms and structures of animals and plants, and their wonderful successions in the history of the world. Sixth, mathematics, or the science of space

and number, that deals with the principles which underlie the order of Nature as expressed at once in the human
understanding and in the material universe. By its use
men were made able to calculate, as in arithmetic, the
problems which concern their ordinary business, as well
as to compute the movements of the celestial bodies, and
a host of actions which take place on the earth that would
be inexplicable except by the aid of this science. Last of
all among the primary sciences we may name that of psy-
chology, which takes account of mental operations among
man and his lower kindred, the animals.

In addition to the seven sciences above mentioned,
which rest in a great measure on the natural divisions of
phenomena, there are many, indeed, indefinitely numerous,
subdivisions which have been made to suit the convenience
of students. Thus astronomy is often separated into
physical and mathematical divisions, which take account
either of the physical phenomena exhibited by the heavenly
bodies or of their motions. In geology there are half a
dozen divisions relating to particular branches of that
subject. In the realm of organic life, in chemistry, and
in physics there are many parts of these sciences which
have received particular names.

It must not be supposed that these sciences have the
independence of each other which their separate names
would imply. In fact, the student of each, however, far
he may succeed in separating his field from that of the
other naturalists, as we may fitly term all students of
Nature, is compelled from time to time to call in the aid
of his brethren who cultivate other branches of learning.
The modern astronomer needs to know much of chemistry,
or else he can not understand many of his observations
on the sun. The geologists have to share their work with
the student of animal and vegetable life, with the physicists; they must, moreover, know something of the celestial spheres in order to interpret the history of the earth.
In fact, day by day, with the advance of learning, we come

2

more clearly to perceive that all the processes of Nature are in a way related to each other, and that in proportion as we understand any part of the great mechanism, we are forced in a manner to comprehend the whole. In other words, we are coming to understand that these divisions of the field of science depend upon the limitations of our knowledge, and not upon the order of Nature itself.

For the purposes of education it is important that every one should know something of the great truths which each science has disclosed. No mortal man can compass the whole realm of this knowledge, but every one can gain some idea of the larger truths which may help him to understand the beauty and grandeur of the sphere in which he dwells, which will enable him the better to meet the ordinary duties of life, that in almost all cases are related to the facts of the world about us. It has been of late the custom to term this body of general knowledge which takes account of the more evident facts and important series of terrestrial actions physiography, or, as the term implies, a description of Nature, with the understanding that the knowledge chosen for the account is that which most intimately concerns the student who seeks information that is at once general and important. Therefore, in this book the effort is made first to give an account as to the ways and means which have led to our understanding of scientific problems, the methods by which each person may make himself an inquirer, and the outline of the knowledge that has been gathered since men first began to observe and criticise the revelations the universe may afford them.

CHAPTER II.

IT is desirable that the student of Nature keep well in mind the means whereby he is able to perceive what goes on in the world about him. He should understand something as to the nature of his senses, and the extent to which these capacities enable him to discern the operations of Nature. Man, in common with his lower kindred, is, by the mechanism of the body, provided with five somewhat different ways by which he may learn something of the things about him. The simplest of these capacities is that of touch, a faculty that is common to the general surface of the body, and which informs us when the surface is affected by contact with some external object. It also enables us to discern differences of temperature. Next is the sense of taste, which is limited to the mouth and the parts about it. This sense is in a way related to that of touch, for the reason that it depends on the contact of our body with material things. Third is the sense of smell, so closely related to that of taste that it is difficult to draw the line between the two. Yet through the apparatus of the nose we can perceive the microscopically small parts of matter borne to us through the air, which could not be appreciated by the nerves of the mouth. Fourth in order of scope comes the hearing, which gives us an account of those waves of matter that we understand as sound. This power is much more far ranging than those before noted; in some cases, as in that of the volcanic explosions from the island of Krakatoa, in the eruption of 1883, the convulsions were audible at the distance of more than a thousand miles away. The greater cannon of modern days may be heard at the distance of more than a hundred miles, so that while the sense of touch, taste, and smell demand contact with the bodies which we appreciate, hearing gives us information concerning objects at a considerable distance. Last and highest of the senses, vastly the most important in all that relates to our understanding of Nature, is sight, or the capacity which enables us to appreciate the movement of those very small waves of ether which constitute light. The eminent peculiarity of sight is that it may give us information concerning things which are inconceivably far away; it enables us to discern the light of suns probably millions of times as remote from us as is the centre of our own solar system.

Although much of the pleasure which the world affords us comes through the other senses, the basis of almost all our accurate knowledge is reported by sight. It is true that what we have observed with our eyes may be set forth in words, and thus find its way to the understanding through the ears; also that in many instances the sense of touch conveys information which extends our perceptions in many important ways; but science rests practically on sight, and on the insight that comes from the training of the mind which the eyes make possible.

The early inquirers had no resources except those their bodies afforded; but man is a tool-making creature, and in very early days he began to invent instruments which helped him in inquiry. The earliest deliberate study was of the stars. Science began with astronomy, and the first instruments which men contrived for the purpose of investigation were astronomical. In the beginning of this search the stars were studied in order to measure the length of the year, and also for the reason that they were supposed in some way to control the fate of men. So far as we know, the first pieces of apparatus for this purpose were invented in Egypt, perhaps about four thousand years before the Christian era. These instruments were of a simple nature, for the magnifying glass was not yet contrived, and so the telescope was impossible. They consisted of arrangements of straight edges and divided circles, so that the observers, by sighting along the instruments, could in a rough way determine the changes in distance between certain stars, or the height of the sun above the horizon at the various seasons of the year. It is likely that each of the great pyramids of Egypt was at first used as an observatory, where the priests, who had some knowledge of astronomy, found a station for the apparatus by which they made the observations that served as a basis for casting the horoscope of the king.

In the progress of science and of the mechanical invention attending its growth, a great number of inventions have been contrived which vastly increase our vision and add inconceivably to the precision it may attain. In fact, something like as much skill and labour has been given to the development of those inventions which add to our learning as to those which serve an immediate economic end. By far the greatest of these scientific inventions are those which depend upon the lens. By combining shaped bits of glass so as to control the direction in which the light waves move through them, naturalists have been able to create the telescope, which in effect may bring distant objects some thousand times nearer to view than they are to the naked eye; and the microscope, which so enlarges minute objects as to make them visible, as they were not before. The result has been enormously to increase our power of vision when applied to distant or to small objects. In fact, for purposes of learning, it is safe to say that these tools have altogether changed man's relation to the visible universe. The naked eye can see at best in the part of the heavens visible from any one point not more than thirty thousand stars. With the telescope somewhere near a hundred million are brought within the limits of vision. Without the help of the microscope an object a thousandth

of an inch in diameter appears as a mere point, the existence of which we can determine only under favourable
circumstances. With that instrument the object may reveal an extended and complicated structure which it may
require a vast labour for the observer fully to explore.

Next in importance to the aid of vision above noted
come the scientific tools which are used in weighing and
measuring. These balances and gauges have attained
such precision that intervals so small as to be quite invisible, and weights as slight as a ten-thousandth of a
grain, can be accurately measured. From these instruments have come all those precise examinations on which
the accuracy of modern science intimately depends. All
these instruments of precision are the inventions of modern
days. The simplest telescopes were made only about two
hundred and fifty years ago, and the earlier compound
microscopes at a yet later date. Accurate balances and
other forms of gauges of space, as well as good means of
dividing time, such as our accurate astronomical clocks
and chronometers, are only about a century old. The instruments have made science accurate, and have immensely
extended its powers in nearly all the fields of inquiry.

Although the most striking modern discoveries are in
the field which was opened to us by the lens in its manifold applications, it is in the chemist's laboratory that we
find that branch of science, long cultivated, but rapidly
advanced only within the last two centuries, which has
done the most for the needs of man. The ancients guessed
that the substances which make up the visible world were
more complicated in their organization than they appear
to our vision. They even suggested the great truth that
matter of all kinds is made up of inconceivably small indi-
visible bits which they and we term atoms. It is likely
that in the classic days of Greece men began to make simple experiments of a chemical nature. A century or two
after the time of Mohammed, the Arabians of his faith, a
people who had acquired Greek science from the libraries

which their conquests gave them, conducted extensive experiments, and named a good many familiar chemical products, such as alcohol, which still bears its Arabic name.

These chemical studies were continued in Europe by the alchemists, a name also of Arabic origin, a set of inquirers who were to a great extent drawn away from scientific studies by vain though unending efforts to change the baser metals into gold and silver, as well as to find a compound which would make men immortal in the body. By the invention of the accurate balance, and by patient weighing of the matters which they submitted to experiment, by the invention of hypotheses or guesses at truth, which were carefully tested by experiment, the majestic science of modern chemistry has come forth from the confused and mystical studies of the alchemists. We have learned to know that there are seventy or more primitive or apparently unchangeable elements which make up the mass of this world, and probably constitute all the celestial spheres, and that these elements in the form of their separate atoms may group themselves in almost inconceivably varied combinations. In the inanimate realm these associations, composed of the atoms of the different substances, forming what are termed molecules, are generally composed of but few units. Thus carbonic-acid gas, as it is commonly called, is made up of an aggregation of molecules, each composed of one atom of carbon and two of oxygen; water, of two atoms of hydrogen and one of oxygen; ordinary iron oxide, of two atoms of iron and three of oxygen. In the realm of organic life, however, these combinations become vastly more complicated, and with each of them the properties of the substance thus produced differ from all others. A distinguished chemist has estimated that in one group of chemical compounds, that of carbon, it would be possible to make such an array of substances that it would require a library of many thousand ordinary volumes to contain their names alone.

It is characteristic of chemical science that it takes account of actions which are almost entirely invisible. No contrivances have been or are likely to be invented which will show the observer what takes place when the atoms of any substance depart from their previous combination and enter on new arrangements. We only know that under certain conditions the old atomic associations break up, and new ones are formed. But though the processes are hidden, the results are manifest in the changes which are brought about upon the masses of material which are subjected to the altering conditions. Gradually the chemists of our day are learning to build up in their laboratories more and more complicated compounds; already they have succeeded in producing many of the materials which of old could only be obtained by extracting them from plants. Thus a number of the perfumes of flowers, and many of the dye-stuffs which a century ago were extracted from vegetables, and were then supposed to be only obtainable in that way, are now readily manufactured. In time it seems likely that important articles of food, for which we now depend upon the seeds of plants, may be directly built up from the mineral kingdom. Thus the result of chemical inquiry has been not only to show us much of the vast realm of actions which go on in the earth, but to give us control of many of these movements so that we may turn them to the needs of man.

Animals and plants were at an early day very naturally the subjects of inquiry. The ancients perceived that there were differences of kind among these creatures, and even in Aristotle's time the sciences of zoölogy and botany had attained the point where there were considerable treatises on those subjects. It was not, however, until a little more than a century ago that men began accurately to describe and classify these species of the organic world. Since the time of Linnæus the growth of our knowledge has gone forward with amazing swiftness. Within a century we have come to know perhaps a hundred times as much concerning these creatures as was learned in all the earlier ages. This knowledge is divisible into two main branches: in one the inquirers have taken account of the different species, genera, families, orders, and classes of living forms with such effect that they have shown the existence at the present time of many hundred thousand distinct species, the vast assemblage being arranged in a classification which shows something as to the relationship which the forms bear to each other, and furthermore that the kinds now living have not been long in existence, but that at each stage in the history of the earth another assemblage of species peopled the waters and the lands.

At first naturalists concerned themselves only with the external forms of living creatures; but they soon came to perceive that the way in which these organisms worked, their physiology, in a word, afforded matters for extended inquiry. These researches have developed the science of physiology, or the laws of bodily action, on many accounts the most modern and extensive of our new acquisitions of natural learning. Through these studies we have come to know something of the laws or principles by which life is handed on from generation to generation, and by which the gradations of structure have been advanced from the simple creatures which appear like bits of animated jelly to the body and mind of man.

The greatest contribution which modern naturalists have made to knowledge concerns the origin of organic species. The students of a century ago believed that all these different kinds had been suddenly created either through natural law or by the immediate will of God. We now know that from the beginning of organic life in the remote past to the present day one kind of animal or plant has been in a natural and essentially gradual way converted into the species which was to be its successor, so that all the vast and complicated assemblage of kinds which now exists has been derived by a process of change from the forms which in earlier ages dwelt upon this planet. The exact manner in which these alterations were produced is not yet determined, but in large part it has evidently been brought about by the method indicated by Mr. Darwin, through the survival of the fittest individuals in the struggle for existence.

Until men came to have a clear conception as to the spherical form of the earth, it was impossible for them to begin any intelligent inquiries concerning its structure or history. The Greeks knew the earth to be a sphere, but this knowledge was lost among the early Christian people, and it was not until about four hundred years ago that men again came to see that they dwelt upon a globe. On the basis of this understanding the science of geology, which had in a way been founded by the Greeks, was revived. As this science depends upon the knowledge which we have gained of astronomy, physics, chemistry, and biology, all of which branches of learning have to be used in explaining the history of the earth, the advance which has been made has been relatively slow. Geology as a whole is the least perfectly organized of all the divisions of learning. A special difficulty peculiar to this science has also served to hinder its development. All the other branches of learning deal mainly, if not altogether, with the conditions of Nature as they now exist. In this alone is it necessary at every step to take account of actions which have been performed in the remote past.

It is an easy matter for the students of to-day to imagine that the earth has long endured; but to our forefathers, who were educated in the view that it had been brought from nothingness into existence about seven thousand years ago, it was most difficult and for a time impossible to believe in its real antiquity. Endeavouring, as they naturally did, to account for all the wonderful revolutions, the history of which is written in the pages of the great stone book, the early geologists supposed this planet to have been the seat of frequent and violent changes, each of which revolutionized its shape and destroyed its living tenants. It was only very gradually that they became convinced that a hundred million years or more have elapsed since the dawn of life on the earth, and that in this vast period the march of events has been steadfast, the changes taking place at about the same rate in which they are now going on. As yet this conception as to the history of our sphere has not become the general property of the people, but the fact of it is recognised by all those who have attentively studied the matter. It is now as well ascertained as any of the other truths which science has disclosed to us.

It is instructive to note the historic outlines of scientific development. The most conspicuous truth which this history discloses is that all science has had its origin and almost all its development among the peoples belonging to the Aryan race. This body of folk appears to have taken on its race characteristics, acquired its original language, its modes of action, and the foundations of its religion in that part of northern Europe which is about the Baltic Sea. Thence the body of this people appear to have wandered toward central Asia, where after ages of pastoral life in the high table lands and mountains of their country it sent forth branches to India, Asia Minor and Greece, to Persia, and to western Europe. It seems ever to have been a characteristic of these Aryan peoples that they had an extreme love for Nature; moreover, they clearly perceived the need of accounting for the things that happened in the world about them. In general they inclined to what is called the pantheistic explanation of the universe. They believed a supreme God in many different forms to be embodied in all the things they saw. Even their own minds and bodies they conceived as manifestations of this supreme power. Among the Aryans who came to dwell in Europe and along the eastern Mediterranean this method of explaining Nature was in time changed to one in which humanlike gods were supposed to control the visible and invisible worlds. In that marvellous centre of culture which was developed among the Greeks this conception of humanlike deities was in time replaced by that of natural law, and in their best days the Greeks were men of science essentially like those of to-day, except that they had not learned by experience how important it was to criticise their theories by patiently comparing them with the facts which they sought to explain. The last of the important Greek men of science, Strabo, who was alive when Christ was born, has left us writings which in quality are essentially like many of the able works of to-day. But for the interruption in the development of Greek learning, natural science would probably have been fifteen hundred years ahead of its present stage. This interruption came in two ways. In one, through the conquest of Greece and the destruction of its intellectual life by the Romans, a people who were singularly incapable of appreciating natural science, and who had no other interest in it except now and then a vacant and unprofitable curiosity as to the processes of the natural world. A second destructive influence came through the fact that Christianity, in its energetic protest against the sins of the pagan civilization, absolutely neglected and in a way despised all forms of science.

The early indifference of Christians to natural learning is partly to be explained by the fact that their religion was developed among the Hebrews, a people remarkable for their lack of interest in the scientific aspects of Nature. To them it was a sufficient explanation that one omnipotent God ruled all things at his will, the heavens and the earth alike being held in the hollow of his hand.

Finding the centre of its development among the Romans, Christianity came mainly into the control of a people who, as we have before remarked, had no scientific interest in the natural world. This condition prolonged the separation of our faith from science for fifteen hundred years after its beginning. In this time the records of Greek scientific learning mostly disappeared. The writ-

ings of Aristotle were preserved in part for the reason that
the Church adopted many of his views concerning questions in moral philosophy and in politics. The rest of
Greek learning was, so far as Europe was concerned, quite
neglected.

A large part of Greek science which has come down
to us owes its preservation to a very singular incident in
the history of learning. In the ninth century, after the
Arabs had been converted to Mohammedanism, and on
the basis of that faith had swiftly organized a great and
cultivated empire, the scholars of that folk became deeply
interested in the remnants of Greek learning which had
survived in the monastic and other libraries about the
eastern Mediterranean. So greatly did they prize these
records, which were contemned by the Christians, that it
was their frequent custom to weigh the old manuscripts
in payment against the coin of their realm. In astronomy,
mathematics, chemistry, and geology the Arabian students,
building on the ancient foundations, made notable and
for a time most important advances. In the tenth century
of our era they seemed fairly in the way to do for science
what western Europe began five centuries later to accomplish. In the fourteenth century the centre of Moham-
medan strength was transferred from the Arabians to the
Turks, from a people naturally given to learning to a folk
of another race, who despised all such culture. Thenceforth in place of the men who had treasured and deciphered
with infinite pains all the records of earlier learning, the
followers of Mohammed zealously destroyed all the records
of the olden days. Some of these records, however, survived among the Arabs of Spain, and others were preserved
by the Christian scholars who dwelt in Byzantium, or
Constantinople, and were brought into western Europe
when that city was captured by the Turks in the fifteenth
century.

Already the advance of the fine arts in Italy and the
general tendency toward the study of Nature, such as

painting and sculpture indicate, had made a beginning, or rather a proper field for a beginning, of scientific inquiry. The result was a new interest in Greek learning in all its branches, and a very rapid awakening of the scientific spirit. At first the Roman Church made no opposition to this new interest which developed among its followers, but in the course of a few years, animated with the fear that science would lead men to doubt many of the dogmas of the Church, it undertook sternly to repress the work of all inquirers.

The conflict between those of the Roman faith and the men of science continued for above two hundred years. In general, the part which the Church took was one of remonstrance, but in a few cases the spirit of fanaticism led to the persecution of the men who did not obey its mandates and disavow all belief in the new opinions which were deemed contrary to the teachings of Scripture. The last instance of such oppression occurred in France in the year 1756, when the great Buffon was required to recant certain opinions concerning the antiquity of the earth which he had published in his work on Natural History. This he promptly did, and in almost servile language withdrew all the opinions to which the fathers had objected. A like conflict between the followers of science and the clerical authorities occurred in Protestant countries. Although in no case were the men of science physically tortured or executed for their opinions, they were nevertheless subjected to great religious and social pressure: they were almost as effectively disciplined as were those who fell under the ban of the Roman Church.

Some historians have criticised the action of the clerical authorities toward science as if the evil which was done had been performed in our own day. It should be remembered, however, that in the earlier centuries the churches regarded themselves as bound to protect all men from the dangers of heresy. For centuries in the early history of Christianity the defenders of the faith had been engaged in a life-and-death struggle with paganism, the followers of which held all that was known of Nature. Quite naturally the priestly class feared that the revival of scientific inquiry would bring with it the evils from which the world had suffered in pagan times. There is no doubt that these persecutions of science were done under what seemed the obligations of duty. They may properly be explained particularly by men of science as one of the symptoms of development in the day in which they were done. It is well for those who harshly criticise the relations of the Church to science to remember that in our own country, about two centuries ago, among the most enlightened and religious people of the time, Quakers were grievously persecuted, and witches hanged, all in the most dutiful and God-fearing way. In considering these relations of science to our faith, the matter should be dealt with in a philosophical way, and with a sense of the differences between our own and earlier ages.

To the student of the relations between Christianity and science it must appear doubtful whether the criticism or the other consequences which the men of science had to meet from the Church was harmful to their work. The early naturalists, like the Greeks whom they followed, were greatly given to speculations concerning the processes of Nature, which, though interesting, were unprofitable. They also showed a curious tendency to mingle their scientific speculations with ancient and base superstitions. They were often given to the absurdity commonly known as the " black art," or witchcraft, and held to the preposterous notions of the astrologists. Even the immortal astronomer Kepler, who lived in the sixteenth century, was a professional astrologer, and still held to the notion that the stars determined the destiny of men. Many other of the famous inquirers in those years which ushered in modern science believed in witchcraft. Thus for a time natural learning was in a way associated with ancient and pernicious beliefs which the Church was seeking to overthrow. One result of the clerical opposition to the advancement of science was that its votaries were driven to prove every step which led to their conclusions. They were forced to abandon the loose speculation of their intellectual guides, the Greeks, and to betake themselves to observation. Thus a part of the laborious fact-gathering habit on which the modern advance of science has absolutely depended was due to the care which men had to exercise in face of the religious authorities.

In our own time, in the latter part of the nineteenth century, the conflict between the religious authority and the men of science has practically ceased. Even the Roman Church permits almost everywhere an untrammelled teaching of the established learning to which it was at one time opposed. Men have come to see that all truth is accordant, and that religion has nothing to fear from the faithful and devoted study of Nature.

The advance of science in general in modern times has been greatly due to the development of mechanical inventions. Among the ancients, the tools which served in the arts were few in number, and these of exceeding simplicity. So far as we can ascertain, in the five hundred years during which the Greeks were in their intellectual vigour, not more than half a dozen new machines were invented, and these were exceedingly simple. The fact seems to be that a talent for mechanical invention is mainly limited to the peoples of France, Germany, and of the English-speaking folk. The first advances in these contrivances were made in those countries, and all our considerable gains have come from their people. Thus, while the spirit of science in general is clearly limited to the Aryan folk, that particular part of the motive which leads to the invention of tools is restricted to western and northern Europe, to the people to whom we give the name of Teutonic.

Mechanical inventions have aided the development of our sciences in several ways. They have furnished inquirers with instruments of precision; they have helped to develop accuracy of observation; best of all, they have served ever to bring before the attention of men a spectacle of the conditions in Nature which we term cause and effect. The influence of these inventions on the development of learning has been particularly great where the machines, such as our wind and water mills, and our steam engine, make use of the forces of Nature, subjugating them to the needs of man. Such instruments give an unending illustration as to the presence in Nature of energy. They have helped men to understand that the machinery of the universe is propelled by the unending application of power. It was, in fact, through such machines that men of science first came to understand that energy, manifested in the natural forces, is something that eternally endures; that we may change its form in our arts as its form is changed in the operations of Nature, but the power endures forever.

It is interesting to note that the first observation which led to this most important scientific conclusion that energy is indestructible however much it may change its form, was made by an American, Benjamin Thompson, who left this country at the time of the Revolution, and after a curious life became the executive officer, and in effect king, of Bavaria. While engaged in superintending the manufacture of cannon, he observed that in boring out the barrel of the gun an amount of heat.was produced which evaporated a certain amount of water. He therefore concluded that the energy required to do the boring of the metal passed into the state of heat, and thus only changed its state, in no wise disappearing from the earth. Other students pursuing the same line of inquiry have clearly demonstrated what is called the law of the conservation of energy, which more than anything has helped us to understand the large operations of Nature. Through these studies we have come to see that, while the universe is a place of ceaseless change, the quantities of energy and of matter remain unaltered.

3

The foregoing brief sketch, which sets forth some of the important conditions which have affected the development of science, may in a way serve to show the student how he can himself become an interpreter of Nature. The evidence indicates that the people of our race have been in a way chosen among all the varieties of mankind to lead in this great task of comprehending the visible universe. The facts, moreover, show that discovery usually begins with the interest which men feel in the world immediately about them, or which is presented to their senses in a daily spectacle. Thus Benjamin Franklin, in the midst of a busy life, became deeply interested in the phenomena of lightning, and by a very simple experiment proved that this wonder of the air was due to electrical action such as we may arouse by rubbing a stick of sealing-wax or a piece of amber with a cloth. All discoveries, in a word, have had their necessary beginnings in an interest in the facts which daily experience discloses. This desire to know something more than the first sight exhibits concerning the actions in the world about us is native in every human soul—at least, in all those who are born with the heritage of our race. It is commonly strong in childhood; if cultivated by use, it will grow throughout a lifetime, and, like other faculties, becomes the stronger and more effective by the exertions which it inspires. It is therefore most important that every one should obey this instinctive command to inquiry, and organize his life and work so that he may not lose but gain more and more as time goes on of this noble capacity to interrogate and understand the world about him.

It is best that all study of Nature should begin not in laboratories, nor with the things which are remote from us, but in the field of Nature which is immediately about us. The student, even if he dwell in the unfavourable conditions of a great city, is surrounded by the world which has yielded immeasurable riches in the way of learning, which he can appropriate by a little study. He can readily come to know something of the movements of the air; the buildings will give him access to a great many different kinds of stone; the smallest park, a little garden, or even a few potted plants and captive animals, may tell him much concerning the forms and actions of living beings. By studying in this way he can come to know something of the differences between things and their relations to each other. He will thus have a standard by which he can measure and make familiar the body of learning concerning Nature which he may find in books. From printed pages alone, however well they be written, he can never hope to catch the spirit that animates the real inquirer, the true lover of Nature.

On many accounts the most attractive way of beginning to form the habit of the naturalist is by the study of living animals and plants. To all of us life adds interest, and growth has a charm. Therefore it is well for the student to start on the way of inquiry by watching the actions of birds and insects or by rearing plants. It is fortunate if he can do both these agreeable things. When the habit of taking an account of that most important part of the world which is immediately about him has been developed in the student, he may profitably proceed to acquire the knowledge of the invisible universe which has been gathered by the host of inquirers of his race. However far he journeys, he should return to the home world that lies immediately and familiarly about him, for there alone can he acquire and preserve that personal acquaintance with things which is at once the inspiration and the test of all knowledge.

Along with this study of the familiar objects about us the student may well combine some reading which may serve to show him how others have been successful in thus dealing with Nature at first hand. For this purpose there are, unfortunately, but few works which are well calculated to serve the needs of the beginner. Perhaps the best naturalist book, though its form is somewhat ancient, is White's

Natural History of Selborne. Hugh Miller's works, particularly his Old Red Sandstone and My Schools and Schoolmasters, show well how a man may become a naturalist under difficulties. Sir John Lubbock's studies on Wasps, and Darwin's work on Animals and Plants under Domestication are also admirable to show how observation should be made. Dr. Asa Gray's little treatise on How Plants Grow will also be useful to the beginner who wishes to approach botany from its most attractive side—that of the development of the creature from the seed to seed.

There is another kind of training which every beginner in the art of observing Nature should obtain, and which many naturalists of repute would do well to give themselves—namely, an education in what we may call the art of distance and geographical forms. With the primitive savage the capacity to remember and to picture to the eye the shape of a country which he knows is native and instinctive. Accustomed to range the woods, and to trust to his recollection to guide him through the wilderness to his home, the primitive man develops an important art which among civilized people is generally dormant. In fact, in our well-trodden ways people may go for many generations without ever being called upon to use this natural sense of geography. The easiest way to cultivate the geographic sense is by practising the art of making sketch maps. This the student, however untrained, can readily do by taking first his own dwelling house, on which he should practise until he can readily from memory make a tolerably correct and proportional plan of all its rooms. Then on a smaller scale he should begin to make also from recollection a map showing the distribution of the roads, streams, and hills with which his daily life makes him familiar. From time to time this work from memory should be compared with the facts. At first the record will be found to be very poor, but with a few months of occasional endeavour the observer will find that his mind takes account of geographic features in a way it did not before, and, moreover, that his mind becomes enriched with impressions of the country which are clear and distinct, in place of the shadowy recollections which he at first possessed.

When the student has attained the point where, after walking or riding over a country, he can readily recall its physical features of the simpler sort, he will find it profitable to undertake the method of mapping with contour lines—that is, by pencilling in indications to show the exact shape of the elevations and depressions. The principle of contour lines is that each of them represents where water would come against the slope if the area were sunk step by step below the sea level—in other words, each contour line marks the intersection of a horizontal plane with the elevation of the country. Practice on this somewhat difficult task will soon give the student some idea as to the complication of the surface of a region, and afford him the basis for a better understanding of what geography means than all the reading he can do will effect. It is most desirable that training such as has been described should be a part of our ordinary school education.

Very few people have clear ideas of distances. Even the men whose trade requires some such knowledge are often without that which a litle training could give them. Without some capacity in this direction, the student is always at a disadvantage in his contact with Nature. He can not make a record of what he sees as long as the element of horizontal and vertical distance is not clearly in mind. To attain this end the student should begin by pacing some length of road where the distances are well known. In this way he will learn the length of his step, which with a grown man generally ranges between two and a half and three feet. Learning the average length of his stride by frequent counting, it is easy to repeat the trial until one can almost unconsciously keep the count as he walks. Properly to secure the training of this sort the observer should first attentively look across the distance which is to be determined. He should notice how houses, fences, people, and trees appear at that distance. He will quickly perceive that each hundred feet of additional interval somewhat changes their aspect. In training soldiers to measure with the eye the distances which they have to know in order effectively to use the modern weapons of war, a common device is to take a squad of men, or sometimes a company, under the command of an officer, who halts one man at each hundred yards until the detachment is strung out with that interval as far as the eye can see them. The men then walk to and fro so that the troops who are watching them may note the effects of increased distance on their appearance, whether standing or in motion. At three thousand yards a man appears as a mere dot, which is not readily distinguishable. Schoolboys may find this experiment amusing and instructive.

After the student has gained, as he readily may, some sense of the divisions of distance within the range of ordinary vision, he should try to form some notion of greater intervals, as of ten, a hundred, and perhaps a thousand miles. The task becomes more difficult as the length of the line increases, but most persons can with a little address manage to bring before their eyes a tolerably clear image of a hundred miles of distance by looking from some elevation which commands a great landscape. It is doubtful, however, whether the best-trained man can get any clear notion of a thousand miles—that is, can present it to himself in imagination as he may readily do with shorter intervals.

The most difficult part of the general education which the student has to give himself is begun when he undertakes to picture long intervals of time. Space we have opportunities to measure, and we come in a way to appreciate it, but the longest lived of men experiences at most a century of life, and this is too small a measure to give any notion as to the duration of such great events as are involved in the history of the earth, where the periods are to be reckoned by the millions of years. The only way in which we can get any aid in picturing to ourselves great lapses of time is by expressing them in units of distance. Let a student walk away on a straight road for the distance of a mile; let him call each step a year; when he has won the first milestone, he may consider that he has gone backward in time to the period of Christ's birth. Two miles more will take him to the station which will represent the age when the oldest pyramids were built. He is still, however, in the later days of man's history on this planet. To attain on the scale the time when man began, he might well have to walk fifty miles away, while a journey which would thus by successive steps describe the years of the earth's history since life appeared upon its surface would probably require him to circle the earth at least four times. We may accept it as impossible for any one to deal with such vast durations save with figures which are never really comprehended. It is well, however, to enlarge our view as to the age of the earth by such efforts as have just been indicated.

When we go beyond the earth into the realm of the stars all efforts toward understanding the ranges of space or the durations of time are quite beyond the efforts of man. Even the distance of about two hundred and forty thousand miles which separates us from the moon can not be grasped by even the greater minds. No human intelligence, however cultivated, can conceive the distance of about ninety-five million miles which separates us from the sun. In the celestial realm we can only deal with relations of space and time in a general and comparative way. We can state the distances if we please in millions of miles, or we can reckon the ampler spaces by using the interval which separates the earth from the sun as we do a foot rule in our ordinary work, but the depths of the starry spaces can only be sounded by the winged imagination.

Although the student has been advised to begin his

studies of Nature on the field whereon he dwells, making that study the basis of his most valuable communications with Nature, it is desirable that he should at the same time gain some idea as to the range and scope of our knowledge concerning the visible universe. As an aid toward this end the following chapters of this book will give a very brief survey of some of the most important truths concerning the heavens and the earth which have rewarded the studies of scientific men. Of remoter things, such as the bodies in the stellar spaces, the account will be brief, for that which is known and important to the general student can be briefly told. So, too, of the earlier ages of the earth's history, although a vast deal is known, the greater part of the knowledge is of interest and value mainly to geologists who cultivate that field. That which is most striking and most important to the mass of mankind is to be found in the existing state of our earth, the conditions which make it a fit abode for our kind, and replete with lessons which he may study with his own eyes without having to travel the difficult paths of the higher sciences.

Although physiography necessarily takes some account of the things which have been, even in the remote past, and this for the reason that everything in this day of the world depends on the events of earlier days, the accent of its teaching is on the immediate, visible, as we may say, living world, which is a part of the life of all its inhabitants.

CHAPTER III.

EVEN before men came to take any careful account of the Nature immediately about them they began to conjecture and in a way to inquire concerning the stars and the other heavenly bodies. It is difficult for us to imagine how hard it was for students to gain any adequate idea of what those lights in the sky really are. At first men imagined the celestial bodies to be, as they seemed, small objects not very far away. Among the Greeks the view grew up that the heavens were formed of crystal spheres in which the lights were placed, much as lanterns may be hung upon a ceiling. These spheres were conceived to be one above the other; the planets were on the lower of them, and the fixed stars on the higher, the several crystal roofs revolving about the earth. So long as the earth was supposed to be a flat and limitless expanse, forming the centre of the universe, it was impossible for the students of the heavens to attain any more rational view as to their plan.

The fact that the earth was globular in form was understood by the Greek men of science. They may, indeed, have derived the opinion from the Egyptian philosophers. The discovery rested upon the readily observed fact that on a given day the shadow of objects of a certain height was longer in high latitude than in low. Within the tropics, when the sun was vertical, there would be no shadow, while as far north as Athens it would be of considerable length. The conclusion that the earth was a sphere appears to have

31

been the first large discovery made by our race. It was, indeed, one of the most important intellectual acquisitions of man.

Understanding the globular form of the earth, the next and most natural step was to learn that the earth was not the centre of the planetary system, much less of the universe, but that that centre was the sun, around which the earth and the other planets revolved. The Greeks appear to have had some idea that this was the case, and their spirit of inquiry would probably have led them to the whole truth but for the overthrow of their thought by the Roman conquest and the spread of Christianity. It was therefore not until after the revival of learning that astronomers won their way to our modern understanding concerning the relation of the planets to the sun. With Galileo this opinion was affirmed. Although for a time the Church, resting its opposition on the interpretation of certain passages of Scripture, resisted this view, and even punished the men who held it, it steadfastly made its way, and for more than two centuries has been the foundation of all the great discoveries in the stellar realm. Yet long after the fact that the sun was the centre of the solar system was well established no one understood why the planets should move in their ceaseless, orderly procession around the central mass. To Newton we owe the studies on the law of gravitation which brought us to our present large conception as to the origin of this order. Starting with the view that bodies attracted each other in proportion to their weight, and in diminishing proportion as they are removed from each other, Newton proceeded by most laborious studies to criticise this view, and in the end definitely proved it by finding that the motions of the moon about the earth, as well as the paths of the planets, exactly agreed with the supposition.

The last great path-breaking discovery which has helped us in our understanding of the stars was made by Fraunhofer and other physicists, who showed us that sub-

Seal Rocks near San Francisco, California, showing slight effect of waves where there is no beach.

stances when in a heated, gaseous, or vaporous state produced, in a way which it is not easy to explain in a work
such as this, certain dark lines in the spectrum, or streak
of divided light which we may make by means of a glass
prism, or, as in the rainbow, by drops of water. Carefully
studying these very numerous lines, those naturalists found
that they could with singular accuracy determine what substances there were in the flame which gave the light. So
accurate is this determination that it has been made to
serve in certain arts where there is no better means of
ascertaining the conditions of a flaming substance except
by the lines which its light exhibits under this kind of
analysis. Thus, in the manufacture of iron by what is
called the Bessemer process, it has been found very convenient to judge as to the state of the molten metal by
such an analysis of the flame which comes forth from it.

No sooner was the spectroscope invented than astronomers hastened by its aid to explore the chemical constitution of the sun. These studies have made it plain that
the light of our solar centre comes forth from an atmosphere composed of highly heated substances, all of which
are known among the materials forming the earth. Although for various reasons we have not been able to recognise in the sun all the elements which are found in our
sphere, it is certain that in general the two bodies are
alike in composition. An extension of the same method
of inquiry to the fixed stars was gradually though with
difficulty attained, and we now know that many of the
elements common to the sun and earth exist in those distant spheres. Still further, this method of inquiry has
shown us, in a way which it is not worth while here to
describe, that among these remoter suns there are many
aggregations of matter which are not consolidated as are
the spheres of our own solar system, but remain in the
gaseous state, receiving the name of nebulæ.

Along with the growth of observational astronomy
which has taken place since the discoveries of Galileo,

there has been developed a view concerning the physical
history of the stellar world, known as the nebular hypothesis, which, though not yet fully proved, is believed by most
astronomers and physicists to give us a tolerably correct
notion as to the way in which the heavenly spheres were
formed from an earlier condition of matter. This majestic conception was first advanced, in modern times at least,
by the German philosopher Immanuel Kant. It was developed by the French astronomer Laplace, and is often
known by his name. The essence of this view rests upon
the fact previously noted that in the realm of the fixed stars
there are many faintly shining aggregations of matter
which are evidently not solid after the manner of the
bodies in our solar system, but are in the state where their
substances are in the condition of dustlike particles, as are
the bits of carbon in flame or the elements which compose
the atmosphere. The view held by Laplace was to the
effect that not only our own solar system, but the centres
of all the other similar systems, the fixed stars, were originally in this gaseous state, the material being disseminated
throughout all parts of the heavenly realm, or at least in
that portion of the universe of which we are permitted
to know something. In this ancient state of matter we
have to suppose that the particles of it were more separated from each other than are the atoms of the atmospheric gases in the most perfect vacuum which we can
produce with the air-pump. Still we have to suppose that
each of these particles attract the other in the gravitative
way, as in the present state of the universe they inevitably do.

Under the influence of the gravitative attraction the
materials of this realm of vapour inevitably tended to fall
in toward the centre. If the process had been perfectly
simple, the result would have been the formation of one
vast mass, including all the matter which was in the original body. In some way, no one has yet been able to make
a reasonable suggestion of just how, there were developed

in the process of concentration a great many separate centres of aggregation, each of which became the beginning of a solar system. The student may form some idea of how readily local centres may be produced in materials disseminated in the vaporous state by watching how fog or the thin, even misty clouds of the sunrise often gather into the separate shapes which make what we term a "mackerel" sky. It is difficult to imagine what makes centres of attraction, but we readily perceive by this instance how they might have occurred.

When the materials of each solar system were thus set apart from the original mass of star dust or vapour, they began an independent development which led step by step, in the case of our own solar system at least, and presumably also in the case of the other suns, the fixed stars, to the formation of planets and their moons or satellites, all moving around the central sun. At this stage of the explanation the nebular hypothesis is more difficult to conceive than in the parts of it which have already been described, for we have now to understand how the planets and satellites had their matter separated from each other and from the solar centre, and why they came to revolve around that central body. These problems are best understood by noting some familiar instances connected with the movement of fluids and gases toward a centre. First let us take the case of a basin in which the water is allowed to flow out through a hole in its centre. When we lift the stopper the fluid for a moment falls straight down through the opening. Very quickly, however, all the particles of the water start to move toward the centre, and almost at once the mass begins to whirl round with such speed that, although it is working toward the middle, it is by its movement pushed away from the centre and forms a conical depression. As often as we try the experiment, the effect is always the same. We thus see that there is some principle which makes particles of fluid that tend toward a

centre fail directly to attain it, but win their way thereto
in a devious, spinning movement.

Although the fact is not so readily made visible to the
eye, the same principle is illustrated in whirling storms,
in which, as we shall hereafter note with more detail, the
air next the surface of the earth is moving in toward a
kind of chimney by which it escapes to the upper regions
of the atmosphere. A study of cyclones and tornadoes,
or even of the little air-whirls which in hot weather lift
the dust of our streets, shows that the particles of the
atmosphere in rushing in toward the centre of upward
movement take on the same whirling motion as do the
molecules of water in the basin—in fact, the two actions
are perfectly comparable in all essential regards, except
that the fluid is moving downward, while the air flows
upward. Briefly stated, the reason for the movement of
fluid and gas in the whirling way is as follows: If every
particle on its way to the centre moved on a perfectly
straight line toward the point of escape, the flow would be
directly converging, and the paths followed would resemble the spokes of a wheel. But when by chance one of
the particles sways ever so little to one side of the direct
way, a slight lateral motion would necessarily be established. This movement would be due to the fact that the
particle which pursued the curved line would press against
the particles on the out-curved side of its path—or, in other
words, shove them a little in that direction—to the extent
that they departed from the direct line they would in turn
communicate the shoving to the next beyond. When two
particles are thus shoving on one side of their paths, the
action which makes for revolution is doubled, and, as we
readily see, the whole mass may in this way become quickly
affected, the particles driven out of their path, moving in a
curve toward the centre. We also see that the action is
accumulative: the more curved the path of each particle, the
more effectively it shoves; and so, in the case of the basin,
we see the whirling rapidly developed before our eyes.

In falling in toward the centre the particles of star dust or vapour would no more have been able one and all to pursue a perfectly straight line than the particles of water in the basin. If a man should spend his lifetime in filling and emptying such a vessel, it is safe to say that he would never fail to observe the whirling movement. As the particles of matter in the nebular mass which was to become a solar system are inconceivably greater than those of water in the basin, or those of air in the atmospheric whirl, the chance of the whirling taking place in the heavenly bodies is so great that we may assume that it would inevitably occur.

As the vapours in the olden day tended in toward the centre of our solar system, and the mass revolved, there is reason to believe that ringlike separations took place in it. Whirling in the manner indicated, the mass of vapour or dust would flatten into a disk or a body of circular shape, with much the greater diameter in the plane of its whirling. As the process of concentration went on, this disk is supposed to have divided into ringlike masses, some approach to which we can discern in the existing nebulæ, which here and there among the farther fixed stars appear to be undergoing such stages of development toward solar systems. It is reasonably supposed that after these rings had been developed they would break to pieces, the matter in them gathering into a sphere, which in time was to become a planet. The outermost of these rings led to the formation of the planet farthest from the sun, and was probably the first to separate from the parent mass. Then in succession rings were formed inwardly, each leading in turn to the creation of another planet, the sun itself being the remnant, by far the greater part of the whole mass of matter, which did not separate in the manner described, but concentrated on its centre. Each of these planetary aggregations of vapour tended to develop, as it whirled upon its centre, rings of its own, which in turn formed, by breaking and concentrating, the satellites or moons which attend the earth, as they do all the planets which lie farther away from the sun than our sphere.

Fig. 1.—Saturn, Jan. 26, 1889 (Antoniadi).

As if to prove that the planets and moons of the solar system were formed somewhat in the manner in which we have described it, one of these spheres, Saturn, retains a ring, or rather a band which appears to be divided obscurely into several rings which lie between its group of satellites and the main sphere. How this ring has been preserved when all the others have disappeared, and what is the exact constitution of the mass, is not yet well ascertained. It seems clear, however, that it can not be composed of solid matter. It is either in the form of dust or of small spheres, which are free to move on each other; otherwise, as computation shows, the strains due to the attraction which Saturn itself and its moons exercise upon it would serve to break it in pieces. Although this ring theory of the formation of the planets and satellites is not completely proved, the occurrence of such a structure as that which girdles Saturn affords presumptive evidence that it is true. Taken in connection with what we know of the nebulæ, the proof of Laplace's nebular hypothesis may fairly be regarded as complete.

It should be said that some of the fixed stars are not isolated suns like our own, but are composed of two great spheres revolving about one another; hence they are termed double stars. The motions of these bodies are very peculiar, and their conditions show us that it is not well to suppose that the solar system in which we dwell is the only type of order which prevails in the celestial families; there may, indeed, be other variations as yet undetected. Still, these differences throw no doubt on the essential truth of the theory as to the process of development of the celestial systems. Though there is much room for debate as to the details of the work there, the general truth of the theory is accepted by nearly all the students of the problem.

A peculiar advantage of the nebular hypothesis is that it serves to account for the energy which appears as light and heat in the sun and the fixed stars, as well as that which still abides in the mass of our earth, and doubtless also in the other large planets. When the matter of which these spheres were composed was disseminated through the realms of space, it is supposed to have had no positive temperature, and to have been dark, realizing the conception which appears in the first chapter of Genesis, " without form, and void." With each stage of the falling in toward the solar centres what is called the " energy of position " of this original matter became converted into light and heat. To understand how this took place, the reader should consider certain simple yet noble generalizations of physics. We readily recognise the fact that when a hammer falls often on an anvil it heats itself and the metal on which it strikes. Those who have been able to observe the descent of meteoric stones from the heavens have remarked that when they came to the earth they were, on their surfaces at least, exceedingly hot. Any one may observe shining meteors now and then flashing in the sky. These are known commonly to be very small bits of matter, probably not larger than grains of sand, which, rushing into our atmosphere. are so heated by the friction which they encounter that they burn to a gas or vapour

4

before they attain the earth. As we know that these particles come from the starry spaces, where the temperature
is somewhere near 500° below 0° Fahr., it is evident that
the light and heat are not brought with them into the atmosphere; it can only be explained by the fact that when
they enter the air they are moving at an average speed
of about twenty miles a second, and that the energy which
this motion represents is by the resistance which the body
encounters converted into heat. This fact will help us to
understand how, as the original star dust fell in toward the
centre of attraction, it was able to convert what we have
termed the energy of position into temperature. We see
clearly that every such particle of dust or larger bit of
matter which falls upon the earth brings about the development of heat, even though it does not actually strike upon
the solid mass of our sphere. The conception of what took
place in the consolidation of the originally disseminated
materials of the sun and planets can be somewhat helped
by a simple experiment. If we fit a piston closely into a
cylinder, and then suddenly drive it down with a heavy
blow, the compressed air is so heated that it may be made
to communicate fire. If the piston should be slowly moved,
the same amount of heat would be generated, or, as we may
better say, liberated by the compression, though the effect
would not be so striking. A host of experiments show
that when a given mass of matter is brought to occupy
a less space the effect is in practically all cases to increase
the temperature. The energy which kept the particles
apart is, when they are driven together, converted into
heat. These two classes of actions are somewhat different
in their nature; in the case of the meteors, or the equivalent star dust, the coming together of the particles is due
to gravitation. In the experiment with the cylinder above
described, the compression is due to mechanical energy,
a force of another nature.

There is little reason to doubt that all our planets, as
well as the sun itself, and also the myriad other orbs of

space, have all passed through the stages of a transition
in which a continually concentrating vapour, drawn together by gravitation, became progressively hotter and
more dense until it assumed the condition of a fluid. This
fluid gradually parted with its heat to the cold spaces of
the heavens, and became more and more concentrated and
of a lower temperature until in the end, as in the case of
our earth and of other planets, it ceased to glow on the
outside, though it remained intensely heated in the inner
parts. It is easy to see that the rate of this cooling would
be in some proportion to the size of the sphere. Thus the
earth, which is relatively small, has become relatively cold,
while the sun itself, because of its vastly greater mass, still
retains an exceedingly high temperature. The reason for
this can readily be conceived by making a comparison of
the rate of cooling which occurs in many of our ordinary
experiences. Thus a vial of hot water will quickly come
down to the temperature of the air, while a large jug filled
with the fluid at the same temperature will retain its heat
many times as long. The reason for this rests upon the
simple principle that the contents of a sphere increase
with its enlargement more rapidly than the surface through
which the cooling takes place.

The modern studies on the physical history of the sun
and other celestial bodies show that their original store
of heat is constantly flowing away into the empty realms
of space. The rate at which this form of energy goes away
from the sun is vast beyond the powers of the imagination
to conceive; thus, in the case of our earth, which viewed
from the sun would appear no more than a small star, the
amount of heat which falls upon it from the great centre
is enough each day to melt, if it all could be put to such
work, about eight thousand cubic miles of ice. Yet the
earth receives only $\frac{1}{2,170,000,000}$ part of the solar radiation. The greater part of this solar heat—in fact, we may
say nearly all of it—slips by the few and relatively small
planets and disappears in the great void.

The destiny of all the celestial spheres seems in time to be that they shall become cooled down to a temperature far below anything which is now experienced on this earth. Even the sun, though its heat will doubtless endure for millions of years to come, must in time, so far as we can see, become dark and cold. So far as we know, we can perceive no certain method by which the life of the slowly decaying suns can be restored. It has, however, been suggested that in many cases a planetary system which has attained the lifeless and lightless stage may by collision with some other association of spheres be by the blow restored to its previous state of vapour, the joint mass of the colliding systems once again to resume the process of concentration through which it had gone before. Now and then stars have been seen to flash suddenly into great brilliancy in a way which suggests that possibly their heat had been refreshed by a collision with some great mass which had fallen into them from the celestial spaces. There is room for much speculation in this field, but no certainty appears to be attainable.

The ancients believed that light and heat were emanations which were given off from the bodies that yielded them substantially as odours are given forth by many substances. Since the days of Newton inquiry has forced us to the conviction that these effects of temperature are produced by vibrations having the general character of waves, which are sent through the spaces with great celerity. When a ray of light departs from the sun or other luminous body, it does not convey any part of the mass; it transmits only motion. A conception of the action can perhaps best be formed by suspending a number of balls of ivory, stone, or other hard substance each by a cord, the series so arranged that they touch each other. Then striking a blow against one end of the line, we observe that the ball at the farther end of the line is set in motion, swinging a little away from the place it occupied before. The movement of the intermediate balls may be so slight as to escape attention. We thus perceive that energy can be transmitted from one to another of these little spheres. Close observation shows us that under the impulse which the blow gives each separate body is made to sway within itself much in the manner of a bell when it is rung, and that the movement is transmitted to the object with which it is in contact. In passing from the sun to the earth, the light and heat traverse a space which we know to be substantially destitute of any such materials as make up the mass of the earth or the sun. Judged by the standards which we can apply, this space must be essentially empty. Yet because motions go through it, we have to believe that it is occupied by something which has certain of the properties of matter. It has, indeed, one of the most important properties of all substances, in that it can vibrate. This practically unknown thing is called ether.

The first important observational work done by the ancients led them to perceive that there was a very characteristic difference between the planets and the fixed stars. They noted the fact that the planets wandered in a ceaseless way across the heavens, while the fixed stars showed little trace of changing position in relation to one another. For a long time it was believed that these, as well as the remoter fixed stars, revolved about the earth. This error, though great, is perfectly comprehensible, for the evident appearance of the movement is substantially what would be brought about if they really coursed around our sphere. It was only when the true nature of the earth and its relations to the sun were understood that men could correct this first view. It was not, indeed, until relatively modern times that the solar system came to be perceived as something independent and widely detached from the fixed stars system; that the spaces which separate the members of our own solar family, inconceivably great as they are, are but trifling as compared with the intervals which part us from the nearer fixed stars. At this stage of our knowledge men came to the noble suggestion that each of the fixed stars was itself a sun, each of the myriad probably attended by planetary bodies such as exist about our own luminary.

It will be well for the student to take an imaginary journey from the sun forth into space, along the plane in which extends that vast aggregation of stars which we term the Milky Way. Let him suppose that his journey could be made with something like the speed of light, or, say, at the rate of about two hundred thousand miles a second. It is fit that the imagination, which is free to go through all things, should essay such excursions. On the fancied outgoing, the observer would pass the interval between the sun and the earth in about eight minutes. It would require some hours before he attained to the outer limit of the solar system. On his direct way he would pass the orbits of the several planets. Some would have their courses on one side or the other of his path; we should say above or below, but for the fact that we leave these terms behind in the celestial realm. On the margin of the solar system the sun would appear shrunken to the state where it was hardly greater than the more brilliant of the other fixed stars. The onward path would then lead through a void which it would require years to traverse. Gradually the sun which happened to lie most directly in his path would grow larger; with nearer approach, it would disclose its planets. Supposing that the way led through this solar system, there would doubtless be revealed planets and satellites in their order somewhat resembling those of our own solar family, yet there would doubtless be many surprises in the view. Arriving near the first sun to be visited, though the heavens would have changed their shape, all the existing constellations having altered with the change in the point of view, there would still be one familiar element in that the new-found planets would be near by, and the nearest fixed stars far away in the firmament.

With the speed of light a stellar voyage could be taken along the path of the Milky Way, which would endure for thousands of years. Through all the course the journeyer would perceive the same vast girdle of stars, faint because they were far away, which gives the dim light of our galaxy. At no point is it probable that he would find the separate suns much more aggregated or greatly farther apart than they are in that part of the Milky Way which our sun now occupies. Looking forth on either side of the " galactic plane," there would be the same scattering of stars which we now behold when we gaze at right angles to the way we are supposing the spirit to traverse.

As the form of the Milky Way is irregular, the mass, indeed, having certain curious divisions and branches, it well might be that the supposed path would occasionally pass on one or the other side of the vast star layer. In such positions the eye would look forth into an empty firmament, except that there might be in the far away, tens of thousands of years perhaps at the rate that light travels away from the observer, other galaxies or Milky Ways essentially like that which he was traversing. At some point the journeyer would attain the margin of our star stratum, whence again he would look forth into the unpeopled heavens, though even there he might discern other remote star groups separated from his own by great void intervals.

The revelations of the telescope show us certain features in the constitution and movements of the fixed stars which now demand our attention. In the first place, it is plain that not all of these bodies are in the same physical condition. Though the greater part of these distant luminous masses are evidently in the state of aggregation displayed by our own sun, many of them retain more or less of that vaporous, it may be dustlike, character which we suppose to have been the ancient state of all the matter in the universe. Some of these masses appear as faint, almost indistinguishable clouds, which even to the greatest telescope and the best-trained vision show no distinct fea-

tures of structure. In other cases the nebulous appearance
is hardly more than a mist about a tolerably distinct central star. Yet again, and most beautifully in the great
nebula of the constellation of Orion, the cloudy mass,
though hardly visible to the naked eye, shows a division
into many separate parts, the whole appearing as if in
process of concentration about many distinct centres.

The nebulæ are reasonably believed by many astronomers to be examples of the ancient condition of the physical universe, masses of matter which for some reason as
yet unknown have not progressed in their consolidation to
the point where they have taken on the characteristics
of suns and their attendant planets.

Many of the fixed stars, the incomplete list of which
now amounts to several hundred, are curiously variable in
the amount of light which they send out to the earth.
Sometimes these variations are apparently irregular, but
in the greater number of cases they have fixed periods,
the star waxing and waning at intervals varying from a few
months to a few years. Although some of the sudden
flashings forth of stars from apparent small size to near
the greatest brilliancy may be due to catastrophes such
as might be brought about by the sudden falling in of
masses of matter upon the luminous spheres, it is more
likely that the changes which we observe are due to the
fact that two suns revolving around a common centre are
in different stages of extinction. It may well be that
one of these orbs, presumably the smaller, has so far lost
temperature that it has ceased to glow. If in its revolution it regularly comes between the earth and its luminous
companion, the effect would be to give about such a change
in the amount of light as we observe.

The supposition that a bright sun and a relatively dark
sun might revolve around a common centre of gravity may
at first sight seem improbable. The fact is, however, that
imperfect as our observations on the stars really are, we
know many instances in which this kind of revolution of

one star about another takes place. In some cases these stars are of the same brilliancy, but in others one of the lights is 'much brighter than the other. From this condition to the state where one of the stars is so nearly dark as to be invisible, the transition is but slight. In a word, the evidence goes to show that while we see only the luminous orbs of space, the dark bodies which people the heavens are perhaps as numerous as those which send us light, and therefore appear as stars.

Besides the greater spheres of space, there is a vast host of lesser bodies, the meteorites and comets, which appear to be in part members of our solar system, and perhaps of other similar systems, and in part wanderers in the vast realm which intervenes between the solar systems. Of these we will first consider the meteors, of which we know by far the most; though even of them, as we shall see, our knowledge is limited.

From time to time on any starry night, and particularly in certain periods of the year, we may behold, at the distance of fifty or more miles above the surface of the earth, what are commonly called " shooting stars." The most of these flashing meteors are evidently very small, probably not larger than tiny sand grains, possibly no greater than the fragments which would be termed dust. They enter the air at a speed of about thirty miles a second. They are so small that they burn to vapour in the very great heat arising from their friction on the air, and do not attain the surface of the earth. These are so numerous that, on the average, some hundreds of thousands' probably strike the earth's atmosphere each day. From time to time larger badies fall—bodies which are of sufficient bulk not to be burned up in the air, but which descend to the ground. These may be from the smallest size which may be observed to masses of many hundred pounds in weight. These are far less numerous than the dust meteorites; it is probable, however, that several hundred fragments each year attain the earth's surface. They come from various directions of space, and there is as yet no means of determining whether they were formed in some manner within our planetary system or whether they wander to us from remoter realms. We know that they are in part composed of metallic iron commingled with nickel and carbon (sometimes as very small diamonds) in a way rarely if ever found on the surface of our sphere, and having a structure substantially unknown in its deposits. In part they are composed of materials which somewhat resemble certain lavas. It is possible that these fragments of iron and stone which constitute the meteorites have been thrown into the planetary spaces by the volcanic eruption of our own and other planets. If hurled forth with a sufficient energy, the fragments would escape from the control of the attraction of the sphere whence they came, and would become independent wanderers in space, moving around the sun in varied orbits until they were again drawn in by some of the greater planets.

As they come to us these meteorites often break up in the atmosphere, the bits being scattered sometimes over a wide area of country. Thus, in the case of the Cocke County meteorite of Tennessee, one of the iron species, the fragments, perhaps thousands in number, which came from the explosion of the body were scattered over an area of some thousand square miles. When they reach the surface in their natural form, these meteors always have a curious wasted and indented appearance, which makes it seem likely that they have been subject to frequent collisions in their journeys after they were formed by some violent rending action.

In some apparent kinship with the meteorites may be classed the comets. The peculiarity of these bodies is that they appear in most cases to be more or less completely vaporous. Rushing down from the depths of the heavens, these bodies commonly appear as faintly shining, cloudlike masses. As they move in toward the sun long trails of vapour stream back from the somewhat consolidated head.

Swinging around that centre, they journey again into the outer realm. As they retreat, their tail-like streamers ap-

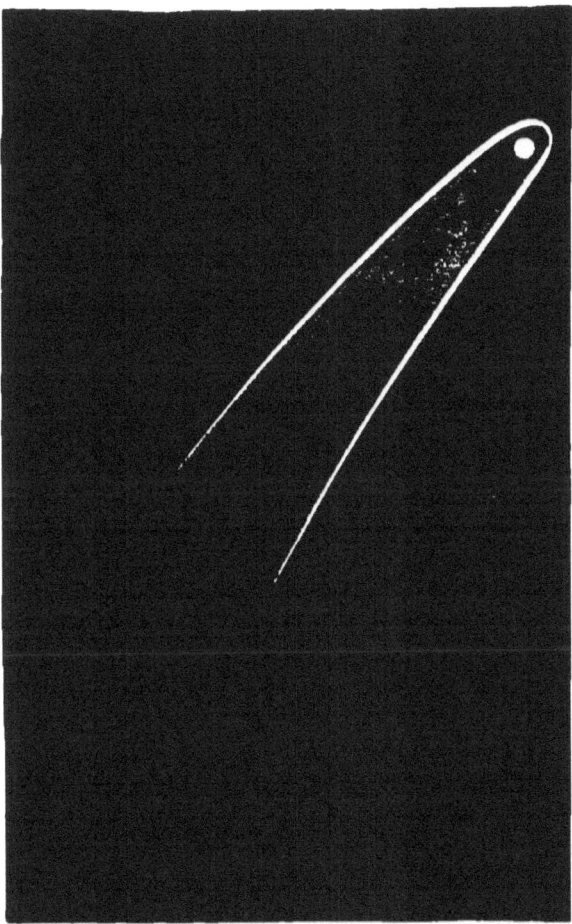

FIG. 2.—The Great Comet of 1811, one of the many varied forms of these bodies.

pear to gather again upon their centres, and when they fade from view they are again consolidated. In some cases it has been suspected that a part at least of the cometary mass was solid. The evidence goes to show, however, that the matter is in a dustlike or vaporous condition, and that the weight of these bodies is relatively very small.

Owing to their strange appearance, comets were to the ancients omens of calamity. Sometimes they were conceived as flaming swords; their forms, indeed, lend themselves to this imagining. They were thought to presage war, famine, and the death of kings. Again, in more modern times, when they were not regarded as portents of calamity, it was feared that these wanderers moving vagariously through our solar system might by chance come in contact with the earth with disastrous results. Such collisions are not impossible, for the reason that the planets would tend to draw these errant bodies toward them if they came near their spheres; yet the chance of such collisions happening to the earth is so small that they may be disregarded.

MOTIONS OF THE SPHERES.

Although little is known of the motions which occur among the celestial bodies beyond the sphere of our solar family, that which has been ascertained is of great importance, and serves to make it likely that all the suns in space are upon swift journeys which in their speed equal, if they do not exceed, the rate of motion among the planetary spheres, which may, in general, be reckoned at about twenty miles a second. Our whole solar system is journeying away from certain stars, and in the direction of others which are situated in the opposite part of the heavens. The proof of this fact is found in the observations which show that on one side of us the stars are apparently coming closer together, while on the other side they are going farther apart. The phenomenon, in a word, is one of perspective, and may be made real to the understanding by noting what takes place when we travel down a street along which there are lights. We readily note that these lights appear to close in behind us, and widen their intervals in the direction in which we journey. By such evidence astronomers have become convinced that our sphere, along with the sun which controls it, is each second a score of miles away from the point where it was before.

There is yet other and most curious evidence which serves to show that certain of the stars are journeying toward our part of the heavens at great speed, while others are moving away from us by their own proper motion. These indications are derived from the study of the lines in the light which the spectrum reveals to us when critically examined. The position of these cross lines is, as we know, affected by the motion of the body whence the light comes, and by close analysis of the facts it has been pretty well determined that the distortion in their positions is due to very swift motions of the several stars. It is not yet certain whether these movements of our sun and of other solar bodies are in straight lines or in great circles.

It should be noted that, although the evidence from the spectroscope serves to show that the matter in the stars is akin to that of our own earth, there is reason to believe that those great spheres differ much from each other in magnitude.

We have now set forth some of the important facts exhibited by the stellar universe. The body of details concerning that realm is vast, and the conclusions drawn from it important; only a part, however, of the matter with which it deals is of a nature to be apprehended by the student who does not approach it in a somewhat professional way. We shall therefore now turn to a description of the portion of the starry world which is found in the limits of our solar system. There the influences of the several spheres upon our planet are matters of vital importance; they in a way affect, if they do not control, all the operations which go on upon the surface of the earth.

THE SOLAR SYSTEM.

We have seen that the matter in the visible universe everywhere tends to gather into vast associations which appear to us as stars, and that these orbs are engaged in ceaseless motion in journeys through space. In only one of these aggregations—that which makes our own solar system—are the bodies sufficiently near to our eyes for us, even with the resources of our telescopes and other instruments, to divine something of the details which they exhibit. In studying what we may concerning the family of the sun, the planets, and their satellites, we may reasonably be assured that we are tracing a history which with many differences is in general repeated in the development of each star in the firmament. Therefore the inquiry is one of vast range and import.

Following, as we may reasonably do, the nebular hypothesis—a view which, though not wholly proved, is eminently probable—we may regard our solar system as having begun when the matter of which it is composed, then in a finely divided, cloudy state, was separated from the similar material which went to make the neighbouring fixed stars. The period when our solar system began its individual life was remote beyond the possibility of conception. Naturalists are pretty well agreed that living beings began to exist upon the earth at least a hundred million years ago; but the beginnings of our solar system must be placed at a date very many times as remote from the present day.*

According to the nebular theory, the original vapour of the solar system began to fall in toward its centre and to whirl about that point at a time long before the mass

---

* Some astronomers, particularly the distinguished Professor Newcomb, hold that the sun can not have been supplying heat as at present for more than about ten million years, and that all geological time must be thus limited. The geologist believes that this reckoning is far too short.

had shrunk to the present limits of the solar system as defined by the path of the outermost planets. At successive stages of the concentration, rings after the manner of those of Saturn separated from the disklike mass, each breaking up and consolidating into a body of nebulous matter which followed in the same path, generally forming rings which became by the same process the moons or satellites of the sphere. In this way the sun produced eight planets which are known, and possibly others of small size on the outer verge of the system which have eluded discovery. According to this view, the planetary masses were born in succession, the farthest away being the oldest. It is, however, held by an able authority that the mass of the solar system would first form a rather flat disk, the several rings forming and breaking into planets at about the same time. The conditions in Saturn, where the inner ring remains parted, favours the view just stated.

Before making a brief statement of the several planets, the asteroids, and the satellites, it will be well to consider in a general way the motions of these bodies about their centres and about the sun. The most characteristic and invariable of these movements is that by which each of the planetary spheres, as well as the satellites, describes an orbit around the gravitative centre which has the most influence upon it—the sun. To conceive the nature of this movement, it will be well to imagine a single planet revolving around the sun, each of these bodies being perfect spheres, and the two the only members of the solar system. In this condition the attraction of the two bodies would cause them to circle around a common centre of gravity, which, if the planet were not larger or the sun smaller than is the case in our solar system, would lie within the mass of the sun. In proportion as the two bodies might approach each other in size, the centre of gravity would come the nearer to the middle point in a line connecting the two spheres. In this condition of a sun with a single planet, whatever were the relative size of sun and planet,

the orbits which they traverse would be circular. In this
state of affairs it should be noted that each of the two
bodies would have its plane of rotation permanently in the
same position. Even if the spheres were more or less flattened about the poles of their axes, as is the case with all
the planets which we have been able carefully to measure,
as well as with the sun, provided the axes of rotation were
precisely parallel to each other, the mutual attraction of
the masses would cause no disturbance of the spheres.
The same would be the case if the polar axis of one sphere
stood precisely at right angles to that of the other. If,
however, the spheres were somewhat flattened at the poles,
and the axes inclined to each other, then the pull of one
mass on the other would cause the polar axes to keep up
a constant movement which is called nutation, or nodding.

The reason why this nodding movement of the polar
axes would occur when these lines were inclined to each
other is not difficult to see if we remember that the attraction of masses upon each other is inversely as the square
of the distance; each sphere, pulling on the equatorial
bulging of the other, pulls most effectively on the part of
it which is nearest, and tends to draw it down toward its
centre. The result is that the axes of the attracted spheres
are given a wobbling movement, such as we may note in the
spinning top, though in the toy the cause of the motion is
not that which we are considering.

If, now, in that excellent field for the experiment we
are essaying, the mind's eye, we add a second planet outside of the single sphere which we have so far supposed to
journey about the sun, or rather about the common centre
of gravity, we perceive at once that we have introduced
an element which leads to a complication of much importance. The new sphere would, of course, pull upon the
others in the measure of its gravitative value—i. e., its
weight. The centre of gravity of the system would now
be determined not by two distinct bodies, but by three.
If we conceive the second planet to journey around the

sun at such a rate that a straight line always connected
the centres of the three orbs, then the only effect on their
gravitative centre would be to draw the first-mentioned
planet a little farther away from the centre of the sun; but
. in our own solar system, and probably in all others, this
supposition is inadmissible, because the planets, although
they move at about the same speed, have longer journeys
to go in proportion to their distance from the sun. Thus
Mercury completes the circle of its year in eighty-eight of
our days, while the outermost planet requires sixty thousand days (more than one hundred and sixty-four years)
for the same task. The result is not only that the centre
of gravity of the system is somewhat displaced—itself a
matter of no great account—but also that the orbit of the
original planet ceases to be circled and becomes elliptical,
and this for the evident reason that the sphere will be drawn
somewhat away from the sun when the second planet happens to lie in the part of its orbit immediately outside of its
position, in which case the pull is away from the solar
centre; while, on the other hand, when the new planet
was on the other side of the sun, its pull would serve to
intensify the attraction which drew the first sphere toward
the centre of gravity. As the pulling action of the three
bodies upon each other, as well as upon their equatorial
protuberances, would vary with every change in their relative position, however slight, the variations in the form
of their orbits, even if the spheres were but three in number, would be very important. The consequences of these
perturbations will appear in the sequel.

In our solar system, though there are but eight great
planets, the group of asteroids, and perhaps a score of
satellites, the variety of orbital and axial movement which
is developed taxes the computing genius of the ablest
astronomer. The path which our earth follows around
the sun, though it may in general and for convenience
be described as a variable ellipse, is, in fact, a line of
such complication that if we should essay a diagram of it

5

on the scale of this page it would not be possible to represent any considerable part of its deviations. These, in fact, would elude depiction, even if the draughtsman had a sheet for his drawing as large as the orbit itself, for every particle of matter in space, even if it be lodged beyond the limits of the farthest stars revealed to us by the telescope, exercises a certain attraction, which, however small, is effective on the mass of the earth. Science has to render its conclusions in general terms, and we can safely take them as such; but in this, as in other instances, it is well to qualify our acceptance of the statements by the memory that all things are infinitely more complicated than we can possibly conceive or represent them to be.

We have next to consider the rotations of the planetary spheres upon their axes, together with the similar movement, or lack of it, in the case of their satellites. This rotation, according to the nebular hypothesis, may be explained by the movements which would set up in the share of matter which was at first a ring of the solar nebulæ, and which afterward gathered into the planetary aggregation. The way of it may be briefly set forth as follows: Such a ring doubtless had a diameter of some million miles; we readily perceive that the particles of matter in the outer part of the belt would have a swifter movement around the sun than those on the inside. When by some disturbance, as possibly by the passage of a great meteoric body of a considerable gravitative power, this ring was broken in two, the particles composing it on either side would, because of their mutual attraction, tend to draw away from the breach, widening that gap until the matter of the broken ring was aggregated into a sphere of the star dust or vapour. When the nebulous matter originally in the ring became aggregated into a spherical form, it would, on account of the different rates at which the particles were moving when they came together, be the surer to fall in toward the centre, not in straight lines, but in curves— in other words, the mass would necessarily take on a movement of rotation essentially like that which we have described in setting forth the nebular hypothesis.

In the stages of concentration the planetary nebulæ might well repeat those through which the greater solar mass proceeded. If the volume of the material were great, subordinate rings would be formed, which when they broke and concentrated would constitute secondary planets or satellites, such as our moon. For some reason as yet unknown the outer planets—in fact, all those in the solar system except the two inner, Venus and Mercury and the asteroids—formed such attendants. All these satellite-forming rings have broken and concentrated except the inner of Saturn, which remains as an intellectual treasure of the solar system to show the history of its development.

To the student who is not seeking the fulness of knowledge which astronomy has to offer, but desires only to acquaint himself with the more critical and important of the heavenly phenomena which help to explain the earth, these features of planetary movement should prove especially interesting for the reason that they shape the history of the spheres. As we shall hereafter see, the machinery of the earth's surface, all the life which it bears, its winds and rains—everything, indeed, save the actions which go on in the depths of the sphere—is determined by the heat and light which come from the sun. The conditions under which this vivifying tide is received have their origin in the planetary motion. If our earth's path around the centre of the system was a perfect circle, and if its polar axis lay at right angles to the plane of its journey, the share of light and heat which would fall upon any one point on the sphere would be perfectly uniform. There would be no variations in the length of day or night; no changes in the seasons; the winds everywhere would blow with exceeding steadiness—in fact, the present atmospheric confusion would be reduced to something like order. From age to age, except so far as the sun itself might vary in the amount of energy which it radiated, or lands rose up into the air or sunk down toward the sea level, the climate of each region would be perfectly stable. In the existing conditions the influences bring about unending variety. First of all, the inclined position of the polar axis causes the sun apparently to move across the heavens, so that it comes in an overhead position once or twice in the year in quite half the area of the lands and seas. This apparent swaying to and fro of the sun, due to the inclination of the axis of rotation, also affects the width of the climatal belts on either side of the equator, so that all parts of the earth receive a considerable share of the sun's influence. If the axis of the earth's rotation were at right angles to the plane of its orbit, there would be a narrow belt of high temperature about the equator, north and south of which the heat would grade off until at about the parallels of fifty degrees we should find a cold so considerable and uniform that life would probably fade away; and from those parallels to the poles the conditions would be those of permanent frost, and of days which would darken into the enduring night or twi-

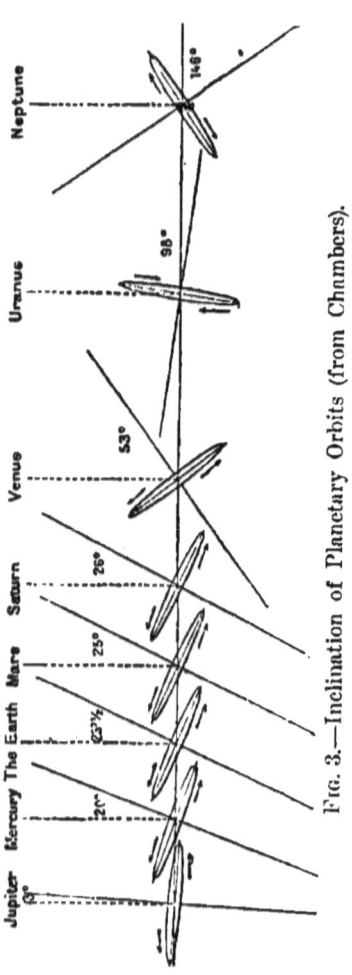

Fig. 3.—Inclination of Planetary Orbits (from Chambers).

light in the realm of the far north and south. Thus the wide habitability of the earth is an effect arising from the inclination of its polar axis.

As the most valuable impression which the student can receive from his study of Nature is that sense of the order which has made possible all life, including his own, it will be well for him to imagine, as he may readily do, what would be the effect arising from changes in relations of earth and sun. Bringing the earth's axis in imagination into a position at right angles to the plane of the orbit, he will see that the effect would be to intensify the equatorial heat, and to rob the high latitudes of the share which they now have. On moving the axis gradually to positions where it approaches the plane of the orbit, he will note that each stage of the change widens the tropic belt. Bringing the polar axis down to the plane of the orbit, one hemisphere would receive unbroken sunshine, the other remaining in perpetual darkness and cold. In this condition, in place of an equatorial line we should have an equatorial point at the pole nearest the sun; thence the temperatures would grade away to the present equator, beyond which half the earth would be in more refrigerating condition than are the poles at the present day. In considering the movements of our planet, we shall see that no great changes in the position of the polar axis can have taken place. On this account the suggested alterations of the axis should not be taken as other than imaginary changes.

It is easy to see that with a circular orbit and with an inclined axis winter and summer would normally come always at the same point in the orbit, and that these seasons would be of perfectly even length. But, as we have before noted, the earth's path around the sun is in its form greatly affected by the attractions which are exercised by the neighbouring planets, principally by those great spheres which lie in the realm without its orbit, Jupiter and Saturn. When these attracting bodies, as is the case from

time to time, though at long intervals, are brought together somewhere near to that part of the solar system
in which the earth is moving around the sun, they draw
our planet toward them, and so make its path very elliptical. When, however, they are so distributed that their
pulling actions neutralize each other, the orbit returns
more nearly to a circular form. The range in its eccentricity which can be brought about by these alterations is
very great. When the path is most nearly circular, the
difference in the major and minor axis may amount to as
little as about five hundred thousand miles, or about one
one hundred and eighty-sixth of its average diameter.
When the variation is greatest the difference in these
measurements may be as much as near thirteen million
miles, or about one seventh of the mean width of the orbit.

The first and most evident effect arising from these
changes of the orbit comes from the difference in the
amount of heat which the earth may receive according as
it is nearer or farther from the sun. As in the case of
other fires, the nearer a body is to it the larger the share
of light and heat which it will receive. In an orbit made
elliptical by the planetary attraction the sun necessarily
occupies one of the foci of the ellipse. The result is, of
course, that the side of the earth which is toward the sun,
while it is thus brought the nearer to the luminary, receives more energy in the form of light and heat than come
to any part which is exposed when the spheres are farther
away from each other in the other part of the orbit. Computations clearly show that the total amount of heat and
the attendant light which the earth receives in a year is
not affected by these changes in the form of its path. While
it is true that it receives heat more rapidly in the half of
the ellipse which is nearest the source of the inundation,
it obtains less while it is farther away, and these two variations just balance each other.

Although the alterations in the eccentricity of its orbit
do not vary the annual supply of heat which the earth re-

ceives, they are capable of changing the character of the
seasons, and this in the way which we will now endeavour
to set forth, though we must do it at the cost of considerable attention on the part of the reader, for the facts are
somewhat complicated. In the first place, we must note
that the ellipticity of the earth's orbit is not developed on
fixed lines, but is endlessly varied, as we can readily imagine it would be for the reason that its form depends upon
the wandering of the outer planetary spheres which pull
the earth about. The longer axis of the ellipse is itself
in constant motion in the direction in which the earth
travels. This movement is slow, and at an irregular rate.
It is easy to see that the effect of this action, which is called
the revolution of the apsides, or, as the word means, the
movement of the poles of the ellipse, is to bring the earth,
when a given hemisphere is turned toward the sun, sometimes in the part of the orbit which is nearest the source
of light and heat, and sometimes farther away. It may
thus well come about that at one time the summer season
of a hemisphere arrives when it is nearest the sun, so that
the season, though hot, will be very short, while at another
time the same season will arrive when the earth is farthest
from the sun, and receives much less heat, which would
tend to make a long and relatively cool summer. The
reason for the difference in length of the seasons is to be
found in the relative swiftness of the earth's revolution
when it is nearest the sun, and the slowness when it is farther away.

There is a further complication arising from that curious phenomenon called the precession of the equinoxes,
which has to be taken into account before we can sufficiently comprehend the effect of the varying eccentricity
of the orbit on the earth's seasons. To understand this
feature of precession we should first note that it means
that each year the change from the winter to the summer—
or, as we phrase it, the passage of the equinoctial line—
occurs a little sooner than the year before. The cause of

this is to be found in the attraction which the heavenly
bodies, practically altogether the moon, exercises on
the equatorial protuberance of the earth. We know that
the diameter of our sphere at the equator is, on the average, something more than twenty-six miles greater than
it is through the poles. We know, furthermore, that
the position of the moon in relation to the earth is such
that it causes the attraction on one half of this protuberance to be greater than it is upon the other. We readily
perceive that this action will cause the polar axis to make
a certain revolution, or, what comes to the same thing,
that the plane of the equator will constantly be altering its
position. Now, as the equinoctial points in the orbit depend for their position upon the attitude of the equatorial
plane, we can conceive that the effect is a change in position of the place in that orbit where summer and winter
begin. The actual result is to bring the seasonal points
backward, step by step, through the orbit in a regular
measure until in twenty-two thousand five hundred years
they return to the place where they were before. This
cycle of change was of old called the Annus Magnus, or
great year.

If the earth's orbit were an ellipse, the major axis of
which remained in the same position, we could readily
reckon all the effects which arise from the variations of
the great year. But this ellipse is ever changing in form,
and in the measure of its departure from a circle the effects
on the seasons distributed over a great period of time are
exceedingly irregular. Now and then, at intervals of hundreds of thousands or millions of years, the orbit becomes
very elliptical; then again for long periods it may in form
approach a circle. When in the state of extreme ellipticity,
the precession of the equinoxes will cause the hemispheres
in turn each to have their winter and summer alternately
near and far from the sun. It is easily seen that when
the summer season comes to a hemisphere in the part of
the orbit which is then nearest the sun the period will be

very hot. When the summer came farthest from the sun that part of the year would have the temperature mitigated by its removal to a greater distance from the source of heat. A corresponding effect would be produced in the winter season. As long as the orbit remained eccentric the tendency would be to give alternately intense seasons to each hemisphere through periods of about twelve thousand years, the other hemisphere having at the same time a relatively slight variation in the summer and winter.

At first sight it may seem to the reader that these studies we have just been making in matters concerning the shape of the orbit and the attendant circumstances which regulate the seasons were of no very great consequence; but, in the opinion of some students of climate, we are to look to these processes for an explanation of certain climatal changes on the earth, including the Glacial periods, accidents which have had the utmost importance in the history of man, as well as of all the other life of the planet.

It is now time to give some account as to what is known concerning the general conditions of the solar bodies—the planets and satellites of our own celestial group. For our purpose we need attend only to the general physical state of these orbs so far as it is known to us by the studies of astronomers. The nearest planet to the sun is Mercury. This little sphere, less than half the diameter of our earth, is so close to the sun that even when most favourably placed for observation it is visible for but a few minutes before sunrise and after sunset. Although it may without much difficulty be found by the ordinary eye, very few people have ever seen it. To the telescope when it is in the *full moon* state it appears as a brilliant disk; it is held by most astronomers that the surface which we see is made up altogether of clouds, but this, as most else that has been stated concerning this planet, is doubtful. The sphere is so near to the sun that if it were possessed of water it would inevitably bear an atmosphere full of vapour. Under any conceivable conditions of a planet placed as Mercury is, provided it had an atmosphere to retain the heat, its temperature would necessarily be very high. Life as we know it could not well exist upon such a sphere.

Next beyond Mercury is Venus, a sphere only a little less in diameter than the earth. Of this sphere we know more than we do of Mercury, for the reason that it is farther from the sun and so appears in the darkened sky. Most astronomers hold that the surface of this planet apparently is almost completely and continually hidden from us by what appears to be a dense cloud envelope, through which from time to time certain spots appear of a dark colour. These, it is claimed, retain their place in a permanent way; it is, indeed, by observing them that the rotation period of the planet has, according to some observers, been determined. It therefore seems likely that these spots are the summits of mountains, which, like many of our own earth, rise above the cloud level.

Recent observations on Venus made by Mr. Percival Lowell appear to show that the previous determinations of the rotation of that planet, as well as regards its cloud wrap, are in error. According to these observations, the sphere moves about the sun, always keeping the same side turned toward the solar centre, just as the moon does in its motion around the earth. Moreover, Mr. Lowell has failed to discover any traces of clouds upon the surface of the planet. As yet these results have not been verified by the work of other astronomers; resting, however, as they do on studies made with an excellent telescope and in the very translucent and steady air of the Flagstaff Station, they are more likely to be correct than those obtained by other students. If it be true that Venus does not turn upon its axis, such is likely to be the case also with the planet Mercury.

Next in the series of the planets is our own earth. As the details of this planet are to occupy us during nearly all the remainder of this work, we shall for the present pass it by.

Beyond the earth we pass first to the planet Mars, a sphere which has already revealed to us much concerning its peculiarities of form and physical state, and which is likely in the future to give more information than we shall obtain from any other of our companions in space, except perhaps the moon. Mars is not only nearer to us than any other planet, but it is so placed that it receives the light of the sun under favourable conditions for our vision. Moreover, its sky appears to be generally almost cloudless, so that when in its orbital course the sphere is nearest our earth it is under favourable conditions for telescopic observation. At such times there is revealed to the astronomer a surface which is covered with an amazing number of shadings and markings which as yet have been incompletely interpreted. The faint nature of these indications has led to very contradictory statements as to their form; no two maps which have been drawn agree except in their generalities. There is reason to believe that Mars has an atmosphere; this is shown by the fact that in the appropriate season the region about either pole is covered by a white coating, presumably snow. This covering extends rather less far toward the planet's equator than does the snow sheet on our continents. Taking into account the colour of the coating, and the fact that it disappears when the summer season comes to the hemisphere in which it was formed, we are, in fact, forced to believe that the deposit is frozen water, though it has been suggested that it may be frozen carbonic acid. Taken in connection with what we have shortly to note concerning the apparent seas of this sphere, the presumption is overwhelmingly to the effect that Mars has seasons not unlike our own.

The existence of snow on any sphere may safely be taken as evidence that there is an atmosphere. In the case of Mars, this supposition is borne out by the appearance of its surface. The ruddy light which it sends back to us, and the appearance on the margin of the sphere, which is somewhat dim, appears to indicate that its atmosphere is dense. In fact, the existence of an atmosphere much denser than that of our own earth appears to be demanded by the fact that the temperatures are such as to permit the coming and going of snow. It is well known that the temperature of any point on the earth, other things being equal, is proportionate to the depth of atmosphere above its surface. If Mars had no more air over its surface than has an equal area of the earth, it would remain at a temperature so low that such seasonal changes as we have observed could not take place. The planet receives one third less heat than an equal area of the earth, and its likeness to our own temperature, if such

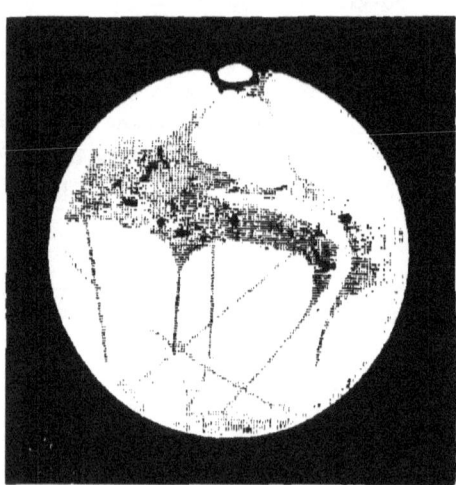

exists, is doubtless brought about by the greater density of its atmosphere, that serves to retain the heat which comes upon its surface. The manner in which this is effected will be set forth in the study of the earth's atmosphere.

As is shown by the maps of Mars, the surface is occupied by shadings which

Fig. 4.—Mars, August 27, 1892 (Guiot), the white patch is the supposed Polar Snow Cap.

seem to indicate the existence of water and lands. Those portions of the area which are taken to be land are very much divided by what appear to be narrow seas. The general geographic conditions differ much from those of our own sphere in that the parts of the planet about the water level are not grouped in great continents, and there are no large oceans. The only likeness to the conditions of our earth which we can perceive is in a general point- ' ing of the somewhat triangular masses of what appears to be land toward one pole. As a whole, the conditions of the Martial lands and seas as regards their form, at least, is more like that of Europe than that of any other part of the earth's surface. Europe in the early Tertiary times had a configuration even more like that of Mars than it exhibits at present, for in that period the land was very much more divided than it now is.

If the lands of Mars are framed as are those of our own earth, there should be ridges of mountains constitut- ing what we may term the backbones of the continent. As yet such have not been discerned, which may be due to the fact that they have not been carefully looked for. The only peculiar physical features which have as yet been discerned on the lands of Mars are certain long, straight, rather narrow crevicelike openings, which have received the name of " canals." These features are very indistinct, and are just on the limit of visibility. As yet they have been carefully observed by but few students, so that their features are not yet well recorded; as far as we know them, these fissures have no likeness in the existing condi- tions of our earth. It is difficult to understand how they are formed or preserved on a surface which is evidently subjected to rainfalls.

It will require much more efficient telescopes than we now have before it will be possible to begin any satisfac- tory study on the geography of this marvellous planet. We can not hope as yet to obtain any indications as to the details of its structure; we can not see closely enough to determine whether rivers exist, or whether there is a coat- ing which we may interpret as vegetation, changing its hues in the different seasons of the year. An advance in our instruments of research during the coming century,

if made with the same speed as during the last, will perhaps enable us to interpret the nature of this neighbour,
and thereby to extend the conception of planetary histories
which we derive from our own earth.

Beyond Mars we find one of the most singular features
of our solar system in a group of small planetary bodies,
the number of which now known amounts to some two
hundred, and the total may be far greater. These bodies
are evidently all small; it is doubtful if the largest is three
hundred and the smaller more than twenty miles in diame-

Fig. 5.—Comparative Sizes of the Planets (Chambers).

ter. So far as it has been determined by the effect of their
aggregate mass in attracting the other spheres, they would,

if put together, make a sphere far less in diameter than our earth, perhaps not more than five hundred miles through. The forms of these asteroids is as yet unknown; we therefore can not determine whether their shapes are spheroidal, as are those of the other planets, or whether they are angular bits like the meteorites. We are thus not in a position to conjecture whether their independence began when the nebulous matter of the ring to which they belonged was in process of consolidation, or whether, after the aggregation of the sphere was accomplished, and the matter solidified, the mass was broken into bits in some way which we can not yet conceive. It has been conjectured that such a solid sphere might have been driven asunder by a collision with some wandering celestial body; but all we can conceive of such actions leads us to suppose that a blow of this nature would tend to melt or convert materials subjected to it into the state of vapour, rather than to drive them asunder in the manner of an explosion.

The four planets which lie beyond the asteroids give us relatively little information concerning their physical condition, though they afford a wide field for the philosophic imagination. From this point of view the reader is advised to consult the writings of the late R. A. Proctor, who has brought to the task of interpreting the planetary conditions the skill of a well-trained astronomer and a remarkable constructive imagination.

The planet Jupiter, by far the largest of the children of the sun, appears to be still in a state where its internal heat has not so far escaped that the surface has cooled down in the manner of our earth. What appear to be good observations show that the equatorial part of its area, at least, still glows from its own heat. The sphere is cloud-wrapped, but it is doubtful whether the envelope be of watery vapour; it is, indeed, quite possible that besides such vapour it may contain some part of the many substances which occupy the atmosphere of the sun. If the Jovian sphere were no larger than the earth, it would, on account of its greater age, long ago have parted with its heat; but on account of its great size it has been able, notwithstanding its antiquity, to retain a measure of temperature which has long since passed away from our earth.

In the case of Saturn, the cloud bands are somewhat less visible than on Jupiter, but there is reason to suppose in this, as in the last-named planet, that we do not behold the more solid surface of the sphere, but see only a cloud wrap, which is probably due rather to the heat of the sphere itself than to that which comes to it from the sun. At the distance of Saturn from the centre of the solar system a given area of surface receives less than one ninetieth of the sun's heat as compared with the earth; therefore we can not conceive that any density of the atmosphere whatever would suffice to hold in enough temperature to produce ordinary clouds. Moreover, from time to time bright spots appear on the surface of the planet, which must be due to some form of eruptions from its interior.

Beyond Saturn the two planets Uranus and Neptune, which occupy the outer part of the solar system, are so remote that even our best telescopes discern little more than their presence, and the fact that they have attendant moons.

From the point of view of astronomical science, the outermost planet Neptune, of peculiar interest for the reason that it was, as we may say, discovered by computation. Astronomers had for many years remarked the fact that the next inner planetary sphere exhibited peculiarities in its orbit which could only be accounted for on the supposition that it was subjected to the attraction of another wandering body which had escaped observation. By skilful computation the place in the heavens in which this disturbing element lay was so accurately determined that when the telescope was turned to the given field a brief study revealed the planet. Nothing else in the history of the science of astronomy, unless it be the computation of eclipses, so clearly and popularly shows the accuracy of the methods by which the work of that science may be done.

As we shall see hereafter, in the chapters which are devoted to terrestrial phenomena, the physical condition of the sun determines the course of all the more important events which take place on the surface of the earth. It is therefore fit that in this preliminary study of the celestial bodies, which is especially designed to make the earth more interpretable to us, we should give a somewhat special attention to what is known under the title of "Solar Physics."

The reader has already been told that the sun is one of many million similar bodies which exist in space, and, furthermore, that these aggregations of matter have been developed from an original nebulous condition. The facts indicate that the natural history of the sun, as well as that of its attendant spheres, exhibits three momentous stages: First, that of vapour; second, that of igneous fluidity; third, that in which the sphere is so far congealed that it becomes dark. Neither of these states is sharply separated from the other; a mass may be partly nebulous and partly fluid; even when it has been converted into fluid, or possibly into the solid state, it may still retain on the exterior some share of its original vaporous condition. In our sun the concentration has long since passed beyond the limits of the nebulous state; the last of the successively developed rings has broken, and has formed itself into the smallest of the planets, which by its distance from the sun seems to indicate that the process of division by rings long ago attained in our solar system its end, the remainder of its nebulous material concentrating on its centre without sign of any remaining tendency to produce these planet-making circles.

6

The Constitution of the Sun.

Before the use of the telescope in astronomical work, which was begun by the illustrious Galileo in 1608, astronomers were unable to approach the problem of the structure of the sun. They could discern no more than can be seen by any one who looks at the great sphere through a bit of smoked glass, as we know this reveals a disklike body of very uniform appearance. The only variation in this simple aspect occurs at the time of a total eclipse, when for a minute or two the moon hides the whole body of the sun. On such occasions even the unaided eye can see that there is about the sphere a broad, rather bright field, of an aspect like a very thin cloud or fog, which rises in streamerlike projections at points to a quarter of a million miles or more above the surface of the sphere. The appearance of this shining field, which is called the corona, reminds one of the aurora which glows in the region about either pole of the earth.

One of the first results of the invention of the telescope was the revelation of the curious dark objects on the sun's disk, known by the name of spots from the time of their discovery, or, at least, from the time when it was clearly perceived that they were not planets, but really on the solar body. The interest in the constitution of the sphere has increased during the last fifty years. This interest has rapidly grown until at the present time a vast body of learning has been gathered for the solution of the many problems concerning the centre of our system. As yet there is great divergence in the views of astronomers as to the interpretation of their observations, but certain points of great general interest have been tolerably well determined. These may be briefly set forth by an account of what would meet the eye if an observer were able to pass from the surface of the earth to the central part of the sun.

In passing from the earth to a point about a quarter

Lava stream, in Hawaiian Islands, flowing into the sea. Note the "ropy" character of the half-frozen rock on the sides of the nearest stream of the lava.

of a million miles from the sun's surface—a distance about
that of the moon from our sphere—the observer would
traverse the uniformly empty spaces of the heavens, where,
but for the rare chance of a passing meteorite or comet,
there would be nothing that we term matter. Arriving at
a point some two or three hundred thousand miles from
the body of the sun, he would enter the realm of the
corona; here he would find scattered particles of matter,
the bits so far apart that there would perhaps be not more
than one or two in the cubic mile; yet, as they would
glow intensely in the central light, they would be sufficient
to give the illumination which is visible in an eclipse.
These particles are most likely driven up from the sun
by some electrical action, and are constantly in motion,
much as are the streamers of the aurora.

Below the corona and sharply separated from it the
observer finds another body of very dense vapour, which
is termed the chromosphere, and which has been regarded
as the atmosphere of the sun. This layer is probably several thousand miles thick. From the manner in which it
moves, in the way the air of our own planet does in great
storms, it is not easy to believe that it is a fluid, yet its
sharply defined upper surface leads us to suppose that
it can not well be a mere mass of vapour. The spectroscope shows us that this chromosphere contains in the state
of vapour a number of metallic substances, such as iron
and magnesium. To an observer who could behold this
envelope of the sun from the distance at which we see the
moon, the spectacle would be more magnificent than the
imagination, guided by the sight of all the relatively trifling
fractures of our earth, can possibly conceive. From the
surface of the fiery sea vast uprushes of heated matter
rise to the height of two or three hundred thousand miles,
and then fall back upon its surface. These jets of heated
matter have the aspect of flames, but they would not be
such in fact, for the materials are not burning, but merely
kept at a high temperature by the heat of the great sphere

beneath. They spring up with such energy that they at times move with a speed of one hundred and fifty miles a second, or at a rate which is attained by no other matter in the visible universe, except that strange, wandering star known to astronomers as "Grombridge, 1830," which is traversing the firmament with a speed of not less than two hundred miles a second.

Below the chromosphere is the photosphere, the lower envelope of the sun, if it be not indeed the body of the sphere itself; from this comes the light and heat of the mass. This, too, can not well be a firm-set mass, for the reason that the spots appear to form in and move over it. It may be regarded as an extremely dense mass of gas, so weighed down by the vast attraction of the great sphere below it that it is in effect a fluid. The near-at-hand observer would doubtless find this photosphere, as it appears in the telescope, to be sharply separated from the thinner and more vaporous envelopes—the chromosphere and the corona—which are, indeed, so thin that they are invisible even with the telescope, except when the full blaze of the sun is cut off in a total eclipse. The fact that the photosphere, except when broken by the so-called spots, lies like a great smooth sea, with no parts which lie above the general line, shows that it has a very different structure from the envelope which lies upon it. If they were both vaporous, there would be a gradation between them.

On the surface of the photosphere, almost altogether within thirty degrees of the equator of the sun, a field corresponding approximately to the tropical belt of the earth, there appear from time to time the curious disturbances which are termed spots. These appear to be uprushes of matter in the gaseous state, the upward movement being upon the margins of the field and a downward motion taking place in the middle of the irregular opening, which is darkened in its central part, thus giving it, when seen by an ordinary telescope, the aspect of a black patch on the glowing surface. These spots, which are from some hundred to some thousand miles in diameter, may endure for months before they fade away. It is clear that they are most abundant at intervals of about eleven years, the last period of abundance being in 1893. The next to come may thus be expected in 1904. In the times of least spotting more than half the days of a year may pass without the surface of the photosphere being broken, while in periods of plenty no day in the year is likely to fail to show them.

It is doubtful if the closest seeing would reveal the cause of the solar spots. The studies of the physicists who have devoted the most skill to the matter show little more than that they are tumults in the photosphere, attended by an uprush of vapours, in which iron and other metals exist; but whether these movements are due to outbreaks from the deeper parts of the sun or to some action like the whirling storms of the earth's atmosphere is uncertain. It is also uncertain what effect these convulsions of the sun have on the amount of the heat and light which is poured forth from the orb. The common opinion that the sun-spot years are the hottest is not yet fully verified.

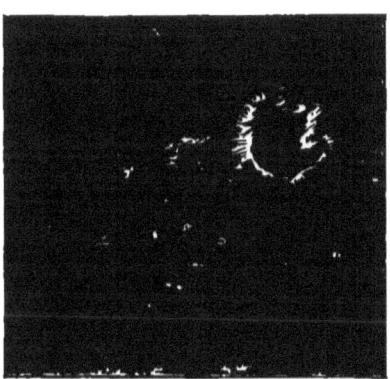

Fig. 6.—Ordinary Sun-spot, June 22, 1885.

Below the photosphere lies the vast unknown mass of the unseen solar realm. It was at one time supposed that the dark colour of the spots was due to the fact that the photosphere was broken through in those spaces, and that we looked down through them upon the surface of the slightly illuminated central part of the sphere. This view is untenable, and in its place we have to assume that for the eight hundred and sixty thousand miles of its diameter the sun is composed of matter such as is found in our earth, but throughout in a state of heat which vastly exceeds that known on or in our planet. Owing to its heat, this matter is possibly not in either the solid or the fluid state, but in that of very compressed gases, which are kept from becoming solid or even fluid by the very high temperature which exists in them. This view is apparently supported by the fact that, while the pressure upon its matter is twenty-seven times greater in the sun than it is in the earth, the weight of the whole mass is less than we should expect under these conditions.

As for the temperature of the sun, we only know that it is hot enough to turn the metals into gases in the manner in which this is done in a strong electric arc, but no satisfactory method of reckoning the scale of this heat has been devised. The probabilities are to the effect that the heat is to be counted by the tens of thousands of degrees Fahrenheit, and it may amount to hundreds of thousands; it has, indeed, been reckoned as high as a million degrees. This vast discharge is not due to any kind of burning action —i. e., to the combustion of substances, as in a fire. It must be produced by the gradual falling in of the materials, due to the gravitation of the mass toward its centre, each particle converting its energy of position into heat, as does the meteorite when it comes into the air.

It is well to close this very imperfect account of the learning which relates to the sun with a brief tabular statement showing the relative masses of the several bodies of the solar system. It should be understood that by mass is meant not the bulk of the object, but the actual amount of matter in it as determined by the gravitative attraction which it exercises on other celestial bodies. In this test the sun is taken as the measure, and its mass is for convenience reckoned at 1,000,000,000.

TABLE OF RELATIVE MASSES OF SUN AND PLANETS.*

The sun	1,000,000,000
Mercury	200
Venus	2,353
Earth	3,060
Mars	339
Asteroids	?
Saturn	285,580
Jupiter	954,305
Uranus	44,250
Neptune	51,600
Combined mass of the four inner planets	5,952
Combined mass of all the planets	1,341,687

It thus appears that the mass of all the planets is about one seven hundredth that of the sun.

Those who wish to make a close study of celestial geography will do well to procure the interesting set of diagrams prepared by the late James Freeman Clarke, in which transparencies placed in a convenient lantern show the grouping of the important stars in each constellation. The advantage of this arrangement is that the little maps can be consulted at night and in the open air in a very convenient manner. After the student has learned the position of a dozen of the constellations visible in the northern hemisphere, he can rapidly advance his knowledge in the admirable method invented by Dr. Clarke.

Having learned the constellations, the student may well proceed to find the several planets, and to trace them in their apparent path across the fixed stars. It will be well for him here to gain if he can the conception that their apparent movement is compounded of their motion around the sun and that of our own sphere; that it would be very different if our earth stood still in the heavens. At this stage he may well begin to take in mind the evidence which the planetary motion supplies that the earth

---

* See Newcomb's Popular Astronomy, p. 234. Harper Brothers, New York.

really moves round the sun, and not the sun and planets round the earth. This discovery was one of the great feats of the human mind; it baffled the wits of the best men for thousands of years. Therefore the inquirer who works over the evidence is treading one of the famous paths by which his race climbed the steeps of science.

The student must not expect to find the evidence that the sun is the centre of the solar system very easy to interpret; and yet any youth of moderate curiosity, and that interest in the world about him which is the foundation of scientific insight, can see through the matter. He will best begin his inquiries by getting a clear notion of the fact that the moon goes round the earth. This is the simplest case of movements of this nature which he can see in the solar system. Noting that the moon occupies a different place at a given hour in the twenty-four, but is evidently at all times at about the same distance from the earth, he readily perceives that it circles about our sphere. This the people knew of old, but they made of it an evidence that the sun also went around our sphere. Here, then, is the critical point. Why does the sun not behave in the same manner as the moon? At this stage of his inquiry the student best notes what takes place in the motions of the planets between the earth and the sun. He observes that those so-called inferior planets Mercury and Venus are never very far away from the central body; that they appear to rise up from it, and then to go back to it, and that they have phases like the moon. Now and then Venus may be observed as a black spot crossing the disk of the sun. A little consideration will show that on the theory that bodies revolve round each other in the solar system these movements of the inner planets can only be explained on the supposition that they at least travel around the great central fire. Now, taking up the outer planets, we observe that they occasionally appear very bright, and that they are then at a place in the heavens where we see that they are far from the solar centre. Gradually they move down toward the sunset and disappear from view. Here, too, the movement, though less clearly so, is best reconcilable with the idea that these bodies travel in orbits, such as those which are traversed by the inner planets. The wonder is that with these simple facts before them, and with ample time to think the matter over, the early astronomers did not learn the great truth about the solar system— namely, that the sun is the centre about which the planets circled. Their difficulty lay mainly in the fact that they did not conceive the earth as a sphere, and even after they attained that conception they believed that our globe was vastly larger than the planets, or even than the sun. This misconception kept even the thoughtful Greeks, who knew that the earth was spherical in form, from a clear notion as to the structure of our system. It was not, indeed, until mathematical astronomy attained a considerable advance, and men began to measure the distances in the solar system, and until the Newtonian theory of gravitation was developed, that the planetary orbits and the relation of the various bodies in the solar system to each other could be perfectly discerned.

Care has been taken in the above statements to give the student indices which may assist him in working out for himself the evidence which may properly lead a person, even without mathematical considerations of a formal kind, to construct a theory as to the relation of the planets to the sun. It is not likely that he can go through all the steps of this argument at once, but it will be most useful to him to ponder upon the problem, and gradually win his way to a full understanding of it. With that purpose in mind, he should avoid reading what astronomers have to say on the matter until he is satisfied that he has done as much as he can with the matter on his own account. He should, however, state his observations, and as far as possible draw the results in his note-book in a diagrammatic form. He should endeavour to see if the facts are reconcilable with any other supposition than that the earth and the other planets move around the sun. When he has done his task, he will have passed over one of the most difficult roads which his predecessors had to traverse on their way to an understanding of the heavens. Even if he fail he will have helped himself to some large understandings.

The student will find it useful to make a map of the heavens, or rather make several representing their condition at different times in the year. On this plot he should put down only the stars whose places and names he has learned, but he should plot the position of the planets at different times. In this way, though at first his efforts will be very awkward, he will soon come to know the general geography of the heavens.

Although the possession or at least the use of a small astronomical telescope is a great advantage to a student after he has made a certain advance in his work, such an instrument is not at all necessary, or, indeed, desirable at the outset of his studies. An ordinary opera-glass, however, will help him in picking out the stars in the constellations, in identifying the planets, and in getting a better idea as to the form of the moon's surface—a matter which will be treated in this work in connection with the structure of the earth.

CHAPTER IV.

THE EARTH.

In beginning the study of the earth it is important that the student should at once form the habit of keeping in mind the spherical form of the planet. Many persons, while they may blindly accept the fact that the earth is a sphere, do not think of it as having that form. Perhaps the simplest way of securing the correct image of the shape is to imagine how the earth would appear as seen from the moon. In its full condition the moon is apt to appear as a disk. When it is new, and also when in its waning stages it is visible in the daytime, the spherical form is very apparent. Imagining himself on the surface of the moon, the student can well perceive how the earth would appear as a vast body in the heavens; its eight thousand miles of diameter, about four times that of the satellite, would give an area sixteen times the size which the moon presents to us. On this scale the continents and oceans would appear very much more plain than do the relatively slight irregularities on the lunar surface.

With the terrestrial globe in hand, the student can readily construct an image which will represent, at least in outline, the appearance which the sphere he inhabits would present when seen from a distance of about a quarter of a million miles away. The continent of Europe-Asia would of itself appear larger than all the lunar surface which is visible to us. Every continent and all the greater islands would be clearly indicated. The snow covering which in

81

the winter of the northern hemisphere wraps so much of
the land would be seen to come and go in the changes of
the seasons; even the permanent ice about either pole,
and the greater regions of glaciers, such as those of the
Alps and the Himalayas, would appear as brilliant patches
of white amid fields of darker hue. Even the changes in
the aspect of the vegetation which at one season clothes
the wide land with a green mantle, and at another assumes the dun hue of winter, would be, to the unaided eye,
very distinct. It is probable that all the greater rivers
would be traceable as lines of light across the relatively
dark surface of the continents. By such exercises of the
constructive imagination—indeed, in no other way—the
student can acquire the habit of considering the earth
as a vast whole. From time to time as he studies the earth
from near by he should endeavour to assemble the phenomena in the general way which we have indicated.

The reader has doubtless already learned that the earth
is a slightly flattened sphere, having an average diameter
of about eight thousand miles, the average section at the
equator being about twenty-six miles greater than that
from pole to pole. In a body of such large proportions this
difference in measurement appears not important; it is,
however, most significant, for it throws light upon the history of the earth's mass. Computation shows that the
measure of flattening at the poles is just what would occur
if the earth were or had been at the time when it assumed
its present form in a fluid condition. We readily conceive
that a soft body revolving in space, while all its particles
by gravitation tended to the centre, would in turning
around, as our earth does upon its axis, tend to bulge out
in those parts which were remote from the line upon which
the turning took place. Thus the flattening of our sphere
at the poles corroborates the opinion that its mass was once
molten—in a word, that its ancient history was such as the
nebular theory suggests.

Although we have for convenience termed the earth

a flattened spheroid, it is only such in a very general sense. It has an infinite number of minor irregularities which it is the province of the geographer to trace and that of the geologist to account for. In the first place, its surface is occupied by a great array of ridges and hollows. The larger of these, the oceans and continents, first deserve our attention. The difference in altitude of the earth's surface from the height of the continents to the deepest part of the sea is probably between ten and eleven miles, thus amounting to about two fifths of the polar flattening before noted. The average difference between the ocean floor and the summits of the neighbouring continents is probably rather less than four miles. It happens, most fortunately for the history of the earth, that the water upon its surface fills its great concavities on the average to about four fifths of their total depth, leaving only about one fifth of the relief projecting above the ocean level. We have termed this arrangement fortunate, for it insures that rainfall visits almost all the land areas, and thereby makes those realms fit for the uses of life. If the ocean had only half its existing area, the lands would be so wide that only their fringes would be fertile. If it were one fifth greater than it is, the dry areas would be reduced to a few scattered islands.

From all points of view the most important feature of the earth's surface arises from its division into land and water areas, and this for the reason that the physical and vital work of our sphere is inevitably determined by this distribution. The shape of the seas and lands is fixed by the positions at which the upper level of the great water comes against the ridges which fret the earth's surface. These elevations are so disposed that about two thirds of the hard mass is at the present time covered with water, and only one third exposed to the atmosphere. This proportion is inconstant. Owing to the endless up-and-down goings of the earth's surface, the place of the shore lines varies from year to year, and in the geological ages great revolutions in the forms and relative area of water and land are brought about.

Noting the greater divisions of land and water as they are shown on a globe, we readily perceive that those parts of the continental ridges which rise above the sea level are mainly accumulated in the northern hemisphere—in fact, far more than half the dry realm is in that part of the world. We furthermore perceive that all the continents more or less distinctly point to the southward; they are, in a word, triangles, with their bases to the northward, and their apices, usually rather acute, directed to the southward. This form is very well indicated in three of the great lands, North and South America and Africa; it is more indistinctly shown in Asia and in Australia. As yet we do not clearly understand the reason why the continents are triangular, why they point toward the south pole, or why they are mainly accumulated in the northern hemisphere. As stated in the chapter on astronomy, some trace of the triangular form appears in the land masses of the planet Mars. There, too, these triangles appear to point toward one pole.

Besides the greater lands, the seas are fretted by a host of smaller dry areas, termed islands. These, as inquiry has shown, are of two very diverse natures. Near the continents, practically never more than a thousand miles from their shores, we find isles, often of great size, such as Madagascar, which in their structure are essentially like the continents—that is, they are built in part or in whole of nonvolcanic rocks, sandstones, limestones, etc. In most cases these islands, to which we may apply the term continental, have at some time been connected with the neighbouring mainland, and afterward separated from it by a depression of the surface which permitted the sea to flow over the lowlands. Geologists have traced many cases where in the past elevations which are now parts of a continent were once islands next its shore. In the deeper seas far removed from the margins of the continents the islands are made up of volcanic ejections of lava, pumice, and dust, which has been thrown up from craters and fallen around their margin or are formed of coral and other organic remains.

Next after this general statement as to the division of sea and land we should note the peculiarities which the earth's surface exhibits where it is bathed by the air, and where it is covered by the water. Beginning with the best-known region, that of the dry land, we observe that the surface is normally made up of continuous slopes of varying declivity, which lead down from the high points to the sea. Here and there, though rarely, these slopes centre in a basin which is occupied by a lake or a dead sea. On the deeper ocean floors, so far as we may judge with the defective information which the plumb line gives us, there is no such continuity in the downward sloping of the surface, the area being cast into numerous basins, each of great extent.

When we examine in some detail the shape of the land surface, we readily perceive that the continuous down slopes are due to the cutting action of rivers. In the basin of a stream the waters act to wear away the original heights, filling them into the hollows, until the whole area has a continuous down grade to the point where the waters discharge into the ocean or perhaps into a lake. On the bottom of the sea, except near the margin of the continent, where the floor may in recent geological times have been elevated into the air, and thus exposed to river action, there is no such agent working to produce continuous down grades.

Looking upon a map of a continent which shows the differences in altitude of the land, we readily perceive that the area is rather clearly divided into two kinds of surface, mountains and plains, each kind being sharply distinguished from the other by many important peculiarities. Mountains are characteristically made up of distinct, more or less parallel ridges and valleys, which are grouped in very elongated belts, which, in the case of the American Cordilleras, extend from the Arctic to the Antarctic Circle. Only in rare instances do we find mountains occupying an area which is not very distinctly elongated, and in such cases the elevations are usually of no great height. Plains, on the other hand, commonly occupy the larger part of the continent, and are distributed around the flanks of the mountain systems. There is no rule as to their shape; they normally grade away from the bases of the mountains toward the sea, and are often prolonged below the level of the water for a considerable distance beyond the shore, forming what is commonly known as the continental shelf or belt of shallows along the coast line. We will now consider some details concerning the form and structure of mountains.

In almost any mountain region a glance over the surface of the country will give the reader a clew to the principal factor which has determined the existence of these elevations. Wherever the bed rocks are revealed he will recognise the fact that they have been much disturbed. Almost everywhere the strata are turned at high angles; often their slopes are steeper than those of house roofs, and not infrequently they stand in attitudes where they appear vertical. Under the surface of plains bedded rocks generally retain the nearly horizontal position in which all such deposits are most likely to be found. If the observer will attentively study the details of position of these tilted rocks of mountainous districts, he will in most cases be able to perceive that the beds have been flexed or folded in the manner indicated by the diagram. Sometimes, though rarely, the tops of these foldings or arches have been preserved, so that the nature of the movement can be clearly discerned. More commonly the upper parts of the upward-arching strata have been cut off by the action of the decay-bringing forces—frost, flowing water, or creeping ice in glaciers—so that only the downward pointing folds which were formed in the mountain-making are well

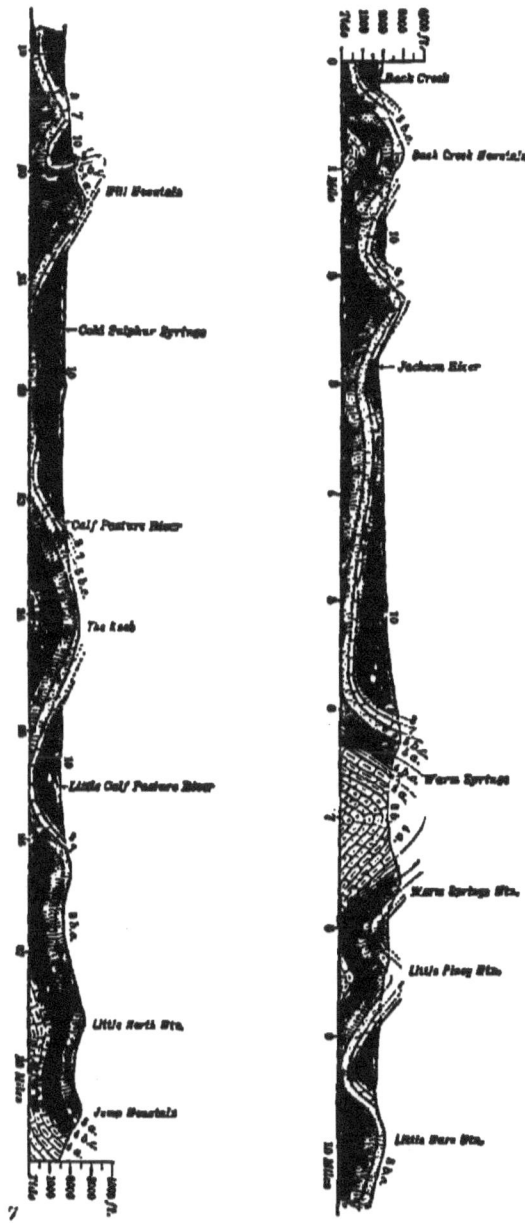

FIG. 7.—Section of mountains. Rockbridge and Bath counties, Va. (from Dana). The numbers indicate the several formations.

preserved, and these are almost invariably hidden within the earth.

By walking across any considerable mountain chain, as, for instance, that of the Alleghanies, it is generally possible to trace a number of these parallel up-and-down folds of the strata, so that we readily perceive that the original beds had been packed together into a much less space than they at first occupied. In some cases we could prove that the shortening of the line has amounted to a hundred miles or more—in other words, points on the plain lands on either side of the mountain range which now exists may have been brought a hundred miles or so nearer together than they were before the elevations were produced. The reader can make for himself a convenient diagram showing what occurred by pressing a number of leaves of this book so that the sheets of paper are thrown into ridges and furrows. By this experiment he also will see that the easiest way to account for such foldings as we observe in mountains is by the supposition that some force residing in the earth tends to shove the beds into a smaller space than they originally occupied. Not only are the rocks composing the mountains much folded, but they are often broken through after the manner of masonry which has been subjected to earthquake shocks, or of ice which has been strained by the expansion that affects it as it becomes warmed before it is melted. In fact, many of our small lakes in New England and in other countries of a long winter show in a miniature way during times of thawing ice folds which much resemble mountain arches.

At first geologists were disposed to attribute all the phenomena of mountain-folding to the progressive cooling of the earth. Although this sphere has already lost a large part of the heat with which it was in the beginning endowed, it is still very hot in its deeper parts, as is shown by the phenomena of volcanoes. This internal heat, which to the present day at the depth of a hundred miles below the surface is probably greater than that of molten iron, is constantly flowing away into space; probably enough of it goes away on the average each day to melt a hundred cubic miles or more of ice, or, in more scientific phrase, the amount of heat rendered latent by melting that volume of frozen water. J. R. Meyer, an eminent physicist, estimated the quantity of heat so escaping each day of the year to be sufficient to melt two hundred and forty cubic miles of ice. The effect of this loss of heat is constantly to shrink the volume of the earth; it has, indeed, been estimated that the sphere on this account contracts on the average to the amount of some inches each thousand years. For the reason that almost all this heat goes from the depths of the earth, the cool outer portion losing no considerable part of it, the contraction that is brought about affects the interior portions of the sphere alone. The inner mass constantly shrinking as it loses heat, the outer, cold part is by its weight forced to settle down, and can only accomplish this result by wrinkling. An analogous action may be seen where an apple or a potato becomes dried; in this case the hard outer rind is forced to wrinkle, because, losing no water, it does not diminish in its extent, and can only accommodate itself to the interior by a wrinkling process. In one case it is water which escapes, in the other heat; but in both contraction of the part which suffers the loss leads to the folding of the outside of the spheroid.

Although this loss of heat on the part of the earth accounts in some measure for the development of mountains, it is not of itself sufficient to explain the phenomena, and this for the reason that mountains appear in no case to develop on the floors of the wide sea. The average depth of the ocean is only fifteen thousand feet, while there are hundreds, if not thousands, of mountain crests which exceed that height above the sea. Therefore if mountains grew on the sea floor as they do upon the land, there should be thousands of peaks rising above the plain of the waters, while, in fact, all of the islands except those near the shores

of continents are of volcanic origin—that is, are lands of
totally different nature.

Whenever a considerable mountain chain is formed, although the actual folding of the beds is limited to the usually narrow field occupied by these disturbances, the elevation takes place over a wide belt of country on one or
both sides of the range. Thus if we approach the Rocky
Mountains from the Mississippi Valley, we begin to mount
up an inclined plane from the time we pass westward from
the Mississippi River. The beds of rock as well as the surface rises gradually until at the foot of the mountain;
though the rocks are still without foldings, they are at a
height of four or five thousand feet above the sea. It
seems probable—indeed, we may say almost certain—that
when the crust is broken, as it is in mountain-building,
by extensive folds and faults, the matter which lies a few
score miles below the crust creeps in toward those fractures, and so lifts up the country on which they lie. When
we examine the forms of any of our continents, we find
that these elevated portions of the earth's crust appear
to be made up of mountains and the table-lands which
fringe those elevations. There is not, as some of our
writers suppose, two different kinds of elevation in our
great lands—the continents and the mountains which they
bear—but one process of elevation by which the foldings
and the massive uplifts which constitute the table-lands
are simultaneously and by one process formed.

Looking upon continents as the result of mountain
growth, we may say that here and there on the earth's crust
these dislocations have occurred in such association and of
such magnitude that great areas have been uplifted above
the plain of the sea. In general, we find these groups of
elevations so arranged that they produce the triangular
form which is characteristic of the great lands. It will
be observed, for instance, that the form of North America
is in general determined by the position of the Appalachian
and Cordilleran systems on its eastern and western mar-

Waterfall near Gadsden, Alabama. The upper shelf of rock is a hard sandstone, the lower beds are soft shale. The conditions are those of most waterfalls, such as Niagara.

gins, though there are a number of smaller chains, such
as the Laurentians in Canada and the ice-covered mountains of Greenland, which have a measure of influence in
fixing its shore lines.

The history of plains, as well as that of mountains,
will have further light thrown upon it when in the next
chapter we come to consider the effect of rain water on the
land. We may here note the fact that the level surfaces
which are above the seashores are divisible into two main
groups—those which have been recently lifted above the
sea level, composed of materials laid down in the shallows next the shore, and which have not yet shared in
mountain-building disturbances, and those which have
been slightly tilted in the manner before indicated in the
case of the plains which border the Rocky Mountains on
the east. The great southern plain of eastern and southern
United States, extending from near New York to Mexico,
is a good specimen of the level lands common on all the
continents which have recently emerged from the sea. The
table-lands on either side of the Mississippi Valley, sloping from the Alleghanies and the Cordilleras, represent
the more ancient type of plain which has already shared
in the elevation which mountain-building brings about.
In rarer cases plains of small area are formed where mountains formerly existed by the complete moving down of
the original ridges.

There is a common opinion that the continents are
liable in the course of the geologic ages to very great
changes of position; that what is now sea may give place
to new great lands, and that those already existing may
utterly disappear. This opinion was indeed generally held
by geologists not more than thirty years ago. Further
study of the problem has shown us that while parts of
each continent may at any time be depressed beneath the
sea, the whole of its surface rarely if ever goes below the
water level. Thus, in the case of North America, we can
readily note very great changes in its form since the land

began to rise above the water. But always, from that ancient day to our own, some portion of the area has been above the level of the sea, thus providing an ark of refuge for the land life when it was disturbed by inundations. The strongest evidence in favour of the opinion that the existing continents have endured for many million years is found in the fact that each of the great lands preserves many distinct groups of animals and plants which have descended from ancient forms dwelling upon the same territory. If at any time the relatively small continent of Australia had gone beneath the sea, all of the curious pouched animals akin to the opossum and kangaroo which abound in that country—creatures belonging in the ancient life of the world—would have been overwhelmed.

We have already noted the fact that the uplifting of mountains and of the table-lands about them, which appears to have been the basis of continental growth, has been due to strains in the rocks sufficiently strong to disturb the beds. At each stage of the mountain-building movement these compressive strains have had to contend with the very great weight of the rocks which they had to move. These lands are not to be regarded as firm set or rigid arches, but as highly elastic structures, the shapes of which may be determined by any actions which put on or take off burden. We see a proof of th's fact from numerous observations which geologists are now engaged in making. Thus during the last ice epoch, when almost all the northern part of this continent, as well as the northern part of Europe, was covered by an ice sheet several thousand feet thick, the lands sank down under their load, and to an extent roughly proportional to the depth of the icy covering. While the northern regions were thus tilted down by the weight which was upon them, the southern section of this land, the region about the Gulf of Mexico, was elevated much above its present level; it seems likely, indeed, that the peninsula of Florida rose to the height of several hundred feet above its present shore line. After the ice passed away the movements were reversed, the northern region rising and the southern sinking down. These movements are attested by the position of the old shore lines formed during the later stages of the Glacial epoch. Thus around Lake Ontario, as well as the other Great Lakes, the beaches which mark the higher positions of those inland seas during the closing stages of the ice time, and which, of course, were when formed horizontal, now rise to the northward at the rate of from two to five feet for each mile of distance. Recent studies by Mr. G. K. Gilbert show that this movement is still in progress.

Other evidence going to show the extent to which the movements of the earth's crust are affected by the weight of materials are found in the fact that wherever along the shores thick deposits of sediments are accumulated the tendency of the region where they lie is gradually to sink downward, so that strata having an aggregate thickness of ten thousand feet or more may be accumulated in a sea which was always shallow. The ocean floor, in general, is the part of the earth's surface where strata are constantly being laid down. In the great reservoir of the waters the *débris* washed from the land, the dust from volcanoes, and that from the stellar spaces, along with the vast accumulation of organic remains, almost everywhere lead to the steadfast accumulation of sedimentary deposits. On the other hand, the realms of the surface above the ocean level are constantly being worn away by the action of the rivers and glaciers, of the waves which beat against the shores, and of the winds which blow over desert regions. The result is that the lands are wearing down at the geologic- ally rapid average rate of somewhere about one foot in five thousand years. All this heavy matter goes to the sea bottoms. Probably to this cause we owe in part the fact that in the wrinklings of the crust due to the contraction of the interior the lands exhibit a prevailing tendency to uprise, while the ocean floors sink down. In this way the continents are maintained above the level of the sea de-

spite the powerful forces which are constantly wearing
their substance away, while the seas remain deep, although
they are continually being burdened with imported materials.

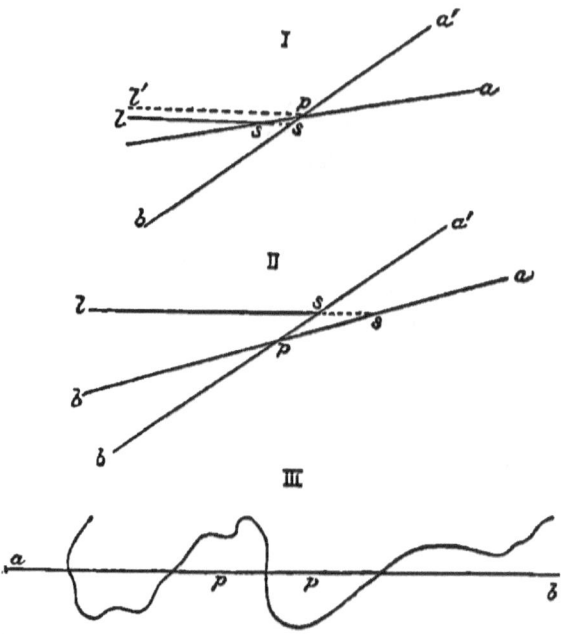

Fɪɢ. 8.—Diagram showing the effect of the position of the fulcrum
    point in the movement of the land masses. In diagrams I and
    II, the lines *a b* represent the land before the movement, and *a' b'*
    its position after the movement; *s, s*, the position of the shore
    line; *p, p*, the pivotal points; *l, s*, the sea line. In diagram III,
    the curved line designates a shore; the line *a b*, connecting the
    pivotal points *p, p*, is partly under the land and partly under
    the sea.

It is easy to see that if the sea floors tend to sink downward, while the continental lands uprise, the movements
which take place may be compared with those which occur
in a lever about a fulcrum point. In this case the sea end

of the bar is descending and the land end ascending. Now, it is evident that the fulcrum point may fall to the seaward or to the landward of the shore; only by chance and here and there would it lie exactly at the coast line. By reference to the diagram (Fig. 8), it will be seen that, while the point of rotation is just at the shore, a considerable movement may take place without altering the position of the coast line. Where the point of no movement is inland of the coast, the sea will gain on the continent; where, however, the point is to seaward, beneath the water, the land will gain on the ocean. In this way we can, in part at least, account for the endless changes in the attitude of the land along the coastal belt without having to suppose that the continents cease to rise or the sea floors to sink downward. It is evident that the bar or section of the rocks from the interior of the land to the bottoms of the seas is not rigid; it is also probable that the matter in the depths of the earth, which moves with the motions of this bar, would change the position of the fulcrum point from time to time. Thus it may well come about that our coast lines are swaying up and down in ceaseless variation.

In very recent geological times, probably since the beginning of the last Glacial period, the region about the Dismal Swamp in Virginia has swayed up and down through four alternating movements to the extent of from fifty to one hundred feet. The coast of New Jersey is now sinking at the rate of about two feet in a hundred years. The coast of New England, though recently elevated to the extent of a hundred feet or more, at a yet later time sank down, so that at some score of points between New York and Eastport, Me., we find the remains of forests with the roots of their trees still standing below high-tide mark in positions where the trees could not have grown. Along all the marine coasts of the world which have been carefully studied from this point of view there are similar evidences of slight or great modern changes in the level of the lands. At some points, particularly on the coast of Alaska and along the coast of Peru, these uplifts of the land have amounted to a thousand feet or more. In the peninsular district of Scandinavia the sway-ings, sometimes up and sometimes down, which are now going on have considerably changed the position of the shore lines since the beginning of the historical period.

There are other causes which serve to modify the shapes and sizes of the continents which may best be considered in the sequel; for the present we may pass from this sub-ject with the statement that our great lands are relatively permanent features; their forms change from age to age, but they have remained for millions of years habitable to the hosts of animals and plants which have adapted their life to the conditions which these fields afford them.

CHAPTER V.

The firm-set portion of the earth, composed of materials which became solid when the heat so far disappeared from the sphere that rocky matter could pass from its previous fluid condition to the solid or frozen state, is wrapped about by two great envelopes, the atmosphere and the waters. Of these we shall first consider the lighter and more universal air; in taking account of its peculiarities we shall have to make some mention of the water with which it is greatly involved; afterward we shall consider the structure and functions of that fluid.

Atmospheric envelopes appear to be common features about the celestial spheres. In the sun there is, as we have noted, a very deep envelope of this sort which is in part composed of the elements which form our own air; but, owing to the high temperature of the sphere, these are commingled with many substances which in our earth— at least in its outer parts—have entered in the solid state. Some of the planets, so far as we can discern their conditions, seem also to have gaseous wraps; this is certainly the case with the planet Mars, and even the little we know of the other like spheres justifies the supposition that Jupiter and Saturn, at least, have a like constitution. We may regard an atmosphere, in a word, as representing a normal and long-continued state in the development of the heavenly orbs. In only one of these considerable bodies of the solar system, the moon, do we find tolerably clear evidence that there is no atmosphere.

97

The atmosphere of the earth is composed mainly of very volatile elements, known as nitrogen and argon. This is commingled with oxygen, also a volatile element. Into this mass a number of other substances enter in varying but always relatively very small proportions. Of these the most considerable are watery vapour and carbon dioxide; the former of these rarely amounts to one per cent of the weight of the air, considering the atmosphere as a whole, and the latter is never more than a small fraction of one per cent in amount. As a whole, the air envelope of the earth should be regarded as a mass of nitrogen and argon, which only rarely, under the influence of conditions which exist in the soil, enters into combinations with other elements by which it assumes a solid form. The oxygen, though a permanent element in the atmosphere, tends constantly to enter into combinations which fix it temporarily or permanently in the earth, in which it forms, indeed, in its combined state about one half the weight of all the mineral substances we know. The carbon dioxide, or carbonic-acid gas, as it is commonly termed, is a most important substance, as it affords plants all that part of their bodies which disappear on burning. It is constantly returned to the atmosphere by the decay of organic matter, as well as by volcanic action.

In addition to the above-noted materials composing the air, all of which are imperatively necessary to the wonderful work accomplished by that envelope, we find a host of other substances which are accidentally, variably, and always in small quantities contained in this realm. Thus near the seashores, and indeed for a considerable distance into the continent, we find the air contains a certain amount of salt so finely divided that it floats in the atmosphere. So, too, we find the air, even on the mountain tops amid eternal snows, charged with small particles of dust, which, though not evident to the unassisted eye, become at once visible when we permit a slender ray of light to enter a dark chamber.

It is commonly asserted that the atmosphere does not effectively extend above the height of forty-five miles; we know that it is densest on the surface of the earth, the most so in those depressions which lie below the level of the sea. This is proved to us by the weight which the air imposes upon the mercury at the open end of a barometric tube. If we could deepen these cavities to the extent of a thousand miles, the pressure would become so great that if the pit were kept free from the heat of the earth the gaseous materials would become liquefied. Upward from the earth's surface at the sea level the atoms and molecules of the air become farther apart until, at the height of somewhere between forty and fifty miles, the quantity of them contained in the ether is so small that we can trace little effect from them on the rays of light which at lower levels are somewhat bent by their action. At yet higher levels, however, meteors appear to inflame by friction against the particles of air, and even at the height of eighty miles very faint clouds have at times been discerned, which are possibly composed of volcanic dust floating in the very rarefied medium, such as must exist at this great elevation.

The air not only exists in the region where we distinctly recognise it; it also occupies the waters and the under earth. In the waters it occurs as a mechanical mixture which is brought about as the rain forms and falls in the air, as the streams flow to the sea, and as the waves roll over the deep and beat against the shores. In the realm of the waters, as well as on the land, the air is necessary for the maintenance of all animal forms; but for its presence such life would vanish from the earth.

Owing to certain peculiarities in its constitution, the atmosphere of our earth, and that doubtless of myriad other spheres, serves as a medium of communication between different regions. It is, as we know, in ceaseless motion at rates which may vary from the speed in the greatest tempests, which may move at the rate of somewhere a hundred and fifty miles an hour, to the very slow movements which occur in caverns, where the transfer is sometimes effected at an almost mocroscopic rate in the space of a day. The motion of the atmosphere is brought about by the action of heat here and there, and in a trifling way, by the heat from the interior of the earth escaping through hot springs or volcanoes, but almost altogether by the heat of the sun. If we can imagine the earth cut off from the solar radiation, the air would cease to move. We often note how the variable winds fall away in the nighttime. Those who in seeking for the North Pole have spent winters in the long-continued dark of that region have noted that the winds almost cease to blow, the air being disturbed only when a storm originated in the sunlit realm forced its way into the circumpolar darkness.

The sun's heat does not directly disturb the atmosphere; if we could take the solid sphere of the world away, leaving the air, the rays would go straight through, and there would be no winds produced. This is due to the fact that the air permits the direct rays of heat, such as come from the sun, to pass through it with very slight resistance. In an aërial globe such as we have imagined, the rays impinging upon its surface would be slightly thrown out of their path as they are in passing through a lens, but they would journey on in space without in any considerable measure warming the mass. Coming, however, upon the solid earth, the heat rays warm the materials on which they are arrested, bringing them to a higher temperature than the air. Then these heated materials radiate the energy into the air; it happens, however, that this radiant heat can not journey back into space as easily as it came in; therefore the particles of air next the surface acquire a relatively high temperature. Thus a thermometer next the ground may rise to over a hundred degrees Fahrenheit, while at the same time the fleecy clouds which we may observe floating at the height of five or six miles above the surface are composed of frozen water.

The effect of the heated air which acquires its temperature by radiation from the earth's surface is to produce the winds. This it brings about in a very simple manner, though the details of the process have a certain complication. The best illustration of the mode in which the winds are produced is obtained by watching what takes place about an ordinary fire at the bottom of a chimney. As soon as the fire is lit, we observe that the air about it, so far as it is heated, tends upward, drawing the smoke with it. If the air in the chimney be cold, it may not draw well at first; but in a few minutes the draught is established, or, in other words, the heated lower air breaks its way up the shaft, gradually pushing the cooler matter out at the top. In still air we may observe the column from the flue extending about the chimney-top, sometimes to the height of a hundred feet or more before it is broken to pieces. It is well here to note the fact that the energy of the draught in a chimney is, with a given heat of fire and amount of air which is permitted to enter the shaft, directly proportionate to the height; thus in very tall flues, between two and three hundred feet high, which are sometimes constructed, the uprush is at the speed of a gale.

Whenever the air next the surface is so far heated that it may overcome the inertia of the cooler air above, it forces its way up through it in the general manner indicated in the chimney flue. When such a place of uprush is established, the hot air next the surface flows in all directions toward the shaft, joining the expedition to the heights of the atmosphere. Owing to the conditions of the earth's surface, which we shall now proceed to trace, these ascents of heated air belong in two distinct classes—those which move upward through more or less cylindrical chimneys in the atmosphere, shafts which are impermanent, which vary in diameter from a few feet to fifty or perhaps a hundred miles, and which move over the surface of the earth; and another which consists of a broad, beltlike shaft in the equatorial regions, which in a way girdles the earth, remains in about the same place, continually endures, and has a width of hundreds of miles. Of these two classes of uprushes we shall first consider the greatest, which occurs in the central portions of the tropical realm.

Under the equator, owing to the fact that the sun for a considerable belt of land and sea maintains the earth at a high temperature, there is a general updraught which began many million years ago, probably before the origin of life, in the age when our atmosphere assumed its present conditions. Into this region the cooler air from the north and south necessarily flows, in part pressed in by the weight of the cold air which overlies it, but aided in its motion by the fact that the particles which ascend leave place for others to occupy. Over the surfaces of the land within the tropical region this draught toward what we may term the equatorial chimney is perturbed by the irregularities of the surface and many local accidents. But on the sea, where the conditions are uniform, the air moving toward the point of ascent is marked in the trade winds, which blow with a steadfast sweep down toward the equator. Many slight actions, such as the movement of the hot and cold currents of the sea, the local air movements from the lands or from detached islands, somewhat perturb the trade winds, but they remain among the most permanent features in this changeable world. It is doubtful if anything on this sphere except the atoms and molecules of matter have varied as little as the trade winds in the centre of the wide ocean. So steadfast and uniform are they that it is said that the helm and sails of a ship may be set near the west coast of South America and be left unchanged for a voyage which will carry the navigator in their belt across the width of the Pacific.

Rising up from the earth in the tropical belt, the air attains the height of several thousand feet; it then begins to curve off toward the north and south, and at the height of somewhere about three to five miles above the surface is again moving horizontally toward either pole; attaining a distance on that journey, it gradually settles down to the surface of the earth, and ceases to move toward higher latitudes. If the earth did not revolve upon its axis the course of these winds along the surface toward the equator, and in the upper air back toward the poles, would be made in what we may call a square manner—that is, the particles of air would move toward the point where they begin to rise upward in due north and south lines, according as they came from the southern or northern hemisphere, and the upper currents or counter trades would retrace their paths also parallel with the meridians or longitude lines. But because the earth revolves from west to east, the course of the trade winds is oblique to the equator, those in the northern hemisphere blowing from northeast to southwest, those in the southern from southeast to northwest. The way in which the motion of the earth affects the direction of these currents is not difficult to understand. It is as follows:

Let us conceive a particle of air situated immediately over the earth's polar axis. Such an atom would by the rotation of the sphere accomplish no motion except, indeed, that it might turn round on its own centre. It would acquire no velocity whatever by virtue of the earth's movement. Then let us imagine the particle moving toward the equator with the speed of an ordinary wind. At every step of its journey toward lower latitudes it would come into regions having a greater movement than those which it had just left. Owing to its inertia, it would thus tend continually to lag behind the particles of matter about it. It would thus fall off to the westward, and, in place of moving due south, would in the northern hemisphere drift to the southwest, and in the southern hemisphere toward the northwest. A good illustration of this action may be obtained from an ordinary turn-table such as is used about railway stations to reverse the position of a locomotive. If the observer will stand in the centre

8

of such a table while it is being turned round he will perceive that his body is not swayed to the right or left. If he will then try to walk toward the periphery of the rotating disk, he will readily note that it is very difficult, if not impossible, to walk along the radius of the circle; he naturally falls behind in the movement, so that his path is a curved line exactly such as is followed by the winds which move toward the equator in the trades. If now he rests a moment on the periphery of the table, so that his body acquires the velocity of the disk at that point, and then endeavours to walk toward the centre, he will find that again he can not go directly; his path deviates in the opposite direction—in other words, the body continually going to a place having a less rate of movement by virtue of the rotation of the earth, on account of its momentum is ever moving faster than the surface over which it passes. This experiment can readily be tried on any small rotating disk, such as a potter's wheel, or by rolling a marble or a shot from the centre to the circumference and from the circumference to the centre. A little reflection will show the inquirer how these illustrations clearly account for the oblique though opposite sets of the trade winds in the upper and lower parts of the air.

The dominating effect of the tropical heat in controlling the movements of the air currents extends, on the ocean surface, in general about as far north and south as the parallels of forty degrees, considerably exceeding the limits of the tropics, those lines where the sun, because of the inclination of the earth's axis, at some time of the year comes just overhead. Between these belts of trade winds there is a strip or belt under the region where the atmosphere is rising from the earth, in which the winds are irregular and have little energy. This region of the " doldrums " or horse latitudes is one of much trouble to sailing ships on their voyages from one hemisphere to another. In passing through it their sails are filled only by the airs of local storms, or winds which make their way

into that part of the sea from the neighbouring continents. Beyond the trade-wind belt, toward the poles, the
movements of the atmosphere are dependent in part on the
counter trades which descend to the surface of the earth
in latitudes higher than that in which the surface or trade
winds flow. Thus along our Atlantic coast, and even in
the body of the continent, at times when the air is not
controlled by some local storm, the counter trade blows
with considerable regularity.

The effect of the trade and counter-trade movements
of the air on the distribution of temperature over the
earth's surface is momentous. In part their influence is
due to the direct heat-carrying power of the atmosphere;
in larger measure it is brought about by the movement of
the ocean waters which they induce. Atmospheric air,
when deprived of the water which it ordinarily contains,
has very little heat-containing capacity. Practically nearly
all the power of conveying heat which it possesses is due
to the vapour of water which it contains. By virtue of
this moisture the winds do a good deal to transfer heat
from the tropical or superheated portion of the earth's
surface to the circumpolar or underheated realms. At
first, the relatively cool air which journeys toward the
equator along the surface of the sea constantly gains in
heat, and in that process takes up more and more water,
for precisely the same reason that causes anything to dry
more rapidly in air which has been warmed next a fire.
The result is that before it begins to ascend in the tropical
updraught, being much moisture-laden, the atmosphere
stores a good deal of heat. As it rises, rarefies, and cools,
the moisture descends in the torrential rains which ordinarily fall when the sun is nearly vertical in the tropical
belt.

Here comes in a very interesting principle which is
of importance in understanding the nature of great storms,
either the continuous storm of the tropics or the local and
irregular whirlings which occur in various parts of the

earth. When the moisture-laden air starts on its upward journey from the earth it has, by virtue of the watery vapour which it contains, a store of energy which becomes applied to promoting the updraught. As it rises, the moisture in the air gathers together or condenses, and in so doing parts with the heat which caused it to evaporate from the ocean surface. For a given weight of water, the amount of heat required to effect the evaporation is very great; this we may roughly judge by observing what a continuous fire is required to send a pint of water into the state of steam. This energy, when it is released by the condensation of water into rain or snow, becomes again heat, and tends somewhat, as does the fire in the chimney, to accelerate the upward passage of the air. The result is that the water which ascends in the equatorial updraught becomes what we may term fuel to promote this important element in the earth's aërial circulation. Trades and counter trades would doubtless exist but for the efficiency of this updraught, which is caused by the condensation of watery vapour, but the movement would be much less than it is.

Whirling Storms.

In the region near the equator, or near the line of highest temperature, which for various reasons does not exactly follow the equator, there is, as we have noticed, a somewhat continuous uprushing current where the air passes upward through an ascending chimney, which in a way girdles the sea-covered part of the earth. In this region the movements of the air are to a great extent under the control of the great continuous updraught. As we go to the north and south we enter realms where the air at the surface of the earth is, by the heat which it acquires from contact with that surface, more or less impelled upward; but there being no permanent updraught for its escape, it from time to time breaks through the roof of cold air which overlies it and makes a temporary channel of passage.

Going polarward from the equator, we first encounter these local and temporary upcastings of the air near the margin of the tropical belt. In these districts, at least over the warmer seas, during the time of the year when it is midsummer, and in the regions where the trade winds are not strong enough to sweep the warm and moisture-laden air down to the equatorial belt, the upward tending strain of the atmosphere next the earth often becomes so strong that the overlying air is displaced, forming a channel through which the air swiftly passes. As the moisture condenses in the way before noted, the energy set free serves to accelerate the updraught, and a hurricane is begun. At first the movement is small and of no great speed, but as the amount of air tending upward is likely to be great, as is also the amount of moisture which it contains, the aërial chimney is rapidly enlarged, and the speed of the rising air increased. The atmosphere next the surface of the sea flows in toward the channel of escape; its passage is marked by winds which are blowing toward the centre. On the periphery of the movement the particles move slowly, but as they win their way toward the centre they travel with accelerating velocity. On the principle which determines the whirling movement of the water escaping through a hole in the bottom of a basin, the particles of the air do not move on straight lines toward the centre, but journey in spiral paths, at first along the surface, and then ascending.

We have noted the fact that in a basin of water the direction of the whirling is what we may term accidental—that is, dependent on conditions so slight that they elude our observation—but in hurricanes a certain fact determines in an arbitrary way the direction in which the spin shall take place. As soon as such a movement of the air attains any considerable diameter, although in its beginning it may have spun in a direction brought about by local accidents, it will be affected by the diverse rates of travel, by virtue of the earth's rotation, of the air on its equatorial and polar sides. On the equatorial side this air is moving more rapidly than it is on the polar side. By observing the water passing from a basin this principle, with a few experiments, can be made plain. The result is to cause these great whirlwinds of the hurricanes of higher latitudes to whirl round from right to left in the northern hemisphere and in the reverse way in the southern. The general system of the air currents still further affects these, as other whirling storms, by driving their centres or chimneys over the surface of the earth. The principle on which this is done may be readily understood by observing how the air shaft above a chimney, through which we may observe the smoke to rise during a time of calm, is drawn off to one side by the slight current which exists even when we feel no wind; it may also be discerned in the little dust whirls which form in the streets on a summer day when the air is not much disturbed. While they spin they move on in the direction of the air drift. In this way a hurricane originating in the Gulf of Mexico may gradually journey under the influence of the counter trades across the Antilles, or over southern Florida, and thence pursue a devious northerly course, generally near the Atlantic coast and in the path of the Gulf Stream, until it has travelled a thousand miles or more toward the North Atlantic. The farther it goes northward the less effectively it is fed with warm and moisture-laden air, the feebler its movement becomes, until at length it is broken up by the variable winds which it encounters.

A very interesting and, from the point of view of the navigator, important peculiarity of these whirls is that at their centre there is a calm, similar in origin and nature to the calm under the equator between the trade-wind belts. Both these areas are in the field where the air is ascending, and therefore at the surface of the earth does not affect the sails of ships, though if men ever come to use flying machines and sail through the tropics at a good height above the sea it will be sensible enough. The dif-

ference between the doldrum of the equator and that of
the hurricane, besides their relative areas, is that one is
a belt and the other a disk. If the seafarer happens to sail
on a path which leads him through the hurricane centre,
he will first discern, as from the untroubled air and sea he
approaches the periphery of the storm, the horizon toward
the disturbance beset by troubled clouds, all moving in
one direction. Entering beneath this pall, he finds a steadily increasing wind, which in twenty miles of sailing may,
and in a hundred miles surely will, compel him to take in
all but his storm sails, and is likely to bring his ship into
grave peril. The most furious winds the mariner knows
are those which he encounters as he approaches the still
centre. These trials are made the more appalling by the
fact that in the furious part of the whirl the rain, condensing from the ascending air, falls in torrents, and the electricity generated in the condensation gives rise to vivid
lightning. If the storm-beset ship can maintain her way,
in a score or two of miles of journey toward the centre,
generally very quickly, it passes into the calm disk, where
the winds, blowing upward, cease to be felt. In this area
the ship is not out of danger, for the waves, rolling in from
the disturbed areas on either side, make a torment of cross
seas, where it is hard to control the movements of a sailing
vessel because the impulse of the winds is lost. Passing
through this disk of calm, the ship re-encounters in reverse order the furious portion of the whirl, afterward the
lessening winds, until it escapes again into the airs which
are not involved in the great torment.

In the old days, before Dove's studies of storms had
shown the laws of hurricane movement, unhappy ship-
masters were likely to be caught and retained in hurricanes, and to battle with them for weeks until their vessels
were beaten to pieces. Now the "Sailing Directions,"
which are the mariner's guide, enable him, from the direction of the winds and the known laws of motion of the
storm centre, to sail out of the danger, so that in most

cases he may escape calamity. It is otherwise with the people who dwell upon the land over which these atmospheric convulsions sweep. Fortunately, where these great whirlwinds trespass on the continent, they quickly die out, because of the relative lack of moisture which serves to stimulate the uprush which creates them. Thus in their more violent forms hurricanes are only felt near the sea, and generally on islands and peninsulas. There the hurricane winds, by the swiftness of their movement, which often attains a speed of a hundred miles or more, apply a great deal of energy to all obstacles in their path. The pressure thus produced is only less destructive than that which is brought about by the tornadoes, which are next to be described.

There is another effect from hurricanes which is even more destructive to life than that caused by the direct action of the wind. In these whirlings great differences in atmospheric pressure are brought about in contiguous areas of sea. The result is a sudden elevation in the level of one part of the water. These disturbances, where the shore lands are low and thickly peopled, as is the case along the western coast of the Bay of Bengal, may produce inundations which are terribly destructive to life and property. They are known also in southern Florida and along the islands of the Caribbean, but in that region are not so often damaging to mankind.

Fortunately, hurricanes are limited to a very small part of the tropical district. They occur only in those regions, on the eastern faces of tropical lands, where the general westerly set of the winds favours the accumulation of great bodies of very warm, moist air next the surface of the sea. The western portion of the Gulf of Mexico and the Caribbean, the Bay of Bengal, and the southeastern portion of Asia are especially liable to their visitations. They sometimes develop, though with less fury, in other parts of the tropics. On the western coast of South America and Africa, where the oceans are visited by the dry land winds, and where the waters are cooled by currents setting in from high latitudes, they are unknown.

Only less in order of magnitude than the hurricanes are the circular storms known as cyclones. These occur on the continents, especially where they afford broad plains little interrupted by mountain ranges. They are particularly well exhibited in that part of North America north of Mexico and south of Hudson Bay. Like the hurricanes, they appear to be due to the inrush of relatively warm air entering an updraught which had been formed in the overlying, cooler portions of the atmosphere. They are, however, much less energetic, and often of greater size than the hurricane whirl. The lack of energy is probably due to the comparative dryness of the air. The greater width of the ascending column may perhaps be accounted for by the fact that, originating at a considerable height above the sea, they have a less thickness of air to break through, and so the upward setting column is readily made broad.

The cyclones of North America appear generally to originate in the region of the Rocky Mountains, though it is probable that in some instances, perhaps in many, the upward set of the air which begins the storm originates in the ocean along the Pacific coast. They gather energy as they descend the great sloping plain leading eastward from the Rocky Mountains to the central portion of the great continental valley. Thence they move on across the country to the Atlantic coast. Not infrequently they continue on over the ocean to the European continent. The eastward passage of the storm centre is due to the prevailing eastward movement of the air in its upper part throughout that portion of the northern hemisphere. Commonly they incline somewhat to the northward of east in their journey. In all cases the winds appear to blow spirally into the common storm centre. There is the same doldrum area or calm field in the centre of the storm that we note between the trade winds and in the middle of a hurricane disk, though this area is less defined than in the other instances, and the forward motion of the storm at a considerable speed is in most cases characteristic of the disturbance. On the front of one of these storms in North America the winds commonly begin in the northeast, thence they veer by the east to the southwest. At this stage in the movement the storm centre has passed by, the rainfall commonly ceases, and cold, dry winds setting to the northwestward set in. This is caused by the fact that the ascending air, having attained a height above the earth, settles down behind the storm, forming an anticyclone or mass of dry air, which presses against the retreating side of the great whirlwind.

In front of the storm the warm and generally moist relatively warm air, pressing in toward the point of uprise and overlaid by the upper cold air, is brought into a condition where it tends to form small subordinate shafts up through which it whirls on the same principle, but with far greater intensity than the main ascending column. The reason for the violence of this movement is that the difference in temperature of the air next the surface and that at the height of a few thousand feet is great. As might be expected, these local spinnings are most apt to occur in the season when the air next the earth is relatively warm, and they are aptest to take place in the half of the advancing front lying between the east and south, for the reason that there the highest temperatures and the greatest humidity are likely to coexist. In that part of the field, during the time when the storm is advancing from the Rocky Mountains to the Atlantic, a dozen or more of these spinning uprushes may be produced, though few of them are likely to be of large size or of great intensity.

The secondary storms of cyclones, such as are above noted, receive the name of tornadoes. They are frequent and terrible visitations of the country from northern Texas, Florida, and Alabama to about the line of the Great Lakes; they are rarely developed in the region west of central Kansas, and only occasionally do they exhibit much energy in the region east of the plain-lands of the Ohio Valley. Although known in other lands, they nowhere, so far as our observations go, exhibit the paroxysmal intensity which they show in the central portion of the North American continent. There the air which they affect acquires a speed of movement and a fury of action unknown in any other atmospheric disturbances, even in those of the hurricanes.

The observer who has a chance to note from an advantageous position the development of a tornado observes that in a tolerably still air, or at least an air unaffected by violent winds—generally in what is termed a "sultry" state of the atmosphere—the storm clouds in the distance begin to form a kind of funnel-shaped dependence, which gradually extends until it appears to touch the earth. As the clouds are low, this downward-growing column probably in no case is observed for the height of more than three or four thousand feet. As the funnel descends, the clouds above and about it may be seen to take on a whirling movement around the centre, and under favourable circumstances an uprush of vapours may be noted in the centre of the swaying shaft. As the whirl comes nearer, the roar of the disturbance, which at a distance is often compared to the sound made by a threshing machine or to that of distant musketry, increases in loudness until it becomes overwhelming. When a storm such as this strikes a building, it is not only likely to be razed by the force of the wind, but it may be exploded, as by the action of gunpowder fired within its walls, through the sudden expansion of the air which it contains. In the centre of the column, although it rarely has a diameter of more than a few hundred feet, the uprush is so swift that it makes a partial vacuum. The air, striving to get into the space which it is eager to occupy, is whirling about at such a rate that the centrifugal motion which it thus acquires restrains its entrance. In this way there may be, as the

column rapidly moves by, a difference of pressure amounting probably to what the mercury of a barometer would
indicate by four or five inches of fall.   Unless the structure
is small and its walls strong, its roof and sides are apt to
be blown apart by this difference of pressure and the consequent expansion of the contained air.   In some cases
where wooden buildings have withstood this curious action
the outer clapboards have been blown off by the expansion
of the small amount of air contained in the interspaces
between that covering and the lath and plaster within
(see Fig. 9).

Fig. 9.—Showing effect of expansion of air contained in a hollow
wall during the passage of the storm.

The blow of the air due to its rotative whirling has in
several cases proved sufficient to throw a heavy locomotive
from the track of a well-constructed railway.   In all cases
where it is intense it will overturn the strongest trees.
The ascending wind in the centre of the column may
sometimes lift the bodies of men and of animals, as well
as the branches and trunks of trees and the timber of
houses, to the height of hundreds of feet above the surface.   One of the most striking exhibitions of the upsucking

action in a tornado is afforded by the effect which it produces when it crosses a small sheet of water. In certain cases where, in the Northwestern States of this country, the path of the storm lay over the pool, the whole of the water from a basin acres in extent has been entirely carried away, leaving the surface, as described by an observer, apparently dry enough to plough.

Fortunately for the interests of man, as well as those of the lower organic life, the paths of these storms, or at least the portion of their track where the violence of the air movement makes them very destructive, often does not exceed five hundred feet in width, and is rarely as great as half a mile in diameter. In most cases the length of the journey of an individual tornado does not exceed thirty miles. It rarely if ever amounts to twice that distance.

In every regard except their small size and their violence these tornadoes closely resemble hurricanes. There is the same broad disk of air next the surface spirally revolving toward the ascending centre, where its motion is rapidly changed from a horizontal to a vertical direction. The energy of the uprush in both cases is increased by the energy set free through the condensation of the water, which tends further to heat and thus to expand the air. The smaller size of the tornado may be accounted for by the fact that we have in their originating conditions a relatively thin layer of warm, moist air next the earth and a relatively very cold layer immediately overlying it. Thus the tension which serves to start the movement is intense, though the masses involved are not very great. The short life of a tornado may be explained by the fact that, though it apparently tends to grow in width and energy, the central spout is small, and is apt to be broken by the movements of the atmosphere, which in the front of a cyclone are in all cases irregular.

On the warmer seas, but often beyond the limits of the tropics, another class of spinning storms, known as waterspouts, may often be observed. In general appearance these air whirls resemble tornadoes, except that they are in all cases smaller than that group of whirlings. As in the tornadoes, the waterspout begins with a funnel, which descends from the sky to the surface of the sea. Up the tube vapours may be seen ascending at great speed, the whole appearing like a gigantic pillar of swiftly revolving smoke. When the whirl reaches the water, it is said that the fluid leaps up into the tube in the form of dense spray, an assertion which, in view of the fact of the action of a tornado on a lake as before described, may well be believed. Like the tornadoes and dust whirls, the life of a waterspout appears to be brief. They rarely endure for more than a few minutes, or journey over the sea for more than two or three miles before the column appears to be broken by some swaying of the atmosphere. As these peculiar storms are likely to damage ships, the old-fashioned sailors were accustomed to fire at them with cannon. It has been claimed that a shot would break the tube and end the little convulsion. This, in view of the fact that they appear to be easily broken up by relatively trifling air currents, may readily be believed. The danger which these disturbances bring to ships is probably not very serious.

The special atmospheric conditions which bring about the formation of waterspouts are not well known; they doubtless include, however, warm, moist air next the surface of the sea and cold air above. Just why these storms never attain greater size or endurance is not yet known. These disturbances have been seen for centuries, but as yet they have not been, in the scientific sense, observed. Their picturesqueness attracts all beholders; it is interesting to note the fact that perhaps the earliest description of their phenomena—one which takes account in the scientific spirit of all the features which they present—was written by the poet Camoëns in the Lusiad, in which he strangely mingles fancy and observation in his account of the great voyage of Vasco da Gama. The poet even

notes that the water which falls when the spout is broken
is not salt, but fresh—a point which clearly proves that
not much of the water which the tube contains is derived
from the sea. It is, in fact, watery vapour drawn from the
air next the surface of the ocean, and condensed in its
ascent through the tube. In this and other descriptions
of Nature Camoëns shows more of the scientific spirit than
any other poet of his time. He was in this regard the first
of modern writers to combine a spiritual admiration for
Nature with some sense of its scientific meaning.

In treating of the atmosphere, meteorologists base their
studies largely on changes in the weight of that medium,
which they determine by barometric observations. In fact,
the science of the air had its beginning in Pascal's admirable observation on the changes in the height of a column
of mercury contained in a bent tube as he ascended the
volcanic peak known as Puy de Dome, in central France.
As before noted, it is to the disturbances in the weight
of the air, brought about mainly by variations in temperature, that we owe all its currents, and it is upon these
winds that the features we term climate in largest measure
depend. Every movement of the winds is not only brought
about by changes in the relative weight of the air at certain points, but the winds themselves, owing to the momentum which the air attains by them, serve to bring
about alterations in the quantity of air over different parts
of the earth, which are marked most distinctly by barometric variations. These changes are exceedingly complicated; a full account of them would demand the space
of this volume. A few of the facts, however, should be
presented here. In the first place, we note that each day
there is normally a range in the pressure which causes the
barometer to be at the lowest at about four o'clock in the
morning and four o'clock in the afternoon, and highest at
about ten o'clock in those divisions of the day. This
change is supposed to be due to the fact that the motes
of dust in the atmosphere in the night, becoming cooled,

condense the water vapour upon their surfaces, thus diminishing the volume of the air. When the sun rises the water evaporated by the heat returns from these little storehouses into the body of the atmosphere. Again in the evening the condensation sets in; at the same time the air tends to drift in from the region to the westward, where the sun is still high, toward the field where the barometer has been thus lowered; the current gradually attains a certain volume, and so brings about the rise of the barometer about ten o'clock at night.

In the winter time, particularly on the well-detached continent of North America, we find a prevailing high barometer in the interior of the country and a corresponding low state of pressure on the Atlantic Ocean. In the summer season these conditions are on the whole reversed.

Under the tropics, in the doldrum belt, there is a zone of low barometer connected to the ascending currents which take place along that line. This is a continuous manifestation of the same action which gives a large area of a disklike form in the centre or eye of the hurricane and in the middle portion of the tornado's whirl. In general, it may be said that the weight of the air is greatest in the regions from which it is blowing toward the points of upward escape, and least in and about those places where the superincumbent air is rising through a temporary or permanent line of escape. In other words, ascending air means generally a relatively low barometer, while descending air is accompanied by greater pressure in the field upon which it falls.

In almost every part of the earth which is affected by a particular physiography we find that the movements of the atmosphere next the surface are qualified by the condition which it encounters. In fact, if a person were possessed of all the knowledge which could be obtained concerning winds, he could probably determine as by a map the place where he might chance to find himself, provided he could extend his observations over a term of years.

In other words, the regimen of the winds—at least those of a superficial nature—is almost as characteristic of the field over which they go as is a map of the country. Of these special winds a number of the more important have been noted, only a few of which we can advert to. First among these may well come the land and sea breezes which are remarked about all islands which are not continuously swept by permanent winds. One of the most characteristic instances of these alternate winds is perhaps that afforded on the island of Jamaica.

The island of Jamaica is so situated within the basin of the Caribbean that it does not feel the full influence of the trades. It has a range of high mountains through its middle part. In the daytime the surface of the land, which has the sun overhead twice each year, and is always exposed to nearly vertical radiation, becomes intensely hot, so that an upcurrent is formed. The formation of this current is favoured by the mountains, which apply a part. of the heat at the height of about a mile above the surface of the sea. This action is parallel to that we notice when, in order to create a draught in the air of a chimney, we put a torch some distance up above the fireplace, thus diminishing the height of the column of air which has to be set in motion. It is further shown by the fact that when miners sought to make an upcurrent in a shaft, in order to lead pure air into the workings through other openings, they found after much experience that it was better to have the fire near the top of the shaft rather than at the bottom.

The ascending current being induced up the mountain sides of Jamaica, the air is forced in from the sea to the relatively free space. Before noon the current, aided in its speed by a certain amount of the condensation of the watery vapour before described, attains the proportions of a strong wind. As the sun begins to sink, the earth's surface pours forth its heat; the radiation being assisted by the extended surfaces of the plants, cooling rapidly takes

9

place. Meanwhile the sea, because of the great heat-storing power of water, is very little cooled, the ascent of the
air ceases, the temporary chimney with its updraught is
replaced by a downward current, and the winds blow from
the land until the sun comes again to reverse the current.
In many cases these movements of the daily winds flowing
into and from islands induce a certain precipitation of
moisture in the form of rain. Generally, however, their
effect is merely to ameliorate the heat by bringing alternately currents from the relatively cool sea and from the
upper atmosphere to lessen the otherwise excessive temperature of the fields which they traverse.

Although characteristic sea and land winds are limited
to regions where the sun's heat is great, they are traceable
even in high latitudes during the periods of long-continued
calm attended with clear skies. Thus on the island of
Martha's Vineyard, in Massachusetts, the writer has noted,
when the atmosphere was in such a state, distinct night
and day, or sea and land, breezes coming in their regular
alternation. During the night when these alternate winds
prevail the central portion of the island, at the distance
of three miles from the sea, is remarkably cold, the low
temperature being due to the descending air current. To
the same physical cause may be attributed the frequent
insets of the sea winds toward midday along the continental shores of various countries. Thus along the coast
of New England in the summer season a clear, still, hot
day is certain to lead to the creation of an ingoing tide
of air, which reaches some miles into the interior. This
stream from the sea enters as a thin wedge, it often being
possible to note next the shore when the movement begins
a difference of ten degrees of temperature between the surface of the ground to which the point of the wedge has
attained, and a position twenty feet higher in the air. This
is a beautiful example to show at once how the relative
weight of the atmosphere, even when the differences are
slight, may bring about motion, and also how masses of the

atmosphere may move by or through the rest of the medium in a way which we do not readily conceive from our observations on the transparent mass. Very few people have any idea how general is the truth that the air, even in continuous winds, tends to move in more or less individualized masses. This, however, is made very evident by watching the gusts of a storm or the wandering patches of wind which disturb the surface of an otherwise smooth sea.

Among the notable local winds are those which from their likeness to the Föhn of the Swiss valleys receive that name. Föhns are produced where a body of air blowing against the slope of a continuous mountain range is lifted to a considerable height, and, on passing over the crest, falls again to a low position. In its ascent the air is cooled, rarefied, and to a great extent deprived of its moisture. In descending it is recondensed, and by the process by which its atoms are brought together its latent heat is made sensible. There being but little watery vapour in the mass, this heat is not much called for by that heat-storing fluid, and so the air is warmed. So far Föhn winds have only been remarked as conspicuous features in Switzerland and on the eastern face of the Rocky Mountains. In the region about the head waters of the Missouri and to the northward their influence in what are called the Chinook winds is distinctly to ameliorate the severe winter climate of the country.

In almost all great desert regions, particularly in the typical Sahara, we find a variety of storm belonging to the whirlwind group, which, owing to the nature of the country, take on special characteristics. These desert storms take up from the verdureless earth great quantities of sand and other fine *débris*, which often so clouds the air as to bring the darkness of night at midday. Their whirlings appear in size to be greater than those which produce tornadoes or waterspouts, but less than hurricanes or cyclones. Little, however, is known about them. They have not been well observed by meteorologists. In some ways they are important, for the reason that they serve to carry the desert sand into regions previously verdure-clad, and thus to extend the bounds of the desolate fields in which they originate. Where they blow off to the sea-ward, they convey large quantities of dust into the ocean, and thus serve to wear down the surface of the land in regions where there are no rivers to effect that action in the normal way.

Notwithstanding its swift motion when impelled by differences in weight, the movements of the air have had but little direct and immediate influence on the surface of the earth. The greater part of the work which it does, as we shall see hereafter, is done through the waters which it impels and bears about. Yet where winds blow over verdureless surfaces the effect of the sand which they sweep before them is often considerable. In regions of arid mountains the winds often drive trains of sand through the valleys, where the sharp particles cut the rocks almost as effectively as torrents of water would, dis-tributing the wearing over the width of the valley. The dust thus blown from a desert region may, when it attains a country covered with vegetation, gradually accumulate on its surface, forming very thick deposits. Thus in north-western China there is a wide area where dust accumula-tions blown from the arid districts of central Asia have gradually heaped up in the course of ages to the depth of thousands of feet, and this although much of the *débris* is continually being borne away by the action of the rain waters as they journey toward the sea. Such dust accumu-lations occur in other parts of the world, particularly in the districts about the upper Mississippi and in the valleys of the Rocky Mountains, but nowhere are they so conspicu-ous as in the region first mentioned.

Where prevailing winds from the sea, from great lakes, and even from considerable rivers, blow against sandy shores or cliffs of the same nature, large quantities of sand

and dust are often driven inland from the coast line. In most cases these wind-borne materials take on the form of dunes, or heaps of sand, varying from a few feet to several hundred feet in height. It is characteristic of these hills of blown sand that they move across the face of the country. Under favourable conditions they may journey scores of miles from the shore. The marching of a dune is effected through the rolling up of the sand on the windward side of the elevation, when it is impelled by the current of air to the crest where it falls into the lee or shelter which the hill makes to the wind. In this way in the course of a day the centre of the dune, if the wind be blowing furiously, may advance a measurable distance from the place it occupied before. By fits and starts this ongoing may be indefinitely continued. A notable and picturesque instance of the march of a great dune may be had from the case in which one of them overwhelmed in the last century the village of Eccles in southeastern England. The advancing sand gradually crept into the hamlet, and in the course of a decade dispossessed the people by burying their houses. In time the summit of the church spire disappeared from view, and for many years thereafter all trace of the hamlet was lost. Of late years, however, the onward march of the sands has disclosed the church spire, and in the course of another century the place may be revealed on its original site, unchanged except that the marching hill will be on its other side.

In the region about the head of the Bay of Biscay the quantity of these marching sands is so great that at one time they jeopardized the agriculture of a large district. The French Government has now succeeded, by carefully planting the surface of the country with grasses and other herbs which will grow in such places, in checking the movement of the wind-blown materials. By so doing they have merely hastened the process by which Nature arrests the march of dunes. As these heaps creep away from the sea, they generally come into regions where a greater variety of plants flourish; moreover, their sand grains become decayed, so that they afford a better soil. Gradually the mat of vegetation binds them down, and in time covers them over so that only the expert eye can recognise their true nature. Only in desert regions can the march of these heaps be maintained for great distances.

Characteristic dunes occur from point to point all along the Atlantic coast from the State of Maine to the northern coast of Florida. They also occur along the coasts of our Great Lakes, being particularly well developed at the southern end of Lake Michigan, where they form, perhaps, the most notable accumulations within the limits of the United States.

When blown sands invade a forest and the deposit is rapidly accumulated, the trees are often buried in an undecayed condition. In this state, with certain chemical reactions which may take place in the mass, the woody matter is apt to become replaced by silex dissolved from the sand, which penetrates the tissues of the plants. In this way salicified forests are produced, such as are found in the region of the Rocky Mountains, where the trunks of the trees, now very hard stone, so perfectly preserve their original structure that when cut and polished they may be used for decorative purposes. Conspicuous as is this work of the dunes, it is in a geological way much less important than that accomplished by the finer dust which drifts from one region of land to another or into the sea. Because of their weight, the sand grains journey over the surface of the earth, except, indeed, where they are uplifted by whirl storms. They thus can not travel very fast or far. Dust, however, rises into the air, and journeys for indefinite distances. We thus see how slight differences in the weight of substances may profoundly affect the conditions of their deportation.

THE SYSTEM OF WATERS.

The envelope of air wraps the earth completely about, and, though varying in thickness, is everywhere present over its surface. That of the waters is much less equally distributed. Because of its weight, it is mainly gathered in the depths of the earth, where it lies in the interstices of the rocks and in the great realm of the seas. Only a very small portion of the fluid is in the atmosphere or on the land. Perhaps less than a ten thousandth part of the whole is at any one time on this round from the seas through the air to the land and back to the great reservoir.

The great water store of the earth is contained in two distinct realms—in the oceans, where the fluid is concentrated in a quantity which fills something like nine tenths of the hollows formed by the corrugations of the earth's surface; and in the rocks, where it is stored in a finely divided form, partly between the grains of the stony matter and partly in the substance of its crystals, where it exists in a combination, the precise nature of which is not well known, but is called water of crystallization. On the average, it seems likely that the materials of the earth, whether under the sea or on the land, have several per cent of their mass of the fluid.

It is not yet known to what depth the water-bearing section of the earth extends; but, as we shall see more particularly hereafter when we come to consider volcanoes, the lavas which they send up to the surface are full of contained water, which passes from them in the form of steam. The very high temperature of these volcanic ejections makes it necessary for us to suppose that they come from a great depth. It is difficult to believe that they originate at less than a hundred miles below the earth's surface. If, then, the rocks contain an average of even five per cent of water to the depth of one hundred miles, the quantity of the fluid stored within the earth is greater than that which is contained in the reservoir of the ocean.

The oceans, on the average, are not more than three miles deep; spread evenly over the surface of the whole earth, their depth would be less than two miles, while the water in the rocks, if it could be added to the seas, would make the total depth seven miles or more. As we shall note hereafter, the processes of formation of strata tend to imprison water in the beds, which in time is returned to the earth's surface by the forces which operate within the crust.

Although the water in the seas is, as we have seen, probably less than one half of the store which the earth possesses, the part it plays in the economy of the planet is in the highest measure important. The underground water operates solely to promote certain changes which take place in the mineral realm. Its effect, except in volcanic processes, are brought about but slowly, and are limited in their action. The movements of this buried water are exceedingly gradual; the forces which impel it about and which bring it to do its work originate in the earth. In the seas the fluid has an exceeding freedom of motion; it can obey the varied impulses which the solar energy imposes upon it. The rôle of these wonderful actions which we are about to trace includes almost everything which goes on upon the surface of the planet—that which relates to the development of animal and vegetable life, as well as to the vast geological changes which the earth is undergoing.

If the surface of the earth were uniformly covered with water to the depth of ten thousand feet or more, every particle of fluid would, in a measure, obey the attraction of the sun, of the moon, and, theoretically, also of all the other bodies in space, on the principle that every particle of matter in the universe exercises a gravitative effect on every other. As it is, owing to the divided condition of the water on the earth's surface, only that which is in the ocean and larger seas exhibits any measurable influence from these distant attractions. In fact, only the tides produced by the moon and sun are of determinable magnitude, and of these the lunar is of greater importance, the reason being the near position of our satellite to our own sphere. The solar tide is four tenths as great as the lunar. The water doubtless obeys in a slight way the attraction of the other celestial bodies, but the motions thus imparted are too small to be discerned; they are lost in the great variety of influences which affect all the matter on the earth.

Although the tides are due to the attraction of the solar bodies, mainly to that of the moon, the mode in which the result is brought about is somewhat complicated. It may briefly and somewhat incompletely be stated as follows: Owing to the fact that the attracting power of the earth is about eighty times greater than that of the moon, the centre of gravity of the two bodies lies within the earth. About this centre the spheres revolve, each in a way swinging around the other. At this point there is no centrifugal motion arising from the revolution of the pair of spheres, but on the side of the earth opposite the moon, some six thousand miles away, the centrifugal force is considerable, becoming constantly greater as we pass away from the turning point. At the same time the attraction of the moon on the water becomes less. Thus the tide opposite the satellite is formed. On the side toward the moon the same centrifugal action operates, though less effectively than in the other case, for the reason that the turning point is nearer the surface; but this action is re-enforced by the greater attraction of the moon, due to the fact that the water is much nearer that body.

In the existing conditions of the earth, what we may call the normal run of the tides is greatly interrupted. Only in the southern ocean can the waters obey the lunar and solar attraction in anything like a normal way. In that part of the earth two sets of tides are discernible, the one and greater due to the moon, the other, much smaller, to the sun. As these tides travel round at different rates, the movements which they produce are sometimes added to each other and sometimes subtracted—that is, at times they come together, while again the elevation of one falls in the hollow of the other. Once again supposing the earth to be all ocean covered, computation shows that the tides in such a sea would be very broad waves, having, indeed, a diameter of half the earth's circumference. Those produced by the moon would have an altitude of about one foot, and those by the sun of about three inches. The geological effects of these swayings would be very slight; the water would pass over the bottom to and fro twice each day, with a maximum journey of a hundred or two feet each way from a fixed point. This movement would be so slow that it could not stir the fine sediment; its only influence would perhaps be to help feed the animals which were fixed upon the bottom by drawing the nurture-bringing water by their mouths.

Although the divided condition of the ocean perturbs the action of the tides, so that except by chance their waves are rarely with their centres where the attracting bodies tend to make them, the influence of these divisions is greatly to increase the geological or change-bringing influences arising from these movements. When from the southern ocean the tides start to the northward up the bays of the Atlantic, the Pacific, or the Indian Ocean, they have, as before noted, a height of perhaps less than two feet. As they pass up the narrowing spaces the waves become compressed—that is, an equal volume of moving water has less horizontal room for its passage, and is forced to rise higher. We see a tolerably good illustration of the same principle when we observe a wind-made wave enter a small recess of the shore, the sides of which converge in the direction of the motion. With the diminished room, the wave gains in height. It thus comes about that the tide throughout the Atlantic basin is much higher than in the southern ocean. On the same principle, when the tide rolls in against the shores every embayment of a distinct kind, whose sides converge toward the head, packs up the tidal wave, often increasing its height in a remarkable way. When these bays are wide-mouthed and of elongate triangular form, with deep bottoms, the tides which on their outer parts have a height of ten or fifteen feet may attain an altitude of forty or fifty feet at the apex of the triangle.

We have already noted the fact that the tide, such as runs in the southern ocean, exercises little or no influence upon the bottom of the sea over which it moves. As the height of the confined waters increases, the range of their journey over the bottom as the wave comes and goes rapidly increases. When they have an elevation of ten feet they can probably stir the finer mud on the ocean floor, and in shallow water move yet heavier particles. In the embayments of the land, where a great body of water journeys like an alternating river into extensive basins, the tidal action becomes intense; the current may be able to sweep along large stones quite as effectively as a mountain torrent. Thus near Eastport, Me., where the tides have a maximum rise and fall of over twenty feet, the waters rush in places so swiftly that at certain stages of the movement they are as much troubled as those at the rapids of the St. Lawrence. In such portions of the shore the tides do important work in carving channels into the lands.

Along the shores of the continents about the North Atlantic, where the tides act in a vigorous manner, we almost everywhere find an underwater shelf extending from the shore with a declivity of only five to ten feet to the mile toward the centre of the sea, until the depth of about five hundred feet is attained; from this point the bottom descends more steeply into the ocean's depth. It is probable that the larger part of the material composing these continental shelves has been brought to its position by tidal action. Each time the tidal wave sweeps in toward the shore it urges the finer particles of sediment along with it. When it moves out it drags them on the return journey toward the depths of the sea. If this shelf were perfectly horizontal, the two journeys of the sand and mud grains would be of the same length; but as the movement takes place up and down a slope, the bits will travel farther under the impulse which leads them downward than under that which impels them up. The result will be that the particles will travel a little farther out from the shore each time it is swung to and fro in the alternating movement of the tide.

The effect of tidal movement in nurturing marine life is very great. It aids the animals fixed on the bottoms of the deep seas to obtain their provision of food and their share of oxygen by drawing the water by their bodies. All regions which are visited by strong tides commonly have in the shallows near the shores a thick growth of seaweed which furnishes an ample provision of food for the fishes and other forms of animal life.

A peculiar effect arising from tidal action is believed by students of the phenomena to be found in the slowing of the earth's rotation on its axis. The tides rotate around the earth from east to west, or rather, we should say, the solid mass of the earth rubs against them as it spins from west to east. As they move over the bottom and as they strike against the shores this push of the great waves tends in a slight measure to use up the original spinning impulse which causes the earth's rotation. Computation shows that the amount of this action should be great enough gradually to lengthen the day, or the time occupied by the earth in making a complete revolution on the polar axis. The effect ought to be great enough to be measurable by astronomers in the course of a thousand years. On the other hand, the records of ancient eclipses appear pretty clearly to show that the length of the day has not changed by as much as a second in the course of three thousand years. This evidence does not require us to abandon the supposition that the tides tend to diminish the earth's rate of rotation. It is more likely that the effect of the reduction in the earth's diameter due to the loss of heat which is continually going on counterbalances the influence of the tidal friction. As the diameter of a rotating body diminishes, the tendency is for the mass to spin more rapidly; if it expands, to turn more slowly, provided in each case the amount of the impulse which leads to the turning remains the same. This can be directly observed by whirling a small weight attached to a string in such a manner that the cord winds around the finger with each revolution; it will be noted that as the line shortens the revolution is more quickly accomplished. We can readily conceive that the earth is made up of weights essentially like that used in the experiment, each being drawn toward the centre by the gravitative stress, which is like that applied to the weight by the cord.

The fact that the days remain of the same length through vast periods of time is probably due to this balance between the effects of tidal action and those arising from the loss of heat—in other words, we have here one of those delicate arrangements in the way of counterpoise which serve to maintain the balanced conditions of the earth's surface amid the great conflicts of diverse energies which are at work in and upon the sphere.

It should be understood that the effects of the attraction which produces tides are much more extensive than they are seen to be in the movements of the sea. So long as the solar and planetary spheres remain fluid, the whole of their masses partake of the movement. It is a consequence of this action, as the computations of Prof. George Darwin has shown, that the moon, once nearer the earth than it is at present, has by a curious action of the tidal force been pushed away from the centre of our sphere, or rather the two bodies have repelled each other. An American student of the problem, Mr. T. J. J. See, has shown that the same action has served to give to the double stars the exceeding eccentricity of their orbits.

Although these recent studies of tidal action in the

celestial sphere are of the utmost importance to the theory
of the universe, for they may lead to changes in the nebular
hypotheses, they are as yet too incomplete and are, moreover, too mathematical to be presented in an elementary
treatise such as this.

We now turn to another class of waves which are of
even more importance than those of the tides—to the undulations which are produced by the action of the wind on
the surface of the water. While the tide waves are limited
to the open ocean, and to the seas and bays which afford
them free entrance, wind waves are produced everywhere
where water is subjected to the friction of air which flows
over it. While tidal waves come upon the shores but twice
each day, the wind waves of ordinary size which roll in
from the ocean deliver their blows at intervals of from three
to ten seconds. Although the tidal waves sometimes, by
a packing-up process, attain the height of fifty feet, their
average altitude where they come in contact with the shore
probably does not much exceed four feet; usually they
come in gently. It is likely that in a general way the ocean
surges which beat against the coast are of greater altitude.
Wind waves are produced and perform their work in
a manner which we shall now describe. When the air
blows over any resisting surface, it tends, in a way which
we can hardly afford here to describe, to produce motions.
If the particle is free to move under the impulse which it
communicates, it bears it along; if it is linked together in
the manner of large masses, which the wind can not trans-
port, it tends to set it in motion in an alternating way.
The sounds of our musical instruments which act by wind
are due to these alternating vibrations, such as all air currents tend to produce. An Æolian harp illustrates the
action which we are considering. Moving over matter
which has the qualities that we denote by the term fluid,
the swayings which the air produces are of a peculiar sort,
though they much resemble those of the fiddle string.

The surface of the liquid rises and falls in what we term waves, the size of which is determined by the measure of fluidity,and by the energy of the wind. Thus, because fresh water is considerably lighter than salt, a given wind will produce in a given distance for the run of the waves heavier surges in a lake than it will in the sea. For this reason the surges in a great storm which roll on the ocean shore, because of the wide water over which they have gathered their impetus, are in size very much greater than those of the largest lakes, which do not afford room for the development of great undulations.

To the eye, a wave in the water appears to indicate that the fluid is borne on before the wind. Examination, however, shows that the amount of motion in the direction in which the wind is blowing is very slight. We may say, indeed, that the essential feature of a wave is found in the transmission of impulse rather than in the movement of the fluid matter. A strip of carpet when shaken sends through its length undulations which are almost exactly like water waves. If we imagine ourselves placed in a particle of water, moving in the swayings of a wave in the open and deep sea, we may conceive ourselves carried around in an ellipse, in each revolution returning through nearly the same orbit. Now and then, when the particle came to the surface, it would experience the slight drift which the continual friction of the wind imposes on the water. If the wave in which the journey was made lay in the trade winds, where the long-continued, steadfast blowing had set the water in motion to great depths, the orbit traversed would be moving forward with some rapidity; where also the wind was strong enough to blow the tops of the waves over, forming white-caps, the advance of the particle very near the surface would be speedy. Notwithstanding these corrections, waves are to be regarded each as a store of energy, urging the water to sway much in the manner of a carpet strip, and by the swaying conveying the energy in the direction of the wave movement.

The rate of movement of wind waves increases with their height. Slight undulations go forward at the rate of less than half a mile an hour. The greater surges of the deeps when swept by the strongest winds move with the speed which, though not accurately determined, has been estimated by the present writer as exceeding forty miles an hour. As these surges often have a length transverse to the wind of a mile or more, a width of about an eighth of a mile, and a height of from thirty-five to forty-five feet, the amount of energy which they transmit is very great. If it could be effectively applied to the shores in the manner in which the energy of exploding gunpowder is applied by cannon shot, it is doubtful whether the lands could have maintained their position against the assaults of the sea. But there are reasons stated below why the ocean waves can use only a very small part of their energy in rending the rocks against which they strike on the coast line.

In the first place, we should note that wind waves have very little influence on the bottom of the deep sea. If an observer could stand on the sea floor at the depth of a mile below a point over which the greatest waves were rolling, he could not with his unaided senses discern that the water was troubled. He would, indeed, require instruments of some delicacy to find out that it moved at all. Making the same observations at the depth of a thousand feet, it is possible that he would note a slight swaying motion in the water, enough sensibly to affect his body. At five hundred feet in depth the movement would probably be sufficient to disturb fine mud. At two hundred feet, the rasping of the surge on the bottom would doubtless be sufficient to push particles of coarse sand to and fro. At one hundred feet in depth, the passage of the surge would be strong enough to urge considerable pebbles before it. Thence up the slope the driving action would become more and more intense until we attained the point where the wave broke. It should furthermore be noted

that, while the movement of the water on the floor of the
deep sea as the wave passes overhead would be to and fro,
with every advance in the shallowing and consequent increased friction on the bottom, the forward element in the
movement would rapidly increase. Near the coast line
the effect of the waves is continually to shove the detritus
up the slopes of the continental shelf. Here we should
note the fact that on this shelf the waves play a part exactly the opposite of that effected by the tides. The tides,
as we have noted, tend to drag the particles down the slope,
while the waves operate to roll them up the declivity.

As the wave in advancing toward the shore ordinarily
comes into continually shallowing water, the friction on
the bottom is ever-increasing, and serves to diminish the
energy the surge contains, and therefore to reduce its proportions. If this action operated alone, the subtraction
which the friction makes would cause the surf waves which
roll in over a continental shelf to be very low, probably
in height less than half that which they now attain. In
fact, however, there is an influence at work to increase the
height of the waves at the expense of its width. Noting
that the friction rapidly increases with the shallowing, it
is easy to see that this resistance is greatest on the advancing front of the wave, and least on its seaward side. The
result is that the front moves more slowly than the rear,
so that the wave is forced to gain in height; but for the
fact that the total friction which the wave encounters
takes away most of its impetus, we might have combers
a hundred feet high rolling upon the shelving shores which
almost everywhere face the seas.

As the wave shortens its width and gains in relative
height, though not in actual elevation, another action is
introduced which has momentous consequences. The water
in the bottom of the wave is greatly retarded in its ongoing
by its friction over the sea floor, while the upper part of
the surge is much less affected in this way. The result is
that at a certain point in the advance, the place of which

10

is determined by the depth, the size, and the speed of the undulation, the front swiftly steepens until it is vertical, and the top shoots forward to a point where it is no longer supported by underlying water, when it plunges down in what is called the surf or breaker. In this part of the wave's work the application of the energy which it transmits differs strikingly from the work previously done. Before the wave breaks, the only geological task which it accomplishes is effected by forcing materials up the slope, in which movement they are slightly ground over each other until they come within the battering zone of the shore, where they may be further divided by the action of the mill which is there in operation.

When the wave breaks on the shore it operates in the following manner: First, the overturning of its crest sends a great mass of water, it may be from the height of ten or more feet, down upon the shore. Thus falling water has not only the force due to its drop from the summit of the wave, but it has a share of the impulse due to the velocity with which the surge moved against the shore. It acts, in a word, like a hammer swung down by a strong arm, where the blow represents not only the force with which the weight would fall of itself, but the impelling power of the man's muscles. Any one who will expose his body to this blow of the surf will recognise how violent it is; he may, if the beach be pebbly, note how it drives the stones about; fragments the size of a man's head may be hurled by the stroke to the distance of twenty feet or more; those as large as the fist may be thrown clear beyond the limits of the wave. So vigorous is this stroke that the sound of it may sometimes be heard ten miles inland from the coast where it is delivered.

Moving forward up the slope of a gently inclined beach, the fragments of the wave are likely to be of sufficient volume to permit them to regather into a secondary surge, which, like the first, though much smaller, again rises into a wall, forming another breaker. Under favourable conditions as many as four or five of these successive diminishing surf lines may be seen. The present writer has seen in certain cases as many as a dozen in the great procession, the lowest and innermost only a few inches high, the outer of all with a height of perhaps twenty feet.

Along with the direct bearing action of the surf goes a to-and-fro movement, due to the rushing up and down of the water on the beach. This swashing affects not only the broken part of the waves, but all the water between the outer breaker and the shore. These swayings in the surf belt often swing the *débris* on the inner margin over a range of a hundred feet or more, the movement taking place with great swiftness, affecting the pebbles to the depth of several inches, and grinding the bits together in a violent way. Listening to the turmoil of a storm, we can on a pebbly beach distinctly hear the sound of the downward stroke, a crashing tone, and the roar of the rolling stones.

As waves are among the interesting things in the world, partly on account of their living quality and partly because of their immediate and often exceeding interest to man, we may here note one or two peculiar features in their action. In the first place, as the reader who has gained a sense of the changes in form of action may readily perceive, the beating of waves on the shore converts the energy which they possess into heat. This probably warms the water during great storms, so that by the hand we may note the difference in temperature next the coast line and in the open waters. This relative warmth of the surf water is perhaps a matter of some importance in limiting the 'development of ice along the shore line; it may also favour the protection of the coast life against the severe cold of the winter season.

The waves which successively come against the shore in any given time, particularly if a violent wind is blowing on to the coast, are usually of about the same size. When, however, in times of calm an old sea, as it is called, is rolling in, the surges may occasionally undergo very great variations in magnitude. Not infrequently these occasional waves are great enough to overwhelm persons who are upon the rocks next the shore. These greater surges are probably to be accounted for by the fact that in the open sea waves produced by winds blowing in different directions may run on with their diverse courses and varied intervals until they come near the shore. Running in together, it very well happens that two of the surges belonging to different sets may combine their forces, thus doubling the swell. The danger which these conjoined waves bring is obviously greatest on cliff shores, where, on account of the depth of water, the waves do not break until they strike the steep.

Having considered in a general way the action of waves as they roll in to the shore, bearing with them the solar energy which was contributed to them by the winds, we shall now take up in some detail the work which goes on along the coast line—work which is mainly accomplished by wave action.

On most coast lines the observer readily notes that the shore is divided into two different kinds of faces—those where the inner margin of the wave-swept belt comes against rocky steeps, and those bordered by a strand altogether composed of materials which the surges have thrown up. These may be termed for convenience cliff shores and wall-beach shores. We shall begin our inquiry with cliff shores, for in those sections of the coast line the sea is doing its most characteristic and important work of assaulting the land. If the student has an opportunity to approach a set of cliffs of hard rock in time of heavy storm, when the waves have somewhere their maximum height, he should seek some headland which may offer him safe foothold whence he can behold the movements which are taking place. If he is so fortunate as to have in view, as well may be the case, cliffs which extend down into deep water, and others which are bordered by rude and generally steeply sloping beaches covered with large stones, he may perceive that the waves come in against the cliffs which plunge into deep water without taking on the breaker form. In this case the undulation strikes but a moderate blow; the wave is not greatly broken. The part next the rock may shoot up as a thin sheet to a considerable height; it is evident that while the ongoing wave applies a good deal of pressure to the steep, it does not deliver its energy in the effective form of a blow as when the wave overturns, or in the consequent rush of the water up a beach slope. It is easy to perceive that firm-set rock cliffs, with no beaches at their bases, can almost indefinitely withstand the assaults. On the steep and stony beach, because of its relatively great declivity, the breaker or surf forms far in, and even in its first plunge often attains the base of the precipice. The blow of the overfalling as well as that of the inrush moves about stones of great size; those three feet or more in diameter are often hurled by the action against the base of the steep, striking blows, the sharp note of which can often be heard above the general roar which the commotion produces. The needlelike crags forming isles standing at a distance from the shore, such as are often found along hard rock coasts, are singularly protected from the action of effective waves. The surges which strike against them are unarmed with stones, and the water at their bases is so deep that it does not sway with the motion with sufficient energy to move them on the bottom. Where a cliff is in this condition, it may endure until an elevation of the coast line brings its base near the level of the sea, or until the process of decay has detached a sufficient quantity of stone to form a talus or inclined plane reaching near to the water level.

As before noted, it is the presence of a sloping beach reaching to about the base of the cliff which makes it possible for the waves to strike at with a hammer instead of with a soft hand. Battering at the base of the cliff, the surges cut a crease along the strip on which they strike, which gradually enters so far that the overhanging rock falls of its own weight. The fragments thus delivered to the sea are in turn broken up and used as battering instruments until they are worn to pieces. We may note that in a few months of heavy weather the stones of such a fall have all been reduced to rudely spherical forms. Observations made on the eastern face of Cape Ann, Mass., where the seas are only moderately heavy, show that the storms of a single winter reduce the fragments thrown into the sea from the granite quarries to spheroidal shapes, more than half of their weight commonly being removed in the form of sand and small pebbles which have been worn from their surfaces.

We can best perceive the effect of battering action which the sea applies to the cliffs by noting the points where, owing to some chance features in the structure in the rock, it has proved most effective. Where a joint or a dike, or perhaps a softer layer, if the rocks be bedded, causes the wear to go on more rapidly, the waves soon excavate a recess in which the pebbles are retained, except in stormy weather, in an unmoved condition. When the surges are heavy, these stones are kept in continuous motion, receding as the wave goes back, and rushing forward with its impulse until they strike against the firm-set rock at the end of the chasm. In this way they may drive in a cut having the length of a hundred feet or more from the face of the precipice. In most cases the roofs over these sea caves fall in, so that the structure is known as a chasm. Occasionally these roofs remain, in which case, for the reason that the floor of the cutting inclines upward, an opening is made to the surface at their upper end, forming what is called in New England a "spouting horn"; from the inland end of the tunnel the spray may be thrown far into the air. As long as the cave is closed at this inner end, and is not so high but that it may be buried beneath a heavy wave, the inrushing water compresses the air in the rear parts of the opening. When the wave begins to retreat this air blows out, sending a gust of spray before it, the action resembling the discharge of a great gun from the face of a fortification. It often happens that two chasms converging separate a rock from the cliff. Then a lowering of the coast may bring the mass to the state of a columnar island, such as abound in the Hebrides and along various other shores.

If a cliff shore retreats rapidly, it may be driven back into the shore, and its face assumes the curve of a small bay. With every step in this change the bottom is sure to become shallower, so that the waves lose more and more of their energy in friction over the bottom. Moreover, in entering a bay the friction which the waves encounter in running along the sides is greater than that which they meet in coming in upon a headland or a straight shore. The result is, with the inward retreat of the steep it enters on conditions which diminish the effectiveness of the wave stroke. The embayment also is apt to hold detritus, and so forms in time a beach at the foot of the cliff, over which the waves rarely are able to mount with such energy as will enable them to strike the wall in an effective manner. With this sketch of the conditions of a cliff shore, we will now consider the fate of the broken-up rock which the waves have produced on that section of the coast land.

By observation of sea-beaten cliffs the student readily perceives that a great amount of rocky matter has been removed from most cliff-faced shores. Not uncommonly it can be shown that such sea faces have retreated for several miles. The question now arises, What becomes of the matter which has been broken up by the wave action? In some part the rock, when pulverized by the pounding to which it is subjected, has dissolved in the water. Probably ninety per cent of it, however, retains the visible state, and has a fate determined by the size of the fragments of which it is composed. If these be as fine as mud,

so that they may float in the water, they are readily borne
away by the currents which are always created along a
storm-swept shore, particularly by the undertow or bottom outcurrent—the "sea-puss," as it is sometimes called—
that sweeps along the bottom from every shore, against
which the waves form a surf. If as coarse as sand grains, or
even very small pebbles, they are likely to be drawn out,
rolling over the bottom to an indefinite distance from the
sea margin. The coarser stones, however, either remain
at the foot of the cliff until they are beaten to pieces, or
are driven along the shore until they find some embayment into which they enter. The journey of such fragments may, when the wind strikes obliquely to the shore,
continue for many miles; the waves, running with the
wind, drive the fragments in oscillating journeys up and
down the beach, sometimes at the rate of a mile or more
a day. The effect of this action can often be seen where a
vessel loaded with brick or coal is wrecked on the coast.
In a month fragments of the materials may be stretched
along for the distance of many miles on either side of the
point where the cargo came ashore. Entering an embayment deep enough to restrain their further journey, the
fragments of rock form a boulder beach, where the bits roll
to and fro whenever they are struck by heavy surges. The
greater portion of them remain in this mill until they are
ground to the state of sand and mud. Now and then one
of the fragments is tossed up beyond the reach of the waves,
and is contributed to the wall of the beach. In very heavy
storms these pebbles which are thrown inland may amount
in weight to many tons for each mile of shore.

The study of a pebbly beach, drawn from crest to the
deep water outside, will give an idea as to the history of
its work. On either horn of the crescent by which the
pebbles are imported into the pocket we find the largest
fragments. If the shore of the bay be long, the innermost
part of the recess may show even only very small pebbles,
or perhaps only fine sand, the coarser material having

been worn out in the journey. On the bottom of the bay, near low tide, we begin to find some sand produced by the grinding action. Yet farther out, below high-tide mark, there is commonly a layer of mud which represents the finer products of the mill.

Boulder beaches are so quick in answering to every slight change in the conditions which affect them that they seem almost alive. If by any chance the supply of detritus is increased, they fill in between the horns, diminish the incurve of the bay, and so cause its beach to be more exposed to heavy waves. If, on the other hand, the supply of grist to the mill is diminished, the beach becomes more deeply incurved, and the wave action is proportionately reduced. We may say, in general, that the curve of these beaches represents a balance between the consumption and supply of the pebbles which they grind up. The supply of pebbles brought along the shore by the waves is in many cases greatly added to by a curious action of seaweeds. If the bottom of the water off the coast is covered by these fragments, as is the case along many coast lines within the old glaciated districts, the spores of algæ are prone to take root upon them. Fastening themselves in those positions, and growing upward, the seaweeds may attain considerable size. Being provided with floats, the plant exercises a certain lifting power on the stone, and finally the tugging action of the waves on the fronds may detach the fragments from the bottom, making them free to journey toward the shore. Observing from near at hand the straight wall of the wave in times of heavy storm, the present writer has seen in one view as many as a dozen of these plant-borne stones, sometimes six inches in diameter, hanging in the walls of water as it was about to topple over. As soon as they strike the wave-beaten part of the shore these stones are apt to become separated from the plants, though we can often notice the remains or prints of the attachments adhering to the surface of the rock. Where the pebbles off the shore are plenty, a rocky beach may be produced by this process of importation through the agency of seaweeds without any supply being brought by the waves along the coast line.

Returning to sand beaches, we enter the most interesting field of contact between seas and lands. Probably nine tenths of all the coast lines of the open ocean are formed of arenaceous material. In general, sand consists of finely broken crystals of silica or quartz. These bits are commonly distinctly facetted; they rarely have a spherical form. Not only do accumulations of sand border most of the shore line, but they protect the land against the assaults of the sea, and this in the following curious manner: When shore waves beat pebbles against each other, they rapidly wear to bits; we can hear the sound of the wearing action as the wave goes to and fro. We can often see that the water is discoloured by the mud or powdered rock. When, however, the waves tumble on a sandy coast, they make but a muffled sound, and produce no mud. In fact, the particles of sand do not touch each other when they receive the blow. Between them there lies a thin film of water, drawn in by the attraction known as capillarity, which sucks the fluid into a sponge or between plates of glass placed near together. The stroke of the waves slightly compresses this capillary water, but the faces of the grains are kept apart as sheets of glass may be observed to be restrained from contact when water is between them. If the reader would convince himself as to the condition of the sand grains and the water which is between them, he may do so by pressing his foot on the wet beach which the wave has just left. He will observe that it whitens and sinks a little under the pressure, but returns in good part to its original form when the foot is lifted. In the experiment he has pushed a part of the contained water aside, but he has not brought the grains together; they do not make the sound which he will often hear when the sand is dry. The result is that the sand on the seashore may wear more in going the dis-

tance of a mile in the dry sand dune than in travelling
for hundreds along the wet shore.

If the rock matter in the state of sand wore as rapidly
under the beating of the waves as it does in the state of
pebbles, the continents would doubtless be much smaller
than they are. Those coasts which have no other protection than is afforded by a low sand beach are often
better guarded against the inroads of the sea than the rock-
girt parts of the continents. It is on account of this remarkable endurance of sand of the action of the waves
that the stratified rocks which make up the crust of the
earth are so thick and are to such an extent composed of
sand grains.

The tendency of the *débris*-making influences along
the coast line is to fill in the irregularities which normally
exist there; to batter off the headlands, close up the bays
and harbours, and generally to reduce the shores to straight
lines. Where the tide has access to these inlets, it is constantly at work in dragging out the detritus which the
waves make and thrust into the recesses. These two actions
contend with each other, and determine the conditions of
the coast line, whether they afford ports for commerce or
are sealed in by sand bars, as are many coast lines which
are not tide-swept, as that of northern Africa, which faces
the Mediterranean, a nearly tideless sea. The same is the
case with the fresh-water lakes; even the greater of them
are often singularly destitute of shelters which can serve
the use of ships, and this because there are no tides to keep
the bays and harbours open.

THE OCEAN CURRENTS.

The system of ocean currents, though it exhibits much
complication in detail, is in the main and primarily dependent on the action of the constant air streams known
as the trade winds. With the breath from the lips over
a basin of water we can readily make an experiment which

shows in a general way the method in which the winds operate in producing the circulation of the sea. Blowing upon the surface of the water in the basin, we find that even this slight impulse at once sets the upper part in motion, the movement being of two kinds—pulsating movements or waves are produced, and at the same time the friction of the air on the surface causes its upper part to slide over the under. With little floats we can shortly note that the stream which forms passes to the farther side of the vessel, there divides, and returns to the point of beginning, forming a double circle, or rather two ellipses, the longer sides of which are parallel with the line of the air current. Watching more closely, aiding the sight by the particles which float at various distances below the surface, we note the fact that the motion which was at first imparted to the surface gradually extends downward until it affects the water to the depth of some inches.

In the trade-wind belt the ocean waters to the depth of some hundreds of feet acquire a continuous movement in the direction in which they are impelled by those winds. This motion is most rapid at the surface and near the tropics. It diminishes downwardly in the water, and also toward the polar sides of the trade-wind districts. Thus the trades produce in the sea two broad, slow-moving, deep currents, flowing in the northern hemisphere toward the southwest, and in the southern hemisphere toward the northwest. Coming down upon each other obliquely, these broad streams meet about the middle of the tropical belt. Here, as before noted, the air of the trade winds leaves the surface and rises upward. The waters being retained on their level, form a current which moves toward the west. If the earth within the tropics were covered by a universal sea, the result of this movement would be the institution of a current which, flowing under the equator, would girdle the sphere.

With a girdling equatorial current, because of the intense heat of the tropics and the extreme cold of the

parallels beyond the fortieth degree of latitude, the earth
would be essentially uninhabitable to man, and hardly so
to any forms of life. Its surface would be visited by fierce
winds induced by the very great differences of temperature which would then prevail. Owing, however, to the
barriers which the continents interpose to the motions of
these windward-setting tropical currents, all the water
which they bear, when it strikes the opposing shores, is
diverted to the right and left, as was the stream in the
experiment with the basin and the breath, the divided
currents seeking ways toward high latitudes, conveying
their store of heat to the circumpolar lands. So effective
is this transfer of temperature that a very large part of the
heat which enters the waters in the tropical region is taken
out of that division of the earth's surface and distributed
over the realms of sea and land which lie beyond the limits
of the vertical sun. Thus the Gulf Stream, the northern
branch of the Atlantic tropical current, by flowing into the
North Atlantic, contributes to the temperature of the
region within the Arctic Circle more heat than actually
comes to that district by the direct influx from the sun.

The above statements as to the climatal effect of the
ocean streams show us how important it is to obtain a
sufficient conception as to the way in which these currents
now move and what we can of their history during the
geologic ages. This task can not yet be adequately done.
The fields of the sea are yet too imperfectly explored to
afford us all the facts required to make out the whole
story. Only in the case of our Gulf Stream can we form
a full conception as to the journey which the waters undergo and the consequence of their motion. In the case of
this current, observations clearly show that it arises from
the junction near the equatorial line of the broad stream
created by the two trade-wind belts. Uniting at the equator, these produce a westerly setting current, having the
width of some hundred miles and a depth of several
hundred feet. Its velocity is somewhat greater than a

mile an hour. The centre of the current, because of the greater strength of the northern as compared with the southern trades, is considerably south of the equator. When this great slow-moving stream comes against the coast of South America, it encounters the projecting shoulder of that land which terminates at Cape St. Roque. There it divides, as does a current on the bows of an anchored ship, a part—rather more than one half—of the stream turning to the northward, the remainder passing toward the southern pole; this northerly portion becomes what is afterward known as the Gulf Stream, the history of which we shall now briefly follow.

Flowing by the northwesterly coast of South America, the northern share of the tropical current, being pressed in against the land by the trade winds, is narrowed, and therefore acquires at once a swifter flow, the increased speed being due to conditions like those which add to the velocity of the water flowing through a hose when it comes to the constriction of the nozzle. Attaining the line of the southeastern or Lesser Antilles, often known as the Windward Islands, a part of this current slips through the interspaces between these isles and enters the Gulf of Mexico. Another portion, failing to find sufficient room through these passages, skirts the Antilles on their eastern and northern sides, passes by and among the Bahama Islands, there to rejoin the part of the stream which entered the Caribbean. This Caribbean portion of the tide spreads widely in that broad sea, is constricted again between Cuba and Yucatan, again expands in the Gulf of Mexico, and is finally poured forth through the Straits of Florida as a stream having the width of forty or fifty miles, a depth of a thousand feet or more, and a speed of from three to five miles an hour, exceeding in its rate of flow the average of the greatest rivers, and conveying more water than do all the land streams of the earth. In this part of its course the deep and swift stream from the Gulf of Mexico, afterward to be named the Gulf Stream, receives the contribution of slower moving and shallower currents which skirted the Antilles on their eastern verge. The conjoined waters then move northward, veering toward the east, at first as a swift river of the sea having a width of less than a hundred miles and of great depth; with each step toward the pole this stream widens, diminishing proportionately in depth; the speed of its current decreases as the original impetus is lost, and the baffling winds set its surface waters to and fro in an irregular way. Where it passes Cape Hatteras it has already lost a large share of its momentum and much of its heat, and is greatly widened.

Although the current of the Gulf Stream becomes more languid as we go northward, it for a very long time retains its distinction from the waters of the sea through which it flows. Sailing eastward from the mouth of the Chesapeake, the navigator can often observe the moment when he enters the waters of this current. This is notable not only in the temperature, but in the hue of the sea. North of that line the sharpness of the parting wall becomes less distinct, the stream spreads out broadly over the surface of the Atlantic, yet its thermometric effects are distinctly traceable to Iceland and Nova Zembla, and the tropical driftwood which it carries affords the principal timber supply of the inhabitants of the first-named isle. Attaining this circumpolar realm, and finally losing the impulse which bore it on, the water of the Gulf Stream partly returns to the southward in a relatively slight current which bears the fluid along the coast of Europe until it re-enters the system of tropical winds and the currents which they produce. A larger portion stagnates in the circumpolar region, in time slowly to return to the tropical district in a manner afterward to be described. Although the Gulf Stream in the region north of Cape Hatteras is so indistinct that its presence was not distinctly recognised until the facts were subjected to the keen eye of Benjamin Franklin, its effects in the way of climate are so great that we must attribute the fitness of northern Europe for the uses of civilized man to its action. But for the heat which this stream brings to the realm of the North Atlantic, Great Britain would be as sterile as Labrador, and the Scandinavian region, the cradle-land of our race, as uninhabitable as the bleakest parts of Siberia.

It is a noteworthy fact that when the equatorial current divides on the continents against which it flows, the separate streams, although they may follow the shores for a certain distance toward the poles, soon diverge from them, just as the Gulf Stream passes to the seaward from the eastern coast of the United States. The reason for this movement is readily found in the same principle which explains the oblique flow of the trades and counter trades in their passage to and from the equatorial belt. The particle of water under the equator, though it flows to the west, has, by virtue of the earth's rotation, an eastward-setting velocity of a thousand miles an hour. Starting toward the poles, the particle is ever coming into regions of the sea where the fluid has a less easterly movement, due to the earth's rotation on its axis. Consequently the journeying water by its momentum tends to move off in an easterly course. Attaining high latitudes and losing its momentum, it abides in the realm long enough to become cooled.

We have already noted the fact that only a portion of the waters sent northward in the Gulf Stream and the other currents which flow from the equator to the poles is returned by the surface flow which sets toward the equator along the eastern side of the basins. The largest share of the tide effects its return journey in other ways. Some portion of this remainder sets equatorward in local cold streams, such as that which pours forth through Davis Strait into Baffin Bay, flowing under the Gulf Stream waters for an unknown distance toward the tropics. There are several of these local as yet little known streams, which doubtless bring about a certain amount of circulation between the polar regions and the tropical districts. Their effect is, however, probably small as compared with that massive drift which we have now to note.

The tropical waters when they attain high latitudes are constantly cooled, and are overlaid by the warmer contributions of that tide, and are thus brought lower and lower in the sea. When they start downward they have, as observations show, a temperature not much above the freezing point of salt water. They do not congeal for the reason that the salt of the ocean lowers the point at which the water solidifies to near 28° Fahr. The effect of this action is gradually to press down the surface cold water until it attains the very bottom in all the circumpolar regions. At the same time this descending water drifts along the bottom of the ocean troughs toward the equatorial realm. As this cold water is heavier than that which is of higher temperature and nearer the surface, it has no tendency to rise. Being below the disturbing influences of any current save its own, it does not tend, except in a very small measure, to mingle with the warmer overlying fluid. The result is that it continues its journey until it may come within the tropics without having gained a temperature of more than 35° Fahr., the increase in heat being due in small measure to that which it receives from the earth's interior and that which it acquires from the overlying warmer water. Attaining the region of the tropical current, this drift water from the poles gradually rises, to take the place of that which goes poleward, becomes warm, and again starts on its surface journey toward the arctic and antarctic regions.

Nothing is known as to the rate of this bottom drift from the polar districts toward the equator, but, from some computation which he has made, the writer is of the opinion that several centuries is doubtless required for the journey from the Arctic Circle to the tropics. The speed of the movement probably varies; it may at times require some thousand years for its accomplishment. The effect of the

11

bottom drift is to withdraw from seas in high latitudes the very cold water which there forms, and to convey it beneath the seas of middle latitudes to a realm where it is well placed for the reheating process. If all the cold water of circumpolar regions had to journey over the surface to the equator, the perturbing effect of its flow on the climates of various lands would be far greater than it is at present. Where such cold currents exist the effect is to chill the air without adding much to the rainfall; while the currents setting northward not only warm the regions near which they flow, but by so doing send from the water surfaces large quantities of moisture which fall as snow or rain. Thus the Gulf Stream, directly and indirectly, probably contributes more than half the rainfall about the Atlantic basin. The lack of this influence on the northern part of North America and Asia causes those lands to be sterilized by cold, although destitute of permanent ice and snow upon their surfaces.

We readily perceive that the effect of the oceanic circulation upon the temperatures of different regions is not only great but widely contrasted. By taking from the equatorial belt a large part of the heat which falls within that realm, it lowers the temperature to the point which makes the district fit for the occupancy of man, perhaps, indeed, tenable to all the higher forms of life. This same heat removed to high latitudes tempers the winter's cold, and thus makes a vast realm inhabitable which otherwise would be locked in almost enduring frosts. Furthermore, this distribution of temperatures tends to reduce the total wind energy by diminishing the trades and counter trades which are due to the variations of heat which are encountered in passing polarward from the equator. Still further, but for this circulation of water in the sea, the oceans about the poles would be frozen to their very bottom, and this vast sheet of ice might be extended southward to within the parallels of fifty degrees north and south latitude, although the waters under the equator might at the

same time be unendurably hot and unfit for the occupancy
of living beings.

A large part of the difficulties which geologists encounter in endeavouring to account for the changes of the
past arise from the evidences of great climatal revolutions
which the earth has undergone. In some chapters of the
great stone book, whose leaves are the strata of the earth,
we find it plainly written in the impressions made by fossils that all the lands beyond the equatorial belt have
undergone changes which can only be explained by the
supposition that the heat and moisture of the countries
have been subjected to sudden and remarkable changes.
Thus in relatively recent times thick-leaved plants which
retained their vegetation in a rather tender state throughout the year have flourished near to the poles, while shortly afterward an ice sheet, such as now covers the greater
part of Greenland, extended down to the line of the Ohio
River at Cincinnati. Although these changes of climate
are, as we shall hereafter note, probably due to entangled
causes, we must look upon the modifications of the ocean
streams as one of the most important elements in the
causation. We can the more readily imagine such changes
to be due to the alterations in the course and volume of
the ocean current when we note how trifling peculiarities
in the geography of the shores—features which are likely
to be altered by the endless changes which occur in the
form of a continent—affect the run of these currents.
Thus the growth of coral reefs in southern Florida, and,
in general, the formation of that peninsula, by narrowing
the exit of the great current from the Gulf of Mexico,
has probably increased its velocity. If Florida should again
sink down, that current would go forth into the North
Atlantic with the speed of about a mile an hour, and would
not have momentum enough to carry its waters over half
the vast region which they now traverse. If the lands
about the western border of the Caribbean Sea, particularly
the Isthmus of Darien, should be depressed to a consider-

able depth below the ocean level, the tropical current would enter the Pacific Ocean, adding to the temperature of its waters all the precious heat which now vitalizes the North Atlantic region. Such a geographic accident would not only profoundly alter the life conditions of that part of the world, but it would make an end of European civilization.

In the chapter on climatal changes further attention will be given to the action of ocean currents from the point of view of their influence on the heat and moisture of different parts of the world. We now have to consider the last important influence of ocean currents—that which they directly exercise on the development of organic life. The most striking effect of this nature which the sea streams bring about is caused by the ceaseless transportation to which they subject the eggs and seeds of animals and plants, as well as the bodies of the mature form which are moved about by the flowing waters. But for the existence of these north and south flowing currents, due to the presence of the continental barriers, the living tenants of the seas would be borne along around the earth, always in the same latitude, and therefore exposed to the same conditions of temperature. In this state of affairs the influences which now make for change in organic species would be far less than they are. Journeying in the great whirlpools which the continental barriers make out of the westward setting tropical currents, these organic species are ever being exposed to alterations in their temperature conditions which we know to be favourable to the creation of those variations on which the advance of organic life so intimately depends. Thus the ocean currents not only help to vary the earth by producing changes in the climate of both sea and land, breaking up the uniformity which would otherwise characterize regions at the same distance from the equator, but they induce, by the consequences of the migrations which they enforce, changes in the organic tenants of the sea.

Another immediate effect of ocean streams arises where their currents of warm water come against shores or shallows of the sea. At these points, if the water have a tropical temperature, we invariably find a vast and rapid development of marine animals and plants, of which the coral-making polyps are the most important. In such positions the growth of forms which secrete solid skeletons is so rapid that great walls of their remains accumulate next the shore, the mass being built outwardly by successive growths until the realm of the land may be extended for scores of miles into the deep. In other cases vast mounds of this organic *débris* may be accumulated in mid ocean until its surface is interspersed with myriads of islands, all of which mark the work due to the combined action of currents and the marine life which they nourish. Probably more than four fifths of all the islands in the tropical belt are due in this way to the life-sustaining action of the currents which the trade winds create.

There are many secondary influences of a less important nature which are due to the ocean streams. The reader will find on most wall-maps of the world certain areas in the central part of the oceans which are noted as Sargassum seas, of which that of the North Atlantic, west and south of the Azore Islands, is one of the most conspicuous. In these tracts, which in extent may almost be compared with the continents, we find great quantities of floating seaweed, the entangled fronds of which often form a mass sufficiently dense to slightly restrain the speed of ships. When the men on the caravels of Columbus entered this tangle, they were alarmed lest they should be unable to escape from its toils. It is a curious fact that these weeds of the sea while floating do not reproduce by spores the structures which answer to the seeds of higher plants, but grow only by budding. It seems certain that they could not maintain their place in the ocean but for the action of the currents which convey the bits rent off from the shores where the plant is truly at home. This vast growth of plant life in the Sargassum basins doubtless contributed considerable and important deposits of sediment to the sea floors beneath the waters which it inhabits. Certain ancient strata, known as the Devonian black shale, occupying the Ohio valley and the neighbouring parts of North America to the east and north of that basin, appear to be accumulations which were made beneath an ancient Sargassum sea.

The ocean currents have greatly favoured and in many instances determined the migrations not only of marine forms, but of land creatures as well. Floating timber may bear the eggs and seeds of many forms of life to great distances until the rafts are cast ashore in a realm where, if the conditions favour, the creatures may find a new seat for their life. Seeds of plants incased in their often dense envelopes may, because they float, be independently carried great distances. So it comes about that no sooner does a coral or other island rise above the waters of the sea than it becomes occupied by a varied array of plants. The migrations of people, even down to the time of the voyages which discovered America, have in large measure been controlled by the run of the ocean streams. The tropical set of the waters to the westward helped Columbus on his way, and enabled him to make a journey which but for their assistance could hardly have been accomplished. This same current in the northern part of the Gulf Stream opposed the passage of ships from northern Europe to the westward, and to this day affects the speed with which their voyages are made.

THE CIRCUIT OF THE RAIN.

We have now to consider those movements of the water which depend upon the fact that at ordinary temperatures the sea yields to the air a continued and large supply of vapour, a contribution which is made in lessened proportion by water in all stages of coldness, and even by ice

when it is exposed to dry air. This evaporation of the sea
water is proportional to the temperature and to the dryness of the air where it rests upon the ocean. It probably amounts on the average to somewhere about three
feet per annum; in regions favourably situated for the
process, as on the west coast of northern Africa, it may
be three or four times as much, while in the cold and
humid air about the poles it may be as little as one foot.
When contributed to the air, the water enters on the state
of vapour, in which state it tends to diffuse itself freely
through the atmosphere by virtue of the motion which is
developed in particles when in the vaporous or gaseous
state.

The greater part of the water evaporated from the
seas probably finds its way as rain at once back into the
deep, yet a considerable portion is borne away horizontally
until it encounters the land. The precipitation of the
water from the air is primarily due to the cooling to which
it is subjected as it rises in the atmosphere. Over the sea
the ascent is accomplished by the simple diffusion of the
vapour or by the uprise through the aërial shaft, such as
that near the equator or over the centres of the whirling
storms. It is when the air strikes the slopes of the land
that we find it brought into a condition which most decidedly tends to precipitate its moisture. Lifted upward,
the air as it ascends the slopes is brought into cooler and
more rarefied conditions. Losing temperature and expand-
ing, it parts with its water for the same reason that it does
in the ascending current in the equatorial belt or in the
chimneys of the whirl storms. A general consequence of
this is that wherever moisture-laden winds from the sea
impinge upon a continent they lay down a considerable
part of the water which they contain.

If all the lands were of the same height, the rain would
generally come in largest proportion upon their coastal
belt, or those portions of the shore-line districts over which
the sea winds swept. But as these winds vary in the

amount of the watery vapour which they contain, and as the surface of the land is very irregular, the rainfall is the most variable feature in the climatal conditions of our sphere. Near the coasts it ranges from two or three inches in arid regions—such as the western part of the Sahara and portions of the coast regions of Chili and Peru—to eight hundred inches about the head waters of the Brahma-pootra River in northern India, where the high mountains are swept over by the moisture-laden airs from the neighbouring sea. Here and there detached mountainous masses produce a singular local increase in the amount of the rainfall. Thus in the lake district in northwestern England the rainfall on the seaward side of mountains, not over four thousand feet high, is very much greater than it is on the other slope, less than a score of miles away. These local variations are common all over the world, though they are but little observed.

In general, the central parts of continents are likely to receive much less rainfall than their peripheral portions. Thus the central districts of North America, Asia, and Australia—three out of the five continental masses—have what we may call interior deserts. Africa has one such, though it is north of the centre, and extends to the shores of the Mediterranean and the Atlantic. The only continent without this central nearly rainless field is South America, where the sole characteristic arid district is situated on the western slope of the Cordilleran range. In this case the peculiarity is due to the fact that the strong westerly setting winds which sweep over the country encounter no high mountains until they strike the Andean chain. They journey up a long and rather gradual slope, where the precipitation is gradually induced, the process being completed when they strike the mountain wall. Passing over its summit, they appear as dry winds on the Pacific coast.

Even while the winds frequently blow in from the sea, as along the western coast of the Americas, they may come over water which is prevailingly colder than the land. This is characteristically the case on the western faces of the American continent, where the sea is cooled by the currents setting toward the equator from high latitudes. Such cool sea air encountering the warm land has its temperature raised, and therefore does not tend to lay down its burden of moisture, but seeks to take up more. On this account the rainfall in countries placed under such conditions is commonly small.

By no means all the moisture which comes upon the earth from the atmosphere descends in the form of rain or snow. A variable, large, though yet undetermined amount falls in the form of dew. Dew is a precipitation of moisture which has not entered the peculiar state which we term fog or cloud, but has remained invisible in the air. It is brought to the earth through the radiation of heat which continually takes place, but which is most effective during the darkened half of the day, when the action is not counterbalanced by the sun's rays. While the sun is high and the air is warm there is a constant absorption of moisture in large part from the ground or from the neighbouring water areas, probably in some part from those suspended stores of water, the clouds, if such there be in the neighbourhood. We can readily notice how clouds drifting in from the sea often melt into the dry air which they encounter. Late in the afternoon, even before the sun has sunk, the radiation of heat from the earth, which has been going on all the while, but has been less considerable than the incurrent of temperature, in a way overtakes that influx. The air next the surface becomes cooled from its contact with the refrigerating earth, and parts with its moisture, forming a coating of water over everything it touches. At the same time the moisture escaping from the warmed under earth likewise drops back upon its cooled surface almost as soon as it has escaped. The thin sheet of water precipitated by this method is quickly returned to the air when it becomes warmed by the morning sunshine, but during the night quantities of it are absorbed by the plants; very often, indeed, with the lowlier vegetation it trickles down the leaves and enters the earth about the base of the stem, so that the roots may appropriate it. Our maize, or Indian corn, affords an excellent example of a plant which, having developed in a land of droughts, is well contrived, through its capacities for gathering dew, to protect itself against arid conditions. In an ordinary dew-making night the leaves of a single stem may gather as much as half a pint of water, which flows down their surfaces to the roots. So efficient is this dew supply, this nocturnal cloudless rain, that on the western coast of South America and elsewhere, where the ordinary supply of moisture is almost wanting, many important plants are able to obtain from it much of the water which they need. The effect is particularly striking along seashores, where the air, although it may not have the humidity necessary for the formation of rain, still contains enough to form dew.

It is interesting to note that the quantity of dew which falls upon an area is generally proportioned to the amount of living vegetation which it bears. The surfaces of leaves are very efficient agents of radiation, and the tangle which they make offers an amount of heat-radiating area many times as great as that afforded by a surface of bared earth. Moreover, the ground itself can not well cool down to the point where it will wring the moisture out of the air, while the thin membranes of the plants readily become so cooled. Thus vegetation by its own structure provides itself with means whereby it may be in a measure independent of the accidental rainfall. We should also note the fact that the dewfall is a concomitant of cloudless skies. The quantity which is precipitated in a cloudy night is very small, and this for the reason that when the heavens are covered the heat from the earth can not readily fly off into space. Under these conditions the temperature of the air rarely descends low enough to favour the precipitation of dew.

Having noted the process by which in the rain circuit the water leaves the sea and the conditions of distribution when it returns to the earth, we may now trace in more detail the steps in this great round. First, we should take note of the fact that the water after it enters the air may come back to the surface of the earth in either of two ways—directly in the manner of dewfall, or in a longer circuit which leads it through the state of clouds. As yet we are not very well informed as to the law of the cloud-making, but certain features in this picturesque and most important process have been tolerably well ascertained.

Rising upward from the sea, the vapour of water commonly remains transparent and invisible until it attains a considerable height above the surface, where the cooling tends to make it assume again the visible state of cloud particles. The formation of these cloud particles is now believed to depend on the fact that the air is full of small dust motes, exceedingly small bits of matter derived from the many actions which tend to bring comminuted solid matter into the air, as, for instance, the combustion of meteoric stones, which are greatly heated by friction in their swift course through the air, the ejections of volcanoes, the smoke of forest and other fires, etc. These tiny bits, floating in the air, because of their solid nature radiate their heat, cool the air which lies against them, and thereby precipitate the water in the manner of dew, exactly as do the leaves and other structures on the surface of the earth. In fact, dew formation is essentially like cloud formation, except that in the one case the water is gathered on fixed bodies, and in the other on floating objects. Each little dust raft with its cargo of condensed water tends, of course, to fall downward toward the earth's surface, and, except for the winds which may blow upward, does so fall, though with exceeding slowness. Its rate of descent may be only a few feet a day. It was falling before it took on the load of water; it will fall a little more rapidly with the added burden, but even in a still air it might be months or years before it would come to the ground. The reason for this slow descent may not at first sight be plain, though a little consideration will make it so.

If we take a shot of small size and a feather of the same weight, we readily note that their rate of falling through the air may vary in the proportion of ten to one or more. It is easy to conceive that this difference is due to the very much less friction which the smaller body encounters in its motion by the particles of air. With this point in mind, the student should observe that the surface presented by solid bodies in relation to their solid contents is the greater the smaller the diameter. A rough, though not very satisfactory, instance of this principle may be had by comparing the surface and interior contents of two boxes, one ten feet square and the other one foot square. The larger has six hundred feet of surface to one thousand cubic feet of interior, or about half a square foot of outer surface to the cubic foot of contents; while the smaller box has six feet of surface for the single cubic foot of interior, or about ten times the proportion of exterior to contents. The result is that the smaller particles encounter more friction in moving toward the earth, until, in the case of finely divided matter, such as the particles of carbon in the smoke from an ordinary fire, the rate of down-falling may be so small as to have little effect in the turbulent conditions of atmospheric motion.

The little drops of water which gather round dust motes, falling but slowly toward the earth, are free to obey the attractions which they exercise upon each other—impulses which are partly gravitative and partly electrical. We have no precise knowledge concerning these movements, further than that they serve to aggregate the myriad little floats into cloud forms, in which the rafts are brought near together, but do not actually touch each other. They are possibly kept apart by electrical repulsion. In this state of association without union the divided water may under-

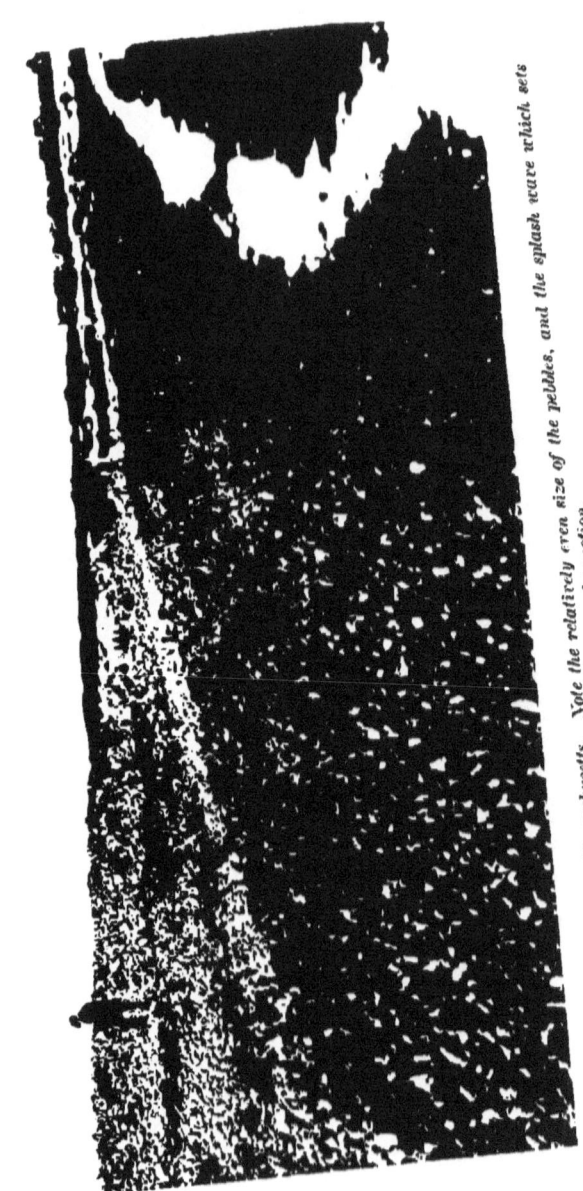

Pocket Creek, Cape Ann, Massachusetts. Note the relatively even size of the pebbles, and the splash wave which sets them in motion.

go the curiously modified aggregations which give us the
varied forms of clouds. As yet we know little as to the
cause of cloud shapes. We remark the fact that in the
higher of these agglomerations of condensed vapour, the
clouds which float at an elevation of from twenty to thirty
thousand feet or more, the masses are generally thin, and
arranged more or less in a leaflike form, though even here
a tendency to produce spherical clouds is apparent. In
this high realm floating water is probably in the frozen
state, answering to the form of dew, which we call hoar
frost. The lower clouds, gathering in the still air, show
very plainly the tendency to agglomerate into spheres,
which appears to be characteristic of all vaporous material
which is free' to move by its own impulses. It is probable
that the spherical shape of clouds is more or less due to
the same conditions as gathered the stellar matter from the
ancient nebular chaos into the celestial spheres. Upon
these spherical aggregations of the clouds the winds act
in extremely varied ways. The cloud may be rubbed between opposite currents, and so flattened out into a long
streamer; it may take the same form by being carried off
by a current in the manner of smoke from a fire; the
spheres may be kept together, so as to form the patchwork
which we call "mackerel" sky; or they may be actually
confounded with each other in a vast common cloud-heap.
In general, where the process of aggregation of two cloud
bodies occurs, changes of temperature are induced in the
masses which are mixed together. If the temperature resulting from this association of cloud masses is an average
increase, the cloud may become lighter, and in the manner
of a balloon move upward. Each of the motes in the cloud
with its charge of vapour may be compared with the ballast of the balloon; if they are warmed, they send forth
a part of their load of condensed water again to the state
of invisible vapour. Rising to a point where it cools, the
vapour gathers back on the rafts and tends again to
weight the cloud downward. The ballast of an ordinary

balloon has to be thrown away from its car; but if some arrangement for condensing the moisture from the air could be contrived, a balloon might be brought into the adjustable state of a cloud, going up or down according as it was heated or cooled.

When the formation of the drop of water or snowflake begins, the mass is very small. If in descending it encounters great thickness of cloud, the bit may grow by further condensation until it becomes relatively large. Generally in this way we may account for the diversities in the size of raindrops or snowflakes. It often happens that the particles after taking on the form of snowflakes encounter in their descent air so warm that they melt into raindrops, or, if only partly melted, reach the surface as sleet. Or, starting as raindrops, they may freeze, and in this simple state may reach the earth, or after freezing they may gather other frozen water about them, so that the hailstone has a complicated structure which, from the point of view of classification, is between a raindrop and a snowflake.

In the process of condensation—indeed, in the steps which precede the formation of rain and snow—there is often more or less trace of electrical action; in fact, a part of the energy which was involved in the vapourization of water, on its condensation, even on the dust motes appears to be converted into electrical action, which probably operates in part to keep the little aggregates of water asunder. When they coalesce in drops or flakes, this electricity often assumes the form of lightning, which represents the swift passage of the electric store from a region where it is most abundant to one where it is less so. The variations in this process of conveying the electricity are probably great. In general, it probably passes, much as an electric current is conveyed, through a wire from the battery which produces the force. In other cases, where the tension is high, or, in other words, where the discharge has to be hastened, we have the phenomena of lightning in which the current burns its way along its path, as it may traverse a slender wire, vapourizing it as it goes. In general, the lightning flash expends its force on the air conductors, or lines of the moist atmosphere along which it breaks its path, its energy returning into the vapour which it forms or the heat which it produces in the other parts of the air. In some cases, probably not one in the thousand of the flashes, the charge is so heavy that it is not used up in its descent toward the earth, and so electrifies, or, as we say, strikes, some object attached to the earth, through which it passes to the underlying moisture, where it finds a convenient place to take on a quiet form. Almost all these hurried movements of electrical energy which intensely heat and light the air which they traverse fly from one part of a cloud to another, or cross from cloud sphere to cloud sphere; of those which start toward the earth, many are exhausted before they reach its surface, and even those that strike convey but a portion of their original impulse to the ground.

The wearing-out effect of lightning in its journey along the air conductors in its flaming passages is well illustrated by what happens when the charge strikes a wire which is not large enough freely to convey it. The wire is heated, generally made white hot, often melted, and perhaps scattered in the form of vapour. In doing this work the electricity may, and often is, utterly dissipated—that is, changed into heat. It has been proposed to take advantage of this principle in protecting buildings from lightning by placing in them many thin wires, along which the current will try to make its way, being exhausted in melting or vaporizing the metal through which it passes.

There are certain other forms of lightning, or at least of electrical discharges, which produce light and which may best be described in this connection. It occasionally happens that the earth becomes so charged that the current proceeds from its surface to the clouds. More rarely, and under conditions which we do not understand, the electric energy is gathered into a ball-like form, which may move slowly along the surface until it suddenly explodes. It is a common feature of all these forms of lightning which we have noted that they ordinarily make in their movement considerable noise. This is due to the sudden displacement of the air which they traverse—displacement due to the action of heat in separating the particles. It is in all essential regards similar to the sounds made by projectiles, such as meteors or swift cannon shots, as they fly through the air. It is even more comparable to the sound produced by exploding gunpowder. The first sound effect from the lightning stroke is a single rending note, which endures no longer—indeed, not as long—as the explosion of a cannon. Heard near by, this note is very sharp, reminding one of the sound made by the breaking of glass. The rolling, continuous sound which we commonly hear in thunder is, as in the case of the noise produced by cannon, due to echo from the clouds and the earth. Thunder is ordinarily much more prolonged and impressive in a mountainous country than in a region of plains, because the steeps about the hearer reverberate the original single crash.

The distribution of thunderstorms is as yet not well understood, but it appears in many cases that they are attendants on the advancing face of cyclones and hurricanes, the area in front of these great whirlstorms being subjected to the condensation and irregular air movements which lead to the development of much electrical energy. There are, however, certain parts of the earth which are particularly subjected to lightning flashes. They are common in the region near the equator, where the ascending currents bring about heavy rains, which mean a rapid condensation and consequent liberation of electrical energy. They diminish in frequency toward the arctic regions. An observer at the pole would probably fail ever to perceive strong flashes. For the same reason thunder-

storms are more frequent in summer, the time when the
difference in temperature between the surface and the
upper air is greatest, when, therefore, the uprushes of air
are likely to be most violent. They appear to be more
common in the night than in the daytime, for the reason
that condensation is favoured by the cooling which occurs
in the dark half of the day. It is rare, indeed, that a
thunderstorm occurs near midday, a period when the air
is in most cases taking up moisture on account of the
swiftly increasing heat.

There are other forms of electrical discharges not distinctly connected with the then existing condensation of
moisture. What the sailors call St. Elmo's fire—a brush
of electric light from the mast tops and other projections
of the ship—indicates the passage of electrical energy between the vessel and the atmosphere. Similar lights are
said sometimes to be seen rising from the surface of the
water. Such phenomena are at present not satisfactorily
explained. Perhaps in the same group of actions comes the
so-called "Jack-o'-lantern" or "Will-o'-the-wisp" fires
flashing from the earth in marshy places, which are often
described by the common people, but have never been
observed by a naturalist. If this class of illuminations
really exists, we have to afford them some other explanation than that they are emanations of self-inflamed phos-
phuretted hydrogen, a method of accounting for them
which illogically finds a place in many treatises on atmospheric phenomena. A gas of any kind would disperse itself
in the air; it could not dance about as these lights are said
to do, and there is no chemical means known whereby it
could be produced in sufficient purity and quantity from
the earth to produce the effects which are described.*

---

* The present writer has made an extended and careful study of
marsh and swamp phenomena, and is very familiar with the aspect of
these fields in the nighttime. He has never been able to see any sign
of the Jack-o'-lantern light. Looking fixedly into any darkness, such

12

In the upper air, or perhaps even beyond the limits of the field which deserves the name, in the regions extending from the poles to near the tropics, there occur electric glowings commonly known as the aurora borealis. This phenomenon occurs in both hemispheres. These illuminations, though in some way akin to those of lightning, and though doubtless due to some form of electrical action, are peculiar in that they are often attended by glows as if from clouds, and by pulsations which indicate movements not at electric speed. As yet but little is known as to the precise nature of these curious storms. It has been claimed, however, that they are related to the sun spots; those periods when the solar spots are plenty, at intervals of about eleven years, are the times of auroral discharges. Still further, it seems probable that the magnetic currents of the earth, that circling energy which encompasses the sphere, moving round in a general way parallel to the equator, are intensified during these illuminations of the circumpolar skies.

Geological Work of Water.

We turn now to the geological work which is performed by falling water. Where the rain or snow returns from the clouds to the sea, the energy of position given to the water by its elevation above the earth through the heat which it acquired from the sun is returned to the air through which it falls or to the ocean surface on which it strikes. In this case the circuit of the rain is short and

---

as is afforded by the depths of a wood, the eye is apt to imagine the appearance of faint lights. Those who have had to do with outpost duty in an army know how the anxious sentry, particularly if he is new to the soldier's trade, will often imagine that he sees lights before him. Sometimes the pickets will be so convinced of the fact that they see lights that they will fire upon the fiction of the imaginations. These facts make it seem probable that the Jack-o'-lantern and his companion, the Will-o'-the-wisp, are stories of the over-credulous.

without geological consequence which it is worth while
to consider, except to note that the heat thus returned is
likely to be delivered in another realm than that in which
the falling water acquired the store, thus in a small way
modifying the climate. When, however, the precipitation
occurs on the surface of the land, the drops of frozen or
fluid water apply a part of their energy in important geological work, the like of which is not done where they
return at once to the sea.

We shall first consider what takes place when the
water in the form of drops of rain comes to the surface of
the land. Descending as they do with a considerable
speed, these raindrops apply a certain amount of energy

Fig. 10.—Showing the diverse action of rain on wooded and cleared
fields. *a*, wooded area; *b*, tilled ground.

to the surface on which they fall. Although the beat of
a raindrop is proverbially light, the stroke is not ineffective. Observing what happens where the action takes
place on the surface of bare rock, we may notice that the
grains of sand or small pebbles which generally abound
on such surfaces, if they be not too steeply inclined, dance
about under the blows which they receive. If we could
cover hard plate glass, a much firmer material than ordinary stone, with such bits, we should soon find that its

surface would become scratched all over by the friction. Moreover, the raindrops perceptibly urge the small detached bits of stone down the slopes toward the streams.

If all the earth's surface were bare rocks, the blow of the raindrops would deserve to be reckoned among the important influences which lead to the wearing of land. As it is, when a country is in a state of Nature, only a small part of its surface is exposed to this kind of wearing. Where there is rain enough to effect any damage, there is sure to be sufficient vegetation to interpose a living and self-renewed covering between the rocks and the rain. Even the lichens which coat what at first sight often seems to be bare rock afford an ample covering for this purpose. It is only where man bares the field by stripping away and overturning this protecting vegetation that the raindrops cut away the earth. The effect of their action can often be noted by observing how on ploughed ground a flat stone or a potsherd comes after a rain to cap a little column. The geologist sometimes finds in soft sandstones that the same action is repeated in a larger way where a thin fragment of hard rock has protected a column many feet in height against the rain work which has shorn down the surrounding rock.

When water strikes the moistened surface it at once loses the droplike form which all fluids assume when they fall through the air.*

When the raindrops coalesce on the surface of the earth, the rôle of what we may call land water begins.

---

* This principle of the spheroidal form in falling fluids is used in making ordinary bird shot. The melted lead drops through sievelike openings, the resulting spheres of the metal being allowed to fall into water which chills them. Iron shot, used in cutting stone, where they are placed between the saw and the surface of the rock, are also made in the same manner. The descending fluid divides into drops because it is drawn out by the ever-increasing speed of the falling particles, which soon make the stream so thin that it can not hold together.

Thenceforward until the fluid arrives at the surface of the sea it is continually at work in effecting a great range of geological changes, only a few of which can well be traced by the general student. The work of land water is due to three classes of properties—to the energy with which it is endowed by virtue of its height above the sea, a power due to the heat of the sun; to the capacity it has for taking substances into solution; and to its property of giving some part of its own substance to other materials with which it comes in contact. The first of these groups of properties may be called dynamical; the others, chemical.

The dynamic value of water when it falls upon the land is the amount of energy it can apply in going down the slope which separates it from the sea. A ton of the fluid, such as may gather in an ordinary rain on a thousand square feet of ground in the highlands of a country—say at an elevation of a thousand feet above the sea—expends before it comes to rest in the great reservoir as much energy as would be required to lift that weight from the ocean's surface to the same height. The ways in which this energy may be expended we shall now proceed in a general way to trace.

As soon as the water has been gathered, from its drop to its sheet state—a process which takes place as soon as it falls—the fluid begins its downward journey. On this way it is at once parted into two distinct divisions, the surface water and the ground water: the former courses more or less swiftly, generally at the rate of a mile or more an hour, in the light of day; the latter enters the interstices of the earth, slowly descends therein to a greater or less depth, and finally, journeying perhaps at the rate of a mile a year, rejoins the surface water, escaping through the springs. The proportion of these two classes, the surface and the ground water, varies greatly, and an intermixture of them is continually going on. Thus on the surface of bare rock or frozen earth all the rain may go away without entering the ground. On very sandy fields the heaviest rainfall may be taken up by the porous earth, so that no streams are found. On such surfaces the present writer has observed that a rainfall amounting to six inches in depth in two hours produced no streams whatever. We shall first follow the history of the surface water, afterward considering the work which the underground movements effect.

If the student will observe what takes place on a level ploughed field—which, after all, will not be perfectly level, for all fields are more or less undulating—he will note that, though the surface may have been smoothed by a roller until it appears like a floor, the first rain, where the fall takes place rapidly enough to produce surface streams, will create a series of little channels which grow larger as they conjoin, the whole appearing to the eye like a very detailed map, or rather model, of a river system; it is, indeed, such a system in miniature. If he will watch the process by which these streamlet beds are carved, he will obtain a tolerably clear idea as to that most important work which the greater streams do in carving the face of the lands. The water is no sooner gathered into a sheet than, guided by the slightest irregularities which it encounters, it begins to flow. At first the motion is so slow that it does not disturb its bed, but at some points in the bottom of the sheet the movement soon becomes swift enough to drag the grains of sand and clay from their adhesions, bearing them onward. As soon as this beginning of a channel is formed the water moves more swiftly in the clearer way; it therefore cuts more rapidly, deepening and enlarging its channel, and making its motion yet more free. The tiny rills join the greater, all their channels sway to and fro as directed this way and that by chance irregularities, until something like river basins are carved out, those gentle slopes which form broad valleys where the carving has been due to the wanderings of many streams. If the field be large, considerable though temporary brooks may be created, which cut channels perhaps a foot in depth.

At the end of this miniature stream system we always find some part of the waste which has been carved out. If the streamlet discharges into a pool, we find the tiny representative of deltas, which form such an important feature on the coast line where large rivers enter seas or lakes. Along the lines of the stream we may observe here and there little benches, which are the equivalent in all save size of the terraces that are generally to be observed along the greater streams. In fact, these accidents of an acre help in a most effective way the student to understand the greater and more complicated processes of continental erosion.

A normal river—in fact, all the greater streams of the earth—originates in high country, generally in a region of mountains. Here, because of the elevation of the region, the streams have cut deep gorges or extensive valleys, all of which have slopes leading steeply downward to torrent beds. Down these inclined surfaces the particles worn off from the hard rock by frost and by chemical decay gradually work their way until they attain the bed of the stream. The agents which assist gravitation in bearing this detritus downward are many, but they all work together for the same end. The stroke of the raindrop accomplishes something, though but little; the direct washing action of the brooklets which form during times of heavy rain, but dry out at the close of the storm, do a good deal of the work; thawing and freezing of the water contained in the mass of detritus help the movement, for, although the thrust is in both directions, it is most effective downhill; the wedges of tree roots, which often penetrate between and under the stones, and there expand in their process of growth, likewise assist the downward motion. The result is that on ordinary mountain slopes the layer of fragments constituting the rude soil is often creeping at the rate of from some inches to some feet a year toward the torrent bed. If there be cliffs at the top of the slope, as is often the case, very extensive falls of rock may take place from it, the masses descending with such speed that they directly attain the stream. If the steeps be low and the rock divided into vertical joints, especially where there is a soft layer at the base of the steep, detached masses from the precipice may move slowly and steadfastly down the slope, so little disturbed in their journey that trees growing upon their summits may continue to develop for the thousands of years before the mass enters the stream bed.

Although the fall of rocks from precipices does not often take place in a conspicuously large way, all great mountain regions which have long been inhabited by man abound in traditions and histories of such accidents. Within a century or two there have been a dozen or more catastrophes of this nature in the inhabited valleys of the Alps. As these accidents are at once instructive and picturesque, it is well to note certain of them in some detail. At Yvorgne, a little parish on the north shore of the Rhône, just above the lake of Geneva, tradition tells that an ancient village of the name was overwhelmed by the fall of a great cliff. The vast *débris* forming the steep slope which was thus produced now bears famous vineyards, but the vintners fancy that they from time to time hear deep in the earth the ringing of the bells which belonged to the overwhelmed church. In 1806 the district of Goldau, just north of Lake Lucerne, was buried beneath the ruins of a peak which, resting upon a layer of clay, slipped away like a launching ship on the surface of the soft material. The *débris* overwhelmed a village and many detached houses, and partly filled a considerable lake. The wind produced by this vast rush of falling rock was so great that people were blown away by it; some, indeed, were killed in this singular manner.

The most interesting field of these Swiss mountain falls is a high mountain valley of amphitheatrical form, known as the Diablerets, or the devil's own district. This great circus, which lies at the height of about four thousand feet above the sea, is walled around on its northern side by a precipice, above which rest, or rather once rested, a number of mountain peaks of great bulk. The region has long been valued for the excellent pasturage which the head of the valley affords. Two costly roads, indeed, have been built into it to afford footpaths for the flocks and herds and their keepers in the summer season. Through this human experience with the valley, we have a record of what has gone on in this part of the mountain wilderness. Within the period of history and tradition, three very great mountain falls have occurred in this field, each having made its memory good by widespread disaster which it brought to the people of the *chalets*. The last of these was brought about by the fall of a great peak which spread itself out in a vast field of ruins in the valley below. The belt of destruction was about half a mile wide and three miles long. When the present writer last saw it, a quarter of a century ago, it was still a wilderness of great rocks, but here and there the process of their decay was giving a foothold for herbage, and in a few centuries the field will doubtless be so verdure-clad that its story will not be told on its face. It is likely, however, to be preserved in the memory of the people, and this through a singular and pathetic tradition which has grown up about the place, one which, if not true, comes at least among the legends which we should like to believe.

As told the present writer by a native of the district, it happened when, in the nighttime the mountain came down, the herdsmen and their cows gathered in the *chalets* —stout buildings which are prepared to resist avalanches of snow. In one of these, which was protected from crushing by the position of the stones which covered it, a solitary herdsman found himself alive in his unharmed dwelling. With him in the darkness were the cows, a store of food and water, and his provisions for the long summer season. With nothing but hope to animate him, he set to work burrowing upward among the rocks, storing the *débris* in the room of the *chalet*. He toiled for some months, but

finally emerged to the light of day, blanched by his long
imprisonment in the darkness, but with the strength to
bear him to his home. In place of the expected warm
welcome, the unhappy man found himself received as a
ghost. He was exorcised by the priest and driven away
to the distance. It was only when long afterward his path
of escape was discovered that his history became known.

Returning to the account of the *débris* which descends
at varied speed into the torrents, we find that when the
detritus encounters the action of these vigorous streams
it is rapidly ground to pieces while it is pushed down the
steep channels to the lower country. Where the stones
are of such size that the stream can urge them on, they
move rapidly; at least in times when the torrent is raging.
They beat over each other and against the firm-set rocks;
the more they wear, the smaller they become, and the more
readily they are urged forward. Where the masses are too
large to be stirred by the violent current, they lie unmoved
until the pounding of the rolling stones reduces them to
the proportions where they may join the great procession.
Ordinarily those who visit mountains behold their torrents
only in their shrunken state, when the waters stir no
stones, and fail even to bear a charge of mud, all detach-
able materials having been swept away when the streams
course with more vigour. In storm seasons the conditions
are quite otherwise; then the swollen torrents, their waters
filled with clay and sand, bear with them great quantities
of boulders, the collisions of which are audible above the
muffled roar of the waters, attesting the very great energy
of the action.

When the waste on a mountain slope lies at a steep
angle, particularly where the accumulation is due to the
action of ancient glaciers, it not infrequently happens that
when the ground is softened with frost great masses of
the material rush down the slope in the manner of landslides. The observer readily notes that in many mountain
regions, as, for instance, in the White Mountains of New

Hampshire, the steep slopes are often seamed by the paths of these great landslides. Their movement, indeed, is often begun by sliding snow, which gives an impulse to the rocks and earth which it encounters in its descent. At a place known as the Wylie Notch, in the White Mountains, in the early part of this century, a family of that name was buried beneath a mass of glacial waste which had hung on the mountain slope from the ancient days until a heavy rain, following on a period of thaw, impelled the mass down the slope. Although there have been few such catastrophes noted in this country, it is because our mountains have not been much dwelt in. As they become thickly inhabited as the Alps are, men are sure to suffer from these accidents.

As the volume of a mountain torrent increases through the junction of many tributaries, the energy of its moving waters becomes sufficient to sweep away the fragments which come to its bed. Before this stage is attained the stream rarely touches the solid under rock of the mountain, the base of the current resting upon the larger loose stones which it was unable to stir. In this pebble-paved section, because the stream could not attack the foundation rock, we find no gorges—in fact, the whole of this upper section of the torrent system is peculiarly conditioned by the fact that the streams are dealing not with bed-rock, but with boulders or smaller loose fragments. If they cut a little channel, the materials from either side slip the faster, and soon repave the bed. But when the streams have by a junction gained strength, and can keep their beds clear, they soon carve down a gorge through which they descend from the upper mountain realm to the larger valleys, where their conjoined waters take on a riverlike aspect. It should be noted here that the cutting power of the water moving in the torrent or in the wave, the capacity it has for abrading rock, resides altogether in the bits of stone or cutting tools with which it is armed. Pure water, because of its fluidity, may move over or against firm-set stones for ages without wearing them; but in proportion as it moves rocky particles of any size, the larger they are, the more effective the work, it wears the rock over which it flows. A capital instance of this may be found where a stream from a hose is used in washing windows. If the water be pure, there is no effect upon the glass; but if it be turbid, containing bits of sand, in a little while the surface will appear cloudy from the multitude of fine scratches which the hard bits impelled by the water have inflicted upon it. A somewhat similar case occurs where the wind bears sand against window panes or a bottle which has long lain on the shore. The glass will soon be deeply carved by the action, assuming the appearance which we term "ground." This principle is made use of in the arts. Glass vessels or sheets are prepared for carving by pasting paper cut into figures on their surfaces. The material is then exposed to a jet of air or steam-impelling sand grains; in a short time all the surface which has not been protected by paper has its polish destroyed and is no longer translucent.

The passage from the torrent to the river, though not in a geographical way distinct, is indicated to the observant eye by a simple feature—namely, the appearance of alluvial terraces, those more or less level heaps of water-borne *débris* which accumulate along the banks of rivers, which, indeed, constitute the difference between those streams and torrents. Where the mountain waters move swiftly, they manage to bear onward the waste which they receive. Even where the blocks of stone cling in the bed, it is only a short time before they are again set in motion or ground to pieces. If by chance the detritus accumulates rapidly, the slope is steepened and the work of the torrent made more efficient. As the torrent comes toward the base of the mountains, where it neither finds nor can create steep slopes over which to flow, its speed necessarily diminishes. With each reduction in this feature its carrying power very rapidly diminishes. Thus water flowing at the rate of ten miles an hour can urge stones four times the mass that it can move when its speed is reduced to half that rate. The result is that on the lowlands, with their relatively gentle slopes, the combined torrents, despite the increase in the volume of the stream arising from their confluence, have to lay down a large part of their load of detritus.

If we watch where a torrent enters a mountain river, we observe that the main stream in a way sorts over the waste contributed to it, bearing on only those portions which its rate of flow will permit it to carry, leaving the remainder to be built into the bank in the form of a rude terrace. This accumulation may not extend far below the point where the torrent which imported the *débris* joins the main stream; a little farther down, however, we are sure to find another such junction and a second accumulation of terrace material. As these contributions increase, the terrace accumulations soon become continuous, lying on one side or the other of the river, sometimes bordering both banks of the stream. In general, it can be said that so long as the rate of fall of the torrent exceeds one hundred feet to the mile it does not usually exhibit these shelves of detritus. Below that rate of descent they are apt to be formed. Much, however, depends upon the amount of detritus which the stream bears and the coarseness of it; moreover, where the water goes through a gorge in the manner of a flume with steep rocky sides, it can urge a larger amount before it than when it traverses a wide valley, through which it passes, it may be, in a winding way.

At first sight it may seem rather a fine distinction to separate torrents from rivers by the presence or absence of terraces. As we follow down the stream, however, and study its action in relation to these terraces, and the peculiar history of the detritus of which they are composed, we perceive that these latter accumulations are very important features. Beginning at first with small and imperfect alluvial plains, the river, as it descends toward the sea, gaining in store of water and in the amount of *débris* which comes with that water from the hills, while the rate of fall and consequent speed of the current are diminished, soon comes to a stage where it is engaged in an endless struggle with the terrace materials. In times of flood, the walls of the terraces compel the tide to flow over the tops of these accumulations. Owing to the relative thinness of the water beyond the bed, and to the growth of vegetation there, the current moves more slowly, and therefore lays down a considerable deposit of the silt and sand which it contains. This may result during a single flood in lifting the level of the terrace by some inches in height, still further serving to restrict the channel. Along the banks of the Mississippi and other large rivers the most of this detritus falls near the stream; a little of it penetrates to the farther side of the plains, which often have a width of ten miles or more. The result is that a broad elevation is constructed, a sort of natural mole or levee, in a measure damming the flood waters, which can now only enter the " back swamps " through the channels of the tributary streams. Each of these back swamps normally discharges into the main stream through a little river of its own, along the banks of which the natural levees do not develop.

We have now to note a curious swinging movement of rivers which was first well observed by the skilful engineers of British India. This movement can best be illustrated by its effects. If on any river which winds through alluvial plains a jetty is so constructed as to deflect the stream at any point, the course which it follows will be altered·during its subsequent flow, it may be, for the distance of hundreds of miles. It will be perceived that in its movements a river normally strikes first against one shore and then against the other. Its water in a general way moves as does a billiard ball when it flies from one cushion to another. It is true that in a torrent we have the same conditions of motion; but there the banks are either of hard rock or, if of detritus, they are continually moving into the stream in the manner before described. In the case of the river, however, its points of collision are often on soft banks, which are readily undermined by the washing action of the stream. In the ordinary course of events, the river beginning, we may imagine, with a straight channel, had its current deflected by some obstacle, it may be even by the slight pressure of a tributary stream, is driven against one bank; thence it rebounds and strikes the other. At each point of impinge it cuts the alluvium away. It can bear on only a small portion of that which it thus obtains; the greater part of the material is deposited on the opposite side of the stream, but a little lower down, where it makes a shallow. On these shallows water-loving plants and even certain trees, such as the willows and poplars, find a foothold. When the stream rises, the sediment settles in this tangle, and soon extends the alluvial plain from the neighbouring bank, or in rarer cases the river comes to flow on either side of an island of its own construction. The natural result of this billiard-ball movement of the waters is that the path of the stream is sinuous. The less its rate of fall and the greater the amount of silt it obtains from its tributaries, the more winding its course becomes. This gain in those parts of the river's curvings where deposition tends to take place may be accelerated by tree-planting. Thus a skilful owner of a tract of land on the south bank of the Ohio River, by assiduously planting willow trees on the front of his property, gained in the course of thirty years more than an acre in the width of his arable land. When told by the present writer that he was robbing his neighbours on the other side of the stream, he claimed that their ignorance of the laws of river motion was sufficient evidence that they did not deserve to own land.

In the primitive state of a country the water-loving plants, particularly the trees which flourish in excessively humid conditions, generally make a certain defence against these incursions of the streams. But when a river has gained an opening in the bank it can, during a flood, extend its width often to the distance of hundreds of feet. During the inundations of the Mississippi the river may at times be seen to eat away acres of land in a single day along one of the outcurves of its banks. The undermined forests falling into the flood join the great procession of drift timber, composed of trees which have been similarly uprooted, which occupies the middle part of the stream. This driftwood belt often has a width of three or four hundred feet, the entangled stems and branches making it difficult for a boat to pass from one side of the river to the other.

Fig. 11.—Oxbows and cut-off. Showing the changes in the course of a river in its alluvial plain.

When the curves of a river have been developed to a certain point (see Fig. 11), when they have attained what is called the "oxbow" form, it often happens that the stream breaks through the isthmus which connects one of the peninsulas with the mainland. Where, as is not infrequently the case, the bend has a length of ten miles or more, the water just above and below the new-made opening is apt to differ in height by some feet. Plunging down the declivity, the stream, flowing with great velocity, soon enlarges the channel so that its whole tide may take the easier way. When this result is accomplished, the old curve is deserted, sand bars are formed across their mouths, which may gradually grow to broad alluvial plains, so that the long-surviving, crescent-shaped lake, the remnant of the river bed, may be seen far from the present course of the ever-changing stream. Gradually the accumulations of vegetable matter and the silt brought in by floods efface this moat or oxbow cut-off, as it is so commonly termed.

As soon as the river breaks through the neck of a peninsula in the manner above described, the current of the stream becomes much swifter for many miles below and above the opening. Slowly, however, the slopes are rearranged throughout its whole course, yet for a time the stream near the seat of the change becomes straighter than before, and this for the reason that its swifter current is better able to dispose of the *débris* which is supplied to it. The effect of a change in the current produced by such new channels as we have described as forming across the isthmuses of bends is to perturb the course of the stream in all its subsequent downward length. Thus an oxbow cut-off formed near the junction of the Ohio and Mississippi may tend more or less to alter the swings of the Mississippi all the way to the Gulf of Mexico.

Although the swayings of the streams to and fro in their alluvial plains will give the reader some idea as to the struggle which the greater rivers have with the *débris* which is committed to them, the full measure of the work and its consequences can only be appreciated by those who have studied the phenomena on the ground. A river

13

such as the Mississippi is endlessly endeavouring to bear
its burden to the sea. If its slope were a uniform inclined plane, the task might readily be accomplished; but
in this, as in almost all other large water ways, the slope
of the bed is ever diminishing with its onward course. The
same water which in the mountain torrent of the Appa-
lachians or Cordilleras rolled along stones several feet in
diameter down slopes of a hundred feet or more to the
mile can in the lower reaches of the stream move no pebbles which are more than one fourth of an inch in diameter
over slopes which descend on the average about half a foot
in a mile. Thus at every stage from the torrent to the sea
the detritus has from time to time to rest within the alluvial banks, there awaiting the decay which slowly comes,
and which may bring it to the state where it may be dissolved in the water, or divided into fragments so small that
the stream may bear them on. A computation which the
present writer has made shows that, on the average, it requires about forty thousand years for a particle of stone
to make its way down the Mississippi to the sea after it has
been detached from its original bed. Of course, some bits
may make the journey straightforwardly; others may require a far greater time to accomplish the course which
the water itself makes at most in a few weeks. This long
delay in the journey of the detritus—a delay caused by its
frequent rests in the alluvial plain—brings about important consequences which we will now consider.

As an alluvial plain is constructed, we generally find
at the base pebbly material which fell to the bottom in
the current of the main stream as the shores grew outward.
Above this level we find the deposits laid down by the
flood waters containing no pebbles, and this for the reason
that those weightier bits remained in the stream bed when
the tide flowed over the plain. As the alluvial deposit is
laid down, a good deal of vegetable matter was built into
it. Generally this has decayed and disappeared. On the
surface of the plain there has always been growing abun-

dant vegetation, the remains of which decayed on the surface in the manner which we may observe at the present
day. This decomposing vegetable matter within and upon
the porous alluvial material produces large quantities of
carbonic acid, a gas which readily enters the rain water,
and gives it a peculiar power of breaking up rock matter.
Acting on the *débris*, this gas-charged water rapidly brings
about a decay of the fragments. Much of the material
passes at once into solution in this water, and drains away
through the multitudinous springs which border the river.
As this matter is completely dissolved, as is sugar in
water, it goes straight away to the sea without ever again
entering the alluvium. In many, if not most, cases this
dissolving work which is going on in alluvial terraces is
sufficient to render a large part of the materials which
they contain into the state where it disappears in an unseen manner; thus while the annual floods are constantly
laying down accumulations on the surface of these plains,
the springs are bearing it away from below.

In this way, through the decomposition which takes
place in them, all those river terraces where much vegetable matter is mingled with the mineral substances, become
laboratories in which substances are brought into solution
and committed to the seas. We find in the water of the
ocean a great array of dissolved mineral substances; it,
indeed, seems probable that the sea water contains some
share, though usually small, of all the materials which
rivers encounter in their journey over and under the lands.
As the waters of the sea obtain but little of this dissolved
matter along the coast, it seems likely that the greater share
of it is brought into the state of solution in the natural
laboratories of the alluvial plains.

Here and there along the sides of the valleys in which
the rivers flow we commonly find the remains of ancient
plains lying at more or less considerable heights above
the level of the streams. Generally these deposits, which
from their form are called terraces, represent the stages of

down-wearing by which the stream has carved out its way through the rocks. The greater part of these ancient alluvial plains has been removed through the ceaseless swinging of the stream to and fro in the valley which it has excavated.

In all the states of alluvial plains, whether they be the fertile deposits near the level of the streams which built them, or the poorer and ruder surfaced higher terraces, they have a great value to mankind. Men early learned that these lands were of singularly uniform goodness for agricultural use. They are so light that they were easily delved with the ancient pointed sticks or stone hoes, or turned by the olden wooden plough. They not only give a rich return when first subjugated, but, owing to the depth of the soil and the frequency with which they are visited by fertilizing inundations, they yield rich harvests without fertilizing for thousands of years. It is therefore not surprising that we find the peoples who depended upon tillage for subsistence first developed on the great river plains. There, indeed, were laid the foundations of our higher civilization; there alone could the state which demands of its citizens fixed abodes and continuous labour take rise. In the conditions which these fields of abundance afforded, dense populations were possible, and all the arts which lead toward culture were greatly favoured. Thus it is that the civilization of China, India, Persia, and Egypt, the beginnings of man's higher development, began near the mouths of the great river valleys. These fields were, moreover, most favourably placed for the institution of commerce, in that the arts of navigation, originating in the sheltered reaches of the streams, readily found its way through the estuaries to the open sea.

Passing down the reaches of a great river as it approaches the sea, we find that the alluvial plains usually widen and become lower. At length we attain a point where the flood waters cover the surface for so large a part of the year that the ground is swampy and untillable unless it is artificially and at great expense of labour won to agriculture in the manner in which this task has been effected in the lower portion of the Rhine Valley. Still farther toward the sea, the plain gradually dips downward until it passes below the level of the waters. Through this mud-flat section the stream continues to cut channels, but with the ever-progressive slowing of its motion the burden of fine mud which it carries drops to the bottom, and constantly closes the paths through which the water escapes. Every few years they tend to break a new way on one side or the other of their former path. Some of the greatest engineering work done in modern times has been accomplished by the engineers engaged in controlling the exits of large rivers to the sea. The outbreak of the Yellow River in 1887, in which the stream, hindered by its own accumulations, forced a new path across its alluvial plains, destroyed a vast deal of life and property, and made the new exit seventy miles from the path which it abandoned.

Below the surface of the open water the alluvial deposits spread out into a broad fan, which slopes gradually to a point where, in the manner of the continental shelf, the bottom descends steeply into deep water.

It is the custom of naturalists to divide the lower section of river deposits—that part of the accumulation which is near the sea—from the other alluvial plains, terming the lower portion the delta. The word originally came into use to describe that part of the alluvium accumulated by the Nile near its mouth, which forms a fertile territory shaped somewhat like the fourth letter of the Greek alphabet. Although the definition is good in the Egyptian instance, and has a certain use elsewhere, we best regard all the detritus in a river valley which is in the state of repose along the stream to its utmost branches as forming one great whole. It is, indeed, one of the most united of the large features which the earth exhibits. The student should consider it as a continuous inclined plane of diminishing slope, extending from the base of the torrents to the sea, and of course ramifying into the several branches of the river system. He should further bear in mind the fact that it is a vast laboratory where rock material is brought into the soluble state for delivery to the seas.

The diversity in the form of river valleys is exceedingly great. Almost all the variety of the landscape is due to this impress of water action which has operated on the surface in past ages. When first elevated above the sea, the surface of the land is but little varied; at this stage in the development the rivers have but shallow valleys, which generally cut rather straight away over the plain toward the sea. It is when the surface has been uplifted to a considerable height, and especially when, as is usually the case, this uplifting action has been associated with mountain-building, that valleys take on their accented and picturesque form. The reason for this is easily perceived: it lies in the fact that the rocks over which the stream flows are guided in the cutting which they effect by the diversities of hardness in the strata that they encounter. The work which it does is performed by the hard substances that are impelled by the current, principally by the sand and pebbles. These materials, driven along by the stream, become eroding tools of very considerable energy. As will be seen when we shortly come to describe waterfalls, the potholes formed at those points afford excellent evidence as to the capacity of stream-impelled bits of stone to cut away the firmest bed rocks. Naturally the case with which this carving work is done is proportionate to the energy of the currents, and also to the relative hardness of the moving bits and the rocks over which they are driven.

So long as the rocks lie horizontally in their natural construction attitude the course of the stream is not much influenced by the variations in hardness which the bed exhibits. Where the strata are very firm there is likely to be a narrow gorge. the steeps of which rise on either side with but slight alluvial plains; where the beds are soft the valley widens, perhaps again to contract where in the course of its descent it encounters another hard layer. Where, however, the beds have been subjected to mountain-building, and have been thrown into very varied attitudes by folding and faulting, the stream now here and now there encounters beds which either restrain its flow or give it freedom. The stream is then forced to cut its way according to the positions of the various underlying strata. This effect upon its course is not only due to the peculiarities of uplifted rocks, but to manifold accidents of other nature: veins and dikes, which often interlace the beds with harder or softer partitions than the country rock; local hardenings in the materials, due to crystallization and other chemical processes, often create indescribable variations which are more or less completely expressed in the path of the stream.

When a land has been newly elevated above the sea there is often—we may say, indeed, generally—a very great difference between the height of its head waters and the ocean level. In this condition of a country the rivers have what we may call a new aspect; their valleys are commonly narrow and rather steep, waterfalls are apt to abound, and the alluvial terraces are relatively small in extent. Stage by stage the torrents cut deeper; the waste which they make embarrasses the course of the lower waters, where no great amount of down-cutting is possible for the reason that the bed of the stream is near sea level. At the same time the alluvial materials, building out to sea, thus diminish the slope of the stream. In the extreme old age of the river system the mountains are eaten down so that the torrent section disappears, and the stream becomes of something like a uniform slope; the higher alluvial plains gradually waste away. until in the end the valley has no salient features. At this stage in the process. or even before it is attained. the valley is likely to be submerged beneath the sea, where it is buried beneath the deposits formed on the floor; or a further uplift of the land may occur with the result that the stream is rejuvenated; or once more en-

dowed with the power to create torrents, build alluvial
plains, and do the other interesting work of a normal
river.

It rarely, if ever, happens that a river valley attains
old age before it has sunk beneath the sea or been refreshed
by further upliftings. In the unstable conditions of the
continents, one or the other of these processes, sometimes
in different places both together, is apt to be going on.
Thus if we take the case of the Mississippi and its principal tributaries, the Ohio and Missouri, we find that for
many geological ages the mountains about their sources
have frequently, if not constantly, grown upward, so that
their torrent sections, though they have worn down tens
of thousands of feet, are still high above the sea level, perhaps on the average as high as they have ever been. At
the same time the slight up-and-down swayings of the
shore lands, amounting in general to less than five hundred
feet, have greatly affected the channels of the main river
and its tributaries in their lower parts. Not long ago the
Mississippi between Cairo and the Gulf flowed in a rather
steep-sided valley probably some hundreds of feet in depth,
which had a width of many miles. Then at the close of the
last Glacial period the region sank down so that the sea
flooded the valley to a point above the present junction of
the Ohio River with the main stream. Since then alluvial
plains have filled this estuary to even beyond the original
mouth. In many other of our Southern rivers, as along the
shore from the Mississippi to the Hudson, the streams have
not brought in enough detritus to fill their drowned valleys,
which have now the name of bays. of which the Delaware
and Chesapeake on the Atlantic coast. and Mobile Bay on
the Gulf of Mexico, are good examples. The failure of
Chesapeake and Delaware Bays to fill with *débris* in the
measure exhibited by the more southern valleys is due to
the fact that the streams which flow into them to a great
extent drain from a region thickly covered with glacial
waste, a mass which holds the flood waters, yielding the

supply but slowly to the torrents, which there have but a slight cutting power.

In our sketch of river valleys no attention has been given to the phenomena of waterfalls, those accidents of the flow which, as we have noted, are particularly apt to characterize rivers which have not yet cut down to near the sea level. Where the normal uniform descent which is characteristic of a river's bed is interrupted by a sudden steep, the fact always indicates the occurrence of one of a number of geological actions. The commonest cause of waterfalls is due to a sudden change in the character of horizontal or at least nearly level beds over which the stream may flow. Where after coursing for a distance over a hard layer the stream comes to its edge and drops on a soft or easily eroded stratum, it will cut this latter bed away, and create a more or less characteristic waterfall. Tumbling down the face of the hard layer, the stream acquires velocity; the *débris* which it conveys is hurled against the bottom, and therefore cuts powerfully, while before, being only rubbed over the stone as it moved along, it cut but slightly. Masses of ice have the same effect as stones. Bits dropping from the ledge are often swept round and round by the eddies, so that they excavate an opening which prevents their chance escape. In these confined spaces they work like augers, boring a deep, well-like cavity. As the bits of stone wear out they are replaced by others, which fall in from above. Working in this way, the fragments often develop regular well-like depressions, the cavities of which work back under the cliffs, and by the undermining process deprive the face of the wall of its support, so that it tumbles in ruin to the base, there to supply more material for the potholing action.

Waterfalls of the type above described are by far the commonest of those which occur out of the torrent districts of a great river system. That of Niagara is an excellent specimen of the type, which, though rarely manifested in anything like the dignity of the great fall, is plentifully shown throughout the Mississippi Valley and the basin of the Great Lakes. Within a hundred miles of Niagara there are at least a hundred small waterfalls of the same type. Probably three quarters of all the larger accidents of this nature are due to the conditions of a hard bed overlying softer strata.

Falls are also produced in very many instances by dikes which cross the stream. So, too, though rarely, only one striking instance being known, an ancient coral reef which has become buried in strata may afford rock of such hardness that when the river comes to cross it it forms a cascade, as at the Falls of the Ohio, at Louisville, Ky. It is a characteristic of all other falls, except those first mentioned, that they rarely plunge with a clean downward leap over the face of a precipice which recedes at its base, but move downward over an irregular sloping surface.

In the torrent district of rivers waterfalls are commonly very numerous, and are generally due to the varying hardness in the rocks which the streams encounter. Here, where the cutting action is going on with great rapidity, slight differences in the resistance which the rocks make to the work will lead to great variations in the form of the bed over which they flow, while on the more gently sloping bottoms of the rivers, where the *débris* moves slowly, such variations would be unimportant in their effect. When the torrents escape into the main river valleys, in regions where the great streams have cut deep gorges, they often descend from a great vertical height, forming wonderful waterfalls, such as those which occur in the famous Lauterbrunnen Valley of Switzerland or in that of the Yosemite in California. This group of cascades is peculiar in that the steep of the fall is made not by the stream itself, but by the action of a greater river or of a glacier which may have some time taken its place.

Waterfalls have an economic as well as a picturesque interest in that they afford sources of power which may be a very great advantage to manufacturers. Thus along the Atlantic coast the streams which come from the Appalachian highlands, and which have hardly escaped from their torrent section before they attain the sea, afford numerous cataracts which have been developed so that. they afford a vast amount of power. Between the James on the south and the Ste. Croix on the north more than a hundred of these Appalachian rivers have been turned to economic use. The industrial arts of this part of the country depend much upon them for the power which drives their machinery. The whole of the United States, because of the considerable size of its rivers and their relatively rapid fall, is richly endowed with this source of energy, which, originating in the sun's heat and conveyed through the rain, may be made to serve the needs of man. In view of the fact that recent inventions have made it possible to convert this energy of falling water into the form of electricity, which may be conveyed to great distances, it seems likely that our rivers will in the future be a great source of national wealth.

We must turn again to river valleys, there to trace certain actions less evident than those already noted, but of great importance in determining these features of the land. First, we have to note that in the valley or region drained by a river there is another degrading or downwearing action than that which is accomplished by the direct work of the visible stream. All over such a valley the underground waters, soaking through the soil and penetrating through the underlying rock, are constantly removing a portion of the mineral matter which they take into solution and bear away to the sea. In this way, deprived of a part of their substance, the rocks are continually settling down by underwear throughout the whole basin, while they are locally being cut down by the action of the stream. Hence in part it comes about that in a river basin we find two contrasted features—the general and often slight slope of a country toward the main stream and its greater tributaries, and the sharp indentation of the gorge in which the streams flow, these latter caused by the immediate and recent action of the streams.

If now the reader will conceive himself standing at any point in a river basin, preferably beyond the realms of the torrents, he may with the guidance of the facts previously noted, with a little use of the imagination, behold the vast perceptive which the history of the river valley may unfold to him. He stands on the surface of the soil, that *débris* of the rocks which is just entering on its way to the ocean. In the same region ten thousand years ago he would have stood upon a surface from one to ten feet higher than the present soil covering. A million years ago his station would have been perhaps five hundred feet higher than the surface. Ten million years in the past, a period less than the lifetime of certain rivers, such as the French Broad River in North Carolina, the soil was probably five thousand feet or more above its present plane. There are, indeed, cases where river valleys appear to have worked down without interruption from the subsidence of the land beneath the sea to the depth of at least two miles. Looking upward through the space which the rocks once occupied, we can conceive the action of the forces in their harmonious coöperation which have brought the surface slowly downward. We can imagine the ceaseless corrosion due to the ground water, bringing about a constant though slow descent of the whole surface. Again and again the streams, swinging to and fro under the guidance of the underlying rock, or from the obstacles which the *débris* they carried imposed upon them, have crossed the surface. Now and then perhaps the wearing was intensified by glacial action, for an ice sheet often cuts with a speed many times as great as that which fluid water can accomplish. On the whole, this exercise of the constructive imagination in conceiving the history of a river valley is one of the most enlarging tasks which the geologist can undertake.

Where in a river valley there are many lateral streams, and especially where the process of solution carried on by the underground waters is most effective, as compared with erosive work done in the bed of the main river, we commonly find the valley sloping gently toward its centre, the rivers having but slight steeps near their banks. On the other hand, where, as occasionally happens, a considerable stream fed by the rain and snow fall in its torrent section courses for a great distance over high, arid plains, on which the ground water and the tributaries do but little work, the basin may slope with very slight declivity to the river margins, and there descend to great depths, forming very deep gorges, of which the Colorado Cañon is the most perfect type. As instances of these contrasted conditions, we may take, on the one hand, the upper Mississippi, where the grades toward the main stream are gentle and the valley gorge but slightly exhibited; on the other, the abovementioned Colorado, which bears a great tide of waters drawn from the high and relatively rainy region of the Rocky Mountains across the vast plateau lying in an almost rainless country. In this section nearly all the down-wearing has been brought about in the direct path of the stream, which has worn the elevated plain into a deep gorge during the slow uprising of the table-land to its present height. In this way a defile nearly a mile in depth has been created in a prevailingly rather flat country. This gorge has embranchments where the few great tributaries have done like work, but, on the whole, this river flows in an almost unbroken channel, the excavation of which has been due to its swift, pebble-bearing waters.

The tendency of a newly formed river is to cut a more or less distinct cañon. As the basin becomes ancient, this element of the gorge tends to disappear, the reason for this being that, while the river bed is high above the sea, the current is swift and the down-cutting rapid, while the slow subsidence of the country on either side—a process which goes on at a uniform rate—causes the surface of that region to be left behind in the race for the sea level. As the stream bed comes nearer the sea level its rate of descent

is diminished, and so the outlying country gradually overtakes it.

In regions where the winters are very cold the effect
of ice on the development of the stream beds both in the
torrent and river sections of the valley is important. This
work is accomplished in several diverse ways. In the first
place, where the stream is clear and the current does not
flow too swiftly, the stones on the bottom radiate their
heat through the water, and thus form ice on their surfaces,
which may attain considerable thickness. As ice is considerably lighter than water, the effect is often to lift up
the stones of the bed if they be not too large; when thus
detached from the bottom, they are easily floated down
stream until the ice melts away. The ice which forms on
the surface of the water likewise imprisons the pebbles
along the banks, and during the subsequent thaw may
carry them hundreds of miles toward the sea. It seems
likely, from certain observations made by the writer, that
considerable stones may thus be carried from the Alle-
ghany River to the main Mississippi.

Perhaps the most important effect of ice on river channels is accomplished when in a time of flood the ice field
which covered the stream, perhaps to the depth of some
feet, is broken up into vast floes, which drift downward
with the current. When, as on the Ohio, these fields sometimes have the area of several hundred acres, they often
collide with the shores, especially where the stream makes
a sharp bend. Urged by their momentum, these ice floes
pack into the semblance of a dam, which may have a thickness of twenty, thirty, or even fifty feet. Beginning on
the shore, where the collision takes place, the dam may
swiftly develop clear across the stream, so that in a few
minutes the way of the waters is completely blocked. The
on-coming ice shoots up upon the accumulation, increases
its height, and extends it up stream, so that in an hour
the mass completely bars the current. The waters then
heap up until they break their way over the obstacle, wash-

ing its top away, until the whole is light enough to be forced down the stream, where, by the friction it encounters on the bottom and sides of the channel, it is broken to pieces. It is easy to see that such moving dams of ice may sweep the bed of a river as with a great broom.

Sometimes where the gorges do not form a stationary dam large cakes of ice become turned on edge and pack together so that they roll down the stream like great wheels, grinding the bed rock as they go.

In high northern countries, as in Siberia, the rivers, even the deepest, often become so far frozen that their channels are entirely obstructed. Where, as in the case of these Siberian rivers, the flow is from south to north, it often happens that the spring thaw sets in before the more northern beds of the main stream are released from their bondage of frost. In this case the inundations have to find new paths on either side of the obstructed way. The result is a type of valleys characterized by very irregular and changeable stream beds, the rivers having no chance to organize themselves into the shapely curves which they ordinarily follow.

The supply which finds its way to a river is composed, as has been already incidentally noted, in part of the water which courses underground for a greater or less distance before it emerges to the surface, and in part of that which moves directly over the ground. These two shares of water have somewhat different histories. On the share of these two depends the stability of the flow. Where, as in New England and other glaciated countries, the surface of the earth is covered with a thick layer of sand and gravel, which, except when frozen, readily admits the water; the rainfall is to a very great extent absorbed by the earth, and only yielded slowly to the streams. In these cases floods are rare and of no great destructive power. Again, where also the river basin is covered by a dense mantle of forests, the ground beneath which is coated, as is the case in primeval woods, with a layer of decomposing vegetation a foot or more in depth, this spongy mass retains the water even more effectively than the open-textured glacial deposits above referred to. When the woods, however, are removed from such an area, the rain may descend to the streams almost as speedily as it finds its way to the gutters from the house roofs. It thus comes about that all regions, when reduced to tillage, and where the rainfall is enough to maintain a good agriculture, are, except when they have a coating of glacial waste, exceedingly liable to destructive inundations.

Unhappily, the risk of river floods is peculiarly great in all the regions of the United States lying much to the east of the Rocky Mountains, except in the basin of the Great Lakes and in the district of New England, where the prevalence of glacial sands and gravels affords the protection which we have noted. Throughout this region the rainfall is heavy, and the larger part of it is apt to come after the ground has become deeply snow-covered. The result is a succession of devastating floods which already are very damaging to the works of man, and promise to become more destructive as time goes on. More than in any other country, we need the protection which forests can give us against these disastrous outgoings of our streams.

LAKES.

In considering the journey of water from the hilltops to the sea, we should take some account of those pauses which it makes on its way when for a time it falls into the basin of a lake. These arrests in the downward motion of water, which we term lakes, are exceedingly numerous; their proper discussion would, indeed, require a considerable volume. We shall here note only the more important of their features, those which are of interest to the general student.

The first and most noteworthy difference in lakes is that which separates the group of dead seas from the living basins of fresh water. When a stream attains a place where its waters have to expand into the lakelike form, the current moves in a slow manner, and the broad surface exposed to the air permits a large amount of evaporation. If the basin be large in proportion to the amount of the incurrent water, this evaporation may exceed the supply, and produce a sea with no outlet, such as we find in the Dead Sea of Judea, in that at Salt Lake, Utah, and in a host of other less important basins. If the rate of evaporation be yet greater in proportion to the flow, the lake may altogether dry away, and the river be evaporated before it attains the basin where it might accumulate. In that case the river is said to sink, but, in place of sinking into the earth, its waters really rise into the air. Many such sinks occur in the central portion of the Rocky Mountain district. It is important to note that the process of evaporation we are describing takes place in the case of all lakes, though only here and there is the air so dry that the evaporation prevents the basin from overflowing at the lowest point on its rim, forming a river which goes thence to the sea. Even in the case of the Great Lakes of North America a considerable part of the water which flows into them does not go to the St. Lawrence and thence to the sea.

As long as the lake finds an outlet to the sea its waters contain but little more dissolved mineral matter than that we find in the rivers. But because all water which has been in contact with the earth has some dissolved mineral substances, while that which goes away by evaporation is pure water, a lake without an outlet gradually becomes so charged with these materials that it can hold no more in solution, but proceeds to lay them down in deposits of that compound substance which from its principal ingredient we name salt. The water of dead seas, because of the additional weight of the substances which it holds, is extraordinarily buoyant. The swimmer notes a difference in this regard in the waters of rivers and fresh-water lakes and those of the sea, due to this same cause. But in those

14

of dead seas, saturated with saline materials, the human body can not sink as it does in the ordinary conditions of immersion. It is easy to understand how the salt deposits which are mined in many parts of the world have generally, if not in all cases, been formed in such dead seas.*

It is an interesting fact that almost all the known dead seas have in recent geological times been living lakes—that is, they poured over their brims. In the Cordilleras from the line between Canada and the United States to central Mexico there are several of these basins. All of those which have been studied show by their old shore lines that they were once brimful, and have only shrunk away in modern times. These conditions point to the conclusion that the rainfall in different regions varies greatly in the course of the geologic ages. Further confirmation of this is found in the fact that very great salt deposits exist on the coast of Louisiana and in northern Europe—regions in which the rainfall is now so great in proportion to the evaporation that dead seas are impossible.

Turning now to the question of how lake basins are formed, we note a great variety in the conditions which may bring about their construction. The greatest agent, or at least that which operates in the construction of the largest basins, are the irregular movements of the earth, due to the mountain-building forces. Where this work goes on on a large scale, basin-shaped depressions are inevitably formed. If all those which have existed remained, the large part of the lands would be covered by them. In most cases, however, the cutting action of the streams has been sufficient to bring the drainage channels down to the bottom of the trough, while the influx of sediments has served to further the work by filling up the cavities. Thus

---

* In some relatively rare cases salt deposits are formed in lagoons along the shores of arid lands, where the sea occasionally breaks over the beach into the basin, affording waters which are evaporated, leaving their salt behind them.

at the close of the Cretaceous period there was a chain of
lakes extending along the eastern base of the Rocky Mountains, constituting fresh-water seas probably as large as
the so-called Great Lakes of North America. But the rivers,
by cutting down and filling up, have long since obliterated
these water areas. In other cases the tiltings of the continent, which sometimes oppose the flow of the streams,
may for a time convert the upper part of a river basin
which originally sloped gently toward the sea into a cavity. Several cases of this description occurred in New
England in the closing stages of the Glacial period, when
the ground rose up to the northward.

We have already noted the fact that the basin of a dead
sea becomes in course of time the seat of extensive salt
deposits. These may, indeed, attain a thickness of many
hundred feet. If now in the later history of the country
the tract of land with the salt beneath it were traversed
by a stream, its underground waters may dissolve out the
salt and in a way restore the basin to its original unfilled
condition, though in the second state that of a living lake.
It seems very probable that a portion at least of the areas
of Lakes Ontario, Erie, and Huron may be due to this
removal of ancient salt deposits, remains of which lie
buried in the earth in the region bordering these basins.

By far the commonest cause of lake basins is found in
the irregularities of the surface which are produced by
the occupation of the country by glaciers. When these
great sheets of ice lie over a land, they are in motion down
the slopes on which they rest; they wear the bed rocks in a
vigorous manner, cutting them down in proportion to their
hardness. As these rocks generally vary in the resistance
which they oppose to the ice, the result is that when the
glacier passes away the surface no longer exhibits the continued down slope which the rivers develop, but is warped
in a very complicated way. These depressions afford natural basins in which lakes gather; they may vary in extent
from a few square feet to many square miles. When a gla-

cier occupies a country, the melting ice deposits on the surface of the earth a vast quantity of rocky *débris*, which was contained in its mass. This detritus is irregularly accumulated; in part it is disposed in the form of moraines or rude mounds made at the margin of the glacier, in part as an irregular sheet, now thick, now thin, which covers the whole of the field over which the ice lay. The result of this action is the formation of innumerable pools, which continue to exist until the streams have cut channels through which their waters may drain away, or the basins have become filled with detritus imported from the surrounding country or by peat accumulations which the plants form in such places.

Doubtless more than nine tenths of all the lake basins, especially those of small size, which exist in the world are due to irregularities of the land surface which are brought about by glacial action. Although the greater part of these small basins have been obliterated since the ice left this country, the number still remaining of sufficient size to be marked on a good map is inconceivably great. In North America alone there are probably over a hundred and fifty thousand of these glacial lakes, although by far the greater part of those which existed when the glacial sheet disappeared have been obliterated.

Yet another interesting group of fresh-water lakes, or rather we should call them lakelets from their small size, owes its origin to the curious underground excavations or caverns which are formed in limestone countries. The water enters these caverns through what are termed "sink holes"—basins in the surface which slope gently toward a central opening through which the water flows into the depths below. The cups of the sink holes rarely exceed half a mile in diameter, and are usually much smaller. Their basins have been excavated by the solvent and cutting actions of the rain water which gathers in them to be discharged into the cavern below. It often happens that after a sink hole is formed some slight accident closes the downward-leading shaft, so that the basin holds water; thus in parts of the United States there are thousands of these nearly circular pools, which in certain districts, as in southern Kentucky, serve to vary the landscape in much the same manner as the glacial lakes of more northern countries.

Some of the most beautiful lakes in the world, though none more than a few miles in diameter, occupy the craters of extinct volcanoes. When for a time, or permanently, a volcano ceases to do its appointed work of pouring forth steam and molten rock from the depths of the earth, the pit in the centre of the cone gathers the rain water, forming a deep circular lake, which is walled round by the precipitous faces of the crater. If the volcano reawakens, the water which blocks its passage may be blown out in a moment, the discharge spreading in some cases to a great distance from the cone, to be accumulated again when the vent ceases to be open. The most beautiful of these volcanic lakes are to be found in the region to the north and south of Rome. The original seat of the Latin state was on the shores of one of these crater pools, south of the Eternal City. Lago Bolsena, which lies to the northward, and is one of the largest known basins of this nature, having a diameter of about eight miles, is a crater lake. The volcanic cone to which it belongs, though low, is of great size, showing that in its time of activity, which did not endure very long, this crater was the seat of mighty ejections. The noblest specimen of this group of basins is found in Crater Lake, Oregon, now contained in one of the national parks of the United States.

Inclosed bodies of water are formed in other ways than those described; the list above given includes all the important classes of action which produce these interesting features. We should now note the fact that, unlike the seas, the lakes are to be regarded as temporary features in the physiography of the land. One and all, they endure for but brief geologic time, for the reason that the streams work to destroy them by filling them with sediment and by carving out channels through which their waters drain away. The nature of this action can well be conceived by considering what will take place in the course of time in the Great Lakes of North America. As Niagara Falls cut back at the average rate of several feet a year, it will be but a brief geologic period before they begin to lower the waters of Lake Erie. It is very probable, indeed, that in twenty thousand years the waters of that basin will be to a great extent drained away. When this occurs, another fall or rapid will be produced in the channel which leads from Lake Huron to Lake Erie. This in turn will go through its process of retreat until the former expanse of waters disappears. The action will then be continued at the outlets of Lakes Michigan and Superior, and in time, but for the interposition of some actions which recreate these basins, their floors will be converted into dry land.

It is interesting to note that lakes owe in a manner the preservation of their basins to an action which they bring about on the waters that flow into them. These rivers or torrents commonly convey great quantities of sediment, which serve to rasp their beds and thus to lower their channels. In all but the smaller lakelets these turbid waters lay down all their sediment before they attain the outlet of the basin. Thus they flow away over the rim rock in a perfectly pure state—a state in which, as we have noted before, water has no capacity for abrading firm rock. Thus where the Niagara River passes from Lake Erie its clean water hardly affects the stone over which it flows. It only begins to do cutting work where it plunges down the precipice of the Falls and sets in motion the fragments which are constantly falling from that rocky face. These Falls could not have begun as they did on the margin of Lake Ontario except for the fact that when the Niagara River began to flow, as in relatively modern times, it found an old precipice on the margin of Lake Ontario, formed by the waves of the lake, down which the waters fell, and where they obtained cutting tools with which to undermine the steep which forms the Falls.

Many great lakes, particularly those which we have just been considering, have repeatedly changed their outlets, according as the surface of the land on which they lie has swayed up and down in various directions, or as glacial sheets have barred or unbarred the original outlets of the basins. Thus in the Laurentian Lakes above Ontario the geologist finds evidence that the drainage lines have again and again been changed. For a time during the Glacial period, when Lake Ontario and the valley of the St. Lawrence was possessed by the ice, the discharge was southward into the upper Mississippi or the Ohio. At a later stage channels were formed leading from Georgian Bay to the eastern part of Ontario. Yet later, when the last-named lake was bared, an ice dam appears to have remained in the St. Lawrence, which held back the waters to such a height that they discharged through the valley of the Mohawk into the Hudson. Furthermore, at some time before the Glacial period, we do not know just when, there appears to have been an old Niagara River, now filled with drift, which ran from Lake Erie to Ontario, a different channel from that occupied by the present stream.

The effects of lakes on the river systems with which they are connected is in many ways most important. Where they are of considerable extent, or where even small they are very numerous, they serve to retain the flood waters, delivering them slowly to the excurrent streams. In rising one foot a lake may store away more water than the river by its consequent rise at the point of outflow will carry away in many months, and this for the simple reason that the lake may be many hundred or even thousand times as wide as the stream. Moreover, as before noted, the sediment gathered by the stream above the level of the lake is deposited in its basin, and does not affect the lower reaches of the river. The result is that great rivers, such as drain from the Laurentian Lakes, flow clear water, are exempt from floods, are essentially without alluvial plains or terraces, and form no delta deposits. In all these features the St. Lawrence River affords a wonderful contrast to the Mississippi. Moreover, owing to the clear waters, though it has flowed for a long time, it has never been able to cut away the slight obstructions which form its rapids, barriers which probably would have been removed if its waters had been charged with sediment.

Muir Glacier, Alaska, showing crevasses and dust layer on surface of ice.

CHAPTER VI.

GLACIERS.

WE have already noted the fact that the water in the clouds is very commonly in the frozen state; a large part of that fluid which is evaporated from the sea attains the solid form before it returns to the earth. Nevertheless, in descending, at least nine tenths of the precipitation returns to the fluid state, and does the kind of work which we have noted in our account of water. Where, however, the water arrives on the earth in the frozen condition, it enters on a rôle totally different from that followed by the fluid material.

Beginning its descent to the earth in a snowflake, the little mass falls slowly, so that when it comes against the earth the blow which it strikes is so slight that it does no effective work. In the state of snow, even in the separate flakes, the frozen water contains a relatively large amount of air. It is this air indeed, which, by dividing the ice into many flakes that reflect the light, gives it the white colour. This important point can be demonstrated by breaking transparent ice into small bits, when we perceive that it has the hue of snow. Much the same effect is given where glass is powdered, and for the same reason.

As the snowflakes accumulate layer on layer they imbed air between them, so that when the material falls in a feathery shape—say to the depth of a foot—more than nine tenths of the mass is taken up by the air-containing spaces. As these cells are very small, the circulation in them is slight, and so the layer becomes an admirable non-conductor, having this quality for the same reason that feathers have it—i. e., because the cells are small enough to prevent the circulation of the air, so that the heat which passes has to go by conduction, and all gases are very poor conductors. The result is that a snow coating is in effect an admirable blanket. When the sun shines upon it, much of the heat is reflected, and as the temperature does not penetrate it to any depth, only the superficial part is melted. This molten water takes up in the process of melting a great deal of heat, so that when it trickles down into the mass it readily refreezes. On the other hand, the heat going out from the earth, the store accumulated in its superficial parts in the last warm season, together with the small share which flows out from the earth's interior, is held in by this blanket, which it melts but slowly. Thus it comes about that in regions of long-enduring snowfall the ground, though frozen to the depth of a foot or more at the time when the accumulation took place, may be thawed out and so far warmed that the vegetation begins to grow before the protecting envelope of snow has melted away. Certain of the early flowers of high latitudes, indeed, begin to blossom beneath the mantle of finely divided ice.

In those parts of the earth which for the most part receive only a temporary coating of snow the effect of this covering is inconsiderable. The snow water is yielded to the earth, from which it has helped to withdraw the frost, so that in the springtime, the growing season of plants, the ground contains an ample store of moisture for their development. Where the snowfall accumulates to a great thickness, especially where it lodges in forests, the influence of the icy covering is somewhat to protract the winter and thus to abbreviate the growing season.

Where snow rests upon a steep slope, and gathers to the depth of several feet, it begins to creep slowly down the declivity in a manner which we may often note on house roofs. This motion is favoured by the gradual though incomplete melting of the flakes as the heat penetrates the mass. Making a section through a mass of snow which has accumulated in many successive falls, we note that the top may still have the flaky character, but that as we go down the flakes are replaced by adherent shotlike bodies, which have arisen from the partial melting and gathering to their centres of the original expanded crystalline bits. In this process of change the mass can move particle by particle in the direction in which gravity impels it. The energy of its motion, however, is slight, yet it can urge loose stones and forest waste down hill. Sometimes, as in the cemetery at Augusta, Me., where stone monuments or other structures, such as iron railings, are entangled in the moving mass, it may break them off and convey them a little distance down the slope.

So long as the summer sun melts the winter's snow, even if the ground be bare but for a day, the rôle of action accomplished by the snowfall is of little geological consequence. When it happens that a portion of the deposit holds through the summer, the region enters on the glacial state, and its conditions undergo a great revolution, the consequences of which are so momentous that we shall have to trace them in some detail. Fortunately, the considerations which are necessary are not recondite, and all the facts are of an extremely picturesque nature.

Taking such a region as New England, where all the earth is life-bearing in the summer season, and where the glacial period of the winter continues but for a short time, we find that here and there on the high mountains the snow endures throughout most of the summer, but that all parts of the surface have a season when life springs into activity. On the top of Mount Washington, in the White Mountains of New Hampshire, in a cleft known as Tuckerman's Ravine, where the deposit accumulates to a great depth, the snow-ice remains until midsummer. It is, indeed, evident that a very slight change in the climatal conditions of this locality would establish a permanent accumulation of frozen water upon the summit of the mountain. If the crest were lifted a thousand feet higher, without any general change in the heat or rainfall of the district, this effect would be produced. If with the same amount of rainfall as now comes to the earth in that region more of it fell as snow, a like condition would be established. Furthermore, with an increase of rainfall to something like double that which now descends the snow bore the same proportion to the precipitation which it does at present, we should almost certainly have the peak above the permanent snow line, that level below which all the winter's fall melts away. These propositions are stated with some care, for the reason that the student should perceive how delicate may be—indeed, commonly is—the balance of forces which make the difference between a seasonal and a perennial snow covering.

As soon as the snow outlasts the summer, the region which it occupies is sterilized to life. From the time the snow begins to hold over the warm period until it finally disappears, that field has to be reckoned out of the habitable earth, not only to man, but to the lowliest organisms.*

If the snow in a glaciated region lay where it fell, the result would be a constant elevation of the deposit year by year in proportion to the annual excess of deposition over the melting or evaporation of the material. But no sooner does the deposit attain any considerable thickness than it begins to move in the directions of least resistance, in accordance with laws which the students of glaciers are just beginning to discern. In small part this motion is accomplished by avalanches or snow slides, phenomena which are in a way important, and therefore merit description.

---

* In certain fields of permanent snow, particularly near their boundaries, some very lowly forms of vegetable life may develop on a frozen surface, drawing their sustenance from the air, and supplied with water by the melting which takes place during the summer time. These forms include the rare phenomenon termed red snow.

Immediately after a heavy snowfall, in regions where the
slopes are steep, it often happens that the deposit which
at first clung to the surface on which it lay becomes so
heavy that it tends to slide down the slope; a trifling
action, the slipping, indeed, of a single flake, may begin
the movement, which at first is gradual and only involves
a little of the snow. Gathering velocity, and with the
materials heaped together from the junction of that already
in motion with that about to be moved, the avalanche in
sliding a few hundred feet down the slope may become
a deep stream of snow-ice, moving with great celerity.
At this stage it begins to break off masses of ice from the
glaciers over which it may flow, or even to move large
stones. Armed with these, it rends the underlying earth.
After it has flowed a mile it may have taken up so much
earth and material that it appears like a river of mud.
Owing to the fact that the energy which bears it downward
is through friction converted into heat, a partial melting of
the mass may take place, which converts it into what we
call slush, or a mixture of snow and water. Finally, the
torrent is precipitated into the bottom of a valley, where
in time the frozen water melts away, leaving only the stony
matter which it bore as a monument to show the termination of its flow.

It was the good fortune of the writer to see in the Swiss
Oberland one very great avalanche, which came from the
high country through a descent of several thousand feet to
the surface of the Upper Grindelwald Glacier. The first
sign of the action was a vague tremor of the air, like that
of a great organ pipe when it begins to vibrate, but before
the pulsations come swiftly enough to make an audible
note. It was impossible to tell when this tremor came, but
the wary guide, noting it before his charge could perceive
anything unusual, made haste for the middle of the glacier. The vibration swelled to a roar, but the seat of the
sound amid the echoing cliffs was indeterminable. Finally,
from a valley high up on the southern face of the glacier,

there leaped forth first a great stone, which sprang with successive rebounds to the floor of ice. Then in succession other stones and masses of ice which had outrun the flood came thicker and thicker, until at the end of about thirty seconds the steep front of the avalanche appeared like a swift-moving wall. Attaining the cliffs, it shot forth as a great cataract, which during the continuance of the flow—which lasted for several minutes—heaped a great mound of commingled stones and ice upon the surface of the glacier. The mass thus brought down the steep was estimated at about three thousand cubic yards, of which probably the fiftieth part was rock material. An avalanche of this volume is unusual, and the proportion of stony matter borne down exceptionally great; but by these sudden motions of the frozen water a large part of the snow deposited above the zone of complete melting is taken to the lower valleys, where it may disappear in the summer season, and much of the erosion accomplished in the mountains is brought about by these falls.

In all Alpine regions avalanches are among the most dreaded accidents. Their occurrence, however, being dependent upon the shape of the surface, it is generally possible to determine in an accurate way the liability of their happening in any particular field. The Swiss take precaution to protect themselves from their ravages as other folk do to procure immunity from floods. Thus the authorities of many of the mountain hamlets maintain extensive forests on the sides of the villages whence the downfall may be expected, experience having shown that there is no other means so well calculated to break the blow which these great snowfalls can deliver, as thick-set trees which, though they are broken down for some distance, gradually arrest the stream.

As long as the region occupied by permanent snow is limited to sharp mountain peaks, relief by the precipitation of large masses to the level below the snow line is easily accomplished, but manifestly this kind of a discharge can

only be effective from a very small field. Where the relief
is not brought about by these tumbles of snow, another
mode of gravitative action accomplishes the result, though
in a more roundabout way, through the mechanism of
glaciers.

We have already noted the fact that the winter's snow
upon our hillsides undergoes a movement in the direction
of the slope. What we have now to describe in a rather
long story concerning glaciers rests upon movements of the
same nature, though they are in certain features peculiarly
dependent on the continuity of the action from year to
year. It is desirable, however, that the student should see
that there is at the foundation no more mystery in glacial
motion than there is in the gradual descent of the snow
after it has lain a week on a hillside. It is only in the scale
and continuity of the action that the greatest glacial envelope exceeds those of our temporary winters—in fact,
whenever the snow falls the earth it covers enters upon an
ice period which differs only in degree from that from
which our hemisphere is just escaping.

Where the reader is so fortunate as to be able to visit
a region of glaciers, he had best begin his study of their
majestic phenomena by ascending to those upper realms
where the snow accumulates from year to year. He will
there find the natural irregularities of the rock surface in a
measure evened over by a vast sheet of snow, from which
only the summits of the greater mountains rise. He may
soon satisfy himself that this sheet is of great depth, for
here and there it is intersected by profound crevices. If
the visit is made in the season when snow falls, which is
commonly during most of the year, he may observe, as
before noted in our winter's snow, that the deposit, though
at first flaky, attains at a short distance below the surface
a somewhat granular character, though the shotlike grains
fall apart when disturbed. Yet deeper, ordinarily a few
feet below the surface, these granules are more or less
cemented together; the mass thus loses the quality of

snow, and begins to appear like a whitish ice. Looking down one of the crevices, where the light penetrates to the depth of a hundred feet or more, he may see that the bluish hue somewhat increases with the depth. A trace of this colour is often visible even in the surface snow on the glacier, and sometimes also in our ordinary winter fields. In a hole made with a stick a foot or more in depth a faint cerulean glimmer may generally be discerned; but the increased blueness of the ice as we go down is conspicuous, and readily leads us to the conclusion that the air, to which, as we before noted, the whiteness of the snow is due, is working out of the mass as the process of compaction goes on. In a glacial district this snow mass above the melting line is called the *névé*.

Remembering that the excess of snow beyond the melting in a *névé* district amounts, it may be, to some feet of material each year, we easily come to the conclusion that the mass works down the slope in the manner which it does even where the coating is impermanent. This supposition is easily confirmed: by observing the field we find that the sheet is everywhere drawing away from the cliffs, leaving a deep fissure between the *névé* and the precipices. This crevice is called by the German-Swiss guides the *Bergschrund*. Passage over it is often one of the most difficult feats to accomplish which the Alpine explorer has to undertake. In fact, the very appearance of the surface, which is that of a river with continuous down slopes, is sufficient evidence that the mass is slowly flowing toward the valleys. Following it down, we almost always come to a place where it passes from the upper valleys to the deeper gorges which pierce the skirts of the mountain. In going over this projection the mass of snow-ice breaks to pieces, forming a crowd of blocks which march down the slope with much more speed than they journeyed when united in the higher-lying fields. In this condition and in this part of the movement the snow-ice forms what are called the *seracs*, or curds, as the word means in the French-Swiss dialect. Slipping and tumbling down the steep slope on which the *seracs* develop, the ice becomes broken into bits, often of small size. These fragments are quickly reknit into the body of ice, which we shall hereafter term the glacier, and in this process the expulsion of the air goes on more rapidly than before, and the mass assumes a more transparent icelike quality.

The action of the ice in the pressures and strains to which it is subjected in joining the main glacier and in the further part of its course demand for their understanding a revision of those notions as to rigidity and plasticity which we derive from our common experience with objects. It is hard to believe that ice can be moulded by pressure into any shape without fracturing, provided the motion is slowly effected, while at the same time it is as brittle as ice to a sudden blow. We see, however, a similar instance of contrasted properties in the confection known as molasses candy, a stick of which may be indefinitely bent if the flexure is slowly made, but will fly to pieces like glass if sharply struck. Ice differs from the sugary substance in many ways; especially we should note that while it may be squeezed into any form, it can not be drawn out, but fractures on the application of a very slight tension. The conditions of its movement we will inquire into further on, when we have seen more of its action.

Entering on the lower part of its course, that where it flows into the region below the snow line, the ice stream is now confined between the walls of the valley, a channel which in most cases has been shaped before the ice time, by a mountain torrent, or perhaps by a slower flowing river. In this part of its course the likeness of a glacial stream to one of fluid water is manifest. We see that it twists with the turn of the gorge, widens where the confining walls are far apart, and narrows where the space is constricted. Although the surface is here and there broken by fractures, it is evident that the movement of the frozen current, though slow, is tolerably free. By placing stakes

15

in a row across the axis of a glacier, and observing their movement from day to day, or even from hour to hour if a good theodolite is used for the purpose, we note that the movement of the stream is fastest in the middle parts, as in the case of a river, and that it slows toward either shore, though it often happens, as in a stream of molten water, that the speediest part of the current is near one side. Further observations have indicated that the movement is most rapid on the surface and least at the bottom, in which the stream is also riverlike. It is evident, in a word, that though the ice is not fluid in strict sense, the bits of which it is made up move in substantially the manner of fluids— that is, they freely slip over each other. We will now turn our attention to some important features of a detailed sort which glaciers exhibit.

If we visit a glacier during the part of the year when the winter snows are upon it, it may appear to have a very uninterrupted surface. But as the summer heat advances, the mask of the winter coating goes away, and we may then see the structure of the ice. First of all we note in all valley glaciers such as we are observing that the stream is overlaid by a quantity of rocky waste, the greater part of which has come down with the avalanches in the manner before described, though a small part may have been worn from the bed over which the ice flows. In many glaciers, particularly as we approach their termination, this sheet of earth and rock materials often covers the ice so completely that the novice in such regions finds it difficult to believe that the ice is under his feet. If the explorer is minded to take the rough scramble, he can often walk for miles on these masses of stone without seeing, much less setting foot on any frozen water. In some of the Alaskan glaciers this coating may bear a forest growth. In general, this material, which is called moraine, is distributed in bands parallel to the sides of the glaciers, and the strips may amount to a half dozen or more. Those on the sides of the ice have evidently been derived from the

precipices which they have passed. Those in the middle
have arisen from the union of the moraines formed in two
or more tributary valleys.

Where the avalanches fall most plentifully, the stones
lie buried with the snow, and only melt out when the
stream attains the region where the annual waste of its
surface exceeds the snowfall. In this section we can see
how the progressive melting gradually brings the rocky
débris into plain view. Here and there we will find a
boulder perched on a pedestal of ice, which indicates a

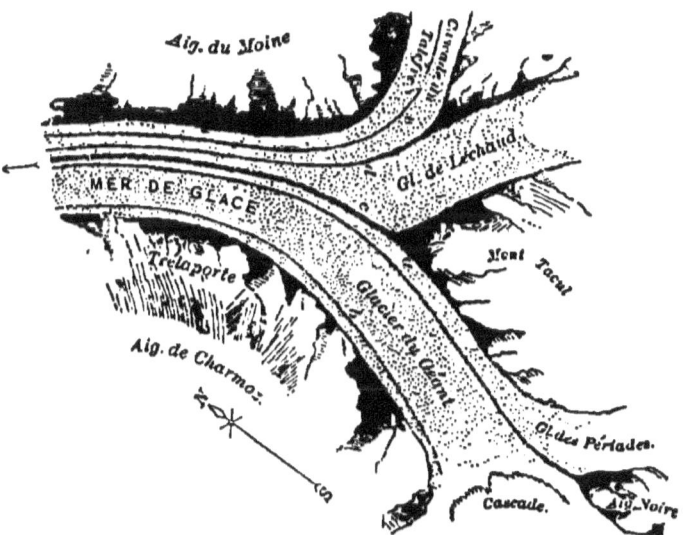

Fig. 12.—Map of glaciers and moraines near Mont Blanc.

recent down-wearing of the field. A frequent sound in
these regions arises from the tumble of the stones from
their pedestals or the slipping of the masses from the sharp
ridge which is formed by the protection given to the ice
through the thick coating of detritus on its surface.
These movements of the moraines often distribute their
waste over the glacier, so that in its lower part we can no

longer trace the contributions from the several valleys, the whole area being covered by the *débris*. At the end of the ice stream, where its forward motion is finally overcome by the warmth which it encounters, it leaves in a rude heap, extending often like a wall across the valley, all the coarse fragments which it conveys. This accumulation, composed of all the lateral moraines which have gathered on the ice by the fall of avalanches, is called the terminal moraine. As the ice stream itself shrinks, a portion of the detritus next the boundary wall is apt to be left clinging against those slopes. It is from the presence of these heaps in valleys now abandoned by glaciers that we obtain some information as to the former greater extent of glacial action.

The next most noticeable feature is the crevasse. These fractures often exist in very great numbers, and constitute a formidable barrier in the explorer's way. The greater part of these ruptures below the *serac* zone run from the sides of the stream toward the centre without attaining that region. These are commonly pointed up stream; their formation is due to the fact that, owing to the swifter motion in the central parts of the stream, the ice in that section draws away from the material which is moving more slowly next the shore. As before noted, these ice fractures when drawn out naturally form fissures at right angles to the direction of the strain. In the middle portions of the ice other fissures form, though more rarely, which appear to depend on local strains brought about through the irregularity of the surface over which the ice is flowing.

If the observer is fortunate, he may in his journey over the glacier have a chance to see and hear what goes on when crevasses are formed. First he will hear a deep, booming sound beneath his feet, which merges into a more splintering note as the crevice, which begins at the bottom or in the distance, comes upward or toward him. When the sound is over, he may not be able to see a trace of the fracture, which at first is very narrow. But if the break intersect any of the numerous shallow pools which in a warm summer's day are apt to cover a large part of the surface, he may note a line of bubbles rushing up through the water, marking the escape of the air from the glacier, some remnant of that which is imprisoned in the original snow. Even where this indication is wanting, he can sometimes trace the crevice by the hissing sound of the air streams where they issue from the ice. If he will take time to note what goes on, he can usually in an hour or two behold the first invisible crack widen until it may be half an inch across. He may see how the surface water hastens down the opening, a little river system being developed on the surface of the ice as the streams make their way to one or more points of descent. In doing this work they excavate a shaft which often becomes many feet in diameter, down which their waters thunder to the base of the glacier. This well-like opening is called a *moulin*, or mill, a name which, as we shall see, is well deserved from the work which falling waters accomplish. Although the institution of the *moulin* shaft depends upon the formation of a crevice, it often happens that as the ice moves farther on its journey its walls are again thrust together, soldered in the manner peculiar to ice, so that no trace of the rupture remains except the shaft which it permitted to form. Like everything else in the glacier, the *moulin* slowly moves down the slope, and remains open as long as it is the seat of descending waters produced by the summer melting. When it ceases to be kept open from the summer, its walls are squeezed together in the fashion that the crevices are closed.

Forming here and there, and generally in considerable numbers, the crevices of a glacier entrap a good deal of the morainal *débris*, which falls through them to the bottom of the glacier. Smaller bits are washed into the *moulin* by the streams arising from the melting ice, which is brought about by the warm sun of the summer, and particularly by the warm rains of that season. On those glaciers where, owing to the irregularity of the bottom over which the ice flows, these fractures are very numerous, it may happen that all the detritus brought upon the surface of the glacier by avalanches finds its way to the floor of the ice.

Although it is difficult to learn what is going on at the under surface of the glacier, it is possible directly and indirectly to ascertain much concerning the peculiar and important work which is there done. The intrepid explorer may work his way in through the lateral fissures, and even with care safely descend some of the fissures which penetrate the central parts of a shallow ice stream. There, it may be at the depth of a hundred feet or more, he will find a quantity of stones, some of which may be in size like to a small house held in the body of the ice, but with one side resting upon the bed rock. He may be so fortunate as to see the stone actually in process of cutting a groove in the bed rock as it is urged forward by the motion of the glacier. The cutting is not altogether in the fixed material, for the boulder itself is also worn and scored in the work. Smaller pebbles are caught in the space between the erratic and the motionless rock and ground to bits. If in his explorations the student finds his way to the part of the floor on which the waters of a *moulin* fall, he may have a chance to observe how the stones set in motion serve to cut the bed rock, forming elongated potholes much as in the case of ordinary waterfalls, or at the base of those shafts which afford the beginnings of limestone caverns.

The best way to penetrate beneath the glacier is through the arch of the stream which always flows from the terminal face of the ice river. Even in winter time every large glacier discharges at its end a considerable brook, the waters of which have been melted from the ice in small part by the outflow of the earth's heat; mainly, however, by the warmth produced in the friction of the ice on itself and on its bottom—in other words, by the conversion of that energy of position, of which we have often to speak, into heat. In the summer time this subglacial stream is swollen by the surface waters descending through the crevices and the *moulins* which come from them, so that the outflow often forms a considerable river, and thus excavates in the ice a large or at least a long cavern, the base of which is the bed rock. In the autumn, when the superficial melting ceases, this gallery can often be penetrated for a considerable distance, and affords an excellent way to the secrets of the under ice. The observer may here see quantities of the rock material held in the grip of the ice, and forced to a rude journey over the bare foundation stones. Now and then he may find the glacial mass in large measure made up of stones, the admixture extending many feet above the bottom of the cavern, perhaps to the very top of the arch. He may perchance find that these stones are crushing each other where they are in contact. The result will be brought about by the difference in the rate of advance of the ice, which moves the faster the higher it is above the surface over which it drags, and thus forces the stones on one level over those below. Where the waters of the subglacial stream have swept the bed rock clean of *débris* its surface is scored, grooved, and here and there polished in a manner which is accomplished only by ice action, though some likeness to it is afforded where stones have been swept over for ages by blowing sand. Here and there, often in a way which interrupts the cavern journey, the shrunken stream, unable to carry forward the *débris*, deposits the material in the chamber, sometimes filling the arch so completely that the waters are forced to make a detour. This action is particularly interesting, for the reason that in regions whence glaciers have disappeared the deposits formed in the old ice arches often afford singularly perfect moulds of those caverns which were produced by the ancient subglacial streams. These moulds are termed *eskers*.

If the observer be attentive, he will note the fact that the waters emerging from beneath the considerable glacier are very much charged with mud. If he will take a glass of the water at the point of escape, he will often find, on permitting it to settle, that the sediment amounts to as much as one twentieth of the volume. While the greater part of this detritus will descend to the bottom of the vessel in the course of a day, a portion of it does not thus fall. He may also note that this mud is not of the yellowish hue which he is accustomed to behold in the materials laid down by ordinary rivers, but has a whitish colour. Further study will reveal the fact that the difference is due to the lack of oxidation in the case of the glacial detritus. River muds forming slowly and during long-continued exposure to the action of the air have their contained iron much oxidized, which gives them a part of their darkened appearance. Moreover, they are somewhat coloured with decayed vegetable matter. The waste from beneath the glacier has been quickly separated from the bed rock, all the faces of the grains are freshly fractured, and there is no admixture of organic matter. The faces of the particles thus reflect light in substantially the same way as powdered glass or pulverized ice, and consequently appear white.

A little observation will show the student that this very muddy character of waters emerging from beneath the glacier is essentially peculiar to such streams as we have described. Ascending any of the principal valleys of Switzerland, he may note that some of the streams flow waters which carry little sediment even in times when they are much swollen, while others at all seasons have the whitish colour. A little further exploration, or the use of a good map, will show him that the pellucid streams receive no contributions of glacial water, while those which look as if they were charged with milk come, in part at least, from the ice arches. From some studies which the writer has made in Swiss valleys, it appears that the amount of erosion accomplished on equal areas of similar rock by the descent of the waters in the form of a glacier or in that of ordinary torrents differs greatly. Moving in the form of ice, or in the state of ice-confined streams, the mass of water applies very many times as much of its energy of position to grinding and bearing away the rocks as is accomplished where the water descends in its fluid state.

The effect of the intense ice action above noted is rapidly to wear away the rocks of the valley in which the glacier is situated. This work is done not only in a larger measure but in a different way from that accomplished by torrents. In the case of the latter, the stream bed is embarrassed by the rubbish which comes into it; only here and there can it attack the bed rock by forcing the stones over its surface. Only in a few days of heavy rain each year is its work at all effective; the greater part of the energy of position of its waters is expended in the endless twistings and turnings of its stream, which result only in the development of heat which flies away into the atmosphere. In the ice stream, owing to its slow movement and to the detritus which it forces along the bottom, a vastly greater part of the energy which impels it down the slope is applied to rock cutting. None of the boulders, even if they are yards in diameter, obstruct its motion; small and great alike are to it good instruments wherewith to attack the bed rocks. The fragments are never left to waste by atmospheric decay, but are to a very great extent used up in mechanical work, while the most of the detritus which comes to a torrent is left in a coarse state when it is delivered to the stream; the larger part of that which the glacier transports is worn out in its journey. To a great extent it is used up in attacking the bed rock. In most cases the *débris* in the terminal moraine is evidently but a small part of what entered the ice during its journey from the uplands; the greater part has been worn out in the rude experiences to which it has been subjected.

It is evident that even in the regions now most extensively occupied by glaciers the drainage systems have been shaped by the movement of ordinary streams—in other words, ice action is almost everywhere, even in the regions about the poles, an incidental feature in the work of water, coming in only to modify the topography, which is mainly moulded by the action of fluid water. When, owing to climatal changes, a valley such as those of the Alps is occupied by a glacial stream, the new current proceeds at once, according to its evident needs, to modify the shape of its channel. An ordinary torrent, because of the swiftness of its motion, which may, in general, be estimated at from three to five miles an hour, can convey away the precipitation over a very narrow bed. Therefore its channel is usually not a hundredth part as wide as the gorge or valley in which it lies. But when the discharge takes place by a glacier, the speed of which rarely exceeds four or five feet a day, the ice stream because of its slow motion has to fill the trough from side to side, it has to be some thousand times as deep and wide as the torrent. The result is that as soon as the glacial condition arises in a country the ice streams proceed to change the old V-shaped torrent beds into those which have a broad U-like form. The practised eye can in a way judge how long a valley has been subjected to glacial action by the extent to which it has been widened by this process.

In the valleys of Switzerland and other mountain districts which have been attentively studied it is evident that glacial action has played a considerable part in determining their forms. But the work has been limited to that part of the basin in which the ice is abundantly provided with cutting tools in the stone which have found their way to the base of the stream. In the region of the *névé*, where the contributions of rocky matter to the surface of the deposit made from the few bare cliffs which rise above the sheet of snow is small, the snow-ice does no cutting of any consequence. Where it passes over the steep at the head of the deep valley into which it drains, and is riven into the *seracs*, such stony matter as it may have gathered is allowed to fall to the bottom, and so comes into a position where it may do effective work. From this *serac* section downward the now distinct ice river, being in general below the snow line, has everywhere cliffs, on either side from which the contributions of rock material are abundant. Hence this part of the glacier, though it is the wasting portion of its length, does all the cutting work of any consequence which is performed. It is there that the underrunning streams become charged with sediment, which, as we have noted, they bear in surprising quantities, and it is therefore in this section of the valley that the impress of the ice work is the strongest. Its effect is not only to widen the valley and deepen it, but also to advance the deep section farther up the stream and its tributaries. The step in the stream beds which we find at the *seracs* appears to mark the point in the course of the glacier where, owing to the falling of stones to its base, as well as to its swifter movements and the firmer state of the ice, it does effective wearing.

There are many other features connected with glaciers which richly repay the study of those who have a mind to explore in the manner of the physicist interested in ice actions the difficult problems which they afford; but as these matters are not important from the point of view of this work, no mention of them will here be made. We will now turn our attention to that other group of glaciers commonly termed continental, which now exist about either pole, and which at various times in the earth's history have extended far toward the equator, mantling over vast extents of land and shallow sea. The difference between the ice streams of the mountains and those which we term continental depends solely on the areas of the fields and the depth of the accumulation. In an ordinary Alpine region the *névé* districts, where the snow gathers, are relatively small. Owing to the rather steep slopes, the frozen water is rapidly discharged into the lower valleys, where it melts away. Both in the *névé* and in the distinct glacier of the lower grounds there are, particularly in the latter, projecting peaks, from which quantities of stone are brought down by avalanches or in ordinary rock falls, so that the ice is abundantly supplied with cutting tools, which work from its surface down to its depths.

As the glacial accumulation grows in depth there are fewer peaks emerging from it, and the streams which it feeds rise the higher until they mantle over the divides between the valleys. Thus by imperceptible stages valley glaciers pass to the larger form, usually but incorrectly termed continental. We can, indeed, in going from the mountains in the tropics to the poles, note every step in this transition, until in Greenland we attain the greatest ice mass in the world, unless that about the southern pole be more extensive. In the Greenland glacier the ice sheet covers a vast extent of what is probably a mountain country, which is certainly of this nature in the southern part of the island, where alone we find portions of the earth not completely covered by the deep envelope. Thanks to the labours of certain hardy explorers, among whom Nansen deserves the foremost place, we now know something as to the conditions of this vast ice field, for it has been crossed from shore to shore. The results of these studies are most interesting, for they afford us a clew as to the conditions which prevail over a large part of the earth during the Glacial period from which the planet is just escaping, and in the earlier ages when glaciation was likewise extensive. We shall therefore consider in a somewhat detailed way the features which the Greenland glacier presents.

Starting from the eastern shore of that land, if we may thus term a region which presents itself mainly in the form of ice, we find next the shore a coast line not completely covered with ice and snow, but here and there exhibiting peaks which indicate that if the frozen mantle were removed the country would appear deeply intersected with fiords in the manner exhibited in the regions to the south of Greenland or the Scandinavian peninsula. The ice

comes down to the sea through the valleys, often facing
the ocean for great distances with its frozen cliffs. Entering on this seaward portion of the glacier, the observer finds that for some distance from the coast line the
ice is more or less rifted with crevices, the formation of
which is doubtless due to irregularities of the rock bottom
over which it moves. These ruptures are so frequent that
for some miles back it is very difficult to find a safe way.
Finally, however, a point is attained where these breaks
rather suddenly disappear, and thence inward the ice rises
at the rate of upward slope of a few feet to the mile in a
broad, nearly smooth incline. In the central portion of
the region for a considerable part of the territory the ice
has very little slope. Thence it declines toward the other
shore, exhibiting the same features as were found on the
eastern versant until near the coast, when again the surface is beset with crevices which continue to the margin
of the sea.

Although the explorations of the central field of Greenland are as yet incomplete, several of these excursions into
or across the interior have been made, and the identity
of the observations is such that we can safely assume the
whole region to be of one type. We can furthermore run
no risk in assuming that what we find in Greenland. at
least so far as the unbroken nature of the central ice field
is concerned, is what must exist in every land where the
glacial envelope becomes very deep. In Greenland it seems
likely that the depth of the ice is on the average more
than half a mile, and in the central part of the realm the
sheet may well have a much greater profundity; it may be
nearly a mile deep. The most striking feature—that of a
vast unbroken expanse, bordered by a region where the ice
is ruptured—is traceable wherever very extensive and presumably deep deposits of ice have been examined. As
we shall see hereafter, these features teach us much as to
the conditions of glacial action—a matter which we shall
have to examine after we have completed our general

survey as to the changes which occur during glacial periods.

In the present state of that wonderful complex of actions which we term climate, glaciers are everywhere, so far as our observations enable us to judge, generally in process of decrease. In Switzerland, although the ancients even in Roman days were in contact with the ice, they were so unobservant that they did not even remark that the ice was in motion. Only during the last two centuries have we any observations of a historic sort which are of value to the geologist. Fortunately, however, the signs written on the rock tell the story, except for its measurement in terms of years, as clearly as any records could give it. From this testimony of the rocks we perceive that in the geological yesterday, though it may have been some tens of thousands of years ago, the Swiss glaciers. vastly thickened, and with their horizontal area immensely expanded, stretched over the Alpine country, so that only here and there did any of the sharper peaks rise above the surface. These vast glaciers, almost continually united on their margins, extended so far that every portion of what is now the Swiss Republic was covered by them. Their front lay on the southern lowlands of Germany, on the Jura district of France; on the south, it stretched across the valley of the Po as far as near Milan. We know this old ice front by the accumulations of rock *débris* which were brought to it from the interior of the mountain realm. We can recognise the peculiar kinds of stone, and with perfect certainty trace them to the bed rock whence they were riven. Moreover, we can follow back through the same evidence the stages of retreat of the glaciers, until they lost their broad continental character and assumed something like their present valley form. Up the valley of any of the great rivers, as, for instance, that of the Rhône above the lake of Geneva, we note successive terminal moraines which clearly indicate stages in the retreat of the ice when for a time it ceased to go backward, or even made a slight temporary

readvance. It is easily seen that on such occasions the
stones carried to the ice front would be accumulated in a
heap, while during the time when day by day the glacier
was retreating the rock waste would be left broadcast over
the valley.

As we go up from the course of the glacial streams we
note that the successive moraines have their materials in
a progressively less decayed state. Far away from the heap
now forming, and in proportion to the distance, the stones
have in a measure rotted, and the heaps which they compose are often covered with soil and occupied by forests.
Within a few miles of the ice front the stones still have
a fresh aspect. When we arrive within, say, half a mile
of the moraine now building, we come to the part of the
glacial retreat of which we have some written or traditional account. This is in general to the effect that the
wasting of the glaciers is going on in this century as it
went on in the past. Occasionally periods of heavy snow
would refresh the ice streams, so that for a little time they
pushed their fronts farther down the valley. The writer
has seen during one of these temporary advances the interesting spectacle of ice destroying and overturning the soil
of a small field which had been planted in grain.

It should be noted that these temporary advances of the
ice are not due to the snowfall of the winter or winters immediately preceding the forward movement. So slow is the
journey of the ice from the *névé* field to the end of a long
glacier that it may require centuries for the store accumulated in the uplands to affect the terminal portion of the
stream. We know that the bodies of the unhappy men
who have been lost in the crevices of the glacier are borne
forward at a uniform and tolerably computable rate until
they emerge at the front, where the ice melts away. In
at least one case the remains have appeared after many
years in the *débris* which is contributed to the moraine. On
account of this slow feeding of the glacial stream, we naturally may expect to find, as we do, in fact, that a great

snowfall of many years ago, and likewise a period when the winter's contribution has been slight, would influence the position of the terminal point of the ice stream at different times, according to its length. If the length of the flow be five miles, it may require twenty or thirty years for the effect to be evident; while if the stream be ten miles long, the influence may not be noted in less than three-score years. Thus it comes about that at the present time in the same glacial district some streams may be advancing while others are receding, though, on the whole, the ice is generally in process of shrinkage. If the present rate of retreat should be maintained, it seems certain that at the end of three centuries the Swiss glaciers as a whole will not have anything like their present area, and many of the smaller streams will entirely disappear.

Following the method of the illustrious Louis Agassiz, who first attentively traced the evidence which shows the geologically recent great extension of glaciers by studying the evidence of the action in fields they no longer occupy, geologists have now inspected a large part of the land areas with a view to finding the proofs of such ice work. So far as these indications are concerned, the indications which they have had to trace are generally of a very unmistakable character. Rarely, indeed, does a skilled student of such phenomena have to search in any region for more than a day before he obtains indubitable evidence which will enable him to determine whether or not the field has recently been occupied by an enduring ice sheet—one which survives the summer season and therefore deserves the name of glacier. The indications which he has to consider consist in the direction and manner in which the surface materials have been carried, the physical conditions of these materials, the shape of the surface of the underlying rock as regards its general contour, and the presence or absence of scratches and groovings on its surface. As these records of ice action are of first importance in dealing with this problem, and as they afford excellent subjects for the study of those who dwell in glaciated regions, we shall note them in some detail.

The geologist recognises several ways in which materials may be transported on the surface of the earth. They may be cast forth by volcanoes, making their journey by being shot through the air, or by flowing in lava streams; it is always easy at a glance, save in very rare instances, to determine whether fragments have thus been conveyed. Again, the detritus may be moved by the wind; this action is limited; it only affects dust, sand, and very small pebbles, and is easily discriminated. The carriage may be effected by river or marine currents; here, again, the size of the fragments moved is small, and the order of their arrangement distinctly traceable. The fragments may be conveyed by ice rafts; here, too, the observer can usually limit the probabilities he has to consider by ascertaining, as he can generally do, whether the region which he is observing has been below a sea or lake. In a word, the before-mentioned agents of transportation are of somewhat exceptional influence, and in most cases can, as explanations of rock transportation, be readily excluded. When, therefore, the geologist finds a country abundantly covered with sand, pebbles, and boulders arranged in an irregular way, he has generally only to inquire whether the material has been carried by rivers or by glaciers. This discrimination can be quickly and critically effected. In the first place, he notes that rivers only in their torrent sections can carry large fragments of rock, and that in all cases the fragments move down hill. Further, that where deposits are formed, they have more or less the form of alluvial deposits. If now the observations show that the rock waste occupying the surface of any region has been carried up hill and down, across the valleys, particularly if there are here and there traces of frontal moraines, the geologist is entitled to suppose—he may, indeed, be sure—that the carriage has been effected by a glacial sheet.

Important corroborative evidence of ice action is gen-
16

erally to be found by inspecting the bed rock below the detritus, which indicates glacial action. Even if it be somewhat decayed, as is apt to be the case where the ice sheet long since passed away, the bed rock is likely to have a warped surface; it is cast into ridges and furrows of a broad, flowing aspect, such as liquid water never produces, which, indeed, can only be created by an ice sheet moving over the surface, cutting its bed in proportion to the hardness of the material. Furthermore, if the bed rock have a firm texture, and be not too much decayed, we almost always find upon it grooves or scratches, channels carved by the stones embedded in the body of the ice, and drawn by its motion over the fixed material. Thus the proof of glacial extension in the last ice epoch is made so clear that accurate maps can be prepared showing the realm of its action. This task is as yet incomplete, although it is already far advanced.

While the study of glaciers began in Europe, inquiries concerning their ancient extension have been carried further and with more accuracy in North America than in any other part of the world. We may therefore well begin our description of the limits of the ice sheets with this continent. Imagining a seafarer to have approached America by the North Atlantic, as did the Scandinavians, and that his voyage came perhaps a hundred thousand years or more before that of Leif Ericsson, he would have found an ice front long before he attained the present shores of the land. This front may have extended from south of Greenland, off the shores of the present Grand Banks of Newfoundland, thence and westward to central or southern New Jersey. This cliff of ice was formed by a sheet which lay on the bottom of the sea. On the New Jersey coast the ice wall left the sea and entered on the body of the continent. We will now suppose that the explorer, animated with the valiant scientific spirit which leads the men of our day to seek the poles, undertook a land journey along the ice front across the continent. From the New Jersey coast the traveller would have passed through central Pennsylvania, where, although there probably detached outlying glaciers lying to the southward as far as central Virginia, the main front extended westward into the Ohio Valley. In southern Ohio a tongue of the ice projected southwardly until it crossed the Ohio River, where Cincinnati now lies, extending a few miles to the southward of the stream. Thence it deflected northwardly, crossing the Mississippi, and again the Missouri, with a tongue or lobe which went far southward in that State. Then again turning to the northwest, it followed in general the northern part of the Missouri basin until it came to within sight of the Rocky Mountains. There the ice front of the main glacier followed the trend of the mountains at some distance from their face for an unknown extent to the northward. In the Cordilleras, as far south as southern Colorado, and probably in the Sierra Nevada to south of San Francisco, the mountain centres developed local glaciers, which in some places were of very great size, perhaps exceeding any of those which now exist in Switzerland. It will thus be seen that nearly one half of the present land area of North America was beneath a glacial covering, though, as before noted, the region about the Gulf of Mexico may have swayed upward when the northern portion of the land was borne down by the vast load of ice which rested upon it. Notwithstanding this possible addition to the land, our imaginary explorer would have found the portion of the continent fit for the occupancy of life not more than half as great as it is at present.

In the Eurasian continent there was no such continuous ice sheet as in North America, but the glaciers developed from a number of different centres, each moving out upon the lowlands, or, if its position was southern, being limited to a particular mountain field. One of these centres included Scandinavia, northern Germany, Great Britain about as far south as London, and a large part of Ireland, the ice covering the intermediate seas and extending to

the westward, so that the passage of the North Atlantic
was greatly restricted between this ice front and that of
North America. Another centre, before noted, was formed
in the Alps; yet another, of considerable area, in the
Pyrenees; other less studied fields existed in the Apennines, in the Caucasus, the Ural, and the other mountains of northern Asia. Curiously enough, however, the
great region of plains in Siberia does not appear to have
been occupied by a continuous ice sheet, though the similar region in North America was deeply embedded in a
glacier.   Coincident with this development of ice in the
eastern part of the continent, the ice streams of the Hima-
layan Mountains, some of which are among the greatest
of our upland glaciers, appear to have undergone but a
moderate extension. Many other of the Eurasian highlands were probably ice-bound during the last Glacial
period, but our knowledge concerning these local fields
is as yet imperfect.

In the southern hemisphere the lands are of less extent
and, on the whole, less studied than in the northern realm.
Here and there where glaciers exist, as in New Zealand
and in the southern part of South America, observant trav-
ellers have noticed that these ice fields have recently shrunk
away. Whether the time of greatest extension and of retreat coincided with that of the ice sheets in the north
is not yet determined; the problem, indeed, is one of some
difficulty, and may long remain undecided. It seems,
however, probable that the glaciers of the southern hemisphere, like those in the north, are in process of retreat.
If this be true, then their time of greatest extension was
probably the same as that of the ice sheets about the southern pole. From certain imperfect reports which we have
concerning evidences of glaciation in Central America and
in the Andean district in the northern part of South
America, it seems possible that at one time the upland ice
along the Cordilleran chain existed from point to point
along that system of elevations, so that the widest interval

between the fields of permanent snow with their attendant glaciers did not much exceed a thousand miles.

Observing the present gradual retreat of those ice remnants which remain mere shreds and patches of the ancient fields, it seems at first sight likely that the extension and recession of the great glaciers took place with exceeding slowness. Measured in terms of human life, in the manner in which we gauge matters of man's history, this process was doubtless slow. There are reasons, however, to believe that the coming and going were, in a geological sense, swift; they may have, indeed, been for a part of the time of startling rapidity. Going back to the time of geological yesterday, before the ice began its development in the northern hemisphere, all the evidence we can find appears to indicate a temperate climate extending far toward the north pole. The Miocene deposits found within twelve degrees, or a little more than seven hundred miles, of the north pole, and fairly within the realm of lowest temperature which now exists on the earth, show by the plant remains which they contain that the conditions permitted the growth of forests, the plants having a tolerably close resemblance to those which now freely develop in the southern portion of the Mississippi Valley. Among them there are species which had the habit of retaining their broad, rather soft leaves throughout the winter season. The climate appears, in a word, to have been one where the mean annual temperature must have been thirty degrees or more higher than the present average of that realm. Although such conditions near the sea level are not inconsistent with the supposition that glaciers existed in the higher mountains of the north, they clearly deny the possibility of the realm being occupied by continental glaciers.

Although the Pliocene deposits formed in high latitudes have to a great extent been swept away by the subsequent glacial wearing, they indicate by their fossils a climatal change in the direction of greater cold. We trace this change, though obscurely, in a progressive manner to a point where the records are interrupted, and the next interpretable indication we have is that the ice sheet had extended to somewhere near the limits which we have noted. We are then driven to seek what we can concerning the sojourn of the ice on the land by the amount of wearing which it has inflicted upon the areas which it occupied. This evidence has a certain, though, as we shall see, a limited value.

When the students of glacial action first began the great task of interpreting these records, they were led to suppose that the amount of rock cutting which was done by the ice was very great. Observing what goes on, in the manner we have noted, beneath a valley glacier such as those of Switzerland, they saw that the ice work went on rapidly, and concluded that if the ice remained long at work in a region it must do a vast deal of erosion. They were right in a part of their premises, but, as we shall see, probably in another part wrong. Looking carefully over the field where the ice has operated, we note that, though at first sight the area appears to have lost all trace of its preglacial river topography, this aspect is due mainly to the irregular way in which the glacial waste is laid down. Close study shows us that we may generally trace the old stream valleys down to those which were no larger than brooks. It is true that these channels are generally and in many places almost altogether filled in with rubbish, but a close study of the question has convinced the writer, and this against a previous view, that the amount of erosion in New England and Canada, where the work was probably as great as anywhere. has not on the average exceeded a hundred feet, and probably was much less than that amount.

Even in the region north of Lake Ontario, over which the ice was deep and remained for a long time, the amount of erosion is singularly small. Thus north of Kingston the little valleys in the limestone rocks which were cut by the preglacial streams, though somewhat encumbered with drift, remain almost as distinct as they are on similar strata in central Kentucky, well south of the field which the ice occupied. In fact, the ice sheet appears to have done the greatest part of its work and to have affected the surface most in the belt of country a few hundred miles in width around the edges of the sheet. It was to be expected that in a continental glacier, as in those of mountain valleys, the most of the *débris* should be accumulated about the margin where the materials dropped from the ice. But why the cutting action should be greatest in that marginal field is not at first sight clear. To explain this and other features as best we may, we shall now consider the probable history of the great ice march in advance and retreat, and then take up the conditions which brought about its development and its disappearance.

Ice is in many ways the most remarkable substance with which the physicist has to deal, and among its eminent peculiarities is that it expands in freezing, while the rule is that substances contract in passing from the fluid to the solid state. On this account frozen water acts in a unique manner when subjected to pressure. For each additional atmosphere of pressure—a weight amounting to about fifteen pounds to the square inch—the temperature at which the ice will melt is lowered to the amount of sixteen thousandths of a degree centigrade. If we take a piece of ice at the temperature of freezing and put upon it a sufficient weight, we inevitably bring about a small amount of melting. Where we can examine the mass under favourable conditions, we can see the fluid gather along the lines of the crystals or other bits of which the ice is composed. We readily note this action by bringing two pieces of ice together with a slight pressure; when the pressure is removed, they will adhere. The adhesion is brought about not by any stickiness of the materials, for the substance has no such property. It is accomplished by melting along the line of contact, which forms a film of water, that at once refreezes when the pressure is withdrawn. When a firm snowball is made by even pressing snow, innumerable similar adhesions grow up in the manner described. The fact is that, given ice at the temperature at which it ordinarily forms, pressure upon it will necessarily develop melting.

The consequences of pressure melting as above described are in glaciers extremely complicated. Because the ice is built into the glacier at a temperature considerably below the freezing point, it requires a great thickness of the mass before the superincumbent weight is sufficient to bring about melting in its lower parts. If we knew the height at which a thermometer would have stood in the surface ice of the ancient glacier which covered the northern part of North America, we could with some accuracy compute how thick it must have been before the effect of pressure alone would have brought about melting; but even then we should have to reckon the temperature derived from the grinding of the ice over the floor and the crushing of rocks there effected, as well as the heat which is constantly though slowly coming forth from the earth's interior. The result is that we can only say that at some depth, probably less than a mile, the slowly accumulating ice would acquire such a temperature that, subjected to the weight above it, the material next the bottom would become molten, or at least converted into a sludgelike state, in which it could not rub against the bottom, or move stones in the manner of ordinary glaciers.

As fast as the ice assumed this liquid or softened state, it would be squeezed out toward the region where, because of the thinning of the glacier, it would enter a field where pressure melting did not occur. It would then resume the solid state, and thence journey to the margin of the ice in the ordinary manner. We thus can imagine how such a glacier as occupied the northern part of this continent could have moved from the central parts toward its periphery, as we can not do if we assume that the glacier everywhere lay upon the bed rock. There is no slope from Lake

Erie to the Ohio River at Cincinnati. Knowing that the ice moved down this line, there are but two methods of accounting for its motion: either the slope of the upper surface to the northward was so steep that the mass would have been thus urged down, the upper parts dragging the bottom along with them, or the ice sheet for the greater part of its extent rested upon pressure-molten water, or sludge ice, which was easily squeezed out toward the front. The first supposition appears inadmissible, for the reason that the ice would have to be many miles deep at Hudson Bay in order that its upper surface should have slope enough to overcome the rigidity of the material and bring about the movement. We know that any such depth is not supposable.

The recent studies in Greenland supply us with strong corroborative evidence for the support of the view which is here urged. The wide central field of that area, where the ice has an exceeding slight declivity, and is unruptured by crevices, can not be explained except on the supposition that it rests on pressure-molten water. The thinner section next the shore, where the glacier is broken up by those irregular movements which its wrestle with the bottom inevitably induces, shows that there it is in contact with the bed rock, for it behaves exactly as do the valley glaciers of like thickness.

The view above suggested as to the condition of continental glaciers enables us to explain not only their movements, but the relatively slight amount of wearing which they brought about on the lands they occupied. Beginning to develop in mountain regions, or near the poles on the lowlands, these sheets, as soon as they attained the thickness where the ice at their bottom became molten, would rapidly advance for great distances until they attained districts where the melting exceeded the supply of frozen material. In this excursion only the marginal portion of the glacier would do erosive work. This would evidently be continued for the greatest amount of time near the front or outer rim of the ice field, for there, we may presume, that for the longest time the cutting rim would rest upon the bed rock of the country. As the ice receded, this rim would fall back; thus in the retreat as in the advance the whole of the field would be subjected to a certain amount of erosion. On this supposition we should expect to find that the front of a continental glacier, fed with pressure-molten water from all its interior district, which became converted into ice, would attain much warmer regions than the valley streams, where all the flow took place in the state of ice, and, furthermore, that the speed of the going on the margin would be much more rapid than in the Alpine streams. These suppositions are well borne out by the study of existing continental ice sheets, which move with singular rapidity at their fronts, and by the ancient glaciers, which evidently extended into rather warm fields. Thus, when the ice front lay at the site of Cincinnati, at six hundred feet above the sea, there were no glaciers in the mountains of North Carolina, though those rise more than five thousand feet higher in the air, and are less than two hundred miles farther south. It is therefore evident that the continental glacier at this time pushed southward into a comparatively warm country in a way that no stream moving in the manner of a valley glacier could possibly have done.

The continental glaciers manage in many cases to convey detritus from a great distance. Thus, when the ice sheet advanced southwardly from the regions north of the Great Lakes, they conveyed quantities of the *débris* from that section as far south as the Ohio River. In part this rubbish was dragged forward by the ice as the sheet advanced; in part it was urged onward by the streams of liquid water formed by the ordinary process of ice melting. Such subglacial rivers appear to have been formed along the margins of all the great glaciers. We can sometimes trace their course by the excavation which they have made, but more commonly by the long ridges of stratified

Front of Muir Glacier, showing ice entering the sea; also small icebergs.

sand and gravel which were packed into the caverns excavated by these subglacial rivers, which are known to
glacialists as *eskers,* or as serpent kames. In many cases
we can trace where these streams flowed up stream in the
old river valleys until they discharged over their head
waters. Thus in the valley of the Genesee, which now flows
from Pennsylvania, where it heads against the tributaries of
the Ohio and Susquehanna, to Lake Ontario, there was
during the Glacial epoch a considerable river which discharged its waters into those of the Ohio and the Susquehanna over the falls at the head of its course.

The effect of widespread glacial action on a country
such as North America appears to have been, in the first
place, to disturb the attitude of the land by bearing down
portions of its surface, a process which led to the uprising
of other parts which lay beyond the realm of the ice.
Within the field of glaciation, so far as the ice rested bodily
on the surface, the rocks were rapidly worn away. A great
deal of the *débris* was ground to fine powder, and went far
with the waters of the under-running streams. A large
part was entangled in the ice, and moved forward toward
the front of the glacier, where it was either dropped at
the margin or, during the recession of the glacier, was
laid upon the surface as the ice melted away. The result
of this erosion and transportation has been to change the
conditions of the surface both as regards soil and drainage.
As the reader has doubtless perceived, ordinary soil is, outside of the river valleys, derived from the rock beneath
where it lies. In glaciated districts the material is commonly brought from a considerable distance, often from
miles away. These ice-made soils are rarely very fertile,
but they commonly have a great endurance for tillage, and
this for the reason that the earth is refreshed by the decay
of the pebbles which they contain. Moreover, while the
tillable earth of other regions usually has a limited depth,
verging downward into the semisoil or subsoil which represent the little changed bed rocks, glacial deposits can

generally be ploughed as deeply as may prove desirable.

The drainage of a country recently affected by glaciers is always imperfect. Owing to the irregular erosion of the bed rocks, and to the yet more irregular deposition of the detritus, there are very numerous lakes which are only slowly filled up or by erosion provided with drainage channels. Though several thousand years have passed by since the ice disappeared from North America, the greater part of the area of these fresh-water basins remains, the greater number of them, mostly those of small size, have become closed.

Where an ice stream descends into the sea or into a large lake, the depth of which is about as great as the ice is thick, the relative lightness of the ice tends to make it float, and it shortly breaks off from the parent mass, forming an iceberg. Where, as is generally the case in those glaciers which enter the ocean, a current sweeps by the place where the berg is formed, it may enter upon a journey which may carry the mass thousands of miles from its origin. The bergs separated from the Greenland glaciers, and from those about the south pole, are often of very great size; sometimes, indeed, they are some thousand feet in thickness, and have a length of several miles. It often happens that these bergs are formed of ice, which contains in its lower part a large amount of rock *débris.* As the submerged portion of the glacier melts in the sea water, these stones are gradually dropped to the bottom, so that the cargo of one berg may be strewed along a line many hundred miles in length. It occasionally happens that the ice mass melts more slowly in those parts which are in the air than in its under-water portions. It thus becomes top-heavy and overturns, in which case such stony matter as remains attains a position where it may be conveyed for a greater distance than if the glacier were not capsized. It is likely, indeed, that now and then fragments of rock from Greenland are dropped on the ocean floor in the part of the

Atlantic which is traversed by steamers between our Atlantic ports and Great Britain.

Except for the risks which they bring to navigators, icebergs have no considerable importance. It is true they somewhat affect the temperature of sea and air, and they also serve to convey fragments of stone far out to sea in a way that no other agent can effect; but, on the whole, their influence on the conditions of the earth is inconsiderable.

Icebergs in certain cases afford interesting indices as to the motion of oceanic currents, which, though moving swiftly at a depth below the surface, do not manifest themselves on the plain of the sea. Thus in the region about Greenland, particularly in Davis Strait, bergs have been seen forcing their way southward at considerable speed through ordinary surface ice, which was either at rest or moving in the opposite direction. The train of these bergs, which moves upward from the south polar continent, west of Patagonia, indicates also in a very emphatic way the existence of a very strong northward-setting current in that part of the ocean.

We have now to consider the causes which could bring about such great extensions of the ice sheet as occurred in the last Glacial period. Here again we are upon the confines of geological knowledge, and in a field where there are no well-cleared ways for the understanding. In facing this problem, we should first note that those who are of the opinion that a Glacial period means a very cold climate in the regions where the ice attained its extension are probably in error. Natural as it may seem to look for exceeding cold as the cause of glaciation, the facts show us that we can not hold this view. In Siberia and in the parts of North America bordering on the Arctic Sea the average cold is so intense that the ground is permanently frozen —as it is, for instance, in the Klondike district—to the depth of hundreds of feet, only the surface thawing out during the warm summers. All this region is cold enough for glaciers, but there is not sufficient snowfall to maintain them. On the other hand, in Greenland, and in a less though conspicuous degree in Scandinavia, where the waters of the North Atlantic somewhat diminish the rigour of the cold, and at the same time bring about a more abundant snowfall, the two actions being intimately related, we have very extensive glaciers. Such facts, which could be very much extended, make it clear that the climate of glacial periods must have been characterized by a great snowfall, and not by the most intense cold.

It is evident that what would be necessary again to envelop the boreal parts of North America with a glacial sheet would not be a considerable decrease of heat, but an increase in the winter's contribution of frozen water. Even if the heat released by this snowfall elevated the average temperature of the winter, as it doubtless would in a considerable measure, it would not melt off the snow. That snowfall tends to warm the air by setting free the heat which was engaged in keeping the water in a state of vapour is familiarly shown by the warming which attends an ordinary snowstorm. Even if the fall begin with a temperature of about 0° Fahr., the air is pretty sure to rise to near the freezing point.

It is evident that no great change of temperature is required in order to bring about a very considerable increase in the amount of snowfall. In the ordinary succession of seasons we often note the occurrence of winters during which the precipitation of snow is much above the average, though it can not be explained by a considerable climatal change. We have to account for these departures from the normal weather by supposing that the atmospheric currents bring in more than the usual amount of moisture from the sea during the period when great falls of snow occur. In fact, in explaining variations in the humidity of the land, whether those of a constant nature or those that are to be termed accidental, we have always to look to those features which determine the importation of vapour from the great field of the ocean where it enters the air. We should furthermore note that these peculiarities of climate are dependent upon rather slight geographic accidents. Thus the snowfall of northern Europe, which serves to maintain the glaciation of that region, and, curiously enough, in some measure its general warmth, depends upon the movement of the Gulf Stream from the tropics to high latitudes. If by any geographical change, such as would occur if Central America were lowered so as to make a free passage for its waters to the westward, the glaciers of Greenland and of Scandinavia would disappear, and at the same time the temperature of those would be greatly lowered. Thus the most evident cause of glaciation must be sought in those alterations of the land which affect the movement of the oceanic currents.

Applying this principle to the northern hemisphere, we can in a way imagine a change which would probably bring about a return of such an ice period as that from which the boreal realm is now escaping. Let us suppose that the region of not very high land about Bering Strait should sink down so as to afford the Kuro Siwo, or North Pacific equivalent of our Gulf Stream, an opportunity to enter the Arctic Sea with something like the freedom with which the North Atlantic current is allowed to penetrate to high latitudes. It seems likely that this Pacific current, which in volume and warmth is comparable to that of the Atlantic, would so far elevate the temperature of the arctic waters that their wide field would be the seat of a great evaporation. Noting once again the fact that the Greenland glaciers, as well as those of Norway, are supplied from seas warmed by the Gulf Stream, we should expect the result of this change would be to develop similar ice fields on all the lands near that ocean.

Applying the data gathered by Dr. Croll for the Gulf Stream, it seems likely that the average annual temperature induced in the Arctic Sea by the free entrance of the Japan current would be between 20° and 30° Fahr. This would convert this wide realm of waters into a field of great evaporation, vastly increasing the annual precipitation. It seems also certain that the greater part of this precipitation would be in the form of snow. It appears to the writer that this cause alone may be sufficient to account for the last Glacial period in the northern hemisphere. As to the probability that the region about Bering Strait may have been lowered in the manner required by this view, it may be said that recent studies on the region about Mount St. Elias show that during or just after the ice epoch the shores in that portion of Alaska were at least four thousand feet lower than at present. As this is but a little way from the land which we should have to suppose to be lowered in order to admit the Japan current, we could fairly conclude that the required change occurred. As for the cause of the land movement, geologists are still in doubt. They know, however, that the altitudes of the land are exceedingly unstable, and that the shores rarely for any considerable time maintain their position. It is probable that these swayings of the earth's surface are due to ever-changing combinations of the weight in different parts of the crust and the strains arising from the contraction of its inner parts.

In the larger operations of Nature the effects which we behold, however simple, are rarely the products of a single cause. In fact, there are few actions so limited that they can fairly be referred to one influence. It is therefore proper to state that there are many other actions besides those above noted which probably enter into those complicated equations which determine the climatal conditions of the earth. To have these would carry us into difficult and speculative inquiries.

As before remarked, all the regions which have been subjected to glaciation are still each year brought temporarily into the glacial state. This fact serves to show us that the changes necessary to produce great ice sheets are not necessarily of a startling nature, however great the consequences may be. Assuming, then, that relatively slight alterations of climate may cause the ice sheet to come and go, we may say that all the influences which have been suggested by the students of glaciation, and various other slighter causes which can not be here noted, may have co-operated to produce the peculiar result. In this equation geographic change has affected the course of the ocean currents, and has probably been the most influential, or at least the commonest, cause to which we must attribute the extension of ice sheets. Next, alterations of the solar heat may be looked to as a change-bringing action; unfortunately, however, we have no direct evidence that this is an efficient cause. Thirdly, the variations in the eccentricity of the earth's orbit, combined with the precession of the equinoxes and the rotation of the apsides, may be regarded as operative. The last of all, changes in the constitution of the atmosphere, have to be taken into account. To these must be added, as before remarked, many less important actions which influence this marvellously delicate machine, the work of which is expressed in the phenomena assembled under the name of climate.

Evidence is slowly accumulating which serves to show that glacial periods of greater or less importance have been of frequent occurrence at all stages in the history of the earth of which we have a distinct record. As these accidents write their history upon the ground alone, and in a way impermanently, it is difficult to trace the ice times of ancient geological periods. The scratches on the bed rocks, and the accumulations of detritus formed as the ice disappeared, have alike been worn away by the agents of decay. Nevertheless, we can trace here and there in the older strata accumulations of pebbly matter often containing large boulders, which clearly were shaped and brought together by glacial action. These are found in

17

some instances far south of the region occupied by the
glaciers during the last ice epoch. They occur in rocks
of the Cambrian or Silurian age in eastern Tennessee and
western North Carolina; they are also found in India beyond the limits to which glaciers have attained in modern
times.

In closing this inadequate account of glacial action,
a story which for its complete telling would require many
volumes, it is well for the reader to consider once again
how slight are the changes of climate which may alternately withdraw large parts of the land from the uses of
life, and again quickly restore the fields to the service
of plants and animals. He may well imagine that these
changes, by driving living creatures to and fro, profoundly
affect the history of their development. This matter will
be dealt with in the volume concerning the history of
organic beings.

When the ice went off from the northern part of this
continent, the surface of the country, which had been
borne down by the weight of the glacier, still remained depressed to a considerable depth below the level of the sea,
the depression varying from somewhere about one hundred feet in southern New England to a thousand feet or
more in high latitudes. Over this region, which lay beneath the level of the sea, the glacier, when it became thin
enough to float, was doubtless broken up into icebergs, in
the manner which we now behold along the coast of
Greenland. Where the shore was swept by a strong current, these bergs doubtless drifted away; but along the
most of the coast line they appear to have lain thickly
grouped next the shores, gradually delivering their loads
of stones and finer *débris* to the bottom. These masses of
floating ice in many cases seem to have prevented the sea
waves from attaining the shore, and thus hindered the
formation of those beaches which in their present elevated
condition enable us to interpret the old position of the sea
along coast lines which have been recently elevated. Here

and there, however, from New Jersey to Greenland, we find bits of these ancient shores which clearly tell the story of that down-sinking of the land beneath the burden of the ice which is such an instructive feature in the history of that period.

CHAPTER VII.

WE have already noted two means by which water finds its way underground. The simplest and largest method by which this action is effected is by building in the fluid as the grains of the rock are laid down on the floors of seas or lakes. The water thus imprisoned is firmly inclosed in the interstices of the stone, it in time takes up into its mass a certain amount of the mineral materials which are contained in the deep-buried rocks. The other portion of the ground water—that with which we are now to be specially concerned—arises from the rain which descends into the crevices of the earth; it is therefore peculiar to the lands. For convenience we shall term the original embedded fluid *rock water,* and that which originates from the rain *crevice water,* the two forming the mass of the earth water.

The crevice water of the earth, although forming at no time more than a very small fraction of the hidden fluid, is an exceedingly potent geological agent, doing work which, though unseen, yet affords the very foundations on which rest the life alike of land and sea. When this water enters the earth, though it is purified of all mineral materials, it has already begun to acquire a share of a gaseous substance, carbonic acid, or, as chemists now term it, carbon dioxide, which enables the fluid to begin its rôle of marvellous activities. In its descent as rain, probably even before it was gathered in drops in the cloud realm,

250

the water absorbs a certain portion of this gas from the atmosphere. Entering the realm of the soil, where the decaying organic matter plentifully gives forth carbon dioxide, a further store of the gas is acquired. At the ordinary pressure of the air, water may take in many times its bulk of the gas.

The immediate effect of carbonic acid when it is absorbed by water is greatly to increase the capacity which that fluid has for taking mineral matters into solution. When charged with this gas, in the measure in which it may be in the soil, water is able to dissolve about fifty times as much limestone as it can in its perfectly pure form take up. A familiar instance of this peculiar capacity which the gas gives may often be seen where the water from a soda-water fountain drips upon the marble slab beneath. In a few years this slab will be considerably corroded, though pure water would in the same time have had no effect upon it.

The first and by far the most important effect of crevice water is exercised upon the soil, which is at once the product of this action, and the laboratory where the larger part of the work is done. Penetrating between the grains of the detrital covering, held in large quantities in the coating, and continually in slow motion, the gas-charged water takes a host of substances into solution, and brings them into a condition where they may react upon each other in the chemical manner. These materials are constantly being offered to the roots of plants and brought in contact with the underlying rock which has not passed into the state of soil. The changes induced in this stony matter lead to its breaking up, or at least to its softening to the point where the roots can penetrate it and complete its destruction. Thus it comes about that the water which to a great extent divides the rocks into the state of soil, which is continually wearing away the material on the surface, or leaching it out through the springs, is also at work in restoring the layer from beneath.

The greater part of the water which enters the soil does not penetrate to any great depth in the underlying rocks, but finds its way to the surface after no long journey in the form of small springs. Generally these superficial springs do not emerge through distinct channels, but move, though slowly, in a massive way down the slopes until they enter a water course. Along the banks of any river, however small, or along the shores of the sea, a pit a few inches deep just above the level of the water will be quickly filled by a flow from this sheet which underlies the earth. At a distance from the stream this sheet spring is in contact with the bed rocks, and may be many feet below the surface, but it comes to the level of the river or the sea near their margins. Here and there the shape of the bed rocks, being like converging house roofs, causes the superficial springs to form small pipelike channels for the escape of their gathered waters, and the flow emerges at a definite point. Almost all these sources of considerable flow are due to the action of the water on the underlying rock, where we shall now follow that portion of the crevice water which penetrates deeply into the earth.

Almost all rocks, however firm they may appear to be, are divided by crevices which extend from the soil level it may be to the depths of thousands of feet. These rents are in part due to the strains of mountain-building, which tend to disrupt the firmest stone, leaving open fractures. They are also formed in other ways, as by the imperfectly understood agencies which produce joint planes. It often happens that where rocks are highly tilted water finds its way downward between the layers, which are imperfectly soldered together, or a bed of coarse material, such as sandstone or conglomerate, may afford an easy way by which the water may descend for miles beneath the surface. Passing through rocks which are not readily soluble, the water, already to a great extent supplied with mineral matter by its journey through the soil, may not do much excavating work, and even after a long time may only slightly enlarge the spaces in which it may be stored or the channels by which it discharges to the surface. Hence it comes about that in many countries, even where the waters penetrate deeply, they do not afford large springs. It is otherwise where the crevice waters enter limestones composed of materials which are readily dissolved. In such places we find the rain so readily entering the underlying rock that no part of the fall goes at once to the brooks, but all has a long underground journey.

In any limestone district where the beds of the material are thick and tolerably pure—as, for instance, in the cavern district of southern Kentucky—the traveller who enters the region notes at once that the usual small streams which in every region of considerable rainfall he is accustomed to see intersecting the surface of the country are entirely absent. In their place he notes everywhere pitlike depressions of bowl-shaped form, the sink holes to which we have already adverted. Through the openings in the bottom of these the rain waters descend into the depths of the earth. Although the most of these depressions have but small openings in their bottom, now and then one occurs with a vertical shaft sufficiently large to permit the explorer to descend into it, though he needs to be lowered down in the manner of a miner who is entering a shaft. In fact, the journey is nearly always one of some hazard; it should not be undertaken save with many precautions to insure safety.

When one is lowered away through an open sink hole, though the descent may at first be somewhat tortuous, the explorer soon finds himself swinging freely in the air, it may be at a point some hundred feet above the base of the bottle-shaped shaft or dome into which he has entered. Commonly the neck of the bottle is formed where the water has worked its way through a rather sandy limestone, a rock which was not readily dissolved by the water. In the pure and therefore easily cut limestone layers the cavity rapidly expands until the light of the lantern may

not disclose its walls. Farther down there is apt to be a
shelf composed of another impure limestone, which extends off near the middle of the shaft. If the explorer
can land upon this shelf, he is sure to find that from this
imperfect floor the cavern extends off in one or more horizontal galleries, which he may follow for a great distance
until he comes to the point where there is again a well-
like opening through the hard layer, with another dome-
shaped base beneath. Returning to the main shaft, the
explorer may continue his descent until he attains the
base of this vertical section of the cave, where he is likely
to find himself delivered in a pool of water of no great
depth, the bottom of which is occupied by a quantity of
small, hard stones of a flinty nature, which have evidently
come from the upper parts of the cavern. The close observer will have noted that here and there in the limestone
there are flinty bits, such as those which he finds in the
pool. From the bottom of the dome a determined inquirer can often make his way along the galleries which
lead from that level, though it may be after a journey of
miles to the point where he emerges from the cavern on
the banks of an open-air river.

Although a journey by way of the sink holes through
a cavern system is to be commended for the reason that
it is the course of the caverning waters, it is, on the whole,
best to approach the cave through their exits along the
banks of a stream or through the chance openings which
are here and there made by the falling in of their roofs.
One advantage of this cavity of entrance is that we can thus
approach the cavern in times of heavy rain when the processes which lead to their construction are in full activity.
Coming in this way to one of the domes formed beneath
a sink hole, we may observe in rainy weather that the
water falling down the deep shaft strikes the bottom with
great force; in many of the Kentucky caves it falls from
a greater height than Niagara. At such times the stones
in the basin at the bottom of the shaft are vigorously

whirled about, and in their motion they cut the rocks in
the bottom of the basin—in fact, this cavity is a great pot
hole, like those at the base of open-air cascades.   It is now
easy to interpret the general principles which determine
the architecture of the cavern realm.

When it first enters the earth all the work which the
water does in the initial steps of cavern formation is effected by solution.   As the crevice enlarges and deepens,
the stream acquires velocity, and begins to use the bits of
hard rock in boring.   It works downward in this way by
the mixed mechanical and chemical action until it encounters a hard layer.   Then the water creeps horizontally
through the soft stratum, doing most of its work by solution, until it finds a crevice in the floor through which
it can excavate farther in the downward direction; so it
goes on in the manner of steps until it burrows channels
to the open stream.   In time the vertical fall under the
sink hole will cut through the hard layer, when the water,
abandoning the first line of exit, will develop another at
a lower level, and so in time it comes about that there may
be several stories of the cave, the lowest being the last to
be excavated.   Of the total work thus done, only a small
part is accomplished by the falling of the water, acting
through the boring action of its tools, the bits of stone
before mentioned; the principal part of the task is done
by the solvent action of the carbonated waters on the limestone.   In the system of caverns known as the Mammoth
Cave, in Kentucky, the writer has estimated that at least
nine tenths of the stone was removed in the state of solution.

When first excavated, the chambers of a limestone cavern have little beauty to attract the eye.   The curves of the
walls are sometimes graceful, but the aspect of the chambers, though in a measure grand, is never charming.   When,
however, the waters have ceased to carve the openings,
when they have been drained away by the formation of
channels on a lower level, there commonly sets in a pro-

cess known as stalactitization, which transforms the scene
into one of singular beauty. We have already noted the
fact that everywhere in ordinary rocks there are crevices
through which water, moving under the pressure of the
fluid which is above, may find its way slowly downward.
In the limestone roofs of caverns, particularly in those
of the upper story, this ooze of water passes through myriads of unseen fissures at a rate so slow that it often evaporates in the dry air without dropping to the floor. When
it comes out of the rocks the water is charged with various
salts of lime; when it evaporates it leaves the material behind on the roof. Where the outflow is so slight that the
fluid does not gather into drops, it forms an incrustation
of limy matter, which often gathers in beautiful flowerlike
forms, or perhaps in the shape of a sheet of alabaster. Where
drops are formed, a small, pendent cone grows downward
from the ceiling, over which the water flows, and on which it
evaporates. This cone grows slowly downward until it may
attain the floor of the chamber, which has a height of thirty
feet or more. If all the water does not evaporate, that
which trickles off the apex of the cone, striking on the
floor, is splashed out into a thin sheet, so that it evaporates
in a speedy manner, lays down its limestone, and thus
builds another and ruder cone, which grows upward toward
that which is pendent above it. Finally, they grow together, enlarge by the process which constructed them,
until a mighty column may be formed, sculptured as if
by the hands of a fantastic architect.

All the while that subterranean streams are cutting
the caverns downward the open-air rivers into which they
discharge are deepening their beds, and thereby preparing
for the construction of yet lower stories of caves. These
open-air streams commonly flow in steep-sided, narrow
valleys, which themselves were caves until the galleries became so wide that they could no longer support the roof.
Thus we often find that for a certain distance the roof
over a large stream has fallen in, so that the water flows in

the open air.   Then it will plunge under an arch and
course, it may be, for some miles, before it again arrives
at a place where the roof has disappeared, or perhaps attains a field occupied by rocks of another character, in

Fig. 13.—Stalactites and stalagmites on roof and floor of a cavern.
The arrows show the direction of the moving water.

which caverns were not formed.   At places these old river
caverns are abandoned by the streams, which find other
courses.   They form natural tunnels, which are not infrequently of considerable length.   One such in southwestern Virginia has been made useful for a railway passing from one valley to another, thus sparing the expense
of a costly excavation.   Where the remnant of the arch is
small, it is commonly known as a natural bridge, of which
that in Rockbridge County, in Virginia, is a very noble

example. Arches of this sort are not uncommon in many cavern countries; five such exist in Carter County, Kentucky, a district in the eastern part of that State which abounds in caverns, though none of them are of conspicuous height or beauty.*

At this stage of his studies on cavern work the student will readily conceive that, as the surface of the country overlying the cave is incessantly wearing down, the upper stories of the system are continually disappearing, while new ones are forming at the present drainage level of the country. In fact, the attentive eye can in such a district find here and there evidences of this progressive destruction. Not only do the caves wear out from above, but their roofs are constantly falling to their floors, a process which is greatly aided by the growth of stalactites. Forming in the crevices or joints between the stones, these rock growths sometimes prize off great blocks. In other cases the weight of the pendent stalactite drags the ill-supported masses of the roof to the floor. In this way a gallery originally a hundred feet below the surface may work its way upward to the light of day. The entrance by which the Mammoth Cave is approached appears to have been formed in this manner, and at several points in that system of caverns the effect of this action may be distinctly observed.

We must now go a step further on the way of subterranean water, and trace its action in the depths below the plane of ordinary caves, which, as we have noted, do not extend below the level of the main streams of the cavern district. The first group of facts to be attended to is that exhibited by artesian wells. These occur where rocks have been folded down into a basinlike form. It often happens that in such a basin the rocks of which it

---

* It is reported that one of these natural bridges of Carter County has recently fallen down. This is the natural end of these features. As before remarked, they are but the remnants of much more extensive roofs which the processes of decay have brought to ruin.

is composed are some of them porous, and others impervious to water, and that the porous layers outcrop on the
high margins of the depression and have water-tight layers
over them.   These conditions can be well represented by
supposing that we have two saucers, one within the other,
with an intervening layer of sand which is full of water.
If now we bore an opening in the bottom of the uppermost
saucer, we readily conceive that the water will flow up
through it.   In Nature we often find these basins with
the equivalent of the sandy layer in the model just described rising hundreds of feet above the valley, so that
the artesian well, so named from the village of Artois, near
Paris, where the first opening of this nature was made, may
yield a stream which will mount upward, especially where
piped, to a great height.   At many places in the world
it is possible by such wells to obtain a large supply of tolerably pure water, but in general it is found to contain too
large a supply of dissolved mineral matter or sulphuretted
gases to be satisfactory for domestic purposes.   It may be
well to note the fact that the greater part of the so-called
artesian wells, or borings which deliver water to a height
above the surface, are not true artesian sources, in that
they do not send up the water by the action of gravitation,
but under the influence of gaseous pressure.

Where, as in the case of upturned porous beds, the
crevice water penetrates far below the earth's surface or
the open-air streams which drain the water away, the fluid
acquires a considerable increase of temperature, on the
average about one degree Fahrenheit for each eighty feet
of descent.   It may, indeed, become so heated that if it
were at the earth's surface it would not only burst into
steam with a vast explosive energy, but would actually
shine in the manner of heated solids.   As the temperature
of water rises, and as the pressure on it increases, it acquires a solvent power, and takes in rocky matter in a
measure unapproached at the earth's surface.   At the
depth of ten miles water beginning as inert rain would

acquire the properties which we are accustomed to associate with strong acids. Passing downward through fissures or porous strata in the manner indicated in the diagram, the water would take up, by virtue of its heat and the gases it contained, a share of many mineral substances which we commonly regard as insoluble. Gold and even platinum—the latter a material which resists all acids at ordinary temperatures—enters into the solution. If now the water thus charged with mineral stores finds in the depths a shorter way to the surface than that which it descended, which may well happen by way of a deep rift in the rocks, it will in its ascent reverse the process which it followed on going down. It will deposit the several minerals in the order of their solubilities—that is, the last to be taken in will be the first to be crystallized on the walls of the fissure through which the upflow is taking place. The result will be the formation of a vein belonging to the variety known as fissure veins.

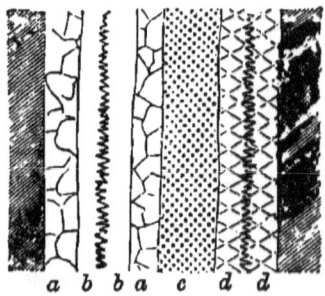

Fig. 14.—Diagram of vein. The different shadings show the variations in the nature of the deposits.

A vein deposit such as we are considering may, though rarely, be composed of a single mineral. Most commonly we find the deposit arranged in a banded form in the manner indicated in the figure (see diagram 14). Sometimes one material will abound in the lower portions of the fissure and another in its higher parts, a feature which is accounted for by the progressive cooling and relinquishment of pressure to which the water is subjected on its way to the surface. With each decrement of those properties some particular substance goes out of the fluid, which may in the end emerge in the form of a warm or hot spring, the water of which contains but little mineral matter. Where, however, the temperature is high, some part of the deposit, even a little gold, may be laid down just about the spring in the deposits known as sinter, which are often formed at such places.

In many cases the ore deposits are formed not only in the main channel of the fissure, but in all the crevices on either side of that way. In this manner, much as in the case of the growth of stalactitic matter between the blocks of stone in the roofs of a cavern, large fragments of rock, known as "horses," are often pushed out into the body of the vein. In some instances the growth of the vein appears to enlarge the fissure or place of the deposit as the accumulation goes on, the process being analogous to that by which a growing root widens the crevice into which it has penetrated. In other instances the fissure formed by the force has remained wide open, or at most has been but partly filled by the action of the water.

It not infrequently happens that the ascending waters of hot springs entering limestones have excavated extensive caves far below the surface of the earth, these caverns being afterward in part filled by the ores of various metals. We can readily imagine that the water at one temperature would excavate the cavern, and long afterward, when at a lower heat, they might proceed to fill it in. At a yet later stage, when the surface of the country had worn down many thousands of feet below the original level, the mineral stores of the caverns may be brought near the surface of the earth. Some of the most important metalliferous deposits of the Cordilleras are found in this group of hot-water caverns. These caverns are essentially like those produced by cold water, with the exception of the temperature of the fluid which does the work and the opposite direction of the flow.

In following crevice water which is free to obey the impulses of gravitation far down into the earth, we enter on a realm where the rock or construction water, that

which was built into the stone at the time of its formation,
is plentiful. Where these two groups of waters come in
contact an admixture occurs, a certain portion of the rock
water joining that in the crevices. Near the surface of
the ground we commonly find that all the construction
water has been washed out by this action. Yet if the rocks
be compact, or if they have layers of a soft and clayey nature, we may find the construction water, even in very
old deposits, remaining near the surface of the ground.
Thus in the ancient Silurian beds of the Ohio Valley a
boring carried a hundred feet below the level of the main
rivers commonly discovers water which is clearly that laid
down in the crevices of the material at the time when the
rocks were formed in the sea. In all cases this water contains a certain amount of gases derived from the decomposition of various substances, but principally from the alteration of iron pyrite, which affords sulphuretted hydrogen.
Thus the water is forced to the surface with considerable
energy, and the well is often named artesian, though it
flows by gas pressure on the principle of the soda-water
fountain, and not by gravity, as in the case of true artesian
wells.

The passage between the work done by the deeply
penetrating surface water and that due to the fluid intimately blended with the rock built into the mass at the
time of its formation is obscure. We are, however, quite
sure that at great depths beneath the earth the construction water acts alone not only in making veins, but in
bringing about many other momentous changes. At a
great depth this water becomes intensely heated, and therefore tends to move in any direction where a chance fissure
or other accident may lessen the pressure. Creeping
through the rocks, and moving from zones of one temperature to another, these waters bring about in the fine interstices chemical changes which lead to great alterations
in the constitution of the rock material. It is probably
in part to these slow driftings of rock water that beds

originally made up of small, shapeless fragments, such as compose clay slates, sandstones, and limestones, may in time be altered into crystalline rocks, where there is no longer a trace of the original bits, all the matter having been taken to pieces by the process of dissolving, and reformed in the regular crystalline order. In many cases we may note how a crystal after being made has been in part dissolved away and replaced by another mineral. In fact, many of our rocks appear to have been again and again made over by the slow-drifting waters, each particular state in their construction being due to some peculiarity of temperature or of mineral contents which the fluid held. These metamorphic phenomena, though important, are obscure, and their elucidation demands some knowledge of petrographic science, that branch of geology which considers the principles of rock formation. They will therefore not be further considered in this work.

VOLCANOES.

Of old it was believed that volcanoes represented the outpouring of fluid rock which came forth from the central realm of the earth, a region which was supposed still to retain the liquid state through which the whole mass of our earth has doubtless passed. Recent studies, however, have brought about a change in the views of geologists which is represented by the fact that we shall treat volcanic phenomena in connection with the history of rock water.

In endeavouring to understand the phenomena of volcanoes it is very desirable that the student should understand what goes on in a normal eruption. The writer may, therefore, be warranted in describing some observations which he had an opportunity to make at an eruption of Vesuvius in 1883, when it was possible to behold far more than can ordinarily be discerned in such outbreaks—in fact, the opportunity of a like nature has probably not

18

been enjoyed by any other person interested in volcanic action. In the winter of 1882–'83 Vesuvius was subjected to a succession of slight outbreaks. At the time of the observations about to be noted the crater had been reduced to a cup about three hundred feet in diameter and about a hundred feet deep. The vertical shaft at the bottom, through which the outbursts were taking place, was about a hundred feet across. Taking advantage of a heavy gale from the northwest, it was practicable, notwithstanding the explosions, to climb to the edge of the crater wall. Looking down into the throat of the volcano, although the pit was full of whirling vapours and the heat was so great that the protection of a mask was necessary, it was possible to see something of what was going on at the moment of an explosion.

The pipe of the volcano was full of white-hot lava. Even in a day of sunshine, which was only partly obscured by the vapours which hung about the opening, the heat of the lava made it very brilliant. This mass of fluid rock was in continuous motion, swaying violently up and down the tube. From four to six times a minute, at the moment of its upswaying, it would burst as by the explosion of a gigantic bubble. The upper portion of the mass was blown upward in fragments, the discharge being like that of shot from a fowling piece; the fragments, varying in size from small, shotlike bits to masses larger than a man's head, were shot up sometimes to the height of fifteen hundred feet above the point of ejection. The wind, blowing at the rate of about forty miles an hour, drove the falling bits of rock to the leeward, so that there was no considerable danger to be apprehended from them. Some seconds after the explosion they could be heard rattling down on the farther slope of the cone. Observations on the interval between the discharge and the fall of the fragments made it easy to compute the height to which they were thrown.

At the moment when the lava in the pipe opened for the passage of the vapour which created the explosion the

movement, though performed in a fraction of a second,
was clearly visible. At first the vapour was colourless; a
few score feet up it began to assume a faint, bluish hue;
yet higher, when it was more expanded, the tint changed
to that of steam, which soon became of the ordinary aspect,
and gathered in swift-revolving clouds. The watery nature
of the vapour was perfectly evident by its odour. Though
commingled with sulphurous-acid gas, it still had the characteristic smell of steam. For a half hour it was possible
to watch the successive explosions, and even to make rough
sketches of the scene. Occasionally the explosions would
come in quick succession, so that the lava was blown out
of the tube; again, the pool would merely sway up and
down in a manner which could be explained only by supposing that great bubbles of vapour were working their
way upward toward the point where they could burst.
Each of these bubbles probably filled a large part of the
diameter of the pipe. In general, the phenomena recalled
the escape of the jet from a geyser, or, to take a familiar
instance, that of steam from the pipe of a high-pressure
engine. When the heat is great, steam may often be seen
at the mouth of the pipe with the same transparent appearance which was observed in the throat of the crater.
In the cold air of the mountain the vapour was rapidly
condensed, giving a rainbow hue in the clouds when they
were viewed at the right angle. The observations were
interrupted by the fact that the wind so far died away that
large balls of the ejected lava began to fall on the windward side of the cone. These fragments, though cooled
and blackened on their outside by their considerable journey up and.down through the air, were still so soft that
they splashed when they struck the surface of cinders.

Watching the cone from a distance, one could note that
from time to time the explosions, increasing in frequency,
finally attained a point where the action appeared to be
continuous. The transition was comparable to that which
we may observe in a locomotive which, when it first gets

under way, gives forth occasional jets of steam, but, slowly gaining speed, finally pours forth what to eye and ear alike seem to be a continuous outrush. All the evidence that we have concerning volcanic outbreaks corroborates that just cited, and is to the effect that the essence of the action consists in the outbreak of water vapour at a high temperature, and therefore endowed with very great expansive force. Along with this steam there are many other gases, which always appear to be but a very small part of the whole escape of a vaporous nature—in fact, the volcanic steam, so far as its chemical composition has been ascertained, has the composition which we should expect to find in rock water which had been forced out from the rock by the tensions that high temperature creates.

Because of its conspicuous nature, the lava which flows from most volcanoes, or is blown out from them in the form of finely divided ash, is commonly regarded as the primary feature in a volcanic outbreak. Such is not really the case. Volcanic explosions may occur with very little output of fluid rock, and that which comes forth may consist altogether of the finely divided bits of rock to which we give the name of ash. In fact, in all very powerful explosions we may expect to find no lava flow, but great quantities of this finely divided rock, which when it started from the depths of the earth was in a fluid state, but was blown to pieces by the contained vapour as it approached the surface.

If the student is so fortunate as to behold a flood of lava coming forth from the flanks of a volcano, he will observe that even at the very points of issue, where the material is white-hot and appears to be as fluid as water, the whole surface gives forth steam. On a still day, viewed from a distance, the path of a lava flow is marked by a dense cloud of this vapour which comes forth from it. Even after the lava has cooled so that it is safe to walk upon it, every crevice continues to pour forth steam. Years after the flowing has ceased, and when the rock surface has

become cool enough for the growth of certain plants upon
it, these crevices still yield steam. It is evident, in a word,
that a considerable part of a lava mass, even after it escapes
from the volcanic .pipes, is water which is intimately commingled with the rock, probably lying between the very
finest grains of the heated substance. Yet this lava which
has come forth from the volcano has only a portion of the
water which it originally contained; a large, perhaps the
greater part, has gone forth in the explosive way through
the crater. It is reasonably believed that the fluidity of
lava is in considerable measure due to the water which it
contains, and which serves to give the mass the consistence
of paste, the partial fluidity of flour and rock grains being
alike brought about in the same manner.

So much of the phenomena of volcanoes as has been
above noted is intended to show the large part which inter-
stitial water plays in volcanic action. We shall now turn
our attention again to the state of the deeply buried rock
water, to see how far we may be able by it to account for
these strange explosive actions. When sediments are laid
down on the sea floor the materials consist of small, irregularly shaped fragments, which lie tumbled together in the
manner of a mass of bricks which have been shot out of a
cart. Water is buried in the plentiful interspaces between
these bits of stone; as before remarked, the amount of this
construction water varies. In general, it is at first not far
from one tenth part of the materials. Besides the fluid contained in the distinct spaces, there is a share which is held
as combined water in the intimate structure of the crystals,
if such there be in the mass. When this water is built into
the stone it has the ordinary temperature of the sea bottom.
As the depositing actions continue to work, other beds are
formed on the top of that which we are considering, and
in time the layer may be buried to the depth of many
thousand feet. There are reasons to believe that on the
floors of the oceans this burial of beds containing water
may have brought great quantities of fluid to the depth

of twenty miles or more below the outer surface of the rocks.

The effect of deep burial is to increase the heat of strata. This result is accomplished in two different ways.

FIG. 15.—Flow of lava invading a forest. A tree in the distance is not completely burned, showing that the molten rock had lost much of its original heat.

The direct effect arising from the imposition of weight, that derived from the mass of stratified material, is, as we know, to bring about a down-sinking of the earth's crust. In the measure of this falling, heat is engendered precisely as it is by the falling of a trip-hammer on the anvil, with which action, as is well known, we may heat an iron bar to a high temperature. It is true that this down-sinking of the surface under weight is in part due to the compression of the rocks, and in part to the slipping away of the soft underpinning of more or less fluid rock. Yet further it is in some measure brought about by the wrinkling of the crust. But all these actions result in the conversion of energy of position into heat, and so far serve to raise the temperature of the rocks which are concerned in the movements. By far the largest source of heat, however, is that which comes forth from the earth's interior, and which was stored there in the olden day when the matter forming the earth gathered into the mass of our sphere. This, which we may term 'the original heat, is constantly flowing forth into space, but makes its way slowly, because of the non-conductive, or, as we may phrase it, the "blanketing" effect of the outer rock. The effect of the strata is the same as that exercised by the non-conductive coatings which are put on steam boilers. A more familiar comparison may be had from the blankets used for bedclothing. If on top of the first blanket we put a second, we keep warmer because the temperature of the lower one is elevated by the heat from our body which is held in. In the crust of the earth each layer of rock resists the outflow of heat, and each addition lifts the temperature of all the layers below.

When water-bearing strata have been buried to the depth of ten miles, the temperature of the mass may be expected to rise to somewhere between seven hundred and a thousand degrees Fahrenheit. If the depth attained should be fifty miles, it is likely that the temperature will be five times as great. At such a heat the water which the rocks contain tends in a very vigorous way to expand and pass into the state of vapour. This it can not readily do, because of its close imprisonment; we may say, however, that the tendency toward explosion is almost as great as that of ignited gunpowder. Such powder, if held in small spaces in a mass of cast steel, could be fired without rending the metal. The gases would be retained in a highly compressed, possibly in a fluid form. If now it happens that any of the strain in the rocks such as lead to the production of faults produce fissures leading from the surface into this zone of heated water, the tendency of the rocks containing the fluid, impelled by its expansion, will be to move with great energy toward the point of relief or lessened pressure which the crevice affords. Where rocks are in any way softened, pressure alone will force them into a cavity, as is shown by the fact that beds of tolerably hard clay stones in deep coal mines may be forced into the spaces by the pressure of the rocks which overlie them—in fact, the expense of cutting out these in-creeping rocks is in some British mines a serious item in the cost of the product.

The expansion of the water contained in the deep-lying heated rocks probably is by far the most efficient agent in urging them toward the plane of escape which the fissure affords. When the motion begins it pervades all parts of the rock at once, so that an actual flow is induced. So far as the movement is due to the superincumbent weight, the tendency is at once to increase the temperature of the moving mass. The result is that it may be urged into the fissure perhaps even hotter than when it started from the original bed place. In proportion as the rocky matter wins its way toward the surface, the pressure upon it diminishes, and the contained vapours are freer to expand. Taking on the vaporous form, the bubbles gather to each other, and when they appear at the throat of the volcano they may, if the explosions be infrequent, assume the character above noted in the little eruption of Vesuvius. Where, however, the lava ascends rapidly through the channel, it often attains the open air with so much vapour in it, and this intimately mingled with the mass, that the explosion rends the materials into an impalpably fine powder, which may float in the air for months before it falls to the earth. With a less violent movement the vapour bubbles expand in the lava, but do not rend it apart, thus forming the porous, spongy rock known as pumice. With a yet slower ascent a large part of the steam may go away, so that we may have a flow of lava welling forth from the vent, still giving forth steam, but with a vapour whose tension is so lowered that the matter is not blown apart, though it may boil violently for a time after it escapes into the air.

Although the foregoing relatively simple explanation of volcanic action can not be said as yet to be generally accepted by geologists, the reasons are sufficient which lead us to believe that it accounts for the main features which we observe in this class of explosions—in other words, it is a good working hypothesis. We shall now proceed in the manner which should be followed in all natural inquiry to see if the facts shown in the distribution of volcanoes in space and time confirm or deny the view.

The most noteworthy feature in the distribution of volcanoes is that, at the present time at least, all active vents are limited to the sea floors or to the shore lands within the narrow range of three hundred miles from the coast. Wherever we find a coast line destitute of volcanoes, as is the case with the eastern coast of North and South America, it appears that the shore has recently been carried into the land for a considerable distance—in other words, old coast lines are normally volcanic; that is, here and there have vents of this nature. Thus the North Atlantic, the coasts of which appear to have gone inland for a great distance in geologically recent times, is non-volcanic; while the Pacific coast, which for a long time has remained in its present position, has a singularly continuous line of craters near the shore extending from Alaska to Tierra del Fuego. So uninterrupted is this line of volcanoes that if they were all in eruption it would very likely be possible to journey down the coast without ever being out of sight of the columns of vapour which they would send forth. On the floor of the sea volcanic peaks appear to be very widely distributed; only a few of them—those which attain the surface of the water—are really known, but soundings show long lines of elevations which doubtless represent cones distributed along fault lines, none of the peaks of sufficient height to break the surface of the sea. It is likely, indeed, that for one marine volcano which appears as an island there are scores which do not attain the surface. Volcanic islands exist and generally abound in the ocean and greater seas; every now and then we observe a new one forming as a small island, which is apt to be washed away by the sea shortly after the eruption ceases, the disappearance being speedy, for the reason that the volcanic ashes of which these cones are composed drift away like snow before the movement of the waves.

If the waters of the ocean and seas were drained away so that we could inspect the portion of the earth's surface which they cover as readily as we do the dry lands, the most conspicuous feature would be the innumerable volcanic eminences which lie hidden in these watery realms. Wherever the observer passed from the centres of the present lands he would note within the limits of those fields only mountains, much modified by river action; hills which the rivers had left in scarfing away the strata; and dales which had been carved out by the flowing waters. Near the shore lines of the vanished seas he would begin to find mountains, hills, and vales occasionally commingled with volcanic peaks, those structures built from the materials ejected from the vents. Passing the coast line to the seaward, the hills and dales would quickly disappear, and before long the mountains would vanish from his way, and he would gradually enter on a region of vast rolling plains beset by volcanic peaks, generally accumulated in long ranges, somewhat after the manner of mountains, but differing from those elevations not only in origin but in aspect, the volcanic set of peaks being altogether made up of conical, cup-topped elevations.

A little consideration will show us that the fact of volcanoes being in the limit to the sea floors and to a narrow fringe of shore next certain ocean borders is reconcilable with the view as to their formation which we have adopted. We have already noted the fact that the continents are old, which implies that the parts of the earth which they occupy have long been the seats of tolerably continuous erosion. Now and then they have swung down partly beneath the sea, and during their submersion they received a share of sediments. But, on the whole, all parts of the lands except strips next the coast may be reckoned as having been subjected to an excess of wearing action far exceeding the depositional work. Therefore, as we readily see, underneath such land areas there has been no blanketing process going on which has served to increase the heat in the deep underlying rocks. On the contrary, it would be easy to show, and the reader may see it himself, that the progressive cooling of the earth has probably brought about a lowering of the temperature in all the section from the surface to very great depths, so that not only is the rock water unaffected by increase of heat, but may be actually losing temperature. In other words, the conditions which we assume bring about volcanic action do not exist beneath the old land.

Beneath the seas, except in their very greatest depths, and perhaps even there, the process of forming strata is continually going on. Next the shores, sometimes for a hundred or two miles away to seaward, the principal contribution may be the sediment worn from the lands by the waves and the rivers. Farther away it is to a large extent made up of the remains of animals and plants, which when dying give their skeletons to form the strata. Much of the materials laid down—perhaps in all more than half—consist of volcanic dust, ashes, and pumice, which drifts very long times before it finds its way to the bottom. We have as yet no data of a precise kind for determining the average rate of accumulation of sediments upon the sea floor, but from what is known of the wearing of the lands, and the amount of volcanic waste which finds its way to the seas, it is probably not less than about a foot in ten thousand years; it is most likely, indeed, much to exceed this amount. From data afforded by the eruptions in Java and in other fields where the quantity of volcanic dust contributed to the seas can be estimated, the writer is disposed to believe that the average rate of sedimentation on the sea floors is twice as great as the estimate above given.

Accumulating at the average rate of one foot in ten thousand years, it would require a million years to produce a hundred feet of sediments; a hundred million to form ten thousand feet, and five hundred million to create the thickness of about ten miles of bed. At the rate of two feet in ten thousand years, the thickness accumulated would be about twenty miles. When we come to consider the duration of the earth's geologic history, we shall find reasons for believing that the formation of sediment may have continued for as much as five hundred million years.

The foregoing inquiries concerning the origin of volcanoes show that at the present time they are clearly connected with some process which goes on beneath the sea. An extension of the inquiry indicates that this relation has existed in earlier geological times; for, although the living volcanoes are limited to places within three hundred miles of the sea, we find lava flows, ashes, and other volcanic accumulations far in the interior of the continents, though the energy which brought them forth to the earth's surface has ceased to operate in those parts of the land. In these cases of continental volcanoes it generally, if not always, appears that the cessation of the activity attended the removal of the shore line of the ocean or the disappearance of great inland seas. Thus the volcanoes of the Yellowstone district may have owed their activity to the immense deposits of sediment which were formed in the vast fresh-water lakes which during the later Cretaceous

and early Tertiary times stretched along the eastern face
of the Rocky Mountains, forming a Mediterranean Sea in
North America comparable to that which borders southern
Europe. It thus appears that the arrangement of volcanoes
with reference to sea basins has held for a considerable
period in the past. Still further, when we look backward
through the successive formations of the earth's crust we
find here and there evidences in old lava flows, in volcanic
ashes, and sometimes in the ruins of ancient cones which
have been buried in the strata, that igneous activity such
as is now displayed in our volcanoes has been, since the
earliest days of which we have any record, a characteristic
feature of the earth. There is no reason to suppose that
this action has in the past been any greater or any less
than in modern days. All these facts point to the conclusion that volcanic action is due to the escape of rock water
which has been heated to high temperatures, and which
drives along with it as it journeys toward a crevice the
rock in which it has been confined.

We will now notice some other explanations of volcanic
action which have obtained a certain credence. First, we
may note the view that these ejections from craters are
forced out from a supposed liquid interior of the earth.
One of the difficulties of this view is that we do not know
that the earth's central parts are fluid—in fact, many considerations indicate that such is not the case. Next, we
observe that we not infrequently find two craters, each containing fluid lava, with the fluid standing at differences
of height of several thousand feet, although the cones are
situated very near each other. If these lavas came from
a common internal reservoir, the principles which control the action of fluids would cause the lavas to be at the
same elevation. Moreover, this view does not provide any
explanation of the fact that volcanoes are in some way
connected with actions which go on on the floors of great
water basins. There is every reason to believe that the
fractures in the rocks under the land are as numerous and

deep-going as those beneath the sea. If it were a mere question of access to a fluid interior, volcanoes should be equally distributed on land and sea floors. Last of all, this explanation in no wise accounts for the intermixture of water with the fluid rock. We can not well believe that water could have formed a part of the deeper earth in the old days of original igneous fusion. In that time the water must have been all above the earth in the vaporous state.

Another supposition somewhat akin to that mentioned is that the water of the seas finds its way down through crevices beneath the floors of the ocean, and, there coming in contact with an internal molten mass, is converted into steam, which, along with the fluid rock, escapes from the volcanic vent. In addition to the objections urged to the preceding view, we may say concerning this that the lava, if it came forth under these circumstances, would emerge by the short way, that by which the water went down, and not by the longer road, by which it may be discharged ten thousand feet or more above the level of the sea.

The foregoing general account of volcanic action should properly be followed by some account of what takes place in characteristic eruptions. This history of these matters is so ample that it would require the space of a great encyclopædia to contain them. We shall therefore be able to make only certain selections which may serve to illustrate the more important facts.

By far the best-known volcanic cone is that of Vesuvius, which has been subjected to tolerably complete record for about twenty-four hundred years. About 500 B. C. the Greeks, who were ever on the search for places where they might advantageously plant colonies, settled on the island of Ischia, which forms the western of what is now termed the Bay of Naples. This island was well placed for tillage as well as for commerce, but the enterprising colonists were again and again disturbed by violent outbreaks of one or more volcanoes which lie in the interior of this island; at one time it appears that the people were driven away by these explosions.

In these pre-Christian days Vesuvius, then known as Monte Somma, was not known to be a volcano, it never having shown any trace of eruption. It appeared as a regularly shaped mountain, somewhat over two thousand feet high, with a central depression about three miles in diameter at the top, and perhaps two miles over at the bottom, which was plainlike in form, with some lakes of bitter water in the centre. The most we know of this central cavity is connected with the insurrection of the slaves led by Spartacus, the army of the revolters having camped for a time on the plain encircled by the crater walls. The outer slopes of the mountain afforded then a remarkably fertile soil; some traces, indeed, of the fertility have withstood the modern eruptions which have desolated its flanks. This wonderful Bay of Naples became the seat of the fairest Roman culture, as well as of a very extended commerce. Toward the close of the first century of our era the region was perhaps richer, more beautifully cultivated, and the seat of a more elaborate luxury than any part of the shore line of Europe at the present day. At the foot of the mountain, on the eastern border of the bay, the city of Pompeii, with a population of about fifty thousand souls, was a considerable port, with an extensive commerce, particularly with Egypt. The charming town was also a place of great resort for rich Egyptians who cared to dwell in Europe. On the flanks of the mountain there was at least one large town, Herculaneum, which appears to have been an association of rich men's residences. On the eastern side of the bay, at a point now known as Baiæ, the Roman Government had a naval station, which in the year 79 was under the command of the celebrated Pliny, a most voluminous though unscientific writer on matters of natural history. With him in that year there was his nephew, commonly known as the younger Pliny, then a student of eighteen years, but afterward himself an author. These facts are stated in some detail, for they are all involved in the great tragedy which we are now to describe.

For many years there had been no eruption about the Bay of Naples. The volcanoes on Ischia had been still for a century or more, and the various circular openings on the mainland had been so far quiet that they were not recognised as volcanoes. Even the inquisitive Pliny, with his great learning, was so little of a geologist that he did not know the signs which indicate the seat of volcanic action, though they are among the most conspicuous features which can meet the eye. The Greeks would doubtless have recognised the meaning of these physical signs. In the year 68, and in the following year, the shores of the Bay of Naples were subject to frequent earthquakes, though these shocks do not appear to have been of a destructive character. In an early morning in the last-named year a servant aroused the elder Pliny at Baiæ with the news that there was a wonderful cloud rising from Monte Somma. The younger Pliny states that in form it was like a pine tree, the common species in Italy having a long trunk with a crown of foliage on its summit, shaped like an umbrella. This crown of the column grew until it spread over the whole landscape, darkening the field of view. Shortly after, a despatch boat brought a message to the admiral, who at once set forth for the seat of the disturbance. He invited his nephew to accompany him, but the prudent young man relates in his letters to Tacitus, from whom we know the little concerning the eruption which has come down to us, that he preferred to do some reading which he had to attend to. His uncle, however, went straight forward, intending to land at some point on the shore at the foot of the cone. He found the sea, however, so high that a landing was impossible; moreover, the fall of rock fragments menaced the ship. He therefore cruised along the shore for some distance, landing at a station probably near the present village of Castellamare. At this point the fall of ashes and pumice was very great, but the sturdy old Roman had his dinner and slept after it. There is testimony that he snored loudly, and was aroused only when his servants began to fear that the fall of ashes and stones would block the way out of his bedchamber. When he came forth with his attendants, their heads protected by planks resting on pillows, he set out toward Pompeii, which was probably the place where he sought to land. After going some distance, the brave man fell dead, probably from heart disease; it is said that he was at the time exceedingly asthmatic. No sooner were his servants satisfied that the life had passed from his body than they fled. The remains were recovered after the eruption had ceased. The younger Pliny further relates that after his uncle left, the cloud from the mountain became so dense that in midday the darkness was that of midnight, and the earthquake shocks were so violent that wagons brought to the courtyard of the dwelling to bear the members of the household away were rolled this way and that by the quakings of the earth.

Save for the above-mentioned few and unimportant details concerning the eruption, we have no other contemporaneous account. We have, indeed, no more extended story until Dion Cassius, writing long after the event, tells us that Herculaneum and Pompeii were overwhelmed; but he mixes his story with fantastic legends concerning the appearance of gods and demons, as is his fashion in his so-called history. Of all the Roman writers, he is perhaps the most untrustworthy. Fortunately, however, we have in the deposits of ashes which were thrown out at the time of this great eruption some basis for interpreting the events which took place. It is evident that for many hours the Vesuvian crater, which had been dormant for at least five hundred years, blew out with exceeding fury. It poured forth no lava streams; the energy of the uprushing vapours was too great for that. The molten rock in their path was blown into fine bits, and all the hard material cast forth as free dust. In the course of the eruption, which probably did not endure more than two days, possibly not more than twenty-four hours, ash enough was poured forth to form a thick layer which spread far over the neighbouring area of land and sea floor. It covered the cities of Herculaneum and Pompeii to a depth of more than twenty feet, and over a circle having a diameter of twenty miles the average thickness may have been something like this amount. So deep was it that, although almost all the people of these towns survived, it did not seem to them worth while to undertake to excavate their dwelling places. At Pompeii the covering did not overtop the higher of the low houses. An amount of labour which may be estimated at not over one thirtieth of the value, or at least the cost which had been incurred in building the city, would have restored it to a perfectly inhabitable state. The fact that it was utterly abandoned probably indicates a certain superstitious view in connection with the eruption.

The fact that the people had time to flee from Herculaneum and Pompeii, bearing with them their more valuable effects, is proved by the excavations at these places which have been made in modern times. The larger part of Pompeii and a considerable portion of Herculaneum have been thus explored; only rarely have human remains been found. Here and there, particularly in the cellars, the labourers engaged in the work of disinterring the cities note that their picks enter a cavity; examining the space, they find they have discovered the remains of a human skeleton. It has recently been learned that by pouring soft plaster of Paris into these openings a mould may be obtained which gives in a surprisingly perfect manner the original form of the body. The explanation of this mould is as follows: Along with the fall of cinders in an eruption there is always a great descent of rain, arising from the condensation of the steam which pours forth from the volcano. This water, mingling with the ashes, forms a pasty mud, which often flows in vast streams, and is sometimes known as mud lava. This material has the qualities of cement—that is, it shortly "sets" in a manner comparable to plaster of Paris or ordinary mortar. During the eruption of 79 this mud penetrated all the low places in Pompeii, covering the bodies of the people, who were suffocated by the fumes of the volcanic emanations. We know that these people were not drowned by the inundation; their attitudes show that they were dead before the flowing matter penetrated to where they lay.

It happened that Pompeii lay beyond the influence of the subsequent great eruptions of Vesuvius, so that it afterward received only slight ash showers. Herculaneum, on the other hand, has century by century been more and more deeply buried until at the present time it is covered by many sheets of lava. This is particularly to be regretted, for the reason that, while Pompeii was a seaport town of no great wealth or culture, Herculaneum was the residence place of the gentry, people who possessed libraries, the records of which can be in many cases deciphered, and from which we might hope to obtain some of the lost treasures of antiquity. The papyrus rolls on which the books of that day were written, though charred by heat and time, are still interpretable.

After the great explosion of 79, Vesuvius sank again into repose. It was not until 1056 that vigorous eruptions again began. From time to time slight explosions occurred, none of which yielded lava flows; it was not until the date last mentioned that this accompaniment of the eruption began to appear. In 1636, after a repose of nearly a century and a half, there came a very great outbreak, which desolated a wide extent of country on the northwestern side of the cone. At this stage in the history of the crater the volcanic flow began to attain the sea. Washing over the edge of the old original crater of Monte Somma, and thus lowering its elevation, these streams devastated, during the eruption just mentioned and in various other outbreaks, a wide field of cultivated

land, overwhelming many villages. The last considerable
eruption which yielded large quantities of lava was that
of 1872, which sent its tide for a distance of about six
miles.

Since 1636 the eruptions of Vesuvius have steadily increased in frequency, and, on the whole, diminished in
violence. In the early years of its history the great outbreaks were usually separated by intervals of a century
or more, and were of such energy that the lava was mostly
blown to dust, forming clouds so vast that on two occasions at least they caused a midnight darkness at Constantinople, nearly twelve hundred miles away. This is
as if a volcano at Chicago should completely hide the sun
in the city of Boston. In the present state of Vesuvius,
the cone may be said to be in slight, almost continuous
eruption. The old central valley which existed before
the eruption of 79, and continued to be distinct for long
after that time, has been filled up by a smaller cone, bearing a relatively tiny crater of vent, the original wall being
visible only on the eastern and northern parts of its circuit,
and here only with much diminished height. On the western face the slope from the base of the mountain to the
summit of the new cone is almost continuous, though the
trained eye can trace the outline of Monte Somma—its position in a kind of bench, which is traceable on that side
of the long slope leading from the summit of the new cone
to the sea. The fact that the lavas of Vesuvius have
broken out on the southwestern side, while the old wall
of the cone has remained unbroken on the eastern versant,
has a curious explanation. The prevailing wind of Naples
is from the southwest, being the strong counter trades
which belong in that latitude. In the old days when the
Monte Somma cone was constructed these winds caused
the larger part of the ashes to fall on the leeward side of
the cone, thus forming a thicker and higher wall around
that part of the crater.

From the nature of the recent eruptions of Vesuvius it

appears likely that the mountain is about to enter on a
second period of inaction. The pipes leading through the
new cone are small, and the mass of this elevation constitutes a great plug, closing the old crater mouth. To give
vent to a large discharge of steam, the whole of this great

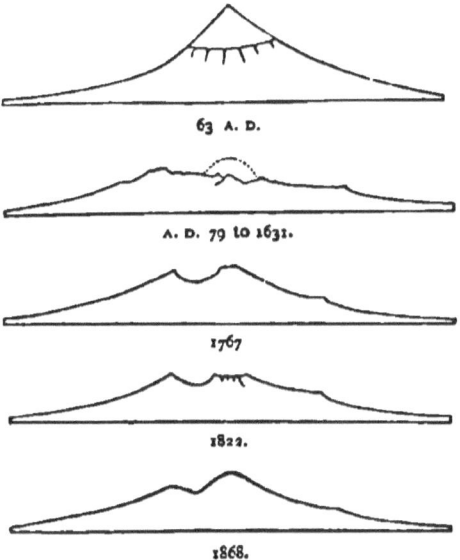

FIG. 16.—Diagrammatic sections through Mount Vesuvius, showing
changes in the form of the cone. (From Phillips.)

mass, having a depth of nearly two thousand feet, would
have to be blown away. It seems most likely that when the
occasion for such a discharge comes, the vapours of the
eruption will seek a vent through some other of the many
volcanic openings which lie to the westward of this great
cone. The history of these lesser volcanoes points to the
conclusion that when the path by way of Vesuvius is obstructed they may give relief to the steam which is forcing
its course to the surface. Two or three times since the
eruption of Pliny, during periods when Vesuvius had

long been quiet, outbreaks have taken place on Ischia or
in the Phlægræn Fields, a region dotted with small craters
which lies to the west of Naples. The last of these occurred in 1552, and led to the formation of the beautiful
little cone known as Monte Nuovo. This eruption took
place near the town of Puzzuoli, a place which was then
the seat of a university, the people of which have left us
records of the accident.

The outbreak which formed Monte Nuovo was slight
but very characteristic. It occurred in and beside a circular pool known as the Lucrine Lake, itself an ancient
crater. At the beginning of the disturbance the ground
opened in ragged cavities, from which mud and ashes and
great fragments of hard rock were hurled high in the air,
some of the stones ascending to a height of several thousand feet. With slight intermissions this outbreak continued for some days, resulting in the formation of a hill
about five hundred feet high, with a crater in its top, the
bottom of which lay near the level of the sea. Although
this volcanic elevation, being made altogether of loose
fragments, is rapidly wearing down, while the crater is
filling up, it remains a beautiful object in the landscape,
and is also noteworthy for the fact that it is the only structure of this nature which we know from its beginning.
In the Phlægræn Field there are a number of other craters
of small size, with very low cones about them. These appear to have been the product of brief, slight eruptions.
That known as the Solfatara, though not in eruption during the historic period, is interesting for the fact that from
the crevices of the rocks about it there comes forth a continued efflux of carbonic-acid gas. This substance probably arises from the effect of heat contained in old lavas
which are in contact with limestone in the deep under-
earth. We know such limestones are covered by the lavas
of Vesuvius, for the reason that numerous blocks of the
rock are thrown out during eruptions, and are often found
embedded in the lava streams. It is an interesting fact

that these craters of the Phlægræn Field, lying between
the seats of vigorous eruption on Ischia and at Vesuvius,
have never been in vigorous eruption. Their slight outbreaks seem to indicate that they have no permanent connection with the sources whence those stronger vents obtain their supply of heated steam.

The facts disclosed by the study of the Vesuvian system
of volcanoes afford the geologist a basis for many interesting conclusions.

In the first place, he notes that the greater part of the
cones, all those of small size, are made up of finely divided
rock, which may have been more or less cemented by the
processes of change which go on within it. It is thus clear
that the lava flows are unessential—indeed, we may say
accidental—contributions to the mass. In the case of
Vesuvius they certainly do not amount to as much as one
tenth of the elevation due to the volcanic action. The
share of the lava in Vesuvius is probably greater than the
average, for during the last six centuries this vent has
been remarkably lavigerous.* Observation on the volcanoes
of other districts show that the Vesuvian group is in this
regard not peculiar. Of nearly two hundred cones which
the writer has examined, not more than one tenth disclose
distinct lavas.

An inspection of the old inner wall of Monte Somma
in that portion where it is best preserved, on the north
side of the Atria del Cavallo, or Horse Gulch—so called
for the reason that those who ascended Vesuvius were accustomed to leave their saddle animals there—we perceive
that the body of the old cone is to a considerable extent
interlaced with dikes or fissures which have been filled
with molten lava that has cooled in its place. It is evident that during the throes of an eruption, when the lava

---

* I venture to use this word in place of the phrase "lava-yielding" for the reason that the term is needed in the description of
volcanoes.

stands high in the crater, these rents are frequently formed, to be filled by the fluid rock. In fact, lava discharges, though they may afterward course for long distances in the open air, generally break their way underground through the cindery cone, and first are disclosed at the distance of a mile or more from the inner walls of the crater. Their path is probably formed by riftings in the compacted ashes, such as we trace on the steep sides of the Atria del Cavallo, as before noted. For the further history of these fissures, we shall have to refer to facts which are better exhibited in the cone of Ætna.

The amount of rock matter which has been thrown forth from the volcanoes about the Bay of Naples is very great. Only a portion of it remains in the region around these cones; by far the greater part has been washed or blown away. After each considerable eruption a wide field is coated with ashes, so that the tilled grounds appear as if entirely sterilized; but in a short time the matter in good part disappears, a portion of it decays and is leached away, and the most of the remainder washes into the sea. Only the showers, which accumulate a deep layer, are apt to be retained on the surface of the country. A great deal of this powdered rock drifts away in the wind, sometimes in great quantities, as in those cases where it darkened the sky more than a thousand miles from the cone. Moreover, the water of the steam which brought about the discharges and the other gases which accompanied the vapour have left no traces of their presence, except in the deep channels which the rain of the condensing steam have formed on the hillsides. Nevertheless, after all these subtractions are made, the quantity of volcanic matter remaining on the surface about the Bay of Naples would, if evenly distributed, form a layer several hundred feet in thickness— perhaps, indeed, a thousand feet in depth—over the territory in which the vents occur. All this matter has been taken in relatively recent times from the depths of the earth. The surprising fact is that no considerable and, indeed, no permanent subsidence of the surface has attended this excavation. We can not believe that this withdrawal of material from the under-earth has resulted in the formation of open underground spaces. We know full well that any such, if it were of considerable size, would quickly be crushed in by the weight of the overlying rocks. We have, indeed, to suppose that these steam-impelled lavas, which are driven toward the vent whence they are to go forth in the state of dust or fluid, come underground from distances away, probably from beneath the floors of the sea to the westward.

Although the shores of the Bay of Naples have remained in general with unchanged elevation for about two thousand years, they have here and there been subjected to slight oscillations which are most likely connected with the movement of volcanic ·matter toward the vents where it is to find escape. The most interesting evidence of this nature is afforded by the studies which have been made on the ruins of the Temple of Serapis at Puzzuoli. This edifice was constructed in pre-Christian times for the worship of the Egyptian god Serapis, whose intervention was sought by sick people. The fact that this divinity of the Nile found a residence in this region shows how intimate was the relation between Rome and Egypt in this ancient day. The Serapeium was built on the edge of the sea, just above its level. When in modern days it began to be studied, its floor was about on its original level, but the few standing columns of the edifice afford indubitable evidence that this part of the shore has been lowered to the amount of twenty feet or more and then re-elevated. The subsidence is proved by the fact that the upper part of the columns which were not protected by the *débris* accumulated about them have been bored by certain shellfish, known as *Lithodomi*, which have the habit of excavating shelters in soft stone, such as these marble columns afford. At present the floor on which the ruin stands appears to be gradually sinking, though the rate of movement is very slow.

Another evidence that the ejections may travel for a great distance underground on their way to the vent is afforded by the fact that Vesuvius and Ætna, though near three hundred miles apart, appear to exchange activities— that is, their periods of outbreak are not simultaneous. Although these elements of the chronology of the two cones may be accidental, taken with similar facts derived from other fields, they appear to indicate that vents, though far separated from each other, may, so to speak, be fed from a common subterranean source. It is a singular fact in this connection that the volcano of Stromboli, though situated between these two cones, is in a state of almost incessant activity. This probably indicates that the last-named vent derives its vapours from another level in the earth than the greater cones. In this regard volcanoes probably behave like springs, of which, indeed, they may be regarded as a group. The reader is doubtless aware that hot and cold springs often escape very near together, the difference in the temperature being due to the depth from which their waters come forth.

As the accidents of volcanic explosion are of a nature to be very damaging to man, as well as to the lower orders of Nature, it is fit that we should note in general the effect of the Neapolitan eruptions on the history of civilization in that region. As stated above, the first Greek settlements in this vicinity—those on the island of Ischia—were much disturbed by volcanic outbreaks, yet the island became the seat of a permanent and prosperous colony. The great eruption of 79 probably cost many hundred lives, and led to the abandonment of two considerable cities, which, however, could at small cost have been recovered to use. Since that day various eruptions have temporarily desolated portions of the territory, but only in very small fields have the ravages been irremediable. Where the ground was covered with dust, it has in most places been again tillable, and so rapid is the decay of the lavas that in a century after their flow has ceased vines can in most cases be

planted on their surfaces.   The city of Naples, which lies
amid the vents, though not immediately in contact with
any of them, has steadfastly grown and prospered from the
pre-Christian times.   It is doubtful if any lives have ever
been lost in the city in consequence of an eruption, and no
great inconvenience has been experienced from them.   Now
and then, after a great ash shower, the volcanic dust has
to be removed, but the labour is less serious than that imposed on many northern cities by a snowstorm.   Through
all these convulsions the tillage of the district has been
maintained.   It has ever been the seat of as rich and
profitable a husbandry as is afforded by any part of Italy.
In fact, the ash showers, as they import fine divided rock
very rich in substances necessary for the growth of plants,
have in a measure served to maintain the fertility of the
soil, and by this action have in some degree compensated
for the injury which they occasionally inflict.   Comparing
the ravages of the eruptions with those inflicted by war,
unnecessary disease, or even bad politics, and we see that
these natural accidents have been most merciful to man.
Many a tyrant has caused more suffering and death than
has been inflicted by these rude operations of Nature.

From the point of view of the naturalist, Ætna is
vastly more interesting than Vesuvius.   The bulk of the
cone is more than twenty times as great as that of the
Neapolitan volcano, and the magnitude of its explosions,
as well as the range of phenomena which they exhibit,
incomparably greater.   It happens, however, that while
human history of the recorded kind has been intimately
bound up with the tiny Vesuvian cone, partly because the
relatively slight nature of its disturbances permitted men
to dwell beside it, the larger Ætna has expelled culture
from the field near its vent, and has done the greater part
of its work in the vast solitude which it has created.*

---

* In part the excellent record of Vesuvius is due to the fact that
since the early Christian centuries the priests of St. Januarius, the patron·

Ætna has been in frequent eruption for a very much longer time than Vesuvius. In the odes of Pindar, in the sixth century before Christ, we find records of eruptions. It is said also that the philosopher Empedocles sought fame and death by casting himself into the fiery crater. There has thus in the case of this mountain been no such long period of repose as occurred in Vesuvius. Though our records of the outbreaks are exceedingly imperfect, they serve to show that the vent has maintained its activity much more continuously than is ordinarily the case with volcanoes. Ætna is characteristically a lava-yielding cone; though the amount of dust put forth is large, the ratio of the fluid rock which flows away from the crater is very much greater than at Vesuvius. Nearly half the cone, indeed, may be composed of this material. Our space does not permit anything like a consecutive story of the Ætnean eruptions since the dawn of history, or even a full account of its majestic cone; we can only note certain features of a particularly instructive nature which have been remarked by the many able men who have studied this structure and the effects of its outbreak.

The most important feature exhibited by Ætna is the vast size of its cone. At its apex its height, though variable from the frequent destruction and rebuilding of the crater walls, may be reckoned as about eleven thousand feet. The base on which the volcanic material lies is probably less than a thousand feet above the sea, so that the maximum thickness of the heap of volcanic ejections is probably about two miles. The average depth of this coating is probably about five thousand feet, and, as the cone has an average diameter of about thirty miles, we may conclude that the cone now contains about a thousand

---

of Naples, have been accustomed to carry his relics in procession whenever an eruption began. The cessation of the outbreak has been written down to the credit of the saint, and thus we are provided with a long story of the successive outbreaks.

Mount Ætna, seen from near Catania. The imperfect cones on the sky line to the left are those of small secondary eruptions.

cubic miles of volcanic materials. Great as is this mass,
it is only a small part of the ejected material which has
gone forth from the vent. All the matter which in its
vaporous state went forth with the eruption, the other
gases and vapours thus discharged, have disappeared. So,
too, a large part of the ash and much of the lava has
been swept away by the streams which drain the region,
and which in times of eruption are greatly swollen by the
accompanying torrential rains. The writer has estimated
that if all the emanations from the volcano—solid, fluid,
and gaseous—could be heaped on the cone, they would
form a mass of between two and three thousand cubic
miles in contents. Yet notwithstanding this enormous
outputting of earthy matter, the earth on which the
Ætnean cone has been constructed has not only failed to
sink down, but has been in process of continuous, slow
uprising, which has lifted the surface more than a thousand feet above the level which it had at the time when
volcanic action began in this field. Here, even more clearly
than in the case of Vesuvius, we see that the materials
driven forth from the crater are derived not from just
beneath its foundation, but from a distance, from realms
which in the case of this insular volcano are beneath the
sea floors. It is certain that here the migration of rock
matter, impelled by the expansion of its contained water
toward the vent, has so far exceeded that which has been
discharged through the crater that an uprising of the surface such as we have observed has been brought about.

There are certain peculiarities of Mount Ætna which
are due in part to its great size and in part to the climatal
conditions of the region in which it lies. The upper part
of the mountain in winter is deeply snow-clad; the frozen
water often, indeed, forms great drifts in the gorges near
the summit. Here it has occasionally happened that a
layer of ashes has deeply buried the mass, so that it has
been preserved for years, becoming gradually more inclosed by the subsequent eruptions. At one point where

this compact snow—which has, indeed, taken on the form of ice—has been revealed to view, it has been quarried and conveyed to the towns upon the seacoast. It is likely that there are many such masses of ice inclosed between the ash layers in the upper part of the mountain, where, owing to the height, the climate is very cold. This curious fact shows how perfect a non-conductor the ash beds of a volcano are to protect the frozen water from the heat of the rocks about the crater.

The furious rains which beset the mountain in times of great eruptions excavate deep channels on its sides. The lava outbreaks which attend almost every eruption, and which descend from the base of the cinder cone at the height of from five to eight thousand feet above the sea, naturally find their way into these channels, where they course in the manner of rivers until the lower and less valleyed section of the cone is reached.

Such a lava flow naturally begins to freeze on the surface, the lava at first becoming viscid, much in the manner of cream on the surface of milk. Urged along by the more fluid lava underneath, this viscid coating takes a ropy or corrugated form. As the freezing goes deeper, a firm stone roof may be formed across the gorge, which, when the current of lava ceases to flow from the crater, permits the lower part of the stream to drain away, leaving a long cavern or series of caves extending far up the cone. The nature of this action is exactly comparable to that which we may observe when on a frosty morning after rain we may find the empty channels which were occupied by rills of water roofed over with ice; the ice roofs are temporary, while those of lava may endure for ages. Some of these lava-stream caves have been disclosed, in the manner of ordinary caverns, by the falling of their roofs; but the greater part are naturally hidden beneath the ever-increasing materials of the cone.

The lava-stream caves of Ætna are not only interesting

because of their peculiarities of form, which we shall not
undertake to describe, but also for the reason that they
help us to account for a very peculiar feature in the history of the great cone. On the slopes of the volcano,
below the upper cindery portion, there are several hundred lesser cones, varying from a few score to seven hundred feet in height. Each of these has its appropriate
crater, and has evidently been the seat of one or more
eruptions. As the greater part of these cones are ancient,
many of them being almost effaced by the rain or buried
beneath the ejections which have surrounded their bases
since the time they were formed, we are led to believe
that many thousands of them have been formed during
the history of the volcano. The history of these subsidiary cones appears to be connected with the lava caves
noted above. These caverns, owing to the irregularities
of their form, contain water. They are, in fact, natural
cisterns, where the abundant rainfall of the mountain finds
here and there storage. When, during the throes of an eruption, dikes such as we know often to penetrate the mountain, are riven outward from the crater through the mass
of the cone, and filled with lava, the heated rock must
often come in contact with these masses of buried water.
The result of this would inevitably be the local generation of steam at a high temperature, which would force
its way out in a brief but vigorous eruption, such as has
been observed to take place when these peripheral volcanoes are formed. Sometimes it has happened that after
the explosion the lava has found its way in a stream from
the fissure thus opened. That this explanation is sufficient is in a measure shown by observations on certain
effects of lava flows from Vesuvius. The writer was informed by a very judicious observer, a resident of Naples,
who had interested himself in the phenomena of that volcano, that the lava streams when they penetrated a cis-
tern, such as they often encounter in passing over villages
or farmsteads, vaporized the water, and gave rise, through

the action of the steam, to small temporary cones, which, though generally washed away by the further flow of the liquid rock, are essentially like those which we find on Ætna. Such subsidiary, or, as they are sometimes called, parasitic cones, are known about other volcanoes, but nowhere are they so characteristic as on the flanks of that wonderful volcano.

A very conspicuous feature in the Ætnean cone consists of a great valley known as the Val del Bove, or Bull Hollow, which extends from the base of the modern and ever-changeable cinder cone down the flanks of the older structure to near its base. This valley has steep sides, in places a thousand or more feet high, and has evidently been formed by the down-settling of portions of the cone which were left without support by the withdrawal from beneath them of materials cast forth in a time of explosion. In an eruption this remarkable valley was the seat of a vast water flood, the fluid being cast forth from the crater at the beginning of the explosion. In the mouths of this and other volcanoes, after a long period of repose, great quantities of water, gathering from rains or condensed from the steam which slowly escapes from these openings, often pours like a flood down the sides of the mountains. In the great eruption of Galongoon, in Java, such a mass of water, cast forth by a terrific explosion, mingled with ashes, so that the mass formed a thick mud, was shot forth with such energy that it ravaged an area nearly eighty miles in diameter, destroying the forests and their wild inhabitants, as well as the people who dwelt within the range of the amazing disaster. So powerfully was this water driven from the crater that the districts immediately at the base of the cone were in a manner overshot by the vast stream, and escaped with relatively little injury.

When it comes forth from the base of the cinder cone, or from one of the small peripheral craters, the lava stream usually appears to be white hot, and to flow with almost the ease of water. It does not really have that measure of fluidity; its condition is rather that of thin paste; but the great weight of the material—near two and a half times that of water—causes the movement down the slope to be speedy. The central portion of the lava stream long retains its high temperature; but the surface, cooling, is first converted into a tough sheet, which, though it may bend, can hardly be said to flow. Further hardening converts these outlying portions of the current into hard, glassy stone, which is broken into fragments in a way resembling the ice on the surface of a river. It thus comes about that the advancing front of the lava stream becomes covered, and its motion hindered by the frozen rock, until the rate of ongoing may not exceed a few feet an hour, and the appearance is that of a heap of stone slowly rolling down a slope. Now and then a crevice is formed, through which a thin stream of liquid lava pours forth, but the material, having already parted with much of its heat, rapidly cools, and in turn becomes covered with the coating of frozen fragments. In this state of the stream the lava flow stands on all sides high above the slope which it is traversing; it is, in fact, walled in by its own solidified parts, though it is urged forward by the contribution which continues to flow in the under arches. In this state of the movement trifling accidents, or even human interference, may direct the current this way or that.

Some of the most interesting chapters in the history of Ætna relate to the efforts of the people to turn these slow-moving streams so that their torrents might flow into wilderness places rather than over the fields and towns. In the great flow of 1669, which menaced the city of Catania, a large place on the seashore to the southeast of the cone, a public-spirited citizen, Señor Papallardo, protecting himself and his servants with clothing made of hides, and with large shields, set forth armed with great hooks with the purpose of diverting the course of the lava

20

mass. He succeeded in pulling away the stones on the flank of the stream, so that a flow of the molten rock was turned in another direction. The expedient would probably have been successful if he had been allowed to continue his labours; but the inhabitants of a neighbouring village, which was threatened by the off-shooting current which Papallardo had created, took up arms and drove him and his retainers away. The flow continued until it reached Catania. The people made haste to build the city walls on the side of danger higher than it was before, but the tide mounted over its summit.

Although the lavas which come forth from the volcano evidently have a high temperature, their capacity for melting other rocks is relatively small. They scour these rocks, because of their weight, even more energetically than do powerful torrents of water, but they are relatively ineffective in melting stone. On Ætna and elsewhere we may often observe lavas which have flowed through forests. When the tide of molten rock has passed by, the trees may be found charred but not entirely burned away; even stems a few inches in diameter retain strength enough to uphold considerable fringes and clots of the lava which has clung to them. These facts bear out the conclusion that the fluidity of the heated stone depends in considerable measure on the water which is contained, either in its fluid or vaporous state, between the particles of the material.

If we consider the Italian volcanoes as a whole, we find that they lie in a long, discontinuous line extending from the northern part of the valley of the Po, within sight of the Alps, to Ætna, and in subterranean cones perhaps to the northern coast of Africa. At the northern end of the line we have a beautiful group of extinct volcanoes, known as the Eugean Mountains. Thence southward to southern Tuscany craters are wanting, but there is evidence of fissures in the earth which give forth thermal waters. From southern Tuscany southward through

Rome to Naples there are many extinct craters, none of which have been active in the historic period. From Naples southward the cones of this system, about a dozen in number, are on islands or close to the margin of the sea. It is a noteworthy fact that the greater part of these shore or insular vents have been active since the dawn of history; several of them frequently and furiously so, while none of those occupying an inland position have been the seat of explosions. This is a striking instance going to show the relation of these processes to conditions which are brought about on the sea bottom.

Ætna is, as we have noticed, a much more powerful volcano than Vesuvius. Its outbreaks are more vigorous, its emanations vastly greater in volume, and the mass of its constructions many times as great as those accumulated in any other European cone. There are, however, a number of volcanoes in the world which in certain features surpass Ætna as much as that crater does Vesuvius. Of these we shall consider but two—Skaptar Jokul, of Iceland, remarkable for the volume of its lava flow, and Krakatoa, an island volcano between Java and Sumatra, which was the seat of the greatest explosion of which we have any record.

The whole of Iceland may be regarded as a volcanic mass composed mainly of lavas and ashes which have been thrown up by a group of volcanoes lying near the northern end of the long igneous axis which extends through the centre of the Atlantic. The island has been the seat of numerous eruptions; in fact, since its settlement by the Northmen in 1070 its sturdy inhabitants have been almost as much distressed by the calamities which have come from the internal heat as they have been by the enduring external cold. They have, indeed, been between frost and fire. The greatest recorded eruption of Iceland occurred in 1783, when the volcano of Skaptar, near the southern border of the island, poured forth, first, a vast discharge of dust and ashes, and afterward in the languid state of eruption inundated a series of valleys with the greatest lava flow of which we have any written record. The dust poured forth into the upper air, being finely divided and in enormous quantity, floated in the air for months, giving a dusky hue to the skies of Europe, which led the common people and many of the learned to fear that the wrath of God was upon them, and that the day of judgment was at hand. Even the poet Cowper, a man of high culture and education, shared in this unreasonable view.

The lava flow in this eruption filled one of the considerable valleys of the island, drying up the river, and inundating the plains on either side. Estimates which have been made as to the volume of this flow appear to indicate that it may have amounted to more than the bulk of the Mont Blanc.

This great eruption, by the direct effect of the calamity, and by the famine due to the ravaging of the fields and the frightening of the fish from the shores which it induced, destroyed nearly one fifth of the Icelandic people. It is, in fact, to be remembered as one of the three or four most calamitous eruptions of which we have any account, and, from the point of view of lava flow, the greatest in history.

Just a hundred years after the great Skaptar eruption, which darkened the skies of Europe, the island of Krakatoa, an isle formed by a small volcano in the straits of Java, was the seat of a vapour explosion which from its intensity is not only unparalleled, but almost unapproached in all accounts of such disturbances. Krakatoa had long been recognised as a volcanic isle; it is doubtful, however, if it had ever been seen in eruption during the three centuries or more since European ships began to sail by it until the month of May of the year above mentioned. Then an outbreak of what may be called ordinary violence took place, which after a few days so far ceased that observers landed and took account of the changes which

the convulsion had brought about. For about three months
there were no further signs of activity, but on the 29th of
August a succession of vast explosions took place, which
blew away a great part of the island, forming in its place a
submarine crater two or three miles in diameter, creating
world-wide disturbances of sea and air.   The sounds of the
outbreak were heard at a distance of sixteen hundred miles
away.   The waves of the air attendant on the explosion
ran round the earth at least once, as was distinctly indicated by the self-recording barometers; it is possible, indeed, that, crossing each other in their east and west
courses, these atmospheric tides twice girdled the sphere.
In effect, the air over the crater was heaved up to the
height of some tens of thousands of feet, and thence rolled
off in great circular waves, such as may be observed in a
pan of milk when a sharp blow pushes the bottom upward.

The violent stroke delivered to the waters of the sea
created a vast wave, which in the region where it originated rolled upon the shores with a surf wall fifty or more
feet high.   In a few minutes about thirty thousand people
were overwhelmed.   The wave rolled on beyond its destructive limits much in the manner of the tide; its influence was felt in a sharp rise and fall of the waters as far
as the Pacific coast of North America, and was indicated
by the tide gauges in the Atlantic as far north as the coast
of Europe.

Owing to the violence of the eruption, Krakatoa poured
forth no lava, but the dust and ashes which ascended into
the air—or, in other words, the finely divided lava which
escaped into the atmosphere—probably amounted in bulk
to more than twenty cubic miles.   The coarser part of this
material, including much pumice, fell upon the seas in the
vicinity, where, owing to its lightness, it was free to drift
in the marine currents far and wide throughout the oceanic
realm.   The finer particles, thrown high into the air, perhaps to the height of nearly a hundred thousand feet—certainly to the elevation of more than half this amount—

drifted far and wide in the atmosphere, so that for years the air of all regions was clouded by it, the sunrise and sunset having a peculiar red glow, which the dust particles produce by the light which they reflect. In this period, at all times when the day was clear, the sun appeared to be surrounded by a dusky halo. In time the greater part of this dust was drawn down by gravity, some portion of it probably falling on every square foot of the earth. Since the disappearance of the characteristic phenomena which it produced in the atmosphere, European observers have noted the existence of faint clouds lying in the upper part of the air at the height of a hundred miles or more above the surface. These clouds, which were at first distinctly visible in the earliest stage of dawn and in the latest period of the sunset glow, seemed to be in rapid motion to the eastward, and to be mounting higher above the earth. It has been not unreasonably supposed that these shining clouds represent portions of the finest dust from Krakatoa, which has been thrown so far above the earth's attraction that it is separating itself from the sphere. If this view be correct, it seems likely that we may look to great volcanic explosions as a source whence the dustlike particles which people the celestial spaces may have come. They may, in a word, be due to volcanic explosions occurring on this and other celestial spheres.

The question suggested above as to the possibility of volcanic ejections throwing matter from the earth beyond the control of its gravitative energy is one of great scientific interest. Computations (not altogether trustworthy) show that a body leaving the earth's surface under the conditions of a cannon ball fired vertically upward would have to possess a velocity at the start of at least seven miles a second in order to go free into space. It would at first sight seem that we should be able to reckon whether volcanoes can propel earth matter upward with this speed. In fact, however, sufficient data are not obtainable; we only know in a general way that the column of vapour rises to the height of thirty or forty thousand feet, and this in eruptions of no great magnitude. In an accident such as that at Krakatoa, even if an observer were near enough to see clearly what was going on, the chance of his surviving the disturbance would be small. Moreover, the ascending vapours, owing to their expansion of the steam in the column, begin to fly out sideways on its periphery, so that the upper part of the central section in the discharge is not visible from the earth.

It is in the central section of the uprushing mass, if anywhere, that the dust might attain the height necessary to put it beyond the earth's attraction, bringing it fairly into the realm of the solar system, or to the position where its own motion and the attraction of the other spheres would give it an independent orbital movement about the sun, or perhaps about the earth. We can only say that observations on the height of volcanic ejections are extremely desirable; they can probably only be made from a balloon. An ascension thus made beyond the cloud disk which the eruption produces might bring the observer where he could discern enough to determine the matter. Although the movements of the rocky particles could not be observed, the colour which they would give to the heavens might tell the story which we wish to know. There is evidence that large masses of stone hurled up by volcanic eruption have fallen seven miles from the base of the cone. Assuming that the masses went straight upward at the beginning of their ascent, and that they were afterward borne outwardly by the expansion of the column, computations which have a general but no absolute value appear to indicate that the masses attained a height of from thirty to fifty miles, and had an initial velocity which, if doubled, might have carried them into space.

Last of all, we shall note the conditions which attend the eruptions of submarine volcanoes. Such explosions have been observed in but a few instances, and only in those cases where there is reason to believe that the crater at the time of its explosion had attained to within a few hundred feet of the sea level. In these cases the ejections, never as yet observed in the state of lava, but in the condition of dust and pumice, have occasionally formed a low island, which has shortly been washed away by the waves. Knowing as we do that volcanoes abound on the sea floor, the question why we do not oftener see their explosions disturbing the surface of the waters is very interesting, but not as yet clearly explicable. It is possible, however, that a volcanic discharge taking place at the depth of several thousand feet below the surface of the water would not be able to blow the fluid aside so as to open a pipe to the surface, but would expend its energy in a hidden manner near the ocean floor. The vapours would have to expand gradually, as they do in passing up through the rock pipe of a volcano, and in their slow upward passage might be absorbed by the water. The solid materials thrown forth would in this case necessarily fall close about the vent, and create a very steep cone, such, indeed, as we find indicated by the soundings off certain volcanic islands which appear only recently to have overtopped the level of the waters.

As will be seen, though inadequately from the diagrams of Vesuvius, volcanic cones have a regularity and symmetry of form far exceeding that afforded by the outlines of any other of the earth's features. Where, as is generally the case, the shape of the cone is determined by the distribution of the falling cinders or divided lava which constitutes the mass of most cones, the slope is in general that known as a catenary curve—i. e., the line formed by a chain hanging between two points at some distance from the vertical. It is interesting to note that this graceful outline is a reflection or consequence of the curve described by the uprushing vapour. The expansion in the ascending column causes it to enlarge at a somewhat steadfast rate, while the speed of the ascent is ever diminishing. Precisely the same action can be seen in the like rush of steam and other gases and vapours from the cannon's mouth; only in the case of the gun, even of the greatest size, we can not trace the movement for more than a few hundred feet. In this column of ejection the outward movement from the centre carries the bits of lava outwardly from the centre of the shaft, so that when they lose their ascending velocity they are drawn downward upon the flanks of the cone, the amount falling upon each part of that surface being in a general way proportional to the thickness of the vaporous mass from which they descend. The result is, that the thickest part of the ash heap is formed on the upper part of the crater, from which point the deposit fades away in depth in every direction. In a certain measure the concentration toward the centre of the cone is brought about by the draught of air which moves in toward the ascending column.

Although, in general, ejections of volcanic matter take place through cones, that being the inevitable form produced by the escaping steam, very extensive outpourings of lava, ejections which in mass probably far exceed those thrown forth through ordinary craters, are occasionally poured out through fissures in the earth's crust. Thus in Oregon, Idaho, and Washington, in eastern Europe, in southern India, and at some other points, vast flows, which apparently took place from fissures, have inundated great realms with lava ejections. The conditions which appear to bring about these fissure eruptions of lava are not yet well understood. A provisional and very probable account of the action can be had in the hypothesis which will now be set forth.

Where any region has been for a long time the seat of volcanic action, it is probable that a large amount of rock in a more or less fluid condition exists beneath its surface. Although the outrushing steam ejects much of this molten material, there are reasons to suppose that a yet greater part lies dormant in the underground spaces. Thus in the case of Ætna we have seen that, though some thousands of miles of rock matter have come forth, the base of the cone has been uplifted, probably by the moving to that region of more or less fluid rock. If now a region thus underlaid by what we may call incipient lavas is subjected to the peculiar compressive actions which lead to mountain-building, we should naturally expect that such soft material would be poured forth, possibly in vast quantities through fault fissures, which are so readily formed in all kinds of rock when subject to irregular and powerful strains, such as are necessarily brought about when rocks are moved in mountain-making. The great eruptions which formed the volcanic table-lands on the west coast of North America appear to have owed the extrusion of their materials to mountain-building actions. This seems to have been the case also in some of those smaller areas where fissure flows occur in Europe. It is likely that this action will explain the greater part of these massive eruptions.

It need not be supposed that the rock beneath these countries, which when forced out became lava, was necessarily in the state of perfect fluidity before it was forced through the fissures. Situated at great depth in the earth, it was under a pressure so great that its particles may have been so brought together that the material was essentially solid, though free to move under the great strains which affected it, and acquiring temperature along with the fluidity which heat induces as it was forced along by the mountain-building pressure. As an illustration of how materials may become highly heated when forced to move particle on particle, it may be well to cite the case in which the iron stringpiece on top of a wooden dam near Holyoke, Mass., was affected when the barrier went away in a flood. The iron stringer, being very well put together, was, it is said, drawn out by the strain until it became sensibly reddened by the motion of its particles, and finally fell hissing into the waters below. A like heating is observable when metal is drawn out in making wire. Thus a mass of imperfectly fluid rock might in a forced journey of a few miles acquire a decided increase of temperature.

Although the most striking volcanic action—all such phenomena, indeed, as commonly receives the name—is exhibited finally on the earth's surface, a great deal of work which belongs in the same group of geological actions is altogether confined to the deep-lying rock, and leads to the formation of dikes which penetrate the strata, but do not rise to the open air. We have already noted the fact that dikes abound in the deeper parts of volcanic cones, though the fissures into which they find their way are seldom riven up to the surface. In the same way beneath the ground in non-volcanic countries we may discover at a great depth in the older, much-changed rock a vast number of these crevices, varying from a few inches to a hundred feet or more in width, which have been filled with lavas, the rock once molten having afterward cooled. In most cases these dikes are disclosed to us through the down-wearing of the earth that has removed the beds into which the dikes did not penetrate, thus disclosing the realm in which the disturbances took place.

Where, as is occasionally the case in deep mines, or on some bare rocky cliff of great height, we can trace a dike in its upward course through a long distance, we find that we can never distinctly discover the lower point of its extension. No one has ever seen in a clear way the point of origin of such an injection. We can, however, often follow it upward to the place where there was no longer a rift into which it could enter. In its upward path the molten matter appears generally to have followed some previously existing fracture, a joint plane or a fault, which generally runs through the rocks on those planes. We can observe evidence that the material was in the state of igneous fluidity by the fact that it has baked the country rocks on either side of the fissure, the amount of baking being in proportion to the width of the dike, and thus to the amount of heat which it could give forth. A dike six

inches in diameter will sometimes barely scar its walls,
while one a hundred feet in width will often alter the
strata for a great distance on either side. In some instances, as in the coal beds near Richmond, Va., dikes occasionally cut through beds of bituminous coal. In these
cases we find that the coal has been converted into coke
for many feet either side of a considerable injection. The
fact that the dike material was molten is still further
shown by the occurrence in it of fragments which it has
taken up from the walls, and which may have been partly
melted, and in most cases have clearly been much heated.

Where dikes extend up through stratified beds which
are separated from each other by distinct layers, along
which the rock is not firmly bound together, it now and
then happens, as noted by Mr. G. K. Gilbert, of the United
States Geological Survey, that the lava has forced its way
horizontally between these layers, gradually uplifting the
overlying mass, which it did not break through, into a
dome-shaped elevation. These side flows from dikes are
termed laccolites, a word which signifies the pool-like nature of the stony mass which they form between the
strata.

In many regions, where the earth has worn down so
as to reveal the zone of dikes which was formed at a great
depth, the surface of the country is fairly laced with these
intrusions. Thus on Cape Ann, a rocky isle on the east
coast of Massachusetts, having an area of about twenty
square miles, the writer, with the assistance of his col-
league, Prof. R. S. Tarr, found about four hundred distinct dikes exhibited on the shore line where the rocks
had been swept bare by the waves. If the census of these
intrusions could have been extended over the whole island,
it would probably have appeared that the total number
exceeded five thousand. In other regions square miles can
be found where the dikes intercepted by the surface occupy
an aggregate area greater than that of the rocks into
which they have been intruded.

Now and then, but rarely, the student of dikes finds one where the bordering walls, in place of having the clean-cut appearance which they usually exhibit, has its sides greatly worn away and much melted, as if by the long-continued passage of the igneous fluid through the crevice. Such dikes are usually very wide, and are probably the paths through which lavas found their way to the surface of the earth, pouring forth in a volcanic eruption. In some cases we can trace their relation to ancient volcanic cones which have worn down in all their part which were made up of incoherent materials, so that there remains only the central pipe, which has been preserved from decay by the coherent character of the lava which filled it.

The hypothesis that dikes are driven upward into strata by the pressure of the beds which overlie materials hot and soft enough to be put in motion when a fissure enters them, and that their movement upward through the crevice is accounted for by this pressure, makes certain features of these intrusions comprehensible. Seeing that very long, slender dikes are found penetrating the rock, which could not have had a high temperature, it becomes difficult to understand how the lava could have maintained its fluidity; but on the supposition that it was impelled forward by a strong pressure, and that the energy thus transmitted through it was converted into heat, we discover a means whereby it could have been retained in the liquid condition, even when forced for long distances through very narrow channels. Moreover, this explanation accounts for the fact which has long remained unexplained that dikes, except those formed about volcanic craters, rarely, if ever, rise to the surface.

The materials contained in dikes differ exceedingly in their chemical and mineral character. These variations are due to the differences in Nature of the deposits whence they come, and also in a measure to exchanges which take place between their own substance and that of the rocks between which they are deposited. This process often has importance of an economic kind, for it not infrequently leads to the formation of metalliferous veins or other aggregations of ores, either in the dike itself or in the country rock. The way in which this is brought about may be easily understood by a familiar example. If flesh be placed in water which has the same temperature, no exchange of materials will take place; but if the water be heated, a circulation will be set up, which in time will bring a large part of the soluble matter into the surrounding water. This movement is primarily dependent on differences of temperature, and consequently differences in the quantity of soluble substances which the water seeks to take up. When a dike is injected into cooler rocks, such a slow circulation is induced. The water contained in the interstices of the stone becomes charged with mineral materials, if such exist in positions where it can obtain possession of them, and as cooling goes on, these dissolved materials are deposited in the manner of veins. These veins are generally laid down on the planes of contact between the two kinds of stone, but they may be formed in any other cavities which exist in the neighbourhood. The formation of such veins is often aided by the considerable shrinkage of the lava in the dike, which, when it cools, tends to lose about fifteen per cent of its volume, and is thus likely to leave a crevice next the boundary walls. Ores thus formed afford some of the commonest and often the richest mineral deposits. At Leadville, in Colorado, the great silver-bearing lodes probably were produced in this manner, wherein lavas, either those of dikes or those which flowed in the open air, have come in contact with limestones. The mineral materials originally in the once molten rock or in the limy beds was, we believe, laid down on ancient sea floors in the remains of organic forms, which for their particular uses took the materials from the old sea water. The vein-making action has served to assemble these scattered bits of metal into

the aggregation which constitutes a workable deposit.   In
time, as the rocks wear down, the materials of the veins
are again taken into solution and returned to the sea,
thence perhaps to tread again the cycle of change.

In certain dikes, and sometimes also, perhaps, in lavas
known as basalts, which have flowed on the surface, the
rock when cooling, from the shrinkage which then occurs,
has broken in a very regular way, forming hexagonal columns which are more or less divided on their length by
joints.   When worn away by the agencies of decay, especially where the material forms steep cliffs, a highly artificial effect is produced, which is often compared, where
cut at right angles to the columns, to pavements, or, where
the division is parallel to the columns, to the pipes of an
organ.

What we know of dikes inclines us to the opinion that
as a whole they represent movements of softened rock
where the motion-compelling agent is not mainly the expansion of the contained water which gives rise to volcanic ejection, but rather in large part due to the weight
of superincumbent strata setting in motion materials which
were somewhat softened, and which tended to creep, as do
the clays in deep coal mines.   It is evident, however; it
is, moreover, quite natural, that dike work is somewhat
mingled with that produced by the volcanic forces; but
while the line between the two actions is not sharp, the
discrimination is important, and occurs with a distinctness
rather unusual on the boundary line between two adjacent
fields of phenomena.

We have now to consider the general effects of the
earth's interior heat so far as that body of temperature
tends to drive materials from the depths of the earth to
the surface.   This group of influences is one of the most
important which operates on our sphere; as we shall
shortly see, without such action the earth would in time
become an unfit theatre for the development of organic

life. To perceive the effect of these movements, we must first note that in the great rock-constructing realm of the seas organic life is constantly extracting from the water substances, such as lime, potash, soda, and a host of other substances necessary for the maintenance of high-grade organisms, depositing these materials in the growing strata. Into these beds, which are buried as fast as they form, goes not only these earthy materials, but a great store of the sea water as well. The result would be in course of time a complete withdrawal into the depths of the earth of those substances which play a necessary part in organic development. The earth would become more or less completely waterless on its surface, and the rocks exposed to view would be composed mainly of silica, the material which to a great extent resists solution, and therefore avoids the dissolving which overtakes most other kinds of rocks. Here comes in the machinery of the hot springs, the dikes, and the volcanoes. These agents, operating under the influence of the internal heat of the earth, are constantly engaged in bearing the earthy matter, particularly its precious more solvent parts, back to the surface. The hot springs and volcanoes work swiftly and directly, and return the water, the carbon dioxide, and a host of other vaporizable and soluble and fusible substances to the realm of solar activity, to the living surface zone of the earth. The dikes operate less immediately, but in the end to the same effect. They lift their materials miles above the level where they were originally laid, probably from a zone which is rarely if ever exposed to view, placing them near the surface, where the erosive agents can readily find access to them.

Of the three agents which serve to export earth materials from its depths, volcanoes are doubtless the most important. They send forth the greater part of the water which is expelled from the rocks. Various computations which the writer has made indicate that an ordinary volcano, such as Ætna, in times of most intense explosion, ' may send forth in the form of steam one fourth of a cubic mile or more of water during each day of its discharge, and in a single great eruption may pour forth several times this quantity. In its history Ætna has probably returned to the atmosphere some hundred cubic miles of water which but for the process would have remained permanently locked up in its rock prison.

The ejection of rock material, though probably on the average less in quantity than the water which escapes, is also of noteworthy importance. The volcanoes of Java and the adjacent isles have, during the last hundred and twenty years, delivered to the seas more earth material than has been carried into those basins by the great rivers. If we could take account of all the volcanic ejections which have occurred in this time, we should doubtless find that the sum of the materials thus cast forth into the oceans was several times as great as that which was delivered from the lands by all the superficial agents which wear them away. Moreover, while the material from the land, except the small part which is in a state of complete solution, all falls close to the shore, the volcanic waste, because of its fine division or because of the blebs of air which its masses contain, may float for many years before it finds its way to the bottom, it may be at the antipodes of the point at which it came from the earth. While thus journeying through the sea the rock matter from the volcanoes is apt to become dissolved in water; it is, indeed, doubtful if any considerable part of that which enters the ocean goes by gravitation to its floor. The greater portion probably enters the state of solution and makes its way thence through the bodies of plants and animals again into the ponderable state.

If an observer could view the earth from the surface of the moon, he would probably each day behold one of these storms which the volcanoes send forth. In the fortnight of darkness, even with the naked eye, it would probably be possible to discern at any time several eruptions,

21

some of which would indicate that the earth's surface was ravaged by great catastrophes. The nearer view of these actions shows us that although locally and in small measure they are harmful to the life of the earth, they are in a large way beneficent.

CHAPTER VIII.

THE SOIL.

THE frequent mention which it has been necessary to make of soil phenomena in the preceding chapters shows how intimately this feature in the structure of the earth is blended with all the elements of its physical history. It is now necessary for us to take up the phenomena of soils in a consecutive manner.

The study of any considerable river basin enables us to trace the more important steps which lead to the destructure and renovation of the earth's detrital coating. In such an interpretation we note that everywhere the rocks which were built on the sea bottom, and more or less made over in the great laboratory of the earth's interior, are at the surface, when exposed to the conditions of the atmosphere, in process of being taken to pieces and returned to the sea. This action goes on everywhere; every drop of rain helps it. It is aided by frost, or even by the changes of expansion and contraction which occur in the rocks from variations of heat. The result is that, except where the slopes are steep, the surface is quickly covered with a layer of fragments, all of which are in the process of decay, and ready to afford some food to plants. Even where the rock appears bare, it is generally covered with lichens, which, adhering to it, obtain a share of nutriment from the decayed material which they help to hold on the slope. When they have retained a thin sheet of the *débris,* mosses and small flowering plants help the work of retaining the

detritus. Soon the strong-rooted bushes and trees win a
foothold, and by sending their rootlets, which are at first
small but rapidly enlarge, into the crevices, they hasten
the disruption of the stones.

If the construction of soil goes on upon a steep cliff,
the quantity retained on the slope may be small, but at the
base we find a talus, composed of the fragments not held
by the vegetation, which gradually increases as the cliff
wears down, until the original precipice may be quite obliterated beneath a soil slope. At first this process is rapid;
it becomes gradually slower and slower as the talus mounts
up the cliff and as the cliff loses its steepness, until finally
a gentle slope takes the place of the steep.

From the highest points in any river valley to the sea
level the broken-up rock, which we term soil, is in process
of continuous motion. Everywhere the rain water, flowing
over the surface or soaking through the porous mass, is
conveying portions of the material which is taken into
solution in a speedy manner to the sea. Everywhere the
expansion of the soil in freezing, or the movements imposed on it by the growth of roots, by the overturning of
trees, or by the innumerable borings and burrowings which
animals make in the mass, is through the action of gravitation slowly working down the slope. Every little disturbance of the grains or fragments of the soil which lifts them
up causes them when they fall to descend a little way farther toward the sea level. Working toward the streams,
the materials of the soil are in time delivered to those
flowing waters, and by them urged speedily, though in
most cases interruptedly, toward the ocean.

There is another element in the movement of the soils
which, though less appreciable, is still of great importance.
The agents of decay which produce and remove the detritus, the chemical changes of the bed rock, and the mechanical action which roots apply to them, along with the
solutional processes, are constantly lowering the surface of
the mass. In this way we can often prove that a soil con-

tinuously existing has worked downward through many thousand feet of strata. In this process of downgoing the country on which the layer rests may have greatly changed its form, but the deposit, under favourable conditions, may continue to retain some trace of the materials which it derived from beds which have long since disappeared, their position having been far up in the spaces now occupied by the air. Where the slopes are steep and streams abound, we rarely find detritus which belonged in rock more than a hundred feet above the present surface of the soil. Where, however, as on those isolated table-lands or buttes which abound in certain portions of the Mississippi Valley, as well as in many other countries, we find a patch of soil lying on a nearly level surface, which for geologic ages has not felt the effect of streams, we may discover, commingled in the *débris*, the harder wreckage derived from the decay of a thousand feet or more of vanished strata.

When we consider the effect of organic life on the processes which go on in the soil, we first note the large fact that the development of all land vegetation depends upon the existence of this detritus—in a word, on the slow movement of the decaying rocky matter from the point where it is disrupted to its field of rest in the depths of the sea. The plants take their food from the portion of this rocky waste which is brought into solution by the waters which penetrate the mass. On the plants the animals feed, and so this vast assemblage of organisms is maintained. Not only does the land life maintain itself on the soil, and give much to the sea, but it serves in various ways to protect this detrital coating from too rapid destruction, and to improve its quality. To see the nature of this work we should visit a region where primeval forests still lie upon the slopes of a hilly region. In the body of such a wood we find next the surface a coating of decayed vegetable matter, made up of the falling leaves, bark, branches, and trunks which are constantly descending to the earth. Ordinarily, this layer is a foot or more in thickness; at the top it is almost altogether composed of vegetable matter; at the bottom it verges into the true soil. An important effect of this decayed vegetation is to restrain the movement of the surface water. Even in the heaviest rains, provided the mass be not frozen, the water is taken into it and delivered in the manner of springs to the larger streams. We can better note the measure of this effect by observing the difference in the ground covered by this primeval forest and that which we find near by which has been converted into tilled fields. With the same degree of rapidity in the flow, the distinct stream channels on the tilled ground are likely to be from twenty to a hundred times in length what they are on the forest bed. The result is that while the brook which drains the forested area maintains a tolerably constant flow of clean water, the other from the tilled ground courses only in times of heavy rain, and then is heavily charged with mud. In the virgin conditions of the soil the downwear is very slow; in its artificial state this wearing goes on so rapidly that the sloping fields are likely to be worn to below the soil level in a few score years.

Not only does the natural coating of vegetation, such as our forests impose upon the country, protect the soil from washing away, but the roots of the larger plants are continually at work in various ways to increase the fertility and depth of the stratum. In the form of slender fibrils these underground branches enter the joints and bed planes of the rock, and there growing they disrupt the materials, giving them a larger surface on which decay may operate. These bits, at first of considerable size, are in turn broken up by the same action. Where the underlying rocks afford nutritious materials, the branches of our tap-rooted trees sometimes find their way ten feet or more below the base of the true soil. Not only do they thus break up the stones, but the nutrition which they obtain in the depths is brought up and deposited in the parts above the ground, as well as in the roots which lie in the true soil, so that

when the tree dies it becomes available for other plants.
Thus in the forest condition of a country the amount of
rock material contributed to the deposit in general so far
exceeds that which is taken away to the rivers by the underground water as to insure the deepening of the soil bed to
the point where only the strongest roots—those belonging to our tap-rooted trees—can penetrate through it to
the bed rocks.

Almost all forests are from time to time visited by
winds which uproot the trees. When they are thus rent
from the earth, the underground branches often form a
disk containing a thick tangle of stones and earth, and
having a diameter of ten or fifteen feet. The writer has
frequently observed a hundred cubic feet of soil matter,
some of it taken from the depth of a yard or more, thus
uplifted into the air. In the path of a hurricane or tornado we may sometimes find thousands of acres which have
been subjected to this rude overturning—a natural ploughing. As the roots rot away, the *débris* which they held
falls outside of the pit, thus forming a little hillock along
the side of the cavity. After a time the thrusting action of
other roots and the slow motion of the soil down the slope
restore the surface from its hillocky character to its original smoothness; but in many cases the naturalist who has
learned to discern with his feet may note these irregularities long after it has been recovered with the forest.

Great as is the effect of plants on the soil, that influence is almost equalled by the action of the animals which
have the habit of entering the earth, finding there a temporary abiding place. The number of these ground forms
is surprisingly great. It includes, indeed, a host of creatures which are efficient agents in enriching the earth.
The species of earthworms, some of which occupy forested
districts as well as the fields, have the habit of passing the
soil material through their bodies, extracting from the
mass such nutriment as it may contain. In this manner
the particles of mineral matter become pulverized, and in

a measure affected by chemical changes in the bodies of the creatures, and are thus better fitted to afford plant food. Sometimes the amount of the earth which the creatures take in in moving through their burrows and void upon the surface is sufficient to form annually a layer on the surface of the ground having a depth of one twentieth of an inch or more. It thus may well happen that the soil to the depth of two or three feet is completely overturned in the course of a few hundred years. As the particles which the creatures devour are rather small, the tendency is to accumulate the finer portions of the soil near the surface of the earth, where by solution they may contribute to the needs of the lowly plants. It is probably due to the action of these creatures that small relics of ancient men, such as stone tools, are commonly found buried at a considerable depth beneath the earth, and rarely appear upon the surface except where it has been subjected to deep ploughing or to the action of running streams.

Along with the earthworms, the ants labour to overturn the soil; frequently they are the more effective of the two agents. The common species, though they make no permanent hillocks, have been observed by the writer to lay upon the surface each year as much as a quarter of an inch of sand and other fine materials which they have brought up from a considerable depth. In many regions, particularly in those occupied by glacial drift, and pebbly alluvium along the rivers, the effect of this action, like that of earthworms, is to bring to the surface the finer materials, leaving the coarser pebbles in the depths. In this way they have changed the superficial character of the soil over great areas; we may say, indeed, over a large part of the earth, and this in a way which fits it better to serve the needs of the wild plants as well as the uses of the farmer.

Many thousand species of insects, particularly the larger beetles, have the habit of passing their larval state in the under earth. Here they generally excavate burrows, and thus in a way delve the soil. As many of them die before reaching maturity, their store of organic matter is contributed to the mass, and serves to nourish the plants. If the student will carefully examine a section of the earth either in its natural or in its tilled state, he will be surprised to find how numerous the grubs are. They may often be found to the number of a score or more of each cubic foot of material. Many of the species which develop underground come from eggs which have carefully been encased in organic matter before their deposition in the earth. Thus some of the carrion beetles are in the habit of laying their eggs in the bodies of dead birds or field mice, which they then bury to the depth of some inches in the earth. In this way nearly all the small birds and mammals of our woods disappear from view in a few hours after they are dead. Other species make balls from the dung of cattle in which they lay their eggs, afterward rolling the little spheres, it may be for hundreds of feet, to the chambers in the soil which they have previously prepared. In this way a great deal of animal matter is introduced into the earth, and contributes to its fertility.

Many of our small mammals have the habit of making their dwelling places in the soil. Some of them, such as the moles, normally abide in the subterranean realm for all their lives. Others use the excavations as places of retreat. In any case, these excavations serve to move the particles of the soil about, and the materials which the animals drag into the earth, as well as the excrement of the creatures, act to enrich it. This habit of taking food underground is not limited to the mammals; it is common with the ants, and even the earthworms, as noted by Charles Darwin in his wonderful essay on these creatures, are accustomed to drag into their burrows bits of grass and the slender leaves of pines. It is not known what purpose they attain by these actions, but it is sufficiently common somewhat to affect the conditions of the soil.

The result of these complicated works done by animals and plants on the soil is that the material to a considerable depth are constantly being supplied with organic matter, which, along with the mineral material, constitutes that part of the earth which can support vegetation. Experiment will readily show that neither crushed rock nor pure vegetable mould will of itself serve to maintain any but the lowliest vegetation. It requires that the two materials be mixed in order that the earth may yield food for ordinary plants, particularly for those which are of use to man, as crops. On this account all the processes above noted whereby the waste of plant and animal life is carried below the surface are of the utmost importance in the creation and preservation of the soil. It has been found, indeed, in almost all cases, necessary for the farmer to maintain the fertility of his fields to plough-in quantities of such organic waste. By so doing he imitates the work which is effected in virgin soil by natural action. As the process is costly in time and material, it is often neglected or imperfectly done, with the result that the fields rapidly diminish in fertility.

The way in which the buried organic matter acts upon the soil is not yet thoroughly understood. In part it accomplishes the results by the materials which on its decay it contributes to the soil in a state in which they may readily be dissolved and taken up by the roots into their sap; in part, however, it is believed that they better the conditions by affording dwelling places for a host of lowly species, such as the forms which are known as bacteria. The organisms probably aid in the decomposition of the mineral matter, and in the conversion of nitrogen, which abounds in the air or the soil, into nitrates of potash and soda—substances which have a very great value as fertilizers. Some effect is produced by the decay of the foreign matter brought into the soil, which as it passes away leaves channels through which the soil water can more readily pass.

By far the most general and important effect arising from the decay of organic matter in the earth is to be found in the carbon dioxide which is formed as the oxygen of the air combines with the carbon which all organic material contains. As before noted, water thus charged has its capacity for taking other substances into solution vastly increased, and on this solvent action depends in large part the decay of the bed rocks and the solution of materials which are to be appropriated by the plants.

Having now sketched the general conditions which lead to the formation of soils, we must take account of certain important variations in their conditions due to differences in the ways in which they are formed and preserved. These matters are not only of interest to the geologist, but are of the utmost importance to the life of mankind, as well as all the lower creatures which dwell upon the lands. First, we should note that soils are divisible into three great groups, which, though not sharply parted from each other, are sufficiently peculiar for the purposes of classification. Where the earth material has been derived from the rocks which nearly or immediately underlie it, we have a group of soils which may be entitled those of immediate derivation—that is, derived from rocks near by, or from beds which once overlaid the level and have since been decayed away. Next, we have alluvial soils, those composed of materials which have been transported by streams, commonly from a great distance, and laid down on their flood plains. Third, the soils the mineral matters of which have been brought into their position by the action of glaciers; these in a way resemble those formed by rivers, but the materials are generally imperfectly sorted, coarse and fine being mingled together. Last of all, we have the soils due to the accumulation of blown dust or blown sand, which, unlike the others, occupy but a small part of the land surface. It would be possible, indeed, to make yet another division, including those areas which when emerging from the sea were cov-

ered with fine, uncemented detritus ready at once to serve
the purposes of a soil. Only here and there, and but seldom, do we find soils of this nature.

It is characteristic of soils belonging to the group to
which we have given the title of immediate derivation that
they have accumulated slowly, that they move very gradually down the slopes on which they lie, and that in all
cases they represent, with a part of their mass at least,
levels of rock which have disappeared from the region
which they occupied. The additions made to their mass
are from below, and that mass is constantly shrinking,
generally at a pretty rapid rate, by the mineral matter
which is dissolved and goes away with the spring water.
They also are characteristically thin on steep slopes, thickening toward the base of the incline, where the diminished
grade permits the soil to move slowly, and therefore to
accumulate.

In alluvial soils we find accumulations which are characterized by growth on their upper surfaces, and by the
distant transportation of the materials of which they are
composed. In these deposits the outleaching removes vast
amounts of the materials, but so long as the floods from
time to time visit their surfaces the growth of the deposits
is continued. This growth rarely takes place from the
waste of the bed rocks on which the alluvium lies. It is
characteristic of alluvial soils that they are generally made
up of *débris* derived from fields where the materials have
undergone the change which we have noted in the last
paragraph; therefore these latter deposits have throughout the character which renders the mineral materials
easily dissolved. Moreover, the mass as it is constructed
is commonly mingled with a great deal of organic waste,
which serves to promote its fertility. On these accounts
alluvial grounds, though they vary considerably in fertility, commonly afford the most fruitful fields of any
region. They have, moreover, the signal advantage that
they often may be refreshed by allowing the flood waters

to visit them, an action which but for the interference of man commonly takes place once each year. Thus in the valley of the Nile there are fields which have been giving rich grain harvests probably for more than four thousand years, without any other effective fertilizing than that derived from the mud of the great river.

The group of glaciated soils differs in many ways from either of those mentioned. In it we find the mineral matter to have been broken up, transported, and accumulated without the influence of those conditions which ordinarily serve to mix rock *débris* with organic matter during the process by which it is broken into bits. When vegetation came to preoccupy the fields made desolate by glacial action, it found in most places more than sufficient material to form soils, but the greater part of the matter was in the condition of pebbles of very hard rock and sand grains, fragments of silex. Fortunately, the broken-up state of this material, by exposing a great surface of the rocky matter to decay, has enabled the plants to convert a portion of the mass into earth fit for the uses of their roots. But as the time which has elapsed since the disappearance of the glaciers is much less than that occupied in the formation of ordinary soil, this decay has in most cases not yet gone very far, so that in a cubic foot of glaciated waste the amount of material available for plants is often only a fraction of that held in the soils of immediate derivation.

In the greater portion of the fields occupied by glacial waste the processes which lead to the introduction of organic matter into the earth have not gone far enough to set in effective work the great laboratory which has to operate in order to give fertile soil. The pebbles hinder the penetration of the roots as well as the movement of insects and other animals. There has not been time enough for the overturning of trees to bring about a certain admixture of vegetable matter with the soil—in a word, the process of soil-making, though the first condition, that of broken-up rock, has been accomplished, is as yet very incomplete. It needs, indeed, care in the introduction of organic matter for its completion.

It is characteristic of glacial soils that they are indefinitely deep. This often is a disadvantageous feature, for the reason that the soil water may pass so far down into the earth that the roots are often deprived of the moisture which they need, and which in ordinary soils is retained near the surface by the hard underlayer. On the other hand, where the glacial waste is made up of pebbles formed from rocks of varied chemical composition, which contain a considerable share of lime, potash, soda, and other substances which are required by plants, the very large surface which they expose to decay provides the soil with a continuous enrichment. In a cubic foot of pebbly glacial earth we often find that the mass offers several hundred times as much surface to the action of decay as is afforded by the underlying solid bed rock from which a soil of immediate derivation has to win its mineral supply. Where the pebbly glacial waste is provided with a mixture of vegetable matter, the process of decay commonly goes forward with considerable rapidity. If the supply of such matter is large, such as may be produced by ploughing in barnyard manure or green crops, the nutritive value of the earth may be brought to a very high point.

It is a familiar experience in regions where glacial soils exist that the earth beneath the swamps when drained is found to be extraordinarily well suited for farming purposes. On inspecting the pebbles from such places, we observe that they are remarkably decayed. Where the masses contain large quantities of feldspar, as is the case in the greater part of our granitic and other crystalline rocks, this material in its decomposition is converted into kaolin or feldspar clay, and gives the stones a peculiar white appearance, which marks the decomposition, and indicates the process by which a great variety of valuable soil ingredients are brought into a state where they may be available for plants.

In certain parts of the glacial areas, particularly in the region near the margin of the ice sheet, where the glacier remained in one position for a considerable time, we find extensive deposits of silicious sand, formed of the materials which settled from the under-ice stream, near where they escaped from the glacial cavern. These kames and sand plains, because of the silicious nature of their materials and the very porous nature of the soil which they afford, are commonly sterile, or at most render a profit to the tiller by dint of exceeding care. Thus in Massachusetts, although the first settlers seized upon these grounds, and planted their villages upon them because the forests there were scanty and the ground free from encumbering boulders, were soon driven to betake themselves to those areas where the drift was less silicious, and where the pebbles afforded a share of clay. Very extensive fields of this sandy nature in southeastern New England have never been brought under tillage. Thus on the island of Martha's Vineyard there is a connected area containing about thirty thousand acres which lies in a very favourable position for tillage, but has been found substantially worthless for such use. The farmers have found it more advantageous to clear away the boulders from the coarser drift in order to win soil which would give them fair returns.

Those areas which are occupied by soil materials which have been brought into their position by the action of the wind may, as regards their character, be divided into two very distinct groups—the dunes and loess deposits. In the former group, where, as we have noted (see page 123), the coarse sea sands or those from the shores of lakes are driven forward as a marching hillock, the grains of the material are almost always silicious. The fragments in the motion are not taken up into the air, but are blown along the surface. Such dune accumulations afford an earth which is even more sterile than that of the glacial sand plains, where there is generally a certain admixture of pebbles from rocks which by their decomposition may afford some elements of fertility. Fortunately for the interests of man, these wind-borne sands occupy but a small area; in North America, in the aggregate, there probably are not more than one thousand square miles of such deposits.

Where the rock material drifted by the winds is so fine that it may rise into the air in the form of dust, the accumulations made of it generally afford a fertile soil, and this for the reason that they are composed of various kinds of rock, and not, as in the case of dunes, of nearly pure silica. In some very rare cases, where the seashore is bordered by coral reefs, as it is in parts of southern Florida, and the strand is made up of limestone bits derived from the hard parts which the polyps secrete, small dunes are made of limy material. Owing, however, in part to the relatively heavy nature of this substance, as well as to the rapid manner in which its grains become cemented together, such limestone dunes never attain great size nor travel any distance from their point of origin.

As before noted, dust accumulations form the soil in extended areas which lie to the leeward of great deserts. Thus a considerable part of western China and much of the United States to the west of the Mississippi is covered by these wind-blown earths. Wherever the rainfall is considerable these loess deposits have proved to have a high agricultural value.

Where a region has an earth which has recently passed from beneath the sea or a great lake, the surface is commonly covered by incoherent detritus which has escaped consolidation into hard rock by the fact that it has not been buried and thus brought into the laboratory of the earth's crust. When such a region becomes dry land, the materials are immediately ready to enter into the state of soil. They commonly contain a good deal of waste derived from the organic life which dwelt upon the sea bottom and was embedded in the strata as they were formed. Where these accumulations are made in a lake, the land vegetation at once possesses the field, even a single year being sufficient for it to effect its establishment. Where the lands emerge from the sea, it requires a few years for the salt water to drain away so that the earth can be fit for the uses of plants. In a general way these sea-bottom soils resemble those formed in the alluvial plains. They are, however, commonly more sandy, and their substances less penetrated by that decay which goes on very freely in the atmosphere because of the abundant supply of oxygen, and but slowly on the sea floor. Moreover, the marine deposits are generally made up in large part of silicious sand, a material which is produced in large quantities by the disruption of the rocks along the sea coast. The largest single field of these ocean-bottom soils of North America is found in the lowland region of the southern United States, a wide belt of country extending along the coast from the Rio Grande to New York. Although the streams have channelled shallow valleys in the beds of this region, the larger part of its surface still has the peculiar features of form and composition which were impressed upon it when it lay below the surface of the sea.

Local variations in the character of the soil covering are exceedingly numerous, and these differences of condition profoundly affect the estate of man. We shall therefore consider some of the more important of these conditions, with special reference to their origin.

The most important and distinctly marked variation in the fertility of soils is that which is produced by differences in the rainfall. No parts of the earth are entirely lacking in rain, but over considerable areas the precipitation does not exceed half a foot a year. In such realms the soil is sterile, and the natural coating of vegetation limited to those plants which can subsist on dew

22

or which can take on an occasional growth at such times
as moisture may come upon them. With a slight increase
in precipitation, the soil rapidly increases in productivity,
so that we may say that where as much as about ten inches
of water enters the earth during the summer half of the
year, it becomes in a considerable measure fit for agriculture. Observations indicate that the conditions of fertility are not satisfied where the rainfall is just sufficient
to fill the pores of the soil; there must be enough water
entering the earth to bring about a certain amount of
outflow in the form of springs. The reason of this need
becomes apparent when we study the evident features of
those soils which, though from season to season charged
with water, do not yield springs, but send the moisture
away through the atmosphere. Wherever these conditions
occur we observe that the soil in dry seasons becomes
coated with a deposit of mineral matter, which, because
of its taste, has received the name of alkali. The origin
of this coating is as follows: The pores of the soil, charged
from year to year with sufficient water to fill them, become stored with a fluid which contains a very large
amount of dissolved mineral matter—too much, indeed,
to permit the roots of plants, save a few species which
have become accustomed to the conditions, to do their
appointed work. In fact, this water is much like that of
the sea, which the roots of only a few of our higher plants
can tolerate. When the dry season comes on, the heat
of the sun evaporates the water at the surface, leaving
behind a coating composed of the substances which the
water contains. The soil below acts in the manner of a
lamp-wick to draw up fluid as rapidly as the heat burns
it away. When the soil water is as far as possible exhausted, the alkali coating may represent a considerable
part of the soluble matter of the soil, and in the next
rainy season it may return in whole or in part to the under-
earth, again to be drawn in the manner before described to
the upper level. It is therefore only when a considerable

share of the ground water goes forth to the streams in each year that the alkaline materials are in quantity kept down to the point where the roots of our crop-giving plants can make due use of the soil. Where, in an arid region, the ground can be watered from the enduring streams or from artificial reservoirs, the main advantage arising from the process is commonly found in the control which it gives the farmer in the amount of the soil water. He can add to the rainfall sufficient to take away the excess of mineral matter. When such soils are first brought under tillage it is necessary to use a large amount of water from the canals, in order to wash away the old store of alkali. After that a comparatively small contribution will often keep the soil in excellent condition for agriculture. It has been found, however, in the irrigated lands beside the Nile that where too much saving is practised in the irrigation, the alkaline coating will appear where it has been unknown before, and with it an unfitness of the earth to bear crops.

Although the crust of mineral matters formed in the manner above described is characteristic of arid countries, and in general peculiar to them, a similar deposit may under peculiar conditions be formed in regions of great rainfall. Thus on the eastern coast of New England, where the tidal marshes have here and there been diked from the sea and brought under tillage, the dissolved mineral matters of the soil, which are excessive in quantity, are drawn to the surface, forming a coating essentially like that which is so common in arid regions. The writer has observed this crust on such diked lands, having a thickness of an eighth of an inch. In fact, this alkali coating represents merely the extreme operation of a process which is going on in all soils, and which contributes much to their fertility. When rain falls and passes downward into the earth, it conveys the soluble matter to a depth below the surface, often to beyond the point where our ordinary crop plants, such as the small grains, can have access to it, and this for the reason that their roots do not penetrate deeply. When dry weather comes and evaporation takes place from the surface, the fluid is drawn up to the upper soil layer, and there, in process of evaporation, deposits the dissolved materials which it contains. Thus the mineral matter which is fit for plant food is constantly set in motion, and in its movement passes the rootlets of the plants. It is probably on this account—at least in part—that very wet weather is almost as unfavourable to the farmer as exceedingly dry, the normal alternation in the conditions being, as is well known, best suited to his needs.

So long as the earth is subjected to conditions in which the rainfall may bring about a variable amount of water in the superficial detrital layer, we find normal fruitful soils, though in their more arid conditions they may be fit for but few species of plants. When, by increasing aridity, we pass to conditions where there is no tolerably permanent store of water in the *débris*, the material ceases to have the qualities of a soil, and becomes mere rock waste. At the other extreme of the scale we pass to conditions where the water is steadfastly maintained in the interstices of the detritus, and there again the characteristic of the soil and its fitness for the uses of land vegetation likewise disappear. In a word, true soil conditions demand the presence of moisture, but that in insufficient quantities, to keep the pores of the earth continually filled; where they are thus filled, we have the condition of swamps. Between these extremes the level at which the water stands in the soil in average seasons is continually varying. In rainy weather it may rise quite to the surface; in a dry season it may sink far down. As this water rises and falls, it not only moves, as before noted, the soluble mineral materials, but it draws the air into and expels it from the earth with each movement. This atmospheric circulation of the soil, as has been proved by experiment, is of great importance in

Mountain gorge, Himalayas, India. Note the difference in the slope of the eroded rocks and the effect of erosion upon them; also the talus slopes at the base of the cliffs which the torrent is cutting away. On the left of the foreground there is a little bench showing a recent higher line of the water.

maintaining its fertility; the successive charges of air supply the needs of the microscopic underground creatures which play a large part in enriching the soil, and the direct effect of the oxygen in promoting decay is likewise considerable. A part of the work which is accomplished by overturning the earth in tillage consists in this introduction of the air into the pores of the soil, where it serves to advance the actions which bring mineral matters into solution.

In the original conditions of any country which is the seat of considerable rainfall, and where the river system is not so far developed as to provide channels for the ready exit of the waters, we commonly find very extensive swamps; these conditions of bad drainage almost invariably exist where a region has recently been elevated above the level of the sea, and still retains the form of an irregular rolling plain common to sea floors, and also in regions where the work done by glaciers has confused the drainage which the antecedent streams may have developed. In an old, well-elaborated river system swamps are commonly absent, or, if they occur, are due to local accidents of an unimportant nature.

For our purpose swamps may be divided into three groups—climbing bogs, lake bogs, and marine marshes. The first two of these groups depend on the movements of the rain water over the land; the third on the action of the tides. Beginning our account with the first and most exceptional of these groups, we note the following features in their interesting history:

Wherever in a humid region, on a gentle slope—say with an inclination not exceeding ten feet to the mile— the soil is possessed by any species of plants whose stems grow closely together, so that from their decayed parts a spongelike mass is produced, we have the conditions which favour the development of climbing bogs. Beginning usually in the shores of a pool, these plants, necessarily of a water-loving species, retain so much moisture

in the spongy mass which they form that they gradually
extend up the slope. Thus extending the margin of their
field, and at the same time thickening the deposit which
they form, these plants may build a climbing bog over
the surface until steeps are attained where the inclination is so great that the necessary amount of water can
not be held in the spongy mass, or where, even if so held,
the whole coating will in time slip down in the manner
of an avalanche.

The greater part of the climbing bogs of the world are
limited to the moist and cool regions of high latitudes,
where species of moss belonging to the genus *Sphagnum*
plentifully flourish. These plants can only grow where
they are continuously supplied with a bath of water about
their roots. They develop in lake bogs as far south as
Mexico, but in the climbing form they are hardly traceable south of New England, and are nowhere extensively
developed within the limits of the United States.   In
more northern parts of this continent, and in northwestern Europe, particularly in the moist climate of Ireland,
climbing bogs occupy great areas, and hold up their lakes
of interstitially contained water over the slopes of hills,
where the surface rises at the rate of thirty feet or more
to the mile. So long as the deposit of decayed vegetable
matter which has accumulated in this manner is thin,
therefore everywhere penetrated by the fibrous roots of the
moss, it may continue to cling to its sloping bed; but when
it attains a considerable thickness, and the roots in the
lower part decay, the pulpy mass, water-laden in some time
of heavy rain, break away in a vast torrent of thick, black
mud, which may inundate the lower lands, causing widespread destruction.

In more southern countries, other water-loving plants
lead to the formation of climbing bogs. Of these, the
commonest and most effective are the species of reeds, of
which our Indian cane is a familiar example. Brakes
of this vegetation, plentifully mingled with other species

of aquatic growth, form those remarkable climbing bogs known as the Dismal and other swamps, which numerously occur along the coast line of the United States from southern Maryland to eastern Texas. Climbing bogs are particularly interesting, not only from the fact that they are eminently peculiar effects of plant growth, but because they give us a vivid picture of those ancient morasses in which grew the plants that formed the beds of vegetable matter now appearing in the state of coal. Each such bed of buried swamp material was, with rare exceptions, where the accumulation took place in lakes, gathered in climbing bogs such as we have described.

Lake bogs occur in all parts of the world, but in their best development are limited to relatively high latitudes, and this for the reason that the plants which form vegetable matter grow most luxuriantly in cool climates and in regions where the level of the basin is subject to less variation than occurs in the alternating wet and dry seasons which exist in nearly all tropical regions. The fittest conditions are found in glaciated regions, where, as before noted, small lakes are usually very abundant. On the shores of one of these pools, of size not so great that the waves may attain a considerable height, or in the sheltered bay of a larger lake, various aquatic plants, especially the species of pond lilies, take root upon the bottom, and spread their expanded leaves on the surface of the water. These flexible-leaved and elastic-stemmed plants can endure waves which attain no more than a foot or two of height, and by the friction which they afford make the swash on the shore very slight. In the quiet water, rushes take root, and still further protect the strand, so that the very delicate vegetation of the mosses, such as the *Sphagnum*, can fix itself on the shore.

As soon as the *Sphagnum* mat has begun its growth, the strength given by its interlaced fibres enables it to extend off from the shore and float upon the water. In this way it may rapidly enlarge, if not broken up by the waves, so that its front advances into the lake at the rate of several inches each year. While growing outwardly it thickens, so that the bottom of the mass gradually works down toward the floor of the basin. At the same

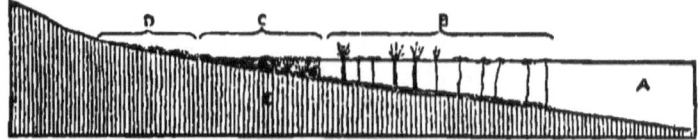

Fig. 17.—Diagram showing beginning of peat bog: A, lake; B, lilies and rushes; c, lake bog; D, climbing bog.

time the lower part of the sheet, decaying, contributes a shower of soft peat mud to the floor of the lake. In this way, growing at its edge, deepening, and contributing to an upgrowth from the bottom, a few centuries may serve entirely to fill a deep basin with peaty accumulation. In general, however, the surface of the bog closes over the lake before the accumulation has completely filled the shoreward portions of the area. In these conditions we have what is familiarly known as a quaking bog, which can be swayed up and down by a person who quickly stoops and rises while standing on the surface. In this state the tough and thick sheet of growing plants is sufficient to uphold a considerable weight, but so elastic that the underlying water can be thrown into waves. Long before the bog has completely filled the lake with the peaty accumulations the growth of trees is apt to take place on its surface, which often reduces the area to the appearance of a very level wet wood.

Climbing and lake bogs in the United States occupy a total area of more than fifty thousand square miles. In all North America the total area is probably more than twice as great. Similar deposits are exceedingly common in the Eurasian continent and in southern Patagonia. It is probable that the total amount of these fields in different parts of the world exceeds half a million square miles. These two groups of fresh-water swamps have an interest, for the reason that when reduced to cultivation by drainage and by subsequent removal of the excess of peaty

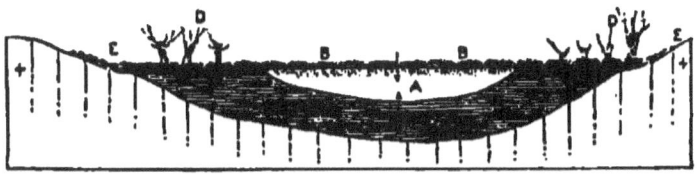

FIG. 18.—Diagram showing development of swamp: A, remains of lake ; B, surface growth; C, peat.

matter, by burning or by natural decay, afford very rich soil. The fairest fields of northern Europe, particularly in Great Britain and Ireland, have been thus won to tillage. In the first centuries of our era a large part of England—perhaps as much as one tenth of the ground now tilled in that country—was occupied by these lands, which retained water in such measure as to make them unfit for tillage, the greater portion of this area being in the condition of thin climbing bog. For many centuries much of the energy of the people was devoted to the reclamation of these valuable lands. This task of winning the swamp lands to agriculture has been more completely accomplished in England than elsewhere, but it has gone far on the continent of Europe, particularly in Germany. In the United States, owing to the fact that lands have been cheap, little of this work of swamp-draining has as yet been accomplished. It is likely that the next great field of improvement to be cultivated by the enterprising people will be found in these excessively humid lands, from which the food-giving resources for the support of many million people can be won.

The group of marine marshes differs in many important regards from those which are formed in fresh water.

Where the tide visits any coast line, and in sheltered positions along that shore, a number of plants, mostly belonging to the group of grasses, species which have become accustomed to having their roots bathed by salt water, begin the formation of a spongy mat, which resembles that composed of *Sphagnum*, only it is much more solid. This mat of the marine marshes soon attains a thickness of a foot or more, the upper or growing surface lying in a position where it is covered for two or three hours at each visit of the tide. Growing rapidly outward from the shore, and having a strength which enables it to resist in a tolerably effective manner waves not more than two or three feet high, this accumulation makes head against the sea. To a certain extent the waves undermine the front of the sheet and break up masses of it, which they distribute over the shallow bottom below the level at which these plants can grow. In this deeper water, also, other marine animals and plants are continually developing, and their remains are added to the accumulations which are ever shallowing the water, thus permitting a further extension of the level, higher-lying marsh. This process continues until the growth has gone as far as the scouring action of the tidal currents will permit. In the end the bay, originally of wide-open water, is only such at high tide. For the greater part of the time it appears as broad savannas, whose brilliant green gives them the aspect of rare fertility.

Owing to the conditions of their growth, the deposits formed in marine marshes contain no distinct peat, the nearest approach to that substance being the tangle of wirelike roots which covers the upper foot or so of the accumulation. The greater part of the mass is composed of fine silt, brought in by the streams of land water which discharge into the basin, and by the remains of animals which dwelt upon the bottom or between the stalks of the plants that occupy the surface of the marshes. These interspaces afford admirable shelter to a host of small marine forms. The result is, that the tidal marshes, as well as the lower-lying mud flats, which have been occupied by the mat of vegetation, afford admirable earth for tillage. Unfortunately, however, there are two disadvantages connected with the redemption of such lands. In the first place, it is necessary to exclude the sea from the area, which can only be accomplished by considerable engineering work; in the second place, the exclusion of the tide inevitably results in the silting up of the passage by which the water found its way to the sea. As these openings are often used for harbours, the effect arising from their destruction is often rather serious. Nevertheless, in some parts of the world very extensive and most fertile tracts of land have thus been won from the sea; a large part of Holland and shore-land districts in northern Europe are made up of fields which were originally covered by the tide. Near the mouth of the Rhine, indeed, the people have found these sea-bottom soils so profitable that they have gone beyond the zone of the marshes, and have drained considerable seas which of old were permanently covered, even at the lowest level of the waters.

On the coast of North America marine marshes have an extensive development, and vary much in character. In the Bay of Fundy, where the tides have an altitude of fifty feet or more, the energy of their currents is such that the marsh mat rarely forms. Its place, however, is taken by vast and ever-changing mud flats, the materials of which are swept to and fro by the moving waters. The people of this region have learned an art of a peculiar nature, by which they win broad fields of excellent land from the sea. Selecting an area of the flats, the surface of which has been brought to within a few feet of high tide, they inclose it with a stout barrier or dike, which has openings for the free admission of the tidal waters. Entering this basin, the tide, moving with considerable velocity, bears in quantities of sediment. In the basin,

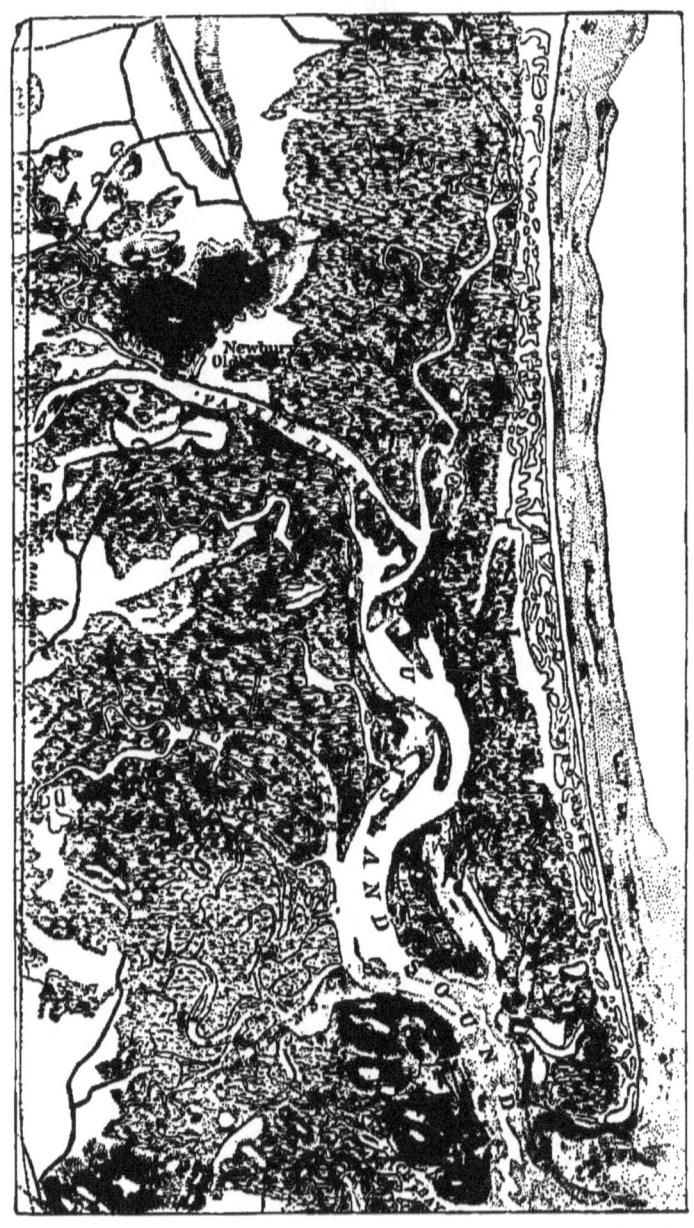

Fig. 10.—Map of Ipswich marshes. Massachusetts, formed behind a barrier beach.

the motion being arrested, this sediment falls to the bottom, and serves to raise its level. In a few months the sheet of sediment is brought near the plane of the tidal movement, then the gates are closed at times when the tide has attained half of its height, so that the ground within the dike is not visited by the sea water, and can be cultivated.

Along the coast of New England the ordinary marine marshes attain an extensive development in the form of broad-grassed savannas. With this aspect, though with a considerable change in the plants which they bear, the fringe of savannas continues southward along the coast to northern Florida. In the region about the mouth of the Savannah River, so named from the vast extent of the tidal marshes, these fields attain their greatest development. In central and southern Florida, however, where the seacoast is admirably suited for their development, these coastal marshes of the grassy type disappear, their place being taken by the peculiar morasses formed by the growth of the mangrove tree.

In the mangrove marshes the tree which gives the areas their name covers all the field which is visited by the tide. This tree grows with its crown supported on stiltlike roots, at a level above high tide. From its horizontal branches there grow off roots, which reach downward into the water, and thence to the bottom. The seeds of the mangrove are admirably devised so as to enable the plant to obtain a foothold on the mud flats, even where they are covered at low tide with a depth of two or three feet of water. They are several inches in length, and arranged with hooklets at their lower ends; floating near the bottom, they thus catch upon it, and in a few weeks' growth push the shoot to the level of the water, thus affording a foundation for a new plantation. In this manner, extending the old forests out into the shallow water of the bays, and forming new colonies wherever the water is not too deep, these plants rapidly occupy all the region which elsewhere would appear in the form of savannas.

The tidal marshes of North America, which may be in time converted to the uses of man, probably occupy an area exceeding twenty thousand square miles. If the work of reclaiming such lands from the sea ever attains the advance in this country that it has done in Holland, the area added to the dry land by engineering devices may amount to as much as fifty thousand square miles —a territory rather greater than the surface of Ken-

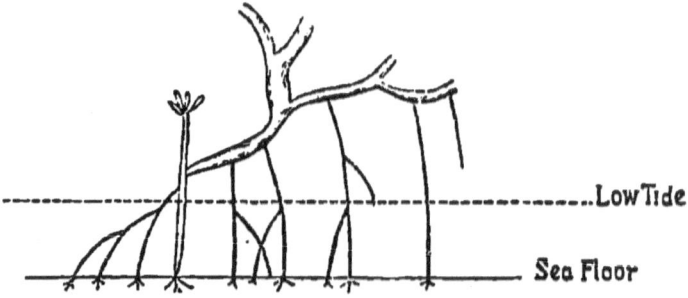

Fig. 20.—Diagram showing mode of growth of mangroves.

tucky, and with a food-yielding power at least five times as great as is afforded by that fertile State. In fact, these conquests from the sea are hereafter to be among the great works which will attract the energies of mankind.

In the arid region of the Cordilleras, as well as in many other countries, the soil, though destitute of those qualities which make it fit for the uses of man, because of the absence of water in sufficient amount, is, as regards its structure and depth, as well as its mineral contents, admirably suited to the needs of agriculture. The development of soils in desert regions is in almost all cases to be accounted for by the former existence in the realms they occupy of a much greater rainfall than now exists. Thus in the Rocky Mountain country, when the

deep soils of the ample valleys were formed, the lakes, as
we have before noted, were no longer dead seas, as is at
present so generally the case, but poured forth great
streams to the sea. Here, as elsewhere, we find evidence
that certain portions of the earth which recently had an
abundant rainfall have now become starved for the lack
of that supply. All the soils of arid regions where the
trial has been made have proved very fertile when subjected to irrigation, which can often be accomplished by
storing the waters of the brief rainy season or by diverting those of rivers which enter the deserts from well-
watered mountain fields. In fact, the soil of these arid
realms yields peculiarly ample returns to the husbandman,
because of certain conditions due to the exceeding dryness of the air. This leads to an absence of cloudy
weather, so that from the time the seed is planted the
growth is stimulated by uninterrupted and intense sunshine. The same dryness of the air leads, as we have
seen, to a rapid evaporation from the surface, by which,
in a manner before noted, the dissolved mineral matter
is brought near the top of the soil, where it can best serve
the greater part of our crop plants. On these accounts
an acre of irrigated soil can be made to yield a far greater
return than can be obtained from land of like chemical
composition in humid regions.

In many parts of the world, particularly in the northern and western portions of the Mississippi Valley, there
are widespread areas, which, though moderately well
watered, were in their virgin state almost without forests.
In the prairie region the early settlers found the country unwooded, except along the margins of the streams.
On the borders of the true prairies, however, they found
considerable areas of a prevailingly forested land, with
here and there a tract of prairie. There were several of
these open fields south of the Ohio, though the country
there is in general forested; one of these prairie areas, in
the Green River district of Kentucky, was several thou-

sand square miles in extent. At first it was supposed that the absence of trees in the open country of the Mississippi Valley was due to some peculiarity of the soil, but experience shows that plantations luxuriantly develop, and that the timber will spread rapidly in the natural way. In fact, if the seeds of the trees which have been planted since the settlement of the country were allowed to develop as they seek to do, it would only be a few centuries before the region would be forest-clad as far west as the rainfall would permit the plants to develop. Probably the woods would attain to near the hundredth meridian.

In the opinion of the writer, the treeless character of the Western plains is mainly to be accounted for by the habit which our Indians had of burning the herbage of a lowly sort each year, so that the large game might obtain better pasturage. It is a well-known fact to all those who have had to deal with cattle on fields which are in the natural state that fire betters the pasturage. Beginning this method of burning in the arid regions to the west of the original forests, the natural action of the fire has been gradually to destroy these woods. Although the older and larger trees, on account of their thick bark and the height of their foliage above the ground, escaped destruction, all the smaller and younger members of the species were constantly swept away. Thus when the old trees died they left no succession, and the country assumed its prairie character. That the prairies were formed in this manner seems to be proved by the testimony which we have concerning the open area before mentioned as having existed in western Kentucky. It is said that around the timberless fields there was a wide fringe of old fire-scarred trees, with no undergrowth beneath their branches, and that as they died no kind of large vegetation took their place. When the Indians who set these fires were driven away, as was the case in the last decade of the last century, the country at once began to resume its timbered condition. From the margin and from every interior point where the trees survived, their seeds spread so that before the open land was all subjugated to the plough it was necessary in many places to clear away a thick growth of the young forest-building trees.

The soils which develop on the lavas and ashes about an active volcano afford interesting subjects for study, for the reason that they show how far the development of the layer which supports vegetation may depend upon the character of the rocks from which it is derived. Where the materials ejected from a volcano lie in a rainy district, the process of decay which converts the rock into soil is commonly very rapid, a few years of exposure to the weather being sufficient to bring about the formation of a fertile soil. This is due to the fact that most lavas, as well as the so-called volcanic ashes, which are of the same material as the lavas, only blown to pieces, are composed of varied minerals, the most of which are readily attacked by the agents of decay. Now and then, however, we find the materials ejected from a particular volcano, or even the lavas and ashes of a single eruption, in such a chemical state that soils form upon them with exceeding slowness.

The foregoing incomplete considerations make it plain that the soil-covering of the earth is the result of very delicate adjustments, which determine the rate at which the broken-down rocks find their path from their original bed places to the sea. The admirable way in which this movement is controlled is indicated by the fact that almost everywhere we find a soil-covering deep enough for the use of a varied vegetation, but rarely averaging more than a dozen feet in depth. Only here and there are the rocks bare or the earth swathed in a profound mass of detritus. This indicates how steadfast and measured is the march of the rock waste from the hills to the sea. Unhappily, man, when by his needs he is forced to till the soil, is compelled to break up this ancient and perfect

23

order. He has to strip the living mantle from the earth, replacing it with growth of those species which serve his needs. Those plants which are most serviceable—which are, indeed, indispensable in the higher civilization, the grains—require for their cultivation that the earth be stripped bare and deeply stirred during the rainy season, and thus subjected to the most destructive effect of the rainfall. The result is, that in almost all grain fields the rate of soil destruction vastly surpasses that at which the accumulation is being made. We may say, indeed, that, except in alluvial plains, where the soil grows by flood-made additions to its upper surface, no field tilled in grain can without exceeding care remain usable for a century. Even though the agriculturist returns to the earth all the chemical substances which he takes away in his crops, the loss of the soil by the washing away of its substance to the stream will inevitably reduce the region to sterility.

It is not fanciful to say that the greatest misfortune which in a large way man has had to meet in his agriculture arises from this peculiar stress which grain crops put upon the soil. If these grains grew upon perennial plants, in the manner of our larger fruits, the problem of man's relation to the soil would be much simpler than it is at present. He might then manage to till the earth without bringing upon it the inevitable destruction which he now inflicts. As it is, he should recognise that his needs imperil this ancient and precious element in the earth's structure, and he should endeavour in every possible way to minimize the damage which he brings about. This result he may accomplish in certain simple ways.

First, as regards the fertility of the soil, as distinguished from the thickness of the coating, it may be said that modern discoveries enable us to see the ways whereby we may for an indefinite period avoid the debasement of our great heritage, the food-giving earth. We now know in various parts of the world extensive and practically inexhaustible deposits, whence may be obtained the phos-

phates, potash, soda, etc., which we take from the soil in
our crops. We also have learned ways in which the materials contained in our sewage may be kept from the sea
and restored to the fields. In fact, the recent developments
of agriculture have made it not only easy, but in most
cases profitable, to avoid this waste of materials which
has reduced so many regions to poverty. We may fairly
look forward to the time, not long distant, when the old
progressive degradation in the fertility of the soil coating
will no longer occur. It is otherwise with the mass of the
soil, that body of commingled decayed rock and vegetable
matter which must possess a certain thickness in order
to serve its needs. As yet no considerable arrest has been
made in the processes which lead to the destruction of
this earthy mass. In all countries where tillage is general the rivers are flowing charged with all they can bear
away of soil material. Thus in the valley of the Po, a
region where, if the soil were forest-clad, the down-wearing
of the surface would probably be at no greater rate than
one foot in five thousand years, the river bears away the
soil detritus so rapidly that at the present time the downgoing is at the rate of one foot in eight hundred years,
and each decade sees the soil disappear from hillsides
which were once fertile, but are now reduced to bare
rocks. All about the Mediterranean the traveller notes
extensive regions which were once covered with luxuriant
forests, and were afterward the seats of prosperous agriculture, where the soil has utterly disappeared, leaving
only the bare rocks, which could not recover its natural
covering in thousands of years of the enforced fallow.

Within the limits of the United States the degradation of the soil, owing to the peculiar conditions of the
country, is in many districts going forward with startling
rapidity. It has been the habit of our people—a habit
favoured by the wide extent of fertile and easily acquired
frontier ground—recklessly to till their farms until the
fields were exhausted, and then to abandon them for new

ground. By shallow ploughing on steep hillsides, by neglect in the beginning of those gulches which form in such
places, it is easy in the hill country of the eastern United
States to have the soil washed away within twenty years
after the protecting forests have been destroyed. The
writer has estimated that in the States south of the Ohio
and James Rivers more than eight thousand square miles
of originally fertile ground have by neglect been brought
into a condition where it will no longer bear crops of any
kind, and over fifteen hundred miles of the area have been
so worn down to the subsoil or the bed rock that it may
never be profitable to win it again to agricultural uses.

Hitherto, in our American agriculture, our people have
been to a great extent pioneers; they have been compelled
to win what they could in the cheapest possible way and
with the rudest implements, and without much regard
to the future of those who were in subsequent generations to occupy the fields which they were conquering
from the wilderness and the savages. The danger is now
that this reckless tillage, in a way justified of old, may
be continued and become habitual with our people. It
is, indeed, already a fixed habit in many parts of the
country, particularly in the South, where a small farmer
expects to wear out two or three plantations in the course
of his natural life. Many of them manage to ruin from
one to two hundred acres of land in the course of half
a century of uninterrupted labour. This system deserves
the reprobation of all good citizens; it would be well,
indeed, if it were possible to do so, to stamp it out by the
law. The same principle which makes it illegal for a
man to burn his own dwelling house may fairly be applied
in restraining him from destroying the land which he
tills.

There are a few simple principles which, if properly
applied, may serve to correct this misuse of our American
soil. The careful tiller should note that all soils whatever which lie on declivities having a slope of more than

one foot in thirty inevitably and rapidly waste when subject to plough tillage. This instrument tends to smear and consolidate the layer of earth over which its heel runs, so that at a depth of a few inches below the surface a layer tolerably impervious to water is formed. The result is that the porous portion of the deposit becomes excessively charged with water in times of heavy rain, and moves down the hillside in a rapid manner. All such steep slopes should be left in their wooded state, or, if brought into use, should be retained as pasture lands.

Where, as is often the case with the farms in hilly countries, all the fields are steeply inclined, it is an excellent precaution to leave the upper part of the slope with a forest covering. In this condition not only is the excessive flow of surface water diminished, but the moisture which creeps down the slope from the wooded area tends to keep the lower-lying fields in a better state for tillage, and promotes the decay of the underlying rocks, and thus adds to the body and richness of the earth.

On those soils which must be tilled, even where they tend to wash away, the aim should be to keep the detritus open to such a depth that it may take in as much as possible of the rainfall, yielding the water to the streams through the springs. This end can generally be accomplished by deep ploughing; it can, in almost all cases, be attained by under-drainage. The effect of allowing the water to penetrate is not only to diminish the superficial wearing, but to maintain the process of subsoil and bedrock decay by which the detrital covering is naturally renewed. Where, as in many parts of the country, the washing away of the soil can not otherwise be arrested, the progress of the destruction can be delayed by forming with the skilful use of the plough ditches of slight declivity leading along the hillsides to the natural waterways. One of the most satisfactory marks of the improvement which is now taking place in the agriculture of the cotton-yielding States of this country is to be found in the rapid increase in the use of the ditch system here mentioned. This system, combined with ploughing in the manner where the earth is with each overturning thrown uphill, will greatly reduce the destructive effect of rainfall on steep-lying fields. But the only effective protection, however, is accomplished by carefully terracing the slopes, so that the tilled ground lies in level benches. This system is extensively followed in the thickly settled portions of Europe, but it may be a century before it will be much used in this country.

The duty of the soil-tiller by the earth with which he deals may be briefly summed up: He should look upon himself as an agent necessarily interfering with the operations which naturally form and preserve the soil. He should see that his work brings two risks; he may impoverish the accumulation of detrital material by taking out the plant food more rapidly than it is prepared for use. This injurious result may be at any time reparable by a proper use of manures. Not so, however, with the other form of destruction, which results in the actual removal of the soil materials. Where neglect has brought about this disaster, it can only be repaired by leaving the area to recover beneath the slowly formed forest coating. This process in almost all cases requires many thousands of years for its accomplishment. The man who has wrought such destruction has harmed the inheritance of life.

CHAPTER IX.

In the preceding chapters of this book the attention of the student has been directed mainly to the operations of those natural forces which act upon the surface of the earth. Incidentally the consequences arising from the applications of energy to the outer part of the planet have been attended to, but the main aim has been to set forth the work which solar energy, operating in the form of heat, accomplishes upon the lands. We have now to consider one of the great results of these actions, which is exhibited in the successive strata that make up the earth's crust.

The most noteworthy effect arising from the action of the solar forces on the earth and their co-operation with those which originate in our sphere is found in the destruction of beds or other deposits of rock, and the removal of the materials to the floors of water basins, where they are again aggregated in strata, and gradually brought once more into a stable condition within the earth. This work is accomplished by water in its various states, the action being directly affected by gravitation. In the form of steam, water which has been built into rocks and volcanically expelled by tensions, due to the heat which it has acquired at great depths below the surface, blows forth great quantities of lava, which is contributed to the formation of strata, either directly in the solid form or indirectly, after having been dissolved in the sea. Acting as waves, water impelled by solar energy transmitted to it by the winds beats against the shores, wearing away great quantities of rock, which is dragged off to the neighbouring sea bottoms, there to resume the bedded form. Moving ice in glaciers, water again applying solar energy given to it by its elevation above the sea, most effectively grinds away the elevated parts of the crust, the *débris* being delivered to the ocean. In the rain the same work is done, and even in the wind the power of the sun serves to abrade the high-lying rocks, making new strata of their fragments.

As gravity enters as an element in all the movements of divided rock, the tendency of the waste worn from the land is to gather on to the bottoms of basins which contain water. Rarely, and only in a small way, this process results in the accumulation of lake deposits; the greater part of the work is done upon the sea floor. When the beds are formed in lake basins, they may be accumulated in either of two very diverse conditions. They may be formed in what are called dead seas, in which case the detrital materials are commonly small in amount, for the reason that the inflowing streams are inconsiderable; in such basins there is normally a large share of saline materials, which are laid down by the evaporation of the water. In ordinary lakes the deposits which are formed are mostly due to the sediment that the rivers import. These materials are usually fine-grained, and the sand or pebbles which they contain are plentifully mingled with clay. Hence lake deposits are usually of an argillaceous nature. As organic life, such as secretes limestone, is rarely developed to any extent in lake basins, limy beds are very rarely formed beneath those areas of water. Where they occur, they are generally due to the fact that rivers charged with limy matter import such quantities of the substance that it is precipitated on the bottom.

As lake deposits are normally formed in basins above the level of the sea, and as the drainage channels of the basins are always cutting down, the effect is to leave such strata at a considerable height above the sea level, where the erosive agents may readily attack them. In consequence of this condition, lacustrine beds are rarely found of great antiquity; they generally disappear soon after they are formed. Where preserved, their endurance is generally to be attributed to the fact that the region they occupy has been lowered beneath the sea and covered by marine strata.

The great laboratory in which the sedimentary deposits are accumulated, the realm in which at least ninety-nine of the hundred parts of these materials are laid down, is the oceanic part of the earth. On the floors of the seas and oceans we have not only the region where the greater part of the sedimentation is effected, but that in which the work assumes the greatest variety. The sea bottoms, as regards the deposits formed upon them, are naturally divided into two regions—the one in which the *débris* from the land forms an important part of the sediment, and the other, where the remoteness of the shores deprives the sediment of land waste, or at least of enough of that material in any such share as can affect the character of the deposits.

What we may term the littoral or shore zone of the sea occupies a belt of prevailingly shallow water, varying in width from a few score to a few hundred miles. Where the bottom descends steeply from the coast, where there are no strong off-shore setting currents, and where the region is not near the mouth of a large river which bears a great tide of sediment to the sea, the land waste may not affect the bottom for more than a mile or two from the shore. Where these conditions are reversed, the *débris* from the air-covered region may be found three or four hundred miles from the coast line. It should also be noted that the incessant up-and-down goings of the land result in a constant change in the position of the coast line, and consequently in the extension of the land sedi-

ment, in the course of a few geological periods over a far
wider field of sea bottom than that to which they would
attain if the shores remained steadfast.

It is characteristic of the sediments deposited within
the influence of the continental detritus that they vary very
much in their action, and that this variation takes place
not only horizontally along the shores in the same stratum,
but vertically, in the succession of the beds. It also may
be traced down the slope from the coast line to deep
water. Thus where all the *débris* comes from the action
of the waves, the deposits formed from the shore outwardly will consist of coarse materials, such as pebbles
near the coast, of sand in the deeper and remoter section, and of finer silt in the part of the deposit which is
farthest out. With each change in the level of the coast
line the position of these belts will necessarily be altered.
Where a great river enters the sea, the changes in the
volume of sediment which it from time to time sends
forth, together with the alternations in the position of its
point of discharge, led to great local complexities in the
strata. Moreover, the turbid water sent forth by the
stream may, as in the case of the tide from the Amazon,
be drifted for hundreds of miles along the coast line or
into the open sea.

The most important variations which occur in the
deposits of the littoral zone are brought about by the
formations of rocks more or less composed of limestone.
Everywhere the sea is, as compared with lake waters, remarkably rich in organic life. Next the shore, partly
because the water is there shallow, but also because of
its relative warmth and the extent to which it is in motion, organic life, both that of animals and plants, commonly develops in a very luxuriant way. Only where the
bottom is composed of drifting sands, which do not afford
a foothold for those species which need to rest upon the
shore, do we fail to find that surface thickly tenanted
with varied forms. These are arranged according to the

depth of the bottom. The species of marine plants which are attached to fixed objects are limited to the depth within which the sunlight effectively penetrates the water; in general, it may be said that they do not extend below a depth of one hundred feet. The animal forms are distributed, according to their kinds, over the floor, but few species having the capacity to endure any great range in the pressure of the sea water. Only a few forms, indeed, extend from low tide to the depth of a thousand feet.

The greatest development of organic life, the realm in which the largest number of species occur, and where their growth is most rapid, lies within about a hundred feet of the low-tide level. Here sunlight, warmth, and motion in the water combine to favour organic development. It is in this region that coral reefs and other great accumulations of limestone, formed from the skeletons of polyps and mollusks, most abundantly occur. These deposits of a limy nature depend upon a very delicate adjustment of the conditions which favour the growth of certain creatures; very slight geographic changes, by inducing movements of sand or mud, are apt to interrupt their formation, bringing about a great and immediate alteration in the character of the deposits. Thus it is that where geologists find considerable fields of rock, where limestones are intercalated with sandstones and deposits of clay, they are justified in assuming that the strata were laid down near some ancient shore. In general, these coast deposits become more and more limy as we go toward the tropical realms, and this for the reason that the species which secrete large amounts of lime are in those regions most abundant and attain the most rapid growth. The stony polyps, the most vigorous of the limestone makers, grow in large quantities only in the tropical realm, or near to it, where ocean streams of great warmth may provide the creatures with the conditions of temperature and food which they need.

As we pass from the shore to the deeper sea, the share of land detritus rapidly diminishes until, as before remarked, at the distance of five hundred miles from the coast line, very little of that waste, except that from volcanoes, attains the bottom of the sea. By far the larger part of the contributions which go to the formation of these deep-sea strata come from organic remains, which are continually falling upon the sea floor. In part, this waste is derived from creatures which dwell upon the bottom; in considerable measure, however, it is from the dead bodies of those forms which live near the surface of the sea, and which when dying sink slowly through the intermediate realm to the bottom.

Owing to the absence of sunlight, the prevailingly cold water of the deeper seas, and the lack of vegetation in those realms, the growth of organic forms on the deep-sea floor is relatively slow. Thus it happens that each shell or other contribution to the sediment lies for some time on the bottom before it is buried. While in this condition it is apt to be devoured by some of the many species which dwell on the bottom and subsist from the remains of animals and plants which they find there. In all cases the fossilization of any form depends upon the accumulation of sediment before the processes of destruction have overtaken them, and among these processes we must give the first place to the creatures which subsist on shells, bones, or other substances of like nature which find their way to the ocean floor. In the absolute darkness, the still water, and the exceeding cold of the deeper seas, animals find difficult conditions for development. Moreover, in this deep realm there is no native vegetation, and, in general, but little material of this nature descends to the bottom from the surface of the sea. The result is, the animals have to subsist on the remains of other animals which at some step in the succession have obtained their provender from the plants which belong on the surface or in the shallow waters of the sea.

This limitation of the food supply causes the depths of the sea to be a realm of continual hunger, a region where every particle of organic matter is apt to be seized upon by some needy creature.

In consequence of the fact that little organic matter on the deeper sea floors escapes being devoured, the most of the material of this nature which goes into strata enters that state in a finely divided condition. In the group of worms alone—forms which in a great diversity of species inhabit the sea floor—we find creatures which are specially adapted to digesting the *débris* which gathers on the sea bottom. Wandering over this surface, much in the manner of our ordinary earthworms, these creatures devour the mud, voiding the matter from their bodies in a yet more perfectly divided form. Hence it comes about that the limestone beds, so commonly formed beneath the open seas, are generally composed of materials which show but few and very imperfect fossils. Studying any series of limestone beds, we commonly find that each layer, in greater or less degree, is made up of rather massive materials, which evidently came to their place in the form of a limy mud. Very often this lime has crystallized, and thus has lost all trace of its original organic structure.

One of the conspicuous features which may be observed in any succession of limestone beds is the partings or divisions into layers which occur with varied frequency. Sometimes at vertical intervals of not more than one or two inches, again with spacings of a score of feet, we find divisional planes, which indicate a sudden change in the process of rock formation. The lime disappears, and in place of it we have a thin layer of very fine detritus, which takes on the form of a clay. Examining these partings with care, we observe that on the upper surface on the limestone the remains of the animal which dwelt on the ancient sea floor are remarkably well preserved, they having evidently escaped the effect of the process which reduced their ancestors, whose remains constitute the layer, to mud. Furthermore, we note that the shaly layer is not only lacking in lime, but commonly contains no trace of animals such as might have dwelt on the bottom. The fossils it bears are usually of species which swam in the overlying water and came to the bottom after death. Following up through the layer of shale, we note that the ordinary bottom life gradually reappears, and shortly becomes so plentiful that the deposit resumes the character which it had before the interruption began. Often, however, we note that the assemblage of species which dwelt on the given area of sea floor has undergone a considerable change. Forms in existence in the lower layer may be lacking in the upper, their place being taken by new varieties.

So far the origin of these divisional planes in marine deposits has received little attention from geologists; they have, indeed, assumed that each of these alterations indicates some sudden disturbance of the life of the sea floors. They have, however, generally assumed that the change was due to alterations in the depth of the sea or in the run of ocean currents. It seems to the writer, however, that while these divisions may in certain cases be due to the above-mentioned and, indeed, to a great variety of causes, they are in general best to be explained by the action of earthquakes. Water being an exceedingly elastic substance, an earthquake passes through it with much greater speed than it traverses the rocks which support the ocean floor. The result is that, when the fluid and solid oscillate in the repeated swingings which a shock causes, they do not move together, but rub over each other, the independent movements having the swing of from a few inches to a foot or two in shocks of considerable energy.

When the sea bottom and the overlying water, vibrating under the impulse of an earthquake shock, move past each other, the inevitable result is the formation of muddy water; the very fine silt of the bottom is shaken up into the fluid, which afterward descends as a sheet to its original position. It is a well-known fact that such muddying of water, in which species accustomed to other conditions dwell, inevitably leads to their death by covering their breathing organs and otherwise disturbing the delicately balanced conditions which enable them to exist. We find, in fact, that most of the tenants of the water, particularly the forms which dwell upon the bottom, are provided with an array of contrivances which enable them to clear away from their bodies such small quantities of silt as may inconvenience them. Thus, in the case of our common clam, the breathing organs are covered with vibratory cilia, which, acting like brooms, sweep off any foreign matter which may come upon their surfaces. Moreover, the creature has a long, double, spoutlike organ, which it can elevate some distance above the bottom, through which it draws and discharges the water from which it obtains food and air. Other forms, such as the crinoids, or sea lilies, elevate the breathing parts on top of tall stems of marvellous construction, which brings those vital organs at the level, it may be, of three or four feet above the zone of mud. In consequence of the peculiar method of growth, the crinoids often escape the damage done by the disturbance of the bottom, and thus form limestone beds of remarkable thickness; sometimes, indeed, we find these layers composed mainly of crinoidal remains, which exhibit only slight traces of partings such as we have described, being essentially united for the depth of ten or twenty feet. Where the layers have been mainly accumulated by shellfish, their average thickness is less than half a foot.

When we examine the partitions between the layers of limestone, we commonly find that, however thin, they generally extend for an indefinite distance in every direction. The writer has traced some of these for miles; never, indeed, has he been able to find where they disappeared.

This fact makes it clear that the destruction which took place at the stage where these partings were formed was widespread; so far as it was due to earthquake shocks, we may fairly believe that in many cases it occurred over areas which were to be measured by tens of thousands of square miles. Indeed, from what we know of earthquake shocks, it seems likely that the devastation may at times have affected millions of square miles.

Another class of accidents connected with earthquakes may also suddenly disturb the mud on the sea bottom. When, as elsewhere noted, a shock originates beneath the sea, the effect is suddenly to elevate the water over the seat of the jarring and the regions thereabouts to the height of some feet. This elevation quickly takes the shape of a ringlike wave, which rolls off in every direction from its point of origin. Where the sea is deep, the effect of this wave on the bottom may be but slight; but as the undulation attains shallower water, and in proportion to the shoaling, the front of the surge is retarded in its advance by the friction of the bottom, while the rear part, being in deeper water, crowds upon the advancing line. The action is precisely that which has been described as occurring in wind-made waves as they approach the beach; but in this last-named group of undulations, because of the great width of the swell, the effect of the shallowing is evident in much deeper water. It is likely that at the depth of a thousand feet the passing of one of these vast surges born of earthquakes may so stir the mud of the sea floor as to bring about a widespread destruction of life, and thus give rise to many of the partitions between strata.

If we examine with the microscope the fine-grained silts which make up the shaly layers between limestones, we find the materials to be mostly of inorganic origin. It is hard to trace the origin of the mineral matter which it contains; some of the fragments are likely to prove of volcanic origin; others, bits of dust from meteorites; yet others, dust blown from the land, which may, as we know, be conveyed for any distance across the seas. Mingled with this sediment of an inorganic origin we almost invariably find a share of organic waste, derived not from creatures which dwelt upon the bottom, but from those which inhabited the higher-lying waters. If, now, we take a portion of the limestone layer which lies above or below the shale parting, and carefully dissolve out with acids the limy matter which it contains, we obtain a residuum which in general character, except so far as the particles may have been affected by the acid, is exactly like the material which forms the claylike partition. We are thus readily led to the conclusion that on the floors of the deeper seas there is constantly descending, in the form of a very slow shower, a mass of mineral detritus. Where organic life belonging to the species which secrete hard shells or skeletons is absent, this accumulation, proceeding with exceeding slowness, gradually accumulates layers, which take on a shaly character. Where limestone-making animals abound, they so increase the rate of deposition that the proportion of the mineral material in the growing strata is very much reduced; it may, indeed, become as small as one per cent of the mass. In this case we may say that the deposit of limestone grew a hundred times as fast as the intervening beds of shale.

The foregoing considerations make it tolerably clear that the sea floor is in receipt of two diverse classes of sediment—those of a mineral and those of an organic origin. The mineral, or inorganic, materials predominate along the shores. They gradually diminish in quantity toward the open sea, where the supply is mainly dependent on the substances thrown forth from volcanoes, on pumice in its massive or its comminuted form—i. e., volcanic dust, states of lava in which the material, because of the vesicles which it contains, can float for ages before it comes to rest on the sea bottom. Variations in the volcanic waste contributed to the sea floor may somewhat

24

affect the quantity of the inorganic sediments, but, as a whole, the downfalling of these fragments is probably at a singularly uniform rate. It is otherwise with the contributions of sediment arising from organic forms. This varies in a surprising measure. On the coral reefs, such as form in the mid oceans, the proportion of matter which has not come into the accumulation through the bodies of animals and plants may be as small as one tenth of one per cent, or less. In the deeper seas, it is doubtful whether the rate of animal growth is such as to permit the formation of any beds which have less than one half of their mass made up of materials which fell through the water.

In certain areas of the open seas the upper part of the water is dwelt in by a host of creatures, mostly foraminifera, which extract limestone from the water, and, on dying, send their shells to the bottom. Thus in the North Atlantic, even where the sea floor is of great depth beneath the surface, there is constantly accumulating a mass of limy matter, which is forming very massive limestone strata, somewhat resembling chalk deposits, such as abundantly occur in Great Britain, in the neighbouring parts of Europe, in Texas, and elsewhere. Accumulations such as this, where the supply is derived from the surface of the water, are not affected by the accidents which divide beds made on the bottom in the manner before described. They may, therefore, have the singularly continuous character which we note in the English chalk, where, for the thickness of hundreds of feet, we may have no evident partitions, except certain divisions, which have evidently originated long after the beds were formed.

We have already noted the fact that, while the floors of the deeper seas appear to lack mountainous elevations, those arising from the folding of strata, they are plentifully scattered over with volcanic cones. We may therefore suppose that, in general, the deposits formed on the sea floor are to a great extent affected by the materials which these vents cast forth. Lava streams and showers represent only a part of the contributions from volcanoes, which finally find their way to the bottom. In larger part, the materials thrown forth are probably first dissolved in the water and then taken up by the organic species; only after the death of these creatures does the waste go to the bottom. As hosts of these creatures have no solid skeleton to contribute to the sea floor, such mineral matter as they may obtain is after their death at once restored to the sea.

Not only does the contribution of organic sediment diminish in quantity with the depth which is attained, but the deeper parts of the ocean bed appear to be in a condition where no accumulations of this nature are made, and this for the reason that the water dissolves the organic matter more rapidly than it is laid down. Thus in place of limestone, which would otherwise form, we have only a claylike residuum, such as is obtained when we dissolve lime rocks in acids. This process of solution, by which the limy matter deposited on the bottom is taken back into the water, goes on everywhere, but at a rate which increases with the depth. This increase is due in part to the augmentation of pressure, and in part to the larger share of carbonic dioxide which the water at great depths holds. The result is, that explorations with the dredge seem to indicate that on certain parts of the deeper sea floors the rocks are undergoing a process of dissolution comparable to that which takes place in limestone caverns. So considerable is the solvent work that a large part of the inorganic waste appears to be taken up by the waters, so as to leave the bottom essentially without sedimentary accumulations. The sea, in a word, appears to be eating into rocks which it laid down before the depression attained its present great depth.

We should here note something of the conditions which determine the supply of food which the marine animals obtain. First of all, we may recur to the point that the ocean waters appear to contain something of all the earth materials which do not readily decompose when they are taken into the state of solution. These mineral substances, including the metals, are obtained in part from the lands, through the action of the rain water and the waves, but perhaps in larger share from the volcanic matter which, in the form of floating lava, pumice, or dust, is plentifully delivered to the sea. Except doubtfully, and at most in a very small way, this chemical store of the sea water can not be directly taken into the structures of animals; it can only be immediately appropriated by the marine plants. These forms can only develop in that superficial realm of the seas which is penetrated by the sunlight, or say within the depth of five hundred feet, mostly within one hundred feet of the surface, about one thirtieth of the average, and about one fiftieth of the maximum ocean depth. On this marine plant life, and in a small measure on the vegetable matter derived from the land, the marine animals primarily depend for their provender. Through the conditions which bring about the formation of *Sargassum* seas, those areas of the ocean where seaweeds grow afloat, as well as by the water-logging and weighting down of other vegetable matter, some part of the plant remains is carried to the sea floor, even to great depths; but the main dependence of the deep-sea forms of animals is upon other animal forms, which themselves may have obtained their store from yet others. In fact, in any deep-sea form we might find it necessary to trace back the food by thousands of steps before we found the creature which had access to the vegetable matter. It is easy to see how such conditions profoundly limit the development of organic being in the abysm of the ocean.

The sedentary animals, or those which are fixed to the sea bottom—a group which includes the larger part of the marine species—have to depend for their sustenance on the movement of the water which passes their station. If the seas were perfectly still, none of these creatures except the most minute could be fed; therefore

the currents of the ocean go far by their speed to determine the rate at which life may flourish. At great depths,
as we have seen, these movements are practically limited
to that which is caused by the slow movement which the
tide brings about. The amount of this motion is proportional to the depth of the sea; in the deeper parts, it carries the water to and fro twice each day for the distance of
about two hundred and fifty feet. In the shallower water
this motion increases in proportion to the shoaling, and
in the regions near the shores the currents of the sea
which, except the massive drift from the poles, do not
usually touch the bottom, begin to have their influence.
Where the water is less than a hundred feet in depth, each
wave contributes to the movement, which attains its maximum near the shore, where every surge sweeps the water
rapidly to and fro. It is in this surge belt, where the
waves are broken, that marine animals are best provided
with food, and it is here that their growth is most rapid.
If the student will obtain a pint of water from the surf,
he will find that it is clouded by fragments of organic
matter, the quantity in a pound of the fluid often amounting to the fiftieth part of its weight. He will thus perceive that along the shore line, though the provision of
victuals is most abundant, the store is made from the animals and plants which are ground up in the mill. In a
word, while the coast is a place of rapid growth, it is
also a region of rapid destruction; only in the case of the
coral animals, which associate their bodies with a number
of myriads in large and elaborately organized communities,
do we find animals which can make such head against the
action of the waves that they can build great deposits in
their realm.

It should be noted that a part of the advantage which
is afforded to organic life by the shore belt is due to the
fact that the waters are there subjected to a constant
process of aëration by the whipping into foam and spray
which occurs where the waves overturn.

It will be interesting to the student to note the great number of mechanical contrivances which have been devised to give security to animals and plants which face these difficult conditions arising from successive violent blows of falling water. Among these may be briefly noted those of the limpets—mollusks which dwell in a conical shell, which faces the water with a domelike outside, and which at the moment of the stroke is drawn down upon the rock by the strong muscle which fastens the creature to its foundation. The barnacles, which with their wedge-shaped prows cut the water at the moment of the stroke, but open in the pauses between the waves, so that the creature may with its branching arms grasp at the food which floats about it; the nullipores, forms of seaweed which are framed of limestone and cling firmly to the rock—afford yet other instances of protective adaptations contrived to insure the safety of creatures which dwell in the field of abundant food supply.

The facts above presented will show the reader that the marine sediments are formed under conditions which permit a great variety in the nature of the materials of which they are composed. As soon as the deposits are built into rocks and covered by later accumulations, their materials enter the laboratory of the under earth, where they are subjected to progressive changes. Even before they have attained a great depth, through the laying down of later deposits upon them, changes begin which serve to alter their structure. The fragments of a soluble kind begin to be dissolved, and are redeposited, so that the mass commonly becomes much more solid, passing from the state of detritus to that of more or less solid rock. When yet more deeply buried, and thereby brought into a realm of greater warmth, or perhaps when penetrated by dikes and thereby heated, these changes go yet further. More of the material is commonly rearranged by solution and redeposition, so that limestone may be converted into crystalline marble, granular sandstones into firm masses, known as quartzites, and clays into the harder form of slate. Where the changes go to the extreme point, rocks originally distinctly bedded probably may be so taken to pieces and made over that all traces of their stratification may be destroyed, all fossils obliterated, and the stone transformed into mica schist, or granite or other crystalline rock. It may be injected into the overlying strata in the form of dikes, or it may be blown forth into the air through volcanoes. Involved in mountain-folding, after being more or less changed in the manner described, the beds may become tangled together like the rumpled leaves of a book, or even with the complexity of snarled thread. All these changes of condition makes it difficult for the geologist to unravel the succession of strata so that he may know the true order of the rocks, and read from them the story of the successive geological periods. This task, though incomplete, has by the labours of many thousand men been so far advanced that we are now able to divide the record into chapters, the divisions of the geologic ages, and to give some account of the succession of events, organic and geographic, which have occurred since life began to write its records.

EARTHQUAKES.

In ordinary experience we seem to behold the greater part of the earth which meets our eyes as fixed in its position. A better understanding shows us that nothing in this world is immovable. In the realm of the inorganic world the atoms and molecules even in solid bodies have to be conceived as endowed with ceaseless though ordered motions. Even when matter is built into the solid rock, it is doubtful whether any grain of it ever comes really to rest. Under the strains which arise from the contraction of the earth's interior and the chemical changes which the rocks undergo, each bit is subject to ever-changing thrusts, which somewhat affect its position. If we in any way could bring a grain of sand from any stratum under a microscope, so that we could perceive its changes of place, we should probably find that it was endlessly swaying this way and that, with reference to an ideally fixed point, such as the centre of the earth. But even that centre, whether of gravity or of figure, is probably never at rest.

Earth movements may be divided into two groups—those which arise from the bodily shifting of matter, which conveys the particles this way or that, or, as we say, change their place, and those which merely produce vibration, in which the particles, after their vibratory movement, return to their original place. For purposes of illustration the first, or translatory motion, may be compared to that which takes place when a bell is carried along upon a locomotive or a ship; and the second, or vibratory movement, to what takes place when the bell is by a blow made to ring. It is with these ringing movements, as we may term them, that we find ourselves concerned when we undertake the study of earthquakes.

It is desirable that the reader should preface his study of earthquakes by noting the great and, at the same time, variable elasticity of rocks. In the extreme form this elasticity is very well shown when a toy marble, which is made of a close-textured rock, such as that from which it derives its name, is thrown upon a pavement composed of like dense material. Experiment will show that the little sphere can often be made to bounce to the height of twenty feet without breaking. If, then, with the same energy the marble is thrown upon a brick floor, the rebound will be very much diminished. It is well to consider what happens to produce the rebound. When the sphere strikes the floor it changes its shape, becoming shorter in the axis at right angles to the point which was struck, and at the same instant expanded along the equator of that axis. The flattening remains for only a small fraction of a second; the sphere vibrates so that it stretches along the line on which it previously shortened, and, as this movement takes place with great swiftness, it may be said to propel itself away from the floor. At the same time a similar movement goes on in the rock of the floor, and, where the rate of vibration is the same, the two kicks are coincident, and so the sphere is impelled violently away from the point of contact. Where the marble comes in contact with brick, in part because of the lesser elasticity of that material, due to its rather porous structure, and partly because it does not vibrate at the same rate as the marble, the expelling blow is much less strong.

All rocks whatever, even those which appear as incoherent sands, are more or less set into vibratory motion whenever they are struck by a blow. In the crust of the earth various accidents occur which may produce that sudden motion which we term a blow. When we have examined into the origin of these impulses, and the way in which they are transmitted through the rocks, we obtain a basis for understanding earthquake shocks. The commonest cause of the jarrings in the earth is found in the formation of fractures, known as faults. If the reader has ever been upon a frozen lake at a time when the weather was growing colder, and the ice, therefore, was shrinking, he may have noted the rending sound and the slight vibration which comes with the formation of a crack traversing the sheet of ice. At such a time he feels a movement which is an earthquake, and which represents the simpler form of those tremors arising from the sudden rupture of fault planes. If he has a mind to make the experiment, he may hang a bullet by a thread from a small frame which rests upon the ice, and note that as the vibration occurs the little pendulum sways to and fro, thus indicating the oscillations of the ice. The same instrument will move in an identical manner when affected by a quaking in the rocks.

Where the rocks are set in vibration by a rent which is formed in them, the phenomena are more complicated, and often on a vastly larger scale than in the simple conditions afforded by a sheet of ice. The rocks on either side of the rupture generally slide over each other, and the opposing masses are rent in their friction upon one another; the result is, not only the first jar formed by the initial fracture, but a great many successive movements from the other breakages which occur. Again, in the deeper parts of the crust, the fault fissures are often at the moment of their formation filled by a violent inrush of liquid rock. This, as it swiftly moves along, tears away masses from the walls, and when it strikes the end of the opening delivers a blow which may be of great violence. The nature of this stroke may be judged by the familiar instance where the relatively slow-flowing stream from a hydrant pipe is suddenly choked by closing the stopcock. Unless the plumber provides a cushion of air to diminish the energy of the blow, it is often strong enough to shake the house. Again, when steam or other gases are by a sudden diminution of pressure enabled to expand, they may deliver a blow which is exactly like that caused by the explosion of gunpowder, which, even when it rushes against the soft cushion of the air, may cause a jarring that may be felt as well as heard to a great distance. Such movements very frequently occur in the eruptions of volcanoes; they cause a quivering of the earth, which may be felt for a great distance from the immediate seat of the disturbance.

When by any of the sudden movements which have been above described a jar is applied to the rocks, the wave flies through the more or less elastic mass until the energy involved in it is exhausted. This may not be brought about until the motion has travelled for the distance of hundreds of miles. In the great earthquake of 1755, known as the Lisbon shock, the records make it seem probable that the movement was felt over one eighth part of the earth's surface. Such great disturbances probably bring about a motion of the rocks near the point of origin, which may be expressed in oscillations having an amplitude of one to two feet; but in the greater number of earthquakes the maximum swing probably does not exceed the tenth of that amount. Very sensible shaking, even such as may produce considerable damage to buildings, are caused by shocks in which the earth vibrates with less than an inch of swing.

When a shock originates, the wave in the rocks due to the compression which the blow inflicts runs at a speed varying with the elasticity of the substance, but at the rate of about fifteen hundred feet a second. The movements of this wave are at right angles to the seat of the originating disturbance, so that the shock may come to the surface in a line forming any angle between the vertical and the nearly horizontal. Where, as in a volcanic eruption, the shock originates with an explosion, these waves go off in circles. Where, however, as is generally the case, the shock originates in a fault plane, which may have a length and depth of many miles, the movement has an elliptical form.

If the earthquake wave ran through a uniform and highly elastic substance, such as glass, it would move everywhere with equal speed, and, in the case of the greater disturbances, the motion might be felt over the whole surface of the earth. But as the motion takes place through rocks of varying elasticity, the rate at which it journeys is very irregular. Moving through materials of one density, and with a rate of vibration determined by those conditions, the impulse is with difficulty communicated to strata which naturally vibrate at another speed. In many cases, as where a shock passing through dense crystalline strata encounters a mass of soft sandstone, the wave, in place of going on, is reflected back toward its point of origin. These earthquake echoes sometimes give rise to very destructive movements. It often happens that before the original tremors of a shock have passed away from a point on the surface the reflex movements rush in, making a very irregular motion, which may be compared to that of the waves in a cross-sea.

The foregoing account of earthquake action will serve to prepare the reader for an understanding of those very curious and important effects which these accidents produce in and on the earth. Below the surface the sensible action of earthquake shocks is limited. It has often been observed that people in mines hardly note a swaying which may be very conspicuous to those on the surface, the reason for this being that underground, where the rocks are firmly bound together, all those swingings which are due to the unsupported position of such objects as buildings, columnar rocks, trees, and the waters of the earth, are absent. The effect of the movements which earthquakes impress on the under earth is mainly due to the fact that in almost every part of the crust tensions or strains of other kinds are continually forming. These may for ages prove without effect until the earth is jarred, when motions will suddenly take place which in a moment may alter the conditions of the rocks throughout a wide field. In a word, a great earthquake caused by the formation of an extensive fault is likely to produce any number of slight dislocations, each of which is in turn shock-making, sending its little wave to complicate the great oscillation. Nor does the perturbing effect of these jarring movements cease with the fractures which they set up and the new strains which are in turn developed by the motions which they induce. The alterations of the rocks which are involved in chemical changes are favoured by such motions. It is a familiar experience that a vessel of water, if kept in the state of repose, may have its temperature lowered three or four degrees below the freezing point without becoming frozen. If the side of the vessel is then tapped with the finger, so as to send a slight quake through the mass, it will instantly congeal. Molecular rearrangements are thus favoured by shocks, and the consequences of those which run through the earth are, from a chemical point of view, probably important.

The reader may help himself to understand something of the complicated problem of earth tensions, and the corresponding movements of the rocks, by considering certain homely illustrations. He may observe how the soil cracks as it shrinks in times of drought, the openings closing when it rains. In a similar way the frozen earth breaks open, sometimes with a shock which is often counted as an earthquake. Again, the ashes in a sifter or the gravel on a sieve show how each shaking may relieve certain tensions established by gravity, while they create others which are in turn to be released by the next shock. An ordinary dwelling house sways and strains with the alternations of temperature and moisture to which it is subjected in the round of climatal alterations. Now and then we note the movements in a cracking sound, but by far the greater part of them escape observation.

With this sketch of the mechanism of earthquake shocks we now turn to consider their effects upon the surface of the earth. From a geological point of view, the most important effect of earthquake shocks is found in the movement of rock masses down steep slopes, which is induced by the shaking. Everywhere on the land the agents of decay and erosion tend to bring heavy masses into position where gravitation naturally leads to their downfall, but where they may remain long suspended, provided they are not disturbed. Thus, wherever there are high and steep cliffs, great falls of rock are likely to occur when the earthquake movements traverse the under earth. In more than one instance observers, so placed that they commanded a view of distant mountains, have noticed the downfall of precipices in the path of the shock before the trembling affected the ground on which they stood. In the famous earthquake of 1783, which devastated southern Italy, the Prince of Scylla persuaded his people to take refuge in their boats, hoping that they might thereby escape the destruction which threatened them on the land. No sooner were the unhappy folk on the water than the fall of neighbouring cliffs near the sea produced a great wave, which overwhelmed the vessels.

Where the soil lies upon steep slopes, in positions in which it has accumulated during ages of tranquillity, a great shock is likely to send it down into the valleys in vast landslides. Thus, in the earthquake of 1692, the Blue Mountains of Jamaica were so violently shaken that the soil and the forests which stood on it were precipitated into the river beds, so that many tree-clad summits became fields of bare rock. The effect of this action is immensely to increase the amount of detritus which the streams convey to the sea. After the great Jamaica shock, above noted, the rivers for a while ceased to flow, their waters being stored in the masses of loose material. Then for weeks they poured forth torrents of mud and the *débris* of vegetation—materials which had to be swept away as the streams formed new channels.

In all regions where earthquake movements are frequent, and the shock of considerable violence, the trained observer notes that the surfaces of bare rock are singularly extensive, the fact being that many of these areas, where the slope lies at angles of from ten to thirty degrees, which in an unshaken region would be thickly soil-covered, are deprived of the coating by the downward movement of the waste which the disturbances bring about. A familiar example of this action may be had by watching the workmen engaged in sifting sand, by casting the material on a sloping grating. The work could not be done but for an occasional blow applied to the sifter. An arrangement for such a jarring motion is commonly found in various ore-dressing machines, where the object is to move fragments of matter over a sloping surface.

Even where the earth is so level that an earthquake shock does not cause a sliding motion of the materials,

such as above described, other consequences of the shaking may readily be noted. As the motion runs through
the mass, provided the movement be one of considerable
violence, crevices several feet in width, and sometimes
having the length of miles, are often formed. In most
cases these fissures, opened by one pulsation of the shock,
are likely to be closed by the return movement, which
occurs the instant thereafter. The consequences of this
action are often singular, and in cases constitute the
most frightful elements of a shock which the sufferer
beholds. In the great earthquake of 1811, which ravaged the section of the Mississippi ·Valley between the
mouth of the Ohio and Vicksburg, these crevices were so
numerously formed that the pioneers protected themselves
from the danger of being caught in their jaws by felling
trees so that they lay at right angles to the direction in
which the rents extended, building on these timbers plat-
forms to support their temporary dwelling places. The
records of earthquakes supply many instances in which
people have been caught in these earth fissures, and in a
single case it is recorded that a man who disappeared into
the cavity was in a moment cast forth in the rush of waters
which in this, as in many other cases, spouts forth as the
walls of the opening come together.

Sometimes these rents are attended by a dislocation,
which brings the earth on one side much higher than on
the other. The step thus produced may be many miles
in length, and may have a height of twenty feet or more.
It needs no argument to show that we have here the top
of a fault such as produced the shock, or it may be one
of a secondary nature, such as any earthquake is likely
to bring about in the strata which it traverses. In certain cases two faults conjoin their action, so that a portion
of the surface disappears beneath the earth, entombing
whatever may have stood on the vanished site. Thus in
the great shock known as that of Lisbon, which occurred in
1755, the stone quay along the harbour, where many thou-

sand people had sought refuge from the falling buildings
of the city, suddenly sank down with the multitude, and
the waters closed over it; no trace of the people or of the
structure was to be found after the shock was over. There
is a story to the effect that during the same earthquake
an Arab village in northern Africa sank down, the earth
on either side closing over it, so that no trace of the
habitations remained. In both these instances the catastrophes are best explained by the diagram.

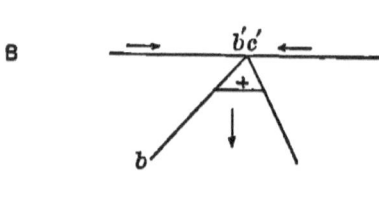

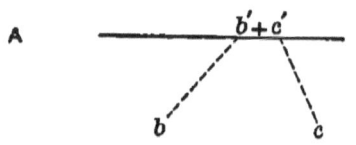

Fig. 21.—Diagram showing how a portion of the earth's surface may be
sunk by faulting. Fig. A shows
the original position; B, the position after faulting; b b' and c c'
the planes of the faults; the arrows
the direction of the movement.

In the earthquake
of 1811 the alluvial
plains on either side of
the Mississippi at many
points sank down so
that arable land was
converted into lakes;
the area of these depres-
sions probably amount-
ed to some hundred
square miles. The
writer, on examining
these sunken lands,
found that the subsi-
dences had occurred
where the old moats or
abandoned channels of
the great river had been
filled in with a mixture
of decaying timber and
river silt. When vio-
lently shaken, this loose-textured *débris* naturally settled
down, so that it formed a basin occupied by a crescent-
shaped lake. The same process of settling plentifully goes
on wherever the rocks are still in an uncemented
state. The result is often the production of changes
which lead to the expulsion of gases. Thus, in the
Charleston earthquake of 1883, the surface over an area

of many hundred square miles was pitted with small craters, formed by the uprush of water impelled by its contained gases. These little water volcanoes—for such we may call them—sometimes occur to the number of a dozen or more on each acre of ground in the violently shaken district. They indicate one result of the physical and chemical alterations which earthquake shocks bring about. As earthquakes increase in violence their effect upon the soil becomes continually greater, until in the most violent shocks all the loose materials on the surface of the earth may be so shaken about as to destroy even the boundaries of fields. After the famous earthquake of Riobamba, which occurred on the west coast of South America in 1797, the people of the district in which the town of that name was situated were forced to redivide their land, the original boundaries having disappeared. Fortunately, shocks of this description are exceedingly rare. They occur in only a few parts of the world.

Certain effects of earthquakes where the shock emerges beneath the sea have been stated in the account of volcanic eruptions (see page 299). We may therefore note here only certain of the more general facts. While passing through the deep seas, this wave may have a height of not more than two or three feet and a width of some score miles. As it rolls in upon the shore the front of the undulation is retarded by the friction of the bottom in such a measure that its speed is diminished, while the following part of the waves, being less checked, crowds up toward this forward part. The result is, that the surge mounts ever higher and higher as it draws near the shore, upon which it may roll as a vast wave having the height of fifty feet or more and a width quite unparalleled by any wave produced from wind action. Waves of this description are most common in the Pacific Ocean. Although but occasional, the damage which they may inflict is very great. As the movement approaches the shore, vessels, however well anchored, are dragged away

25 ·

to seaward by the great back lash of the wave, a phenomenon which may be perceived even in the case of the
ordinary surf. Thus forced to seaward, the crews of the
ships may find their vessels drawn out for the distance of
some miles, until they come near the face of the advancing billow. This, as it approaches the shore, straight-
ens up to the wall-fronted form, and then topples upon
the land. Those vessels which are not at once crushed
down by the blow are generally hurled far inland by the
rush of waters. In the great Jamaica earthquake of
1692 a British man-of-war was borne over the tops of certain warehouses and deposited at a distance from the shore.

Owing to the fact that water is a highly elastic material, the shocks transmitted to it from the bottom are
sent onward with their energy but little diminished. While
the impulse is very violent, these oscillations may prove
damaging to shipping. The log-books of mariners abound
in stories of how vessels were dismasted or otherwise
badly shaken by a sudden blow received in the midst
of a quiet sea. The impression commonly conveyed to
the sailors is that the craft has struck upon a rock. The
explanation is that an earthquake jar, in traversing the
water, has delivered its blow to the ship. As the speed
of this jarring movement is very much greater than that
of any ordinary wave, the blow which it may strike may
be most destructive. There seems, indeed, little reason
to doubt that a portion of the vessels which are ever disappearing in the wilderness of the ocean are lost by the
crushing effect of these quakings which pass through the
waters of the deep.

We have already spoken of the earthquake shock as
an oscillation. It is a quality of all bodies which oscillate under the influence of a blow, such as originates in
earthquake shocks, to swing to and fro, after the manner
of the metal in a bell or a tuning fork, in a succession
of movements, each less than the preceding, until the
impulse is worn out, or rather, we should in strict sense

say, changed to other forms of energy. The result is, that
even in the slightest earthquake shock the earth moves
not once to and fro, but very many times. In a considerable shock the successive diminishing swingings amount
to dozens before they become so slight as to elude per-
ception. Although the first swaying is the strongest, and
generally the most destructive, the quick to-and-fro motions are apt to continue and to complete the devastation
which the first brings about. The vibrations due to any
one shock take place with great rapidity. They may,
indeed, be compared to those movements which we perceive in the margin of a large bell when it has received
a heavy blow from the clapper. The reader has perhaps
seen that for a moment the rim of the bell vibrates with
such rapidity that it has a misty look—that is, the motions
elude the sight. It is easy to see that a shaking of this
kind is particularly calculated to disrupt any bodies which
stand free in the air and are supported only at their base.

In what we may call the natural architecture of the
earth, the pinnacles and obelisks, such as are formed in
many high countries, the effect of these shakings is destructive, and, as we have seen, even the firmer-placed
objects, such as the strong-walled cliffs and steep slopes
of earth, break down under the assaults. It is therefore
no matter of surprise that the buildings which man erects,
where they are composed of masonry, suffer greatly from
these tremblings. In almost all cases human edifices are
constructed without regard to other problems of strength
than those which may be measured by their weight and
the resistance to fracture from gravitation alone. They
are not built with expectation of a quaking, but of a firm-
set earth.

The damage which earthquakes do to buildings is in
most cases due to the fact that they sway their walls out
of plumb, so that they are no longer in position to support the weight which they have to bear. The amount
of this swaying is naturally very much greater than that

which the earth itself experiences in the movement. A building of any height with its walls unsupported by neighbouring structures may find its roof rocked to and fro through an arc which has a length of feet, while its base moves only through a length of inches. The reader may see an example of this nature if he will poise a thin book or a bit of plank a foot long on top of a small table; then jarring the table so that it swings through a distance of say a quarter of an inch, he will see that the columnar object swings at its top through a much greater distance, and is pretty sure to be overturned.

Where a building carries a load in its upper parts, such as may be afforded by its heavy roof or the stores which it contains, the effect of an earthquake shock such as carries the earth to and fro becomes much more destructive than it might otherwise be. This weight lags behind when the earth slips forward in the first movement of the oscillation, with the effect that the walls of the building are pretty sure to be thrust so far beyond the perpendicular that they give way and are carried down by the weight which they bore. It has often been remarked in earthquake shocks that tall columns, even where composed of many blocks, survive a shock which overturns lower buildings where thin walls support several floors, on each of which is accumulated a considerable amount of weight. In the case of the column, the strains are even, and the whole structure may rock to and fro without toppling over. As the energy of the undulations diminish, it gradually regains the quiet state without damage. In the ordinary edifice the irregular disposition of the weight does not permit the uniform movement which may insure safety. Thus, if the city of Washington should ever be violently shaken, the great obelisk, notwithstanding that it is five hundred feet high, may survive a disturbance which would wreck the lower and more massive edifices which lie about it.

Where, as is fortunately rarely the case, the great shock

comes to the earth in a vertical direction, the effect upon all movable objects is in the highest measure disastrous. In such a case buildings are crushed as if by the stroke of a giant's hand. The roofs and floors are at one stroke thrown to the foundations, and all the parts of the walls which are not supported by strong masonry continuous from top to bottom are broken to pieces. In such cases it has been remarked that the bodies of men are often thrown considerable distances. It is asserted, indeed, that in the Riobamba shock they were cast upward to the height of more than ninety feet. It is related that the sole survivor of a congregation which had hastened at the outset of the disturbance into a church was thrown by the greatest and most destructive shock upward and through a window the base of which was at the height of more than twenty feet from the ground.

It is readily understood that an earthquake shock may enter a building in any direction between the vertical and the horizontal. As the movement exhausts itself in passing from the place of its origin, the horizontal shocks are usually of least energy. Those which are accurately vertical are only experienced where the edifices are placed immediately over the point where the motion originates. It follows, therefore, that the destructive work of earthquakes is mainly performed in that part of the field where the motion is, as regards its direction, between the vertical and the horizontal—a position in which the edifice is likely to receive at once the destructive effect arising from the sharp upward thrust of the vertical movement and the oscillating action of that which is in a horizontal direction. Against strains of this description, where the movements have an amplitude of more than a few inches, no ordinary masonry edifice can be made perfectly safe; the only tolerable security is attained where the building is of well-framed timber, which by its elasticity permits a good deal of motion without destructive consequences. Even such buildings, however,

those of the strongest type, may be ruined by the greater
earthquakes. Thus, in the Mississippi Valley earthquake
of 1811, the log huts of the frontiersmen, which are about
as strong as any buildings can be made, were shaken to
pieces by the sharp and reiterated shocks.

It is by no means surprising to find that the style
of architecture adopted in earthquake countries differs
from that which is developed in regions where the earth
is firm-set. The people generally learn that where their
buildings must meet the trials of earthquakes they have
to be low and strong, framed in the manner of fortifica-
tions, to withstand the assault of this enemy. We observe
that Gothic architecture, where a great weight of masonry
is carried upon slender columns and walls divided by tall
windows, though it became the dominant style in the relatively stable lands of northern Europe, never gained a
firm foothold in those regions about the Mediterranean
which are frequently visited by severe convulsions of the
earth. There the Grecian or the Romanesque styles,
which are of a much more massive type, retain their places
and are the fashions to the present day. Even this manner of building, though affording a certain security against
slight tremblings, is not safe in the greater shocks. Again
and again large areas in southern Italy have been almost
swept of their buildings by the destructive movements
which occur in that realm. The only people who have
systematically adapted their architectural methods to
earthquake strains are the Japanese, who in certain districts where such risks are to be encountered construct
their dwellings of wood, and place them upon rollers, so
that they may readily move to and fro as the shock passes
beneath them. In a measure the people of San Francisco have also provided against this danger by avoiding
dangerous weights in the upper parts of their buildings, as
well as the excessive height to which these structures are
lifted in some of our American towns.

Earthquakes of sensible energy appear to be limited

to particular parts of the earth's crust. The regions, indeed, where within the period of human history shocks of devastating energy have occurred do not include more than one fifteenth part of the earth's surface. There is a common notion that these movements are most apt to happen in volcanic regions. It is, indeed, true that sensible shocks commonly attend the explosions from great craters, but the records clearly show that these movements are very rarely of destructive energy. Thus in the regions about the base of Vesuvius and of Ætna, the two volcanoes of which most is known, the shocks have never been productive of extensive disaster. In fact, the reiterated slight jarrings which attend volcanic action appear to prevent the formation of those great and slowly accumulated strains which in their discharge produce the most violent tremblings of the earth. The greatest and most continuous earthquake disturbances of history—that before noted in the early days of this century, in the Mississippi Valley, where shocks of considerable violence continued for two years—came about in a field very far removed from active volcanoes. So, too, the disturbances beneath the Atlantic floor which originated the shocks that led to the destruction of Lisbon, and many other similar though less violent movements, are developed in a field apparently remote from living volcanoes. Eastern New England, which has been the seat of several considerable earthquakes, is about as far away from active vents as any place on the habitable globe. We may therefore conclude that, while volcanoes necessarily produce shocks resulting from the discharge of their gases and the intrusion of lava into the dikes which are formed about them, the greater part of the important shocks are in no wise connected with volcanic explosions.

With the exception of the earthquake in the Mississippi Valley, all the great shocks of which we have a record have occurred in or near regions where the rocks have been extensively disturbed by mountain-building

forces, and where the indications lead us to believe that
dislocations of strata, such as are competent to rive the beds
asunder, may still be in progress. This, taken in connection with the fact that many of these shocks are attended by the formation of fault planes, which appear
on the surface, lead us to the conclusion that earthquakes
of the stronger kind are generally formed by the riving
of fissures, which may or may not be developed upward
to the surface. This view is supported by many careful
observations on the effect which certain great earthquakes
have exercised on the buildings which they have ravaged. The distinguished observer, Mr. Charles Mallet, who
visited the seat of the earthquake which, in 1854, occurred in the province of Calabria in Italy, with great
labour and skill determined the direction in which the
shock moved through some hundreds of edifices on which
it left the marks of its passage. Plotting these lines of
motion, he found that they were all referred to a vertical
plane lying at the depth of some miles beneath the surface, and extending for a great distance in a north and
south direction. This method of inquiry has been applied
to other fields, with the result that in the case of all the
instances which have been subjected to this inquiry the
seat of the shock has been traced to such a plane, which
can best be accounted for by the supposition of a fault.

The method pursued by Mr. Mallet in his studies of
the origin of earthquakes, and by those who have continued his inquiry, may be briefly indicated as follows:
Examining disrupted buildings, it is easy to determine
those which have been wrecked by a shock that emerged
from the earth in a vertical direction. In these cases,
though tall walls may remain standing, the roofs and
floors are thrown into the cellars. With a dozen such instances the plane of what is called the seismic vertical
is established (*seismos* is the Greek for earthquake). Then
on either side of this plane, which indicates the line but
not the depth of the disturbance, other observations may

be made which give the clew to the depth. Thus a building may be found where the northwest corner at its
upper part has been thrown off. Such a rupture was clearly
caused by an upward but oblique movement, which in the
first half of the oscillation heaved the structure upwardly
into the northwest, and then in the second half, or rebound,
drew the mass of the building away from the unsupported
corner, allowing that part of the masonry to fly off and
fall to the ground. Constructing a line at right angles
to the plane of the fracture, it will be found to intersect
the plane, the position of which has been in part determined by finding the line where it intersects the earth,
or the seismic vertical before noted. Multiplying such
observations on either side of the last-mentioned line,
the attitude of the underground parts of the plane, as
well as the depth to which it attained, can be approximately determined. ·

It is worth while to consider the extent to which
earthquake shocks may affect the general quality of the
people who dwell in countries where these disturbances
occur with such frequency and violence as to influence
their lives. There can be no question that wherever
earthquakes occur in such a measure as to produce widespread terror, where, recurring from time to time, they
develop in men a sense of abiding insecurity, they become potent agents of degradation. All the best which
men do in creating a civilization rests upon a sense of con-
fidence that their efforts may be accumulated from year
to year, and that even after death the work of each man
may remain as a heritage to his kind. It is likely, indeed,
that in certain realms, as in southern Italy, a part of
the failure of the people to advance in culture is due to
their long experience of such calamities, and the natural
expectation that they will from time to time recur. In
a similar way the Spanish settlements in Central and
South America, which lie mostly in lands that are subject to disastrous shocks, may have been retarded by

the despair, as well as the loss of property and life, which these accidents have so frequently inflicted upon them. It will not do, however, to attribute too much to such terrestrial influences. By far the most important element in determining the destiny of a people is to be found in their native quality, that which they owe to their ancestors of distant generations. In this connection it is well to consider the history of the Icelandic people, where a small folk has for a thousand years been exposed to a range and severity of trials, such as earthquakes, volcanic explosions, and dearth of harvests may produce, and all these in a measure that few if any other countries experience. Notwithstanding these misfortunes, the Icelanders have developed and maintained a civilization which in all else, except its material results, on the average transcends that which has been won by any other folk in modern times. If a people have the determining spirit which leads to high living, they can successfully face calamities far greater than those which earthquakes inflict.

It was long supposed that the regions where earthquakes are not noticeable by the unaided senses were exempt from all such disturbances. The observations which seismologists have made in recent years point to the conclusion that no part of the earth's surface is quite exempt from movements which, though not readily perceived, can be made visible by the use of appropriate instruments. With an apparatus known as the horizontal pendulum it is possible to observe vibrations which do not exceed in amplitude the hundredth part of an inch. This mechanism consists essentially of a slender bar supported near one end by two wires, one from above, the other from below. It may readily be conceived that any measurable movement will cause the longer end of the rod to sway through a considerable arc. Wherever such a pendulum has been carefully observed in any district, it has been found that it indicates the occurrence of slight tremors. Even certain changes of the barometer, which alter the weight of the atmosphere that rests upon the earth to the amount indicated by an inch in the height of the mercury column, appears in all cases to create such tremors. Many of these slight shocks may be due to the effect of more violent quakings, which have run perhaps for thousands of miles from their point of origin, and have thus been reduced in the amplitude of their movement. Others are probably due to the slight motion brought about through the chemical changes of the rocks, which are continuously going on. The ease with which even small motions are carried to a great distance may be judged by the fact that when the ground is frozen the horizontal pendulum will indicate the jarring due to a railway train at the distance of a mile or more from the track.

In connection with the earth jarring, it would bo well to note the occurrence of another, though physically different, kind of movement, which we may term earth swayings, or massive movements, which slowly dislocate the vertical, and doubtless also the horizontal, position of points upon its surface. It has more than once been remarked that in mountain countries, where accurate sights have been taken, the heights of points between the extremities of a long line appear somewhat to vary in the course of a term of years. Thus at a place in the Apennines, where two buildings separated by some miles of distance are commonly intervisible over the crest of a neighbouring peak, it has happened that a change of level of some one of the points has made it impossible to see the one edifice from the other. Knowing as we do that the line of the seacoast is ever-changing, uprising taking place at some points and down-sinking at others, it seems not unlikely that these irregular swayings are of very common occurrence. Moreover, astronomers are beginning to remark the fact that their observatories appear not to remain permanently in the same position—that is, they do not have exactly the same latitude and longitude. Certain of these changes have recently been explained by the discovery of a new and hitherto unnoted movement of the polar axis. It is not improbable, however, that the irregular swaying of the earth's crust, due to the folding of strata and to the alterations in the volume of rocks which are continually going on, may have some share in bringing about these dislocations.

Measured by the destruction which was wrought to the interests of man, earthquakes deserve to be reckoned among the direst calamities of Nature. Since the dawn of history the records show us that the destruction of life which is to be attributed to them is to be counted by the millions. A catalogue of the loss of life in the accidents of this description which have occurred during the Christian era has led the writer to suppose that probably over two million persons have perished from these shocks in the last nineteen centuries. Nevertheless, as compared with other agents of destruction, such as preventable disease, war, or famine, the loss which has been inflicted by earth movements is really trifling, and almost all of it is due to an obstinate carelessness in the construction of buildings without reference to the risks which are known to exist in earthquake-ridden countries.

Although all our exact knowledge concerning the distribution of earthquakes is limited to the imperfect records of two or three thousand years, it is commonly possible to measure in a general way the liability to such accidents which may exist in any country by a careful study of the details of its topography. In almost every large area the process of erosion naturally leaves quantities of rock, either in the form of detached columns or as detrital accumulations deposited on steep slopes. These features are of relatively slow formation, and it is often possible to determine that they have been in their positions for a time which is to be measured by thousands of years. Thus, on inspecting a country such as North America, where the historic records cover but a brief time, we may on inquiry determine which portions of its area have long been exempt from powerful shocks. Where natural obelisks and steep taluses abound—features which would have disappeared if the region had been moved by great shocks —we may be sure that the field under inspection has for a great period been exempt from powerful shaking. Judged by this standard, we may safely say that the region occupied by the Appalachian Mountains has been exempt from serious trouble. So, too, the section of the Cordilleras lying to the east of what is commonly called the Great Basin, between the Rocky Mountains and the Sierra Nevada, has also enjoyed a long reign of peace. In glaciated countries the record is naturally less clear than in those parts of the world which have been subjected to long-continued, slow decay of the rocks. Nevertheless, in those fields boulders are often found poised in position which they could not have maintained if subjected to violent shaking. Judged by this evidence, we may say that a large part of the northern section of this continent, particularly the area about the Great Lakes, has been exempt from considerable shocks since the glacier passed away.

The shores which are subject to the visitations of the great marine waves, caused by earthquake shocks occurring beneath the bottom of the neighbouring ocean, are so swept by those violent inundations that they lose many features which are often found along coasts that have been exempted from such visitations. Thus wherever we find extensive and delicately moulded dunes, poised stones, or slender pinnacled rocks along a coast, we may be sure that since these features were formed the district has not been swept by these great waves.

Around the northern Atlantic we almost everywhere find the glacial waste here and there accumulated near the margin of the sea in the complicated sculptured outlines which are assumed by kame sands and gravels. From

Fig. 22.—Poised rocks indicating a long exemption from strong earthquakes in the places where such features occur.

a study of these features just above the level of high tide, the writer has become convinced that the North Atlantic district has long been exempt from the assaults of other waves than those which are produced during heavy storms.

At the present time the waves formed by earthquakes appear to be of destructive violence only on the west coast of South America, where they roll in from a region of the Pacific lying to the south of the equator and a few hundred miles from the shore of the continent, which appears to be the seat of exceedingly violent shocks. A similar field occurs in the Atlantic between the Lesser Antilles and the Spanish peninsula, but no great waves have come thence since the time of the Lisbon earthquake. The basin of the Caribbean and the region about Java appear to be also fields where these disturbances may be expected, though in each but one wave of this nature has been recorded. Therefore we may regard these secondary results of a submarine earthquake as seldom phenomena.

DURATION OF GEOLOGICAL TIME.

Although it is beyond the power of man to conceive any such lapses of time as have taken place in the history of this earth, it is interesting, and in certain ways profitable, to determine as near as possible in the measure of years the duration of the events which are recorded in the rocks. Some astronomers, basing their conclusions on the heat-containing power of matter, and on the rate at which energy in this form flows from the sun, have come to the conclusion that our planet could not have been in independent existence for more than about twenty million years. The geologist, however, resting his conclusions on the records which are the subject of his inquiry, comes on many different lines to an opinion which traverses that entertained by some distinguished astronomers. The ways in which the student of the earth arrives at this opinion will now be set forth.

By noting the amount of sediment carried forth to the sea by the rivers, the geologist finds that the lands of the earth—those, at least, which are protected by their natural envelopes of vegetation—are wearing down at a rate which pretty certainly does not exceed one foot in about five thousand years, or two hundred feet in a million years. Discovering at many places on the earth's surface deposits which originally had a thickness of five thousand feet or more, which have been worn down to the depths of thousands of feet in a single rather brief section of geological time, the student readily finds himself prepared to claim that a period of from five to ten million years has often been required for the accomplishment of but a very small part of the changes which he knows to have occurred on this earth.

As the geologist follows down through the sections of the stratified rocks, and from the remains of strata determines the erosion which has borne away the greater part of the thick deposits which have been exposed to erosion, he comes upon one of those breaks in the succession, or encounters what is called an unconformity, as when horizontal strata lie against those which are tilted. In many cases he may observe that at this time there was a great interval unrepresented by deposits at the place where his observations are made, yet a great lapse of time is indicated by the fact that a large amount of erosion took place in the interval between the two sets of beds.

Putting together the bits of record, and assuming that the rate of erosion accomplished by the agents which operate on the land has always been about the same, the geologist comes to the conclusion that the section of the rocks from the present day to the lowest strata of the Laurentian represents in the time required for their formation not less than a hundred million years; more likely twice that duration. To this argument objection is made by some naturalists that the agents of erosion may have been more active in the past than they are at present. They suggest that the rainfall may have been much greater or the tides higher than they now are. Granting all that can be claimed on this score, we note the fact that the rate of erosion evidently does not increase in anything like a proportionate way with the amount of rainfall. Where a country is protected by its natural coating of vegetation, the rain is delivered to the streams without making any considerable assault upon the surface of the earth, however large the fall may be. Moreover, the tides have little direct cutting power; they can only remove detritus which other agents have brought into a condition to be borne away. The direct cutting power of the tidal movement does not seem to 'be much greater in the Bay of Fundy, where the maximum height of the waves amounts to fifty feet, than on the southern coast of Massachusetts, where the range is not more than five. So far as the observer can judge, the climatal conditions and the other influences which affect the wear of rocks have not greatly varied in the past from what they are at the present day. Now and then there have been periods of excessive erosion; again, ages in which large fields were in the conditions of exceeding drought. It is, however, a fair presumption that these periods in a way balance each other, and that the average state was much like that which we find at present.

If after studying the erosive phenomena exhibited in the structure of the earth the student takes up the study of the accumulations of strata, and endeavours to determine the time required for the laying down of the sediments, he finds similar evidence of the earth's great antiquity. Although the process of deposition, which has given us the rocks visible in the land masses, has been very much interrupted, the section which is made by grouping the observations made in various fields shows that something like a maximum thickness of a hundred and fifty thousand feet of beds has been accumulated in that part of geologic time during which strata were being laid down in the fields that are subjected to our study. Although in these rocks there are many sets of beds which were rapidly formed, the greater part of them have been accumulated with exceeding slowness. Many fine shales,
26

such as those which plentifully occur in the Devonian beds of this country, must have required a thousand years or more for the deposition of the materials that now occupy an inch in depth. In those sections a single foot of the rock may well represent a period of ten thousand years. In many of the limestones the rate of accumulation could hardly have been more speedy. The reckoning has to be rough, but the impression which such studies make upon the mind of the unprejudiced observer is to the effect that the thirty miles or so of sedimentary deposits could not have been formed in less than a hundred million years. In this reckoning it should be noted that no account is taken of those great intervals of unrecorded time, such as elapsed between the close of the Laurentian and the beginning of the Cambrian periods.

There is a third way in which we may seek an interpretation of duration from the rocks. In each successive stage of the earth's history, in different measure in the various ages, mountains were formed which in time, during their exposure to the conditions of the land, were worn down to their roots and covered by deposits accumulated during the succeeding ages. A score or more of these successively constructed series of elevations may readily be observed. Of old, it was believed that mountain ranges were suddenly formed, but there is, however, ample evidence to prove that these disturbed portions of the strata were very gradually dislocated, the rate of the mountainous growth having been, in general, no greater in the past than it is at the present day, when, as we know full well, the movements are going on so slowly that they escape observation. Only here and there, as an attendant on earthquake shocks or other related movements of the crust, do we find any trace of the upward march which produces these elevations. Although not a subject for exact measurements, these features of mountain growth indicate a vast lapse of time, during which the elevations were formed and worn away.

Yet another and very different method by which we may obtain some gauge of the depths of the past is to be found in the steps which have led organic life from its lowest and earliest known forms to the present state of advancement. Taking the changes of species which have occurred since the beginning of the last ice epoch, we find that the changes which have been made in the organic life have been very small; no naturalist who has obtained a clear idea of the facts will question the statement that they are not a thousandth part of the alterations which have occurred since the Laurentian time. The writer is of the opinion that they do not represent the ten thousandth part of those vast changes. These changes are limited in the main to the disappearance of a few forms, and to slight modifications in those previously in existence which have survived to the present day. So far as we can judge, no considerable step in the organic series has taken place in this last great period of the earth's history, although it has been a period when, as before noted, all the conditions have combined to induce rapid modifications in both animals and plants. If, then, we can determine the duration of this period, we may obtain a gauge of some general value.

Although we can not measure in any accurate way the duration of the events which have taken place since the last Glacial period began to wane, a study of the facts seems to show that less than a hundred thousand years can not well be assumed for this interval. Some of the students who have approached the subject are disposed to allow a period of at least twice this length as necessary for the perspective which the train of events exhibits. Reckoning on the lowest estimate, and counting the organic changes which take place during the age as amounting to the thousandth part of the organic changes since the Laurentian age, we find ourselves in face once again of that inconceivable sum which was indicated by the physical record.

Here, again, the critics assert that there may have been periods in the history of the earth when the changes of organic life occurred in a far swifter manner than in this last section of the earth's history. This supposition is inadmissible, for it rests on no kind of proof; it is, moreover, contraindicated by the evident fact that the advance in the organic series has been more rapid in recent time than at any stage of the past. In a word, all the facts with which the geologist deals are decidedly against the assumption that terrestrial changes in the organic or the inorganic world ever proceed in a spasmodic manner. Here and there, and from time to time, local revolutions of a violent nature undoubtedly occur, but, so far as we may judge from the aspect of the present or the records of the past, these accidents are strictly local; the earth has gone forward in its changes much as it is now advancing. Its revolutions have been those of order rather than those of accident.

The first duty of the naturalist is to take Nature as he finds it. He must avoid supposing any methods of action which are not clearly indicated in the facts that he observes. The history of his own and of all other sciences clearly shows that danger is always incurred where suppositions as to peculiar methods of action are introduced into the interpretation. It required many centuries of labour before the students of the earth came to adopt the principle of explaining the problems with which they had to deal by the evidence that the earth submitted to them. Wherever they trusted to their imaginations for guidance, they fell into error. Those who endeavour to abbreviate our conception of geologic time by supposing that in the olden days the order of events was other than that we now behold are going counter to the best traditions of the science.

Although the aspect of the record of life since the beginning of the Cambrian time indicates a period of at least a hundred million years, it must not be supposed

that this is the limit of the time required for the development of the organic series. All the important types of
animals were already in existence in that ancient period
with the exception of the vertebrates, the remains of
which have apparently now been traced down to near the
Cambrian level. In other words, at the stage where we
first find evidence of living beings the series to which they
belong had already climbed very far above the level of
lifeless matter. Few naturalists will question the statement that half the work of organic advance had been
accomplished at the beginning of the Cambrian rocks.
The writer is of the opinion that the development which
took place before that age must have required a much
longer period than has elapsed ·from that epoch to the
present day. We thus come to the conclusion that the
measurement of duration afforded by organic life indicates a yet more lengthened claim of events, and demands
more time than appears to be required for the formation
of the stratified rocks.

The index of duration afforded by the organic series is
probably more trustworthy than that which is found in
the sedimentary strata, and this for the reason that the
records of those strata have been subjected to numerous
and immeasurable breaks, while the development of organic life has of necessity been perfectly continuous. The
one record can at any point be broken without interrupting
the sequences; the other does not admit of any breaches
in the continuity.

THE MOON.

Set over against the earth—related to, yet contrasted
with it in many ways—the moon offers a most profitable
object to the student of geology. He should often turn
to it for those lessons which will be briefly noted.

In the beginning of their mutual history the materials of earth and moon doubtless formed one vaporous
body which had been parted from the concentrating mass

of the sun in the manner noted in the sketch of the history of the solar system. After the earth-moon body had gathered into a nebulous sphere, it is most likely that a ring resembling that still existing about Saturn was formed about the earth, which in time consolidated into the satellite. Thenceforth the two bodies were parted, except for the gravitative attraction which impelled them to revolve about their common centre of gravity, and except for the light and heat they might exchange with one another.

The first stages after the parting of the spheres of earth and moon appear to have been essentially the same in each body. Concentrating upon their centres, they became in time fluid by heat; further on, they entered the rigid state —in a word, they froze—at least in their outer parts. At this point in their existence their histories utterly diverge; or rather, we may say, the development of the earth continued in a vast unfolding, while that of the moon appears to have been absolutely arrested in ways which we will now describe.

With the naked eye we see on the moon a considerable variation in the light of different parts of its surface; we discern that the darker patches appear to be rudely circular, and that they run together on their margins. Seeing this little, the ancients fancied that our satellite had seas and lands like the earth. The first telescopes did not dispel their fancies; even down to the early part of this century there were astronomers who believed the moon to be habitable; indeed, they thought to find evidence that it was the dwelling place of intelligent beings who built cities, and who tried to signal their intellectual kindred of this planet. When, however, strong glasses were applied to the exploration, these pleasing fancies were rudely dispelled.

Seen with a telescope of the better sort, the moon reveals itself to be in large part made up of circular depressions, each surrounded by a ringlike wall, with nearly level but rough places between. The largest of these walled areas is some four hundred miles in diameter; thence they grade down to the smallest pits which the glass can disclose, which are probably not over as many feet across. The writer, from a careful study of these pits, has come to the conclusion that the wider are the older and the smaller the last formed. The rude elevations about these pits—some of which rise to the height of ten thousand feet or more—con-stitute the principal top-ographic reliefs of the lunar surface. Besides the pits above men-tioned, there are numer-ous fractures in the sur-face of the plains and ringlike ridges; on the most of these the walls have separated, forming trenches not unlike what we find in the case of some terrestrial breaks such as have been noted about volcanoes and else-where. It may be that the so-called canals of Mars are of the same nature.

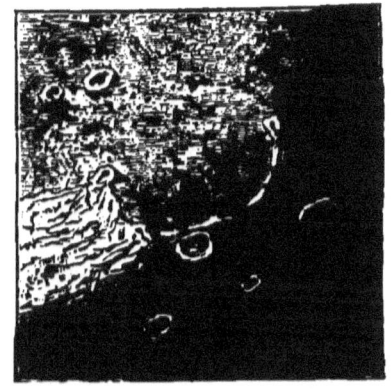

Fig. 23.—Lunar mountains near the Gulf of Iris.

The most curious feature on the moon's surface are the bands of lighter colour, which, radiating from certain of the volcanolike pits—those of lesser size and probably of latest origin—extend in some cases for five hundred miles or more across the surface. These light bands have never been adequately explained. It seems most likely that they are stains along the sides of cracks, such as are sometimes observed about volcanoes.

The eminent peculiarity of the moon is that it is desti-tute of any kind of gaseous or aqueous envelope. That there is no distinct atmosphere is clearly shown by the

perfectly sharp and sudden way in which the light of a
star disappears when it goes behind the moon and the clear
lines of the edge of the satellite in a solar eclipse.   The
same evidence shows that there is no vapour of water;
moreover, a careful search which the writer has made shows
that the surface has none of those continuous down grades
which mark the work of water flowing over the land.
Nearly all of the surface consists of shallow or deep pits,
such as could not have been formed by water action.   We
therefore have not only to conclude that the moon is
waterless, but that it has been in this condition ever since
the part that is turned toward us was shaped.

As the moon, except for the slight movement termed
its " libration," always turns the same face to us, so that
we see in all only about four sevenths of its surface, it
has naturally been conjectured that the unseen side, which
is probably some miles lower than that turned toward us,
might have a different character from that which we behold.   There are reasons why this is improbable.   In the
first place, we see on the extreme border of the moon,
when the libration turns one side the farthest around
toward the earth, the edge of a number of the great walled
pits such as are so plenty on the visible area; it is fair to
assume that these rings are completed in the invisible
realm.   On this basis we can partly map about a third
of the hidden side.   Furthermore, there are certain bands
of light which, though appearing on the visible side, evidently converge to some points on the other.   It is reasonable to suppose that, as all other bands radiate from walled
pits, these also start from such topographic features.   In
this way certain likenesses of the hidden area to that which
is visible is established, thus making it probable that the
whole surface of the satellite has the same character.

Clearly as the greater part of the moon is revealed to
us—so clearly, indeed, that it is possible to map any elevation of its surface that attains the height of five hundred feet—the interpretation of its features in the light

of geology is a matter of very great difficulty. The main points seem to be tolerably clear; they are as follows: The surface of the moon as we see it is that which was formed when that body, passing from the state of fluidity from heat, formed a solid crust. The pits which we observe on its surface are the depressions which were formed as the mass gradually ceased to boil. The later formed of these openings are the smaller, as would be the case in such a slowing down of a boiling process.

As the diameter of the moon is only about one fourth of that of the earth, its bulk is only about one sixteenth of that of its planet; consequently, it must have cooled to the point of solidification ages before the larger sphere attained that state. It is probable that the same changeless face that we see looked down for millions of years on an earth which was still a seething, fiery mass. In a word, all that vast history which is traceable in the rocks beneath our feet—which is in progress in the seas and lands and is to endure for an inconceivable time to come—has been denied our satellite, for the reason that it had no air with which to entrap the solar heat and no water to apply the solar energy to evolutionary processes. The heat which comes upon the moon as large a share for each equal area as it comes upon the earth flies at once away from the airless surface, at most giving it a temporary warmth, but instituting no geological work unless it be a little movement from the expansion and contraction of the rocks. During the ages in which the moon has remained thus lifeless the earth, owing to its air and water, has applied a vast amount of solar energy to geological work in the development and redevelopment of its geological features and to the processes of organic life. We thus see the fundamental importance of the volatile envelopes of our sphere, how absolutely they have determined its history.

It would be interesting to consider the causes which led to the absence of air and water on the moon, but this

matter is one of the most debatable of all that relates to
that sphere; we shall therefore have to content ourselves
with the above brief statements as to the vast and far-act-
ing effects which have arisen from the non-existence of
those envelopes on our nearest neighbour of the heavens.

METHODS IN STUDYING GEOLOGY.

So far as possible the preceding pages, by the method
adopted in the presentation of facts, will serve to show
the student the ways in which he may best undertake
to trace the order of events exhibited in the phenomena
of the earth. Following the plan pursued, we shall now
consider certain special points which need to be noted by
those who would adopt the methods of the geologist.

At the outset of his studies it may be well for the inquirer to note the fact that familiarity with the world
about him leads the man in all cases to a certain neglect
and contempt of all the familiar presentations of Nature.
We inevitably forget that those points of light in the
firmament are vast suns, and we overlook the fact that
the soil beneath our feet is not mere dirt, but a marvellous structure, more complicated in its processes than the
chemist's laboratory, from which the sustenance of our
own and all other lives is drawn. We feel our own bodies
as dear but commonplace possessions, though we should
understand them as inheritances from the inconceivable
past, which have come to us through tens of thousands
of different species and hundreds of millions of individual
ancestors. We must overlook these things in our common
life. If we could take them into account, each soul would
carry the universe as an intellectual burden.

It is, however, well from time to time to contemplate
the truth, and to force ourselves to see that all this apparently simple and ordinary medley of the world about
us is a part of a vast procession of events, coming forth
from the darkness of the past and moving on beyond the

light of the present day. Even in his professional work
the naturalist of necessity falls into the commonplace way
of regarding the facts with which he deals. If he be an
astronomer, he catalogues the stars with little more sense
of the immensities than the man who keeps a shop takes
account of his wares. Nevertheless, the real profit of all
learning is in the largeness of the understanding which it
develops in man. The periods of growth in knowledge
are those in which the mind, enriched by its store, enlarges
its conception while it escapes from commonplace ways of
thought. With this brief mention of what is by far the
most important principle of guidance which the student
can follow, we will turn to the questions of method that
the student need follow in his ordinary work.

With almost all students a difficulty is encountered
which hinders them in acquiring any large views as to
the world about them. This is due to the fact that they
can not make and retain in memory clear pictures of the
things they see. They remember words rather than things
—in fact, the training in language, which is so large a part
of an education, tends ever to diminish the element of visual
memory. The first task of the student who would become
a naturalist is to take his knowledge from the thing, and
to remember it by the mental picture of the thing. In
all education in Nature, whether the student is guided by
his own understanding or that of the teacher, a first and
very continuous aim should be to enforce the habit of
recalling very distinct images of all objects which it is
desired to remember. To this end the student should
practise himself by looking intently upon a landscape or
any other object; then, turning away, he should try to
recall what he has beheld. After a moment the impression
by the sight should be repeated, and the study of the
memory renewed. The writer knows by his own experience that even in middle-aged people, where it is hard to
breed new habits, such deliberate training can greatly increase the capacity of the memory for taking in and repro-

ducing images which are deemed of importance. Practice of this kind should form a part of every naturalist's daily routine. After a certain time, it need not be consciously done. The movements of thought and action will, indeed, become as automatic as those which the trained fencer makes with his foil.

Along with the habit of visualizing memories, and of storing them without the use of words, the student should undertake to enlarge his powers of conceiving spaces and directions as they exist in the field about him. Among savages and animals below the grade of man, this understanding of spacial relations is very clear and strong. It enables the primitive man to find his way through the trackless forest, and the carrier pigeon to recover his mate and dwelling place from the distance of hundreds of miles away. In civilized men, however, the habit of the home and street and the disuse of the ancient freedom has dulled, and in some instances almost destroyed, all sense of this shape of the external world. The best training to recover this precious capacity will now be set forth.

The student should begin by drawing a map on a true scale, however roughly the work may be done, of those features of the earth about him with which he is necessarily most familiar. The task may well be begun with his own dwelling or his schoolroom. Thence it may be extended so as to include the plan of the neighbouring streets or fields. At first, only directions and distances should be platted. After a time to these indications should be added on the map lines indicating in a general way contours or the lines formed by horizontal planes intersecting the area subject to delineation. After attaining certain rude skill in such work, the student may advantageously make excursions to districts which he can see only in a hurried way. As he goes, he should endeavour to note on a sketch map the positions of the hills and streams and the directions of the roads. A year of holiday practice in such work will, if the tasks occupy somewhere about a hundred hours of his time, serve greatly to extend or reawaken what may be called the topographic sense, and enable him to place in terms of space the observations of Nature which he may make.

In his more detailed work the student should select some particular field for his inquiry. If he be specially interested in geologic phenomena, he will best begin by noting two classes of facts—those exhibited in the rocks as they actually appear in the state of repose as shown in the outcrops of his neighbourhood, and those shown in the active manifestations of geological work, the decay of the rocks and the transportation of their waste, or, if the conditions favour, the complicated phenomena of the seashores.

As soon as the student begins to observe, he should begin to make a record of his studies. To the novice in any science written, and particularly sketched, notes are of the utmost importance. These, whether in words or in drawings, should be made in face of the facts; they should, indeed, be set down at the close of an observation, though not until the observer feels that the object he is studying has yielded to him all which it can at that time give. It is well to remark that where a record is made at the outset of a study the student is apt to feel that he is in some way pledged to shape all he may see to fit that which he has first written. In his early experience as a teacher, the writer was accustomed to have students compare their work of observation and delineation with that done by trained men on the same ground. It now seems to him best for the beginner at first to avoid all such reference of his own work to that of others. So great is the need of developing independent motive that it is better at the outset to make many blunders than to secure accuracy by trust in a leader. The skilful teacher can give fitting words of caution which may help a student to find the true way, but any reference of his undertakings to masterpieces is sure to breed a servile habit. Therefore such comparisons are fitting only after the habit of free work has been well formed. The student who can afford the help of a master, or, better, the assistance of many, such as some of our universities offer, should by all means avail himself of this resource. More than any other science, geology, because of the complexity of the considerations with which it has to deal, depends upon methods of labour which are to a great extent traditional, and which can not, indeed, be well transmitted except in the personal way. In the distinctly limited sciences, such as mathematics, physics, or even those which deal with organic bodies, the methods of work can be so far set forth in printed directions that the student may to a great extent acquire sound ways of work without the help of a teacher.

Although there is a vast and important literature concerning geology, the greater part of it is of a very special nature, and will convey to the beginner no substantial information whatever. It is not until he has become familiar with the field with which he is enabled to deal in the actual way that he can transfer experience thus acquired to other grounds. Therefore beyond the pleasing views which he may obtain by reading certain general works on the science, the student should at the outset of his inquiry limit his work as far as possible to his field of practice, using a good text-book, such as Dana's Manual of Geology, as a source of suggestions as to the problems which his field may afford.

The main aim of the student in this, as in other branches of inquiry, is to gain practice in following out the natural series of actions. To the primitive man the phenomenal world presents itself as a mere phantasmagoria, a vast show in which the things seen are only related to each other by the fact that they come at once into view. The end of science is to divine the order of this host, and the ways in which it is marshalled in its onward movement and the ends to which its march appears to be directed. So far as the student observes well, and thus gains a clear

notion of separated facts, he is in a fair way to gather the
data of knowledge which may be useful; but the real
value of these discernments is not gained until the observations go together, so as to make something with a perspective.   Until the store of separate facts is thus arranged,
it is merely crude material for thought; it is not in the
true meaning science, any more than a store of stone and
mortar is architecture.   When the student has developed
an appetite for the appreciation of order and sources of
energy in phenomena, he has passed his novitiate, and
becomes one of that happy body of men who not only see
what is perceived by the mass of their fellows, but are
enabled to look through those chains of action which,
when comprehended, serve to rationalize and ennoble all
that the senses of man, aided by the instruments which he
has devised, tell us concerning the visible world.

INDEX.

through coal, 306 ; driven upward, 307 : formation of, 305, 310 ; material of, 307, 308 ; representing movements of softened rock, 309 ; their relation to volcanic cones, 307 ; variations of the materials of, 307, 308 ; waterfalls produced by, 192 ; zone of, 306.

Dismal Swamp, 95, 333.

Distances, general idea of, 27 ; good way to study, 27, 28 ; training soldiers to measure, 28.

Doldrums, 104, 109 ; doldrum of the equator, 109 ; of the hurricane, 109.

Drainage, imperfect, of a country affected by glaciers, 242.

Dunes, 123, 124, 325, 326, 387 ; moulded, 387.

Duration of geological time, 389.

Dust accumulations from wind, in China, 122.

Earth, a flattened sphere, 82 ; air envelope of the, 98 ; amount of heat falling from the sun on the, 41 ; antiquity of the, 391 ; atmosphere of the, 98 ; attracting power of the, 127 ; axis of the rotation of the, 58 ; composition of the atmosphere of the, 98 ; crust of the, affected by weight, 98 ; deviation of the path of the, varied, 61 ; diameter of the, 82 ; of the, affected by loss of heat, 131 ; difference in altitude of the surface of the, 83 ; discovery that it was globular, 31, 32 ; effect of imaginary changes in the relations of sun and, 59 ; effect of the interior heat of the, 309, 310 ; effect of the sun on the, 60, 61 ; formerly in a fluid state, 82 ; imaginary view of the, from the moon, 81 ; important feature of the surface of the, 83 ; jarring caused by faults, 367 ; surface of the, determined by heat and light from the sun, 57 ; most im-

portant feature of the surface of the, 83 ; motion of the, affecting the direction of trade winds, 103 ; movements, 366 ; natural architecture of the, 377 ; no part of the, exempt from movement, 384 ; parting of the moon and, 396 ; path of the, around the sun, 55, 56, 59, 60 ; revolving from east to west, 103 ; shrinking of the, from daily escape of heat, 59 ; soil-covering of the, 343 ; study of the, 81-96 ; swaying, 385 ; tensions, problem of, 371 ; tremors, caused by chemical changes in the rocks, 365 ; tropical belt of the, 74 ; viewed from the surface of the moon, 311, 312 ; water store of the, 125.

Earthquakes, 277, 278, 280, 356, 358, 370-384, 388-390 ; accidents of, 358 : action of, 356 ; agents of degradation, 383, 384 ; basis of, 367 ; certain limitations to, 380, 381 ; Charleston, of 1883, 374, 375 ; countries, architecture in, 381 ; echoes, 369, 370 ; damages of, 377, 390 : effect of, on the soil, 375 ; the surface of the earth, 371 ; formed by riving of fissures, 382 ; great, occurring where rocks have been disturbed by mountain-building, 381, 382 ; Herculaneum and Pompeii destroyed by an, 277, 280 ; Italian, in 1783, 371, 372 ; important, not connected with volcanic explosions, 381 ; Jamaica, in 1692, 372, 376 ; Lisbon, in 1755, 368, 369, 373, 374, 381 ; maximum swing of, 369 ; measuring the liability to, 386, 387 ; mechanism of, 370, 371 ; method of the study of, followed by Mr. Charles Mallet, 382, 383 ; Mississippi, in 1811, 373, 374, 380, 381 ; movement of the earth during, 377 ; originating from a fault plane, 367, 369, 370 ; originating from the seas, 358, 375 ; oscilla-